VIRGIL'S FIRE

Dr. Druid Book Two

MAXWELL FARMER

MOUNTAINDALE
PRESS

To my future child, you are loved. If you believe it's possible, have faith in the big man above, and put the work in, you can accomplish anything!

CHAPTER ONE

Westbound

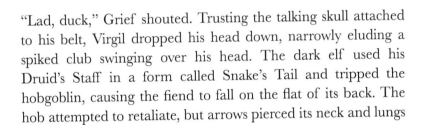

"Lad, duck," Grief shouted. Trusting the talking skull attached to his belt, Virgil dropped his head down, narrowly eluding a spiked club swinging over his head. The dark elf used his Druid's Staff in a form called Snake's Tail and tripped the hobgoblin, causing the fiend to fall on the flat of its back. The hob attempted to retaliate, but arrows pierced its neck and lungs in rapid succession. Within seconds, it had bled out.

Virgil turned to Gwen, the high elf archer and Hunter Druid gave him a wink before nocking another arrow and firing past him at a goblin.

Ahead of the elf druids was a contingent of around twenty small green goblins accompanied by two taller and brutish hobgoblins. Their numbers were half of what they originally were due to the rest of the druids' companions. In between the goblins and druids, fighting against the fiendish creatures, were three animals, all very different yet equally deadly.

To the right was a large boar, Gwen's pet. The porcine animal possessed the thick, curled horns of a ram in conjunction with sharp tusks. The beast was a terror boar, Christopher P. Bacon, Chris P. Bacon for short, and he was crashing through the goblin ranks. The boar was shattering leg bones with his thick horns, tossing goblins up in the air for Gwen to pick off with her arrows, and goring any nearby foes with his tusks.

To the left was a rodent the size of a housecat. It was the stego rat, Splinter. Unlike the brutish methods of Christopher, she fought using speed like a graceful assassin. Adorned with sharp bony spikes on her body and a single horn on her head, the stego rat swiftly dodged club strikes and kicks from nearby goblins. Splinter clawed straight through a goblin's exposed abdomen, eviscerating the small green fiend on the spot, then jumped and rammed her horn into the left eye of another. The goblin's kin began swinging their clubs at the rat, but Splinter quickly dislodged herself, causing the small fiends to accidentally attack their comrade and cave in its face, killing it on the spot.

In the center was the biggest and baddest animal of the group. Standing nine feet tall while on all four feet, the beast had purple skin with large sections of its body covered in thick brown fur. It had two forward-facing antlers on each side of its head and possessed the face of a moose with a large metal ring pierced through the septum of its nose. Its mouth was not that of an herbivore though; no, in addition to blunt incisors, it contained many sharp, serrated teeth like that of a wolf.

That was Baphomet the beastking, a former demon-beast hybrid purified and evolved into the literal alpha predator of the Yggdra Timberland. Baphomet let out a roar, intimidating most of the goblins, then bit down on the head of a nearby fiend. It flailed for just a moment before its head popped like a water balloon. Baphomet flung the goblin's body into some of its comrades then charged at the two remaining hobs. The red-skinned larger goblinoids, unaffected by the beastking's intimidating roar, charged in kind, wielding large greatswords.

Baphomet was able to block one swing with its antlers and backhanded the hob away, but the other swung true and cut into the thick hide of the beast. Baphomet roared in pain, turning to attack the hob, who dodged backwards. Baphomet scowled as every breath it took caused it pain. A cocky smile graced the hob's face as he noticed the beast was injured. The smile quickly turned to fear as Baphomet's body glowed slightly and its wound healed completely in a matter of seconds.

The beastking turned to its master, Virgil the Healer Druid, and nodded gratefully. Virgil pushed up his round glasses and gave a slight nod in reply. Baphomet turned as the first hob ran back in to attack him.

Fortunately, Virgil cast his Yggdrashield spell and a wall of thorny sticks and vines erupted from the ground, creating a wall in front of Baphomet. The hob wasn't fast enough to stop the swing and its blade lodged into the tough wood. Baphomet jumped to the shield's side, flanking the nearby hob. The beastking inhaled a deep breath, using its unique ability—Demon-Beast Flame—then exhaled a gout of blue flame, engulfing the two hobs. They both screamed in pain before collapsing to the ground, having taken the full attack. Seeing their leaders killed, the small green goblins dropped their weapons and ran for their lives.

The running fiends quickly fell victim to Gwen's Master-ranked Archery skill. The Hunter Druid's Tracking skill made sure none escaped. "That's all of them," Gwen stated as she returned. "Is everyone alright?"

Virgil nodded. "Nobody was badly injured, and with my healing they are as good as new." He looked over the small party appreciatively. "I think our teamwork is getting even better."

"Haha! Ye be right 'bout that, lad, and it all be thanks to me," Grief said.

Virgil looked down to his soulbound companion, Grief Devilslayer. The animated skull was once a dwarven warrior from a clan famously known for their knowledge of fiends and their ability to kill them. The long-story-short was that he was left at the altar by a spiteful elf, and was subsequently cursed by that elf for sleeping with her sister not long after. Now the dwarf was a repository of information on demons; he used the foramen magnum in the back of his head as a portal to an isolated pocket of space to essentially be a bag of holding, and took credit for things that he was not even remotely responsible for.

"All thanks to you?" Virgil asked. "Please explain how you're solely responsible, my friend."

"Well, without me that hob would've clobbered yer face in an' crushed those fancy glasses of yers," Grief retorted.

"And for that, I'm grateful, but everyone else?" he asked, trying to get Grief to face the facts.

"Ah… well, maybe I exaggerated a bit…" the skull admitted uncomfortably.

"Don't worry, bud," Virgil said. "You're still very valuable to this group, just not so much when it comes to direct stuff. You have great storage and information," Virgil said, patting atop the skull's head.

"Sigh, yeah yeah, ye be right, lad," Grief admitted, sounding like a defeated child.

Virgil chuckled, then looked back to the rest of his party. All of them had some blood on them, but none were worse-for-wear. "Good job, everyone," he said, then pulled out a couple pieces of dried meat and tossed one to each of the animals. They each caught their treat mid-air and ate happily.

Gwen came up and gave Virgil a kiss on the cheek. "Good job yourself, Virgil. I'm going to go loot the bodies. Check any notifications you got, then come help me. Afterward, we need to figure out where we go next."

Virgil blushed and nodded, smiling at the beautiful elf.

Your party has successfully defeated a force that outnumbered your own at a greater than 5-to-1 disadvantage.

For successfully defeating 30 goblins and 4 hobgoblin brutes, you have received 400 Experience.

Danger Sense has reached Level 12!

Restoration Magic has reached Level 23!

Name: Virgil
Level: 13 (463/6560 experience to next level.)
Unallocated Stat Points: 8
Race: Elf **Subrace:** Dark Elf
Class: Druid
Specialization: Healer Druid
Attunement: A Veterinarian's Pact
Languages: Common, Elven
Companions: Grief (Soulbound), Splinter, Baphomet

Pools & Resistances

Health: 102
Manna: 290
Stamina: 210
Armor: 119
Life Magic: 50%
Earth Magic: 50%
Nature Magic: 50%
Light Magic: -50%

Statistics

Strength: 10
Agility: 45
Intelligence: 29
Endurance: 27
Charisma: 13

Traits

True Healer
Darkvision
Increased Hearing
Ally of Darkness
Beast Commander

Skills
Medicine Level 53
Herbology Level 53
Nature Magic (Restoration) Level 23
Spells: Restore, Leeching Vines, Yggdrashield, Nature Bolt, Barkskin
Stealth Level 15 — Subskill: Sneak Attack Level 3
Analyze Level 10
Danger Sense Level 12 — Subskill: Detect Hostile Intent Level 5
Skinning Level 4
Trade Level 4
Alchemy Level 23
Taunt Level 3
Soulbound Recall

Virgil dismissed the notifications, satisfied with his progress, and went to check on the goblin loot. There were a few copper and silver coins, random animal claws and teeth, and some shoddy-looking weaponry. Seriously, the spiked clubs looked like baseball bats with nails embedded in the top. The most valuable item to Virgil were the few herbs and a couple of potions that some had on them.

The herbs were a mix of Tulitan which could be a lubricant or digestive aid, some stamina-replenishing herbs, and something called Shimmerleaf. When Virgil examined it, he was notified that it had stealth-aiding properties and possibly even could be used to make an invisibility potion! The potions were nothing fancy, just a minor health and a stamina-replenishing one.

They left the weapons, as they had no use for them. Their roles as druid champions locked them into only using their class weapon given by the world tree. Gwen, being the Hunter Druid, had her bow. Virgil, being the Healer Druid, had his staff. Unfortunately, being the Healer Druid also meant that he had barely any offensive ability with the weapon. His class restriction even prevented him from getting any kind of staff-based skill despite him receiving training in its use. Fortunately, he was allowed to use magic. Though still not an offensive powerhouse, with some of his spells he could hold his own. His real power was his attunement, allowing him to bind animal companions.

"Alright, Virgil," Gwen said as she finished going through the bodies, wiping her hands and leaning against a nearby tree. "Where do we go now? We certainly can't go back to Kygor."

"No doubt about that," Virgil agreed, thinking about the capital city of the Rubasal Kingdom that housed the world tree Yggdrasil. The king and much of the city was notably discriminatory towards dark elves like Virgil, and had tried to arrest him unjustly, then kill Baphomet in retribution since Virgil managed to purify the former demon general instead. Long story short, he and his party were now fugitives from the kingdom that ruled most of the land they were summoned to protect. It was obviously a messed-up situation, but the druids were making the best of it.

"Well, we have two options," Virgil said. "We can go back to the Northern Wastes to find the dark elf village and meet up with them. The other option is going west."

"What's out west?" Gwen asked.

"The Mage College. I found a secret abandoned warlock lab in the capital's sewers. There, I found this," he said as he pulled out a tattered journal covered in runic carvings. "It's a journal detailing a plan by a group of warlocks at the Mage College a while ago. According to the book, some of the staff have been replaced by demons. I received a quest to bring this journal back to the college, and remove the imposters."

Gwen put her hand to her chin and tapped her foot, thinking deeply about the options. "So, up north are the dark elves. There we can hopefully form an alliance and have a safe place free from the Rubasal Kingdom's influence and any hopeful bounty hunters." She shook her head, "Though I like the idea, that doesn't put us any closer to finding the demon generals we need to eliminate."

"Aye. I agree with the lass," Grief added. "Headin' to the Mage College is yer only definitive lead to findin' and slayin' more demons. My vote is to head west to Amthoon. It be the coastal city where the college be located."

"Not seeing any obvious reason to not go west versus north," Virgil agreed.

The party headed towards Amthoon. During their trek, Gwen's Tracking skill activated, quickly helping her realize that she had been on this path before.

"Ooh! I've been down this trail. This path leads to Ginterbacher!" Gwen said.

"Gi... Ginterbacher?" Virgil asked, clearly confused.

Gwen chuckled. "Yes. It's a weird name, but translated to Common it means, 'Haven That Gives.' It's the village where I met my trainer," she said excitedly. "It is not a big village, but it's a safe place where we can relax and shouldn't have to worry about a bunch of racist elves. Plus, I think they'll appreciate you in particular. They have a wildlife preserve nearby where the last population of an endangered species remains."

"Cool!" Virgil replied happily. Discovering and caring for rare animals was so exciting to him. It was one of the reasons he had become a veterinarian in the first place. For the next few hours, the party continued west. As they progressed, the pines and spruces transitioned into terrain that reminded Virgil of a short stint he did in the rainforests of Sumatra. The air even became notably more humid. He figured it was going to be just as dangerous.

The Yggdra Timberland was truly fascinating as it possessed more than one type of microbiome such as coniferous forests, swampland, dry savannah grassland, and now tropical rainforests. That didn't account for the wasteland just outside the forest's boundaries.

Fortunately, their journey was mostly uneventful. They did end up fighting a small pack of vile stalkers. Though their appearance was nightmare fuel, the druids had fought them before, so they did not flinch in fear upon seeing them. They were able to handle the pack in just under two minutes. Virgil took the time to collect some of the stalkers' venom. He figured he could potentially experiment with it to make some sort of demonic anti-venom, or maybe he could reverse engineer it to make it deadly to demons instead?

Name: Vile Stalker Venom x2
Item Class: Ingredient
Rarity: Rare
Demonic venom from a vile stalker. It will do -1 point of health/second for 50 seconds. If the afflicted target dies while poisoned, they will be reincarnated as a demon.

Virgil *carefully* put the venom into some empty vials then stored them inside the back of Grief's skull.

As the group headed westward, Gwen pointed out a large volcano in the distance. "That volcano is called Brandios. According to my teacher, it's a dangerous place, but it is warded off by a set of protective totems. Seeing the volcano now also means that we're not far from the village."

"Who is your teacher, anyway? How did you happen to find a teacher out here?" Virgil asked.

"Did ye find another druid out here? I was under the impression that you five were the only druids left on this world," Grief added.

"She's not a druid," Gwen answered. "You're right, we are the only druids. No, my teacher is a ranger. She specializes in archery. Since my soulbound weapon is a bow, I thought it would be beneficial that I try to learn from her. Though she is a warg living in a kingdom of elves, she is one of the best in the entire timberland."

"What's a warg?" Virgil asked.

Grief answered that question for her. "Wargs be one of the three beastkin races. Beastkin be a name for the groups of peoples that primarily share animal-like features. Wargs look like canines—wolves and foxes. There also be those that look like birds called flooms, and the lizard-like reptiles."

"And these beastkin are part of the kingdom? I don't remember seeing any of them in the capital."

"Yes," Gwen said, nodding. She then took on an uncomfortable look. "They... are not valued very highly by the royal family, so they usually avoid large settlements."

Virgil could believe that. "Well, then we should likely not run into any problems while we spend time in this village." They continued walking for another fifteen minutes until Christopher stopped in his tracks. The boar's fur raised slightly, and he lifted his large snout up in the air and sniffed loudly. A scent then struck the terror boar's nose, and he turned back to Gwen, grunting and snorting nervously.

"What is it, love?" Gwen asked as she knelt down to pet her animal companion. Christopher grunted some more and turned his head back toward the direction they were going. Gwen looked around, but when she didn't see anything, she closed her eyes and took in a deep inhale to smell the air. "Smoke?" she asked in surprise.

"How close is Ginterbacher from here?" Virgil asked.

"Not far, just a few minutes down the path. Why?"

Virgil pushed his glasses back up the bridge of his nose and pointed above a large nearby tree. In the sky were multiple columns of smoke rising through the air. A scream cut through the forest from the direction of the smoke.

CHAPTER TWO

Raiders

The party sprinted towards the direction of the village, stopping when they made it to the hill that overlooked the small village. Under normal circumstances, this would have been a pleasant sight, but this was anything but normal. The villagers were screaming, fleeing towards the village entrance. At the back of the village, five buildings were burning, their thatch roofs ablaze.

Large brutish creatures fought small clusters of a few armed citizens in the dirt streets, attacking with reckless abandon.

"We need to help them," Gwen said.

They raced down the hill towards the attackers. As they made it down to the village's border, Virgil cast Barkskin on the party. They ran past civilians running in the opposite direction. Virgil was grateful he was notified about the beastkin. If he saw animal-like humanoids running by him in the chaos, he would have been concerned about new types of demons.

As the group ran towards the edge of the village, they were able to get a good look at the raiders. There was a warg that looked like a fox adorned in a plaid kilt, wielding an axe, fighting against a hulking, shirtless barbarian who stood at least seven and a half feet tall. The orc was wielding a greatsword and wore only a leather only loincloth and was adorned with various tribal style piercings on his face. His chest, shoulders, and arms were covered in a variety of brands in repeated patterns, as if he had undergone some sort of ritual.

Something about the orc sent a shiver up Virgil's spine as he focused on it. Instead of a look of anger or hatred as it fought, it had a crazed smile showing its sharp teeth. Its red skin also had bulging pulsing black vessels atop it.

Virgil used Analyze.
Name: Firebrand Orc
Level: 18
Race: Monster Type: Orc
Health: 395/395 Manna: 0 Stamina: 350/350
Resistances: Fire 50%, Slashing Damage 25%, Piercing Damage 25%

Orcs are a strong and usually barbaric people whose entire culture revolves around combat. After generations of such violence, their bodies have grown to become both tough and deadly. They are able to kill an adult humanoid by the time they reach the age of 5. This orc is a raider from the Firebrand Tribe who make their home in the Scorched Lands by the volcano Brandios. Firebrands are a unique specimen among the orcish race as their culture has an obsession with, you guessed it, fire. They will often burn their bodies to toughen their skin and believe their god lays dormant inside Brandios, waiting until it is time to burn the world in renewing flame.

Virgil quickly dismissed the info and saw the orc deflect the warg's axe swing into the ground. The orc backhanded the warg, sending him flying into the side of a building, his axe still stuck in the ground.

The orc smiled as he approached the downed warg and raised his weapon to strike, bellowing, "You will burn!"

Before the orc's swing could land, Gwen activated Rapid Fire Archery, shooting the firebrand in the left eye and forearm.

The orc recoiled slightly, then turned to the incoming druids, still brandishing a wide smile and seemingly unfazed by the embedded arrows. "Burn!" the orc shouted, and swung his sword down. Virgil quickly cast Yggdrashield and it arose to block the weapon, causing the blade to embed itself into the construct skull with a crunch, saving the unconscious warg's life.

"Shit," Virgil spat as he saw three more firebrands emerge from burning buildings behind the one Gwen had just shot. He really wished Baphomet was ready to fight again. After the beastking used its demon fire attack, it could take considerable time before it had the energy to transform to its massive form again. While having a hulking behemoth join the fight would be ideal, Baphomet hadn't fully recharged yet. They had to make do with what they had. "We have to get in there. Go!"

On Virgil's command, the party charged. Splinter hopped off Virgil's pauldron, and the cat-sized rat sprinted toward the injured orc who was still smiling despite blood and ocular fluid running down his face from the arrow stuck in his eye. The other orcs turned to the party, looking similar to their comrade in appearance outside of their hair choices. All of the firebrands had the same pulsing veins and crazed smiles. The raiders all gripped their swords and were murmuring the word 'burn' quietly.

Christopher lowered his head and charged at the nearest orc. The orc was swinging his greatsword down at the terror boar, but Gwen used a spell called Air Strike Arrow to hit the bulky weapon and deflect the sword backward. That gave Christopher the opportunity he needed to ram straight into the tibia of the orc's right leg. The orc's bones were thick and tough, but the boar's curled horns were tougher. As Christopher made contact, both tibia and fibula leg bones shattered, piercing through muscle and skin and protruding through the back of the orc's calf.

Instead of groaning or crying out in pain from the obviously terrible injury, the orc just yelled 'burn' in a more shrilled and angry manner.

Another orc swung his sword at Christopher who was preoccupied with the newly downed firebrand. Virgil cast his Yggdrashield spell and a five-foot-tall construct of wood, dirt, and vines with thorns grew out of the ground in between the orc and his intended victim, blocking his blow.

Virgil wasn't quick enough to stop the third orc though.

The orc in the rear was at Christopher's flank, where the shield was not protecting the boar, and charged. He was carrying a torch in one hand and a sword in the other. Gwen cast a spell and a spear made out of solid stone emerged from the ground like a defensive pike, piercing through the charging orc's bicep deeply.

To everyone's surprise, the orc dropped his sword and kept charging, causing the firebrand's arm to be amputated grotesquely in the process.

The orc didn't stop, and swung his torch at Christopher like a club yelling, "BURN!"

The boar squealed in pain as both the torch's heat and momentum struck him solidly, causing him to fly backwards.

Virgil ran over to the boar, immediately casting his Restore spell and assessing the damage. The Healer Druid's magic was already working well, and both the bruising and burns on Christopher's skin were already regressing back to normal.

Splinter had finished off the orc she was fighting against earlier, and attacked the one-armed orc before it could continue its assault on Christopher. She ran behind the orc and bit straight through its Achilles tendon, cleaving it in two. The orc fell to one leg, as it was no longer able to bear weight on the other. The orc turned its head back. It swung its torch back at Splinter and kicked uselessly at the stego rat with its injured leg to get her off.

He should have been paying attention to his front. Gwen, angered at the damage done to her beloved pet, pulled out a special arrow to finish off the orc. The arrowhead was made of ignitum, a rust-colored metal that was very reactive and easily flammable.

"You want to burn things? Why don't you get a taste of how it feels to burn?" She snarled and released the arrow. It struck true, landing just above the collar bone and penetrating the orc's chest. The heat from the impact set the metal ablaze and quickly the orc began to burn from the inside. Its roar was cut short as its lungs began to burn away. It gritted its teeth and began to laugh despite it flailing in pain as its entire body was set on fire. The sight was uncomfortable to the druid's eyes as it seemed like the orc was possessed before it died and its laughs finally went silent.

Suddenly, an orc jumped out of one of the windows of the burning building and bolted away from the battle towards the forest, quickly followed by two others. All three looked to be carrying something in one of their arms. Gwen used her elven grace to climb up atop a roof then used her vantage point to fire. Though a skilled archer and druid, her range was not far enough to get the leader.

She pulled back, activating her Multi-Shot subskill, and fired. The Hunter Druid hit one of the two rear orcs in the calf, but narrowly missed the second, flying just above its shoulder.

The struck orc groaned slightly, but kept hobbling forward, showing a true testament to the race's endurance.

"Damn," Gwen uttered and pulled another arrow from her quiver and fired. The second shot struck the ground five feet behind the orc. The orc turned back and grinned smugly at Gwen just as the frontrunner made it to the tree line.

Both it and its comrade were just about to get away safely when a large, five foot long arrow made of some sort of black metal launched out of the window of the burning barn like a missile. Both Gwen and the orcs barely had time to register the projectile in the air as it rapidly flew across the open field. The orcs didn't even have the time to dodge.

The arrow descended and penetrated the injured orc straight through its bare chest, piercing through its body and striking the side of the other orc's body. The first orc died instantly, but the second orc managed to avoid death. The dead orc dropped whatever it was carrying to the ground, while its injured but living comrade pulled out the arrow embedded in its side.

More arrows flew out from the burning building, but were much smaller. The remaining raider picked up what its dead comrade dropped, then used the deceased orc's body as a literal meat shield as it dragged itself to the forest edge. All ten of the arrows fired pierced the dead orc's body but did not go further like the large black one had.

The orc made it to the forest, dropping its dead comrade, now a giant pin cushion, and disappeared into the thick jungle.

CHAPTER THREE

The Ranger

Gwen was wondering who was still in the burning building when another form jumped out from the window. They were covered in a large cloak and rolled gracefully as they made contact with the ground. As soon as the figure stood up, the barn collapsed to the ground. Still uncertain if they were friend or foe, Gwen nocked another arrow and drew back, keeping her aim locked.

The figure seemed to be aware of Gwen, and quickly turned to face the druid. "Your aim has improved since last I saw you, Gwendolyn, but you still need practice, my young pupil," a deep but feminine voice said as the figure pulled down her hood and revealed the face of a white wolf with red eyes. A chunk was missing out of her right ear and her left was heavily pierced. It was a warg ranger. Specifically, it was Valgorna the White, an albino warg and Gwen's teacher in the Archery skill.

"Master? You're okay!" Gwen exclaimed as she quickly hopped down from the roof. Virgil and company followed behind her, still keeping an eye out for any more orcs. Gwen ran up to Valgorna and asked, "Are there any more attackers?"

"No, Gwendolyn," she replied in between heavy breaths.

"Those three were the last of them." Satisfied that they were now reasonably safe, Gwen walked up and hugged the warg, who stood slightly smaller than her elf pupil.

"What are orcs doing here, and what do they want? I thought they couldn't get out of the Scorched Lands," Gwen said.

Valgorna nodded. "You're right, they shouldn't. So, something is definitely not right." The ranger then turned to see Virgil. "Is this not the dark elf you were tasked in bringing to the king?"

"Yes…" Gwen responded. "I discovered that he was actually innocent, though. How did you know it was him?"

The warg chuckled. "Easy. I've never seen a dark elf wear glasses in my life. When you told me he wore glasses, it wasn't hard to figure out who he was. You're right too. He is a cute one, even with his long ears." Gwen began to blush and Virgil chuckled a little at that. Valgorna just continued, "Come, let us check on the others, and keep any other buildings from burning down."

For the next few hours, the druids and ranger worked to gather the citizens together by the town hall, saving a few from burning buildings, healing wounds, and preventing the fires from overtaking any more homes. None of them had any water-based magic like the Moon Druid, Pierre, so they had to resort to destroying the buildings and corralling the flames away from other constructs. Virgil's healing skills came in very handy when it came to the injured citizens. He soon became a favorite of the townspeople, especially the kids, who liked to tug on his overly large ears.

Unfortunately, some injuries were too severe for some of the people, and there were at least five dead from the orc attacks before Virgil could get to them. Their families cried over the dead bodies, and he left them to mourn, not wishing to disturb them. Seeing their bodies with such grievous wounds was tough. He had become a veterinarian because, while he liked people, seeing them suffer and die was not something he was too comfortable with. On Imeria though, he was not only a healer of animals, but also of people. Gwen depended on him to help keep her healthy and alive.

Seeing the families' losses gave him newfound determination to help his party and to seek justice against the orcs.

"Is that everyone?" Virgil asked Valgorna as she and Gwen entered the large stone and wood town hall. The sun had just set, giving way to a clear sky. Some torches were providing most of the illumination for people. Fortunately for Virgil, his dark elf eyes granted him Darkvision, rendering the torchlight unnecessary. Behind the ranger was the foxlike warg in a plaid kilt that the druids had saved earlier. His head was bandaged and his left shoulder appeared to be injured as that arm was now in a sling. *Maybe from the orc deflecting his axe,* Virgil thought.

"We haven't finished accounting for everyone yet," the ranger replied. "Still, I want to thank you for saving my mate," she said and made way for the warg behind her to make his way toward Virgil.

"I am Maldraxx, and thank you, honorable druid," he said, extending his right hand out to Virgil. Virgil mirrored the gesture and the two clasped wrists.

"I'm Virgil, and you're welcome." Now that Virgil was closer, he could see the red fur of the fox definitely had a good bit of white mixed in, indicating the warg was not on the younger side. "You did good out there, fighting a brutish orc like that one-on-one."

"I'm just a lumberjack, no warrior or leader of a people like my Valgorna, but I thank you for your kind words," Maldraxx replied.

"Speaking of the people, how many didn't make it?" Valgorna asked Virgil.

"Five. By the time I got here, they were already gone. I was able to help the others, but for some it is merely just stabilization. I have great healing abilities, but my magic can't fix shattered bones or dislocations. I will need some extra hands and equipment in order to realign them properly. If I don't before I try to use a healing spell, the bone may heal permanently disfigured."

He continued but with a more somber tone, "There's also a boy, I believe he is what is called a floom. His bird-like bones are hollow and not as strong, so he has many fractures. His right arm had already lost a lot of blood, was almost separated from his body, and covered in severe burns. By the time I got to him the arm was... not salvageable." Virgil's face turned both serious and grim. "I gave the boy a sleeping powder, then I... removed the arm completely. Afterward, I applied a numbing ointment, used my Restore spell, and applied a wrap for him. I'm... sorry I couldn't do more," he said, almost crying.

Valgorna put a comforting hand on Virgil's shoulder. "You have nothing to apologize for, Virgil. You saved that boy's life and many more. Don't fret. I know someone who may be able to regrow the floom's arm."

Virgil's eyes widened. "Really?"

The ranger nodded. "Yes, now, you two go rest," she said to the druids. "I'm going to check on the people and finish our headcount. We may have more need of you yet."

Virgil, exhausted from the fighting and the emotional toll of healing injured people, readily agreed. He felt like he now had a better understanding of how combat medics felt in the field, choosing who got priority and making grim calls. It was almost too much for him. He, Gwen, and the animals all sat on a porch of a nearby building and leaned back against the wall.

"You did great out there, Virgil," Gwen said as she held his hand and gave him a kiss on the cheek. "Really, you helped so many people out there when they needed it most. You're a real hero, and don't you forget."

"Thanks, Gwen," Virgil said, grateful for the kind words from the cute elf. He knew he'd done all he could, but his conscience was really putting in work to try to make him feel like he could've done more. Despite Valgorna's request, he helped to repair the dislocated bones and stabilize broken limbs. His Master-ranked Medicine skill provided great benefit to his ability to heal during that time, for which he was grateful. After he was done, Virgil took some comfort in remembering Gwen's encouraging words from earlier. That helped to give him the peace of mind he needed, and he quickly fell asleep.

––––––

A few hours later, Virgil awoke to Gwen shaking his shoulder.

"Come on now," she said.

Virgil put his glasses back on and blinked his eyes clear. Standing in front of him were Valgorna and Maldraxx.

"Is everyone accounted for?" he asked.

The ranger shook her head somberly. "No, unfortunately not."

"We have discovered that the orcs kidnapped two of our children, and one of our blood rhynorns."

"What's a… blood rhynorn?" Virgil asked.

"Remember that endangered species I told you about? That's it," Gwen answered.

"Yes." Valgorna continued, "The rhynorns are a creature on the brink of extinction, and we possess the last known population in all of the Yggdra Timberland. They are scavenging creatures, responsible for eating much of the dead and rotten carrion that other predators won't eat. When there is a healthy number of them, they help protect the woods from disease and infections that could kill both people and animals. They are also known for their coat that is a deep red, the color of blood."

"Sounds charming," Virgil said sarcastically.

"They can be, if you know how to handle them," Valgorna replied, then continued with the main subject. "They captured a young female rhynorn, one floom girl, and a reptil boy. I don't know why they were captured, but we need to go get them back."

"Can we do that safely, master?" Gwen asked. "What if some of the orcs double back while we're gone? Who will defend the people?"

"I have sent word to my ranger allies and to a healer friend of mine. They will be here shortly. Rest assured, we can leave now, and the people will be safe."

Quest Unlocked
Raid The Raiders
Orc raiders from the Firebrand Tribe have kidnapped 2 beastkin children and 1 rare and endangered blood rhynorn. The village leader Valgorna is asking that you assist her in tracking the raiders and recovering what was stolen.
Requirements:
Rescue at least 1 of the 3 kidnapped.
Reward:
Variable depending on the number rescued.
Do you accept?
Yes or No

Though tired, the druids agreed with the ranger's logic and accepted the quest. Wanting to make sure they had the best chance to succeed, and remembering his recent experience gained from the earlier fighting, Virgil took time to allocate his eight unused stat points. Looking at his current stats, he decided to play to his strengths. He put four points into agility and the other four into intelligence, boosting his overall Manna pool to three-hundred and thirty points.

They set out to find where the orcs' basecamp was at. With both Gwen's Master-ranked Tracking skill, a professional ranger at their side, and an obvious trail of orc blood from the one injured by Valgorna's arrow, it was not hard to follow the path. Enough time had also elapsed that Baphomet could transform back into its larger form, though Virgil still kept his animal companion in his satchel, as the bulkier version would likely be heard crashing through the jungle.

During their trek, Virgil and Gwen took the time to add Valgorna to their party and ask about the orcs, particularly the Firebrand Tribe raiders that attacked them.

"Most orcs will work for anyone if there's enough coin or blood in it, but not the firebrands. They are a zealous tribe of pyromaniacs that were deemed too dangerous to fight against or ally with. Even other orc and ogre tribes couldn't make peace with them, so they were quarantined in the Scorched Lands encompassing the volcano Brandios. Supposedly, they even worship the thing."

Virgil recalled the information when he Analyzed one of the firebrands, and that all matched up. Maybe he was just being paranoid, but there was something unnatural about the orcs. He was highly suspicious of demonic interference. *"Hey Grief, are orcs demons or 'demon adjacent' like distant cousins of goblins or something?"* he asked through their Soulbound Communication.

"What? No, lad, they not be associatin' with demons to me knowledge. Quite frankly, it sounds absurd. Though orcs like to spill blood, they won't be fightin' fer nothin' without some coin. I say yer bein' too suspicious. Orcs will never work fer demons."

Virgil forced himself not to roll his eyes at Grief. From an analytical perspective, it made sense to wonder if there was some connection between orcs and fiends. They definitely seemed 'demon-y' to him.

After a few hours going through the dark and humid jungle, the party found the orc encampment. It wasn't too hard, as the monsters weren't being quiet and there was a large pyre illuminating the dark jungle. Stealthily, the group made it to the edge of the camp. Before they got too close, Virgil cast Barkskin on everyone to provide some extra protection.

Twenty red orcs with the bulging, pulsating, black veins all kneeled around an altar perched atop a wooden platform. They all still had unnaturally wide grins on their faces. Atop the altar was what looked to be a wooden totem of an eye with tentacles emerging out of it. Virgil was getting some major demon vibes from the altar. He lifted the skull up to see the creepy sight. *"What was that you said about orcs never working for demons?"*

Grief sent the mental equivalent of a shrug. *"It's been five-hundred years, lad, give me some leeway. I guess not everythin' is the same since I last been out. It looks like people have changed since I was trapped in Kygor.*"

Beside the altar was a thin, hooded figure wearing a brown robe that covered their entire body. It was obvious that the person was some kind of cult leader-caster type. On the other side were three steel cages. Two had the missing beastkin children in them. The other had a strange looking animal. It looked like a North American opossum, but with an elongated snout, multi-pointed antlers, and dark red fur. It was clear that the beast was the blood rhynorn.

The orcs began bowing up and down in unison at the altar, quietly chanting the same word, 'Burn.'

Virgil did *not* like where this was going. "Are orcs known to work with demons?" he asked, whispering to Valgorna.

The ranger shrugged and tilted her head slightly. "A typical orc will work for anyone, but it would be strange if the firebrands were working with demons, given their isolation. These orcs are definitely strange though, even compared to firebrands."

"Why is that? The smiling?" Virgil asked.

"Yes, orcs normally don't have such strange forced smiles or pulsing vessels on their bodies."

"Well, you did say they are also known to worship the volcano, so maybe these are some religious outcasts?" Virgil suggested.

"Better than any other idea I can think of," the warg replied before looking back at the ritual. The party's eyes widened in shock as the tentacles on the totem set on fire, grew, and moved independently as if they were alive. The orcs ceased their chanting and the hooded figure addressed the group. It was a light but masculine voice, and the figure spoke in a harsh language. Virgil presumed it was orcish. Both druids had something called an 'Earring of the Adept' equipped, and the piercings allowed them to understand any language they heard. It couldn't help them speak it, mind you, but it was still incredibly useful.

"Brothers, sisters, the time of fire has begun!"

"Burn, burn, burn!" The orcs chanted in unison in response.

"Yes, yes, firebrands, you have borne witness and have now seen the power which our master provides. Together, fueled by his fires, we all shall bathe in flames!"

"Burn, burn, burn!"

"Now, as you know, the master requires... specific sacrifices for his flame. These three will do nicely. As such, you will be rewarded." The hooded figure raised a staff in the air, and the four tentacles of flame shot out and struck four of the orcs on the front row. The orcs' bodies seized as heat emanated from them, making even the hiding druids uncomfortable, and were raised slightly off the ground. Their already large muscles began to bulge and grow in size. Their skin began to darken to a red hue and the vessels wriggled on their bodies like worms.

The other orcs' vessels began to glow bright red, even brighter than their blood red skin, and pulsate rhythmically in unison as they began to chant something new, "Zinthos, Zinthos, Zinthos!"

"Lad, I don't know what that totem be, but if I had a body still, I'd bet me left nut that the fire be hateflame," Grief communicated through his mental link to Virgil.

"What's hateflame?" Virgil asked.

"It be a unique type of demonic fire caused by hatred that can alter the body. Point bein', ye need to stop it now!"

"Crap," Virgil muttered after learning that. He then activated Party Chat and sent a message to the others. *Take out the caster and totem now!* he said and then fired a Nature Bolt from his staff at the robed thin figure. Virgil's offensive capability was not strong, but the magic bolt did hit its mark, striking the figure unexpectedly in the chest and causing him to stagger backwards. The flames instantly dissipated, the empowered orcs fell back to the ground, and the other orcs stopped their chanting.

The two archers followed Virgil's order and fired at the caster. They were much more effective and struck him in the left shoulder and right side of the chest, launching the caster backwards and into the totem. Both fell off the altar. The twenty orcs then turned back to face the threat in their midst, crazed smiles plastered on their faces.

Virgil wasn't sure if the monster race had Darkvision, but it seemed that they noticed where the party was hiding as they brandished their weapons with the four larger red orcs standing behind them.

The party was gearing up for a major fight when something unexpected happened. All the orcs suddenly stopped moving. They all began to shake and convulse and… shrivel. The bright red veins began to dull and regress to black. Their red skin started to turn a deathly gray, their muscles shrank, and their skin started looking like raisins. Their smiling faces were replaced with exhausted and tired expressions.

Virgil didn't know what was happening, but he wasn't going to look a gift horse in the mouth. He reached in his satchel, grabbing Baphomet still in small puppy form, and took the beastking out. "You ready for a fight?" he asked. The tiny creature just nodded, ready for the battle. Virgil threw the beastking forward and up into the air above the heads of the weakened orcs and yelled, "Sic' em!"

The beastking transformed into its massive form and descended onto the orcs like a comet to a dinosaur. Baphomet landed with a crash, instantly squashing four of the orcs with its massive size. The orcs, though weakened, were still not going down without a fight. They gave a roar and charged at Baphomet. The large beastking swung its antlers and claws, cutting through and eviscerating some of the incoming attackers.

The two archers began to fire arrows, peppering the distracted orcs in vulnerable, unprotected spots while both Christopher and Splinter stayed at the edge of the fighting, picking off some of the orcs not in the heat of battle. Virgil was focused mainly on Baphomet; casting Restore multiple times as well as Yggdrashield to protect his pet. In only half a minute, twelve of the orcs were dead. Then, something surprising happened. The caster whom the archers shot stood back up.

The hood was pulled back, revealing the face of a thin, male dawn elf with beady black eyes. A trail of blood came from his mouth, and he held the totem in his hands. It was broken into two pieces from the fall. The elf gave the party a malicious smile and pressed the two halves together. Immediately, the wooden tentacles turned into ones of flame again. They did not reach out to strike any orc, but it had an immediate effect on the eight remaining monsters.

Their lethargy was resolved and their forms returned to the veiny, musclebound, smiling versions they were. They all began laughing while gripping their weapons, promising retribution for their fallen comrades. "Kill the fools, and take the prisoners to the master!" the elf shouted. Three of the orcs ran for the cages, while the other five reinvigorated orcs attacked with reckless abandon.

Valgorna fired a set of arrows, but the elf caster conjured a wall of flame to block it. While the fire burned the wood of the arrows, Gwen knew it did not burn stone. The Hunter Druid cast Stone Spear. Her Predator Magic proved successful as it pierced the flame wall with ease and impaled a firebrand through the chest and dissipated part of the flame as well.

Taking in the situation, Virgil let his gamer instincts take over. "Crap. Valgorna, take out the orcs trying to get away. Gwen, you and Christopher take care of the caster. My companions and I will take care of the rest," he said out loud, ignoring Party Chat.

The party jumped into action. The warg ranger took off and followed the fleeing orcs into the darkness of the jungle. Christopher lowered his head, and the boar charged at the caster. The dawn elf somehow channeled magic through the totem, and the flame tentacles lashed out at the terror boar. The porcine creature dodged one while Gwen used an Air Strike Arrow spell to intercept another.

The four remaining firebrands charged at Baphomet. With

newfound speed and power, they closed the distance on the beastking. Baphomet was able to block two of their swords with its antlers, but was not quick enough to get the other two. Both unblocked orcs, one male and one female, swung hard with their crude greatswords, biting deep into the thick hide of the animal. Baphomet roared in pain, but was quickly healed by Virgil. The two orcs dislodged their weapons, causing blood to pour out of the wounds, and were about to swing again when an Yggdrashield appeared in front of one, and Splinter flanked the other.

The stego rat was not above fighting dirty. After all, she had grown up in the sewers. The cat-sized rodent ran and jumped at the unexpected orc's scrotum, biting down with her large incisors and neutering the orc on the spot. It was not how Virgil would've professionally neutered an animal, but this was a fight to the death, so he approved.

The orc, still smiling, fell to his knees as blood rapidly poured out from the wound. The stego rat quickly took advantage of the prone orc's condition by jumping on his back and biting down on his neck right by the brainstem. The orc's groans disappeared in an instant.

Virgil promptly cast Leeching Vines on the orc he used the shield on before she could take a second swing. Vines surged from the ground under her, wrapping around her arms and legs. Thorns from the vines embedded in the orc's flesh and began leeching her health. The spell had a bonus effect; it provided a fifty to one-hundred percent decrease in speed of the target for three to five seconds. The orc strained against her bindings, already causing the vines to fray some.

"Splinter," Virgil said and pointed to the bound orc. "Spike Wheel." The stego rat nodded and ran at the she-orc. Right before she broke out of the vines, Splinter jumped into the air and spun, turning into a spiked wheel of death. The stego rat spun forward and managed to cut clean through the calf of one of the orc's legs.

Despite that grievous injury, the orc was not fazed. She

turned back to face Splinter and was about to swing her greatsword down at the rat. Virgil quickly fired off a Nature Bolt spell, striking the orc in the face. The orc quickly snapped her head at Virgil, still showing a smiling face, and charged at him.

Virgil's eyes widened in fear as the crazed orc jumped and crawled at him at a surprising speed despite her bleeding stump leg. She quickly flung herself at him, swinging her greatsword with just one hand. Virgil backstepped and raised his crystalline buckler, just barely able to block the swing. Having only ten points in his strength stat, Virgil's arm was flung down, and the dark elf fell to the ground. The orc was on top of him. She laughed as she pulled out a wicked-looking dagger that was made from a strange-looking, reflective black metal and raised it to strike.

Virgil's distraction did provide one thing. The orc had completely ignored Splinter. The stego rat used Spike Wheel again and amputated the arm holding the dagger above the elbow. Virgil jammed his staff into the orc's mouth and cast Nature Bolt. To the orc's surprise, the spell tore out of the back of her neck, killing her on the spot.

"Thanks, girl," he said to Splinter as he forced the heavy orc body off him. He then surveyed how the battle was going. Baphomet had just killed the last orc opponent by biting her head off completely.

Virgil surveyed the rest of the fight and noticed the elven caster had one more arrow in his body, this time completely through his bicep. He held onto the totem with one hand while using the staff to cast spells with the other.

Gwen cast her Lighting Arrows spell, but they were unable to get past another conjured flame wall.

The flame tentacles of the totem were still lashing out at Christopher, who was doing a great job distracting them. Virgil was confident the duo could take the cult leader, but Virgil would rather be safe than sorry. "Baphomet, Instill Fear on the elf."

The beastking dropped the partially eaten orc, faced the cultist, and roared, using its animalistic presence to assert dominance in the mind of the caster. The dawn elf turned to face the beastking, wide-eyed and shaking in fear. He forced the eye of the totem to turn and face Baphomet.

The four flame tentacles from the totem launched out at the beast and wrapped around its forearms. Baphomet roared in anger at the flames.

Gwen and Christopher used the distraction and charged in. The terror boar, using his long tusks, gored the cultist's abdomen while Gwen fired an arrow which struck the totem, knocking it out of the elf's hand and causing it to break into two pieces once more as it hit the ground.

As it broke, the tentacles instantly dissipated.

The Hunter Druid then kicked the elf to the ground, putting a foot on his chest, and pointed a nocked arrow right at his face.

The elf smirked as the Instill Fear effect faded. "Hahaha, you think this is it? You think you've won?" His voice was weak as the wound from the boar was likely fatal. "You saw the power that one totem brought. That is just a taste of what our master has in store. All will burn!" the elf declared, and then a surge of heat radiated from his body, forcing Gwen to hop off and back away.

The elf's body raised up in the air and began to glow like he was on fire. A large slitted eye appeared on the center of the elf's forehead, focusing on Virgil as he began to speak again. This time the voice was much deeper and menacing. "How dare you steal from me!"

"Steal?! You're the one who's fucking stealing!" Virgil spat. "Who are you, and what do you want?" His Danger Sense was going off, and the druid could somehow feel the demonic energy coming off the possessed elf.

The 'elf' shook his head. "Pitiful mortal. I am Zinthos, and I am the fires of hatred incarnate!" he pronounced as the elf's hair went up in flame and turned into four tentacles of fire.

"With every new thing I devour, my flame grows, and soon, my hate will burn the entirety of Yggdrasil," Zinthos said, still holding Virgil's gaze.

Virgil was somehow paralyzed, staring into the large central eye of Zinthos. He shivered as he felt his thoughts being invaded. He felt the being trying to force him to move, but he fought desperately, causing his body to shake. He wasn't sure how much longer he could hold out.

Fortunately, the druid didn't have to worry about that as an arrow from deep in the forest struck Zinthos. It burned as it made contact with the body, so it just bounced off the being instead, but it freed up Virgil's mind.

"Don't look at its eye directly!" he shouted as he looked away, desperate to save everyone else from the same trap he had fallen into. He looked to where the arrow was fired from and saw the warg ranger with two beastkin children behind. Virgil smiled, grateful for the skilled archer.

Virgil then heard Zinthos speak in his mind, "*Hahahaha, do not worry, druid. This servant's body is about to expire. We shall meet again, but don't keep me waiting. I'm oh so hungry, and a dark elf would fuel my fires even more.*"

The possessed dawn elf had veins bulging out from his head before it burst into flames.

CHAPTER FOUR

Recovery

"Is everyone okay?" Virgil asked as he looked around.

"All good here," Gwen replied.

"We are okay as well," Valgorna called out as she walked up to the group, two beastkin children in tow.

"Great, where is the rhynorn?" Virgil asked.

The warg's face took on an uncomfortable expression. "Eh, I was... unable to free the beast. The orcs split up in two different directions, and I had to choose between the rhynorn or the children."

Virgil put his hand up. "Say no more. It's alright. I would have made the same decision in your shoes." Though Virgil dedicated his professional life to helping animals, and in truth liked a lot of animals more than people, the lives of people always were a higher priority than the lives of animals in his book.

Valgorna squinted her eyes and cocked her head to the side. "My shoes? But I don't wear shoes," she said, lifting up and showing one of her white fur-covered feet.

"He means in your situation, master," Gwen explained.

The warg nodded, then looked to Virgil. "I see. Well, hurry

and loot these invaders. We need to get the children back to Ginterbacher."

There was not much of value to be looted from the orcs. Most of the weapons were of poor quality, and Virgil was concerned he may get tetanus if he touched them. There was, however, one weapon that they thought to take.

Name: Tribal Glass Dagger
Item Type: Weapon
Damage: +10–20
Durability: 75/85
Item Class: Great
Description: A dagger used by a firebrand orc raider made from the rare volcanic metal, Glass.
Effect: +200% damage to unarmored foes, +15% chance to gain a critical hit to unarmored foes.

There were also a few healing herbs, as well as an extremely rare fruit called a dragonberry. When ingested, it would allow the user to breathe a gout of flame for five seconds. When Virgil thought as to why the orcs would have it, he quickly realized that being from the firebrand tribe made it more likely that they would be in possession of such a fruit. Regardless, he stored that immediately in Grief's storage pocket. The now-headless elf had some interesting loot.

Name: Shaman's Staff
Item Type: Weapon
Damage: +5–10
Durability: 75/85
Item Class: Uncommon
Effect: Provides +15% damage & -10% cost to all elemental-based spells (water, earth, fire, air).
Description: A wooden staff wrapped by a curling swirl of the green metal, Elementum.

Name: Zinthos Totem (Damaged)
Item Type: Totem
Durability: 0/50
Item Class: Epic
Description: A totem used to channel the demonic power of the demon Zinthos. If fire, blood, corruption, or demonic summoning magic is channeled through the totem when it's intact, a portion of the demon's conscience and power will appear.

Name: Elemental Mage Robes
Item Type: Clothing
Durability: 20/20
Item Class: Uncommon
Effect: -10% cost to all elemental-based spells (water, earth, fire, air).
Description: A robe enchanted to provide a bonus to all elemental-based spells.

Name: Manna Restoration Potion
Item Type: Potion
Durability: 10/10
Item Class: Exceptional
Effect: Restores entire manna pool of the imbiber over the course of 10 seconds.
Description: One of the best types of manna potions in all of Imeria, restoring the entire pool of the imbiber.

Name: Mummified Fire Sprite
Item Type: Alchemical Ingredient
Durability: 10/10
Item Class: Rare
Effect: A unique ingredient that can provide a variety of fire-based effects.
Description: The charred and mummified husk of a fire sprite. Be warned that, while powerful ingredients, if any sprite

discovers you have used their brethren for experimentation instead of allowing nature to reclaim it, you will be a hated enemy of all sprites, and they will attack you on sight.

Virgil had major demon vibes from Zinthos earlier, but the totem now confirmed that the malevolent being was a demon. Virgil also had a sneaking suspicion that he may very well be the second general they were looking for. He'd have to talk with Grief later about the being. Lastly, the potion and sprite body intrigued him; with his Herbology and Alchemy skills, he was excited to see what he could do with them. Sure, if a sprite discovered him using it, he may have a mortal enemy with the race, but right now, the reward outweighed the risk. So, he felt unperturbed as he stored all of the items in Grief.

Afterward, the party headed back to Ginterbacher. During their journey back, Virgil looked at the rest of his notifications.

For your part in defeating 20 firebrand orcs and the Zinthos cult leader, you have been awarded +2500 Experience.

Stealth has reached Level 16!

Restoration Magic has reached Level 24!

Despite not being able to save one of the endangered animals, the townsfolk were still very grateful at the recovery of the children.

A contingent of hooded rangers surrounded the city and even took up watch on the remaining roofs of the town. Valgorna was right, her allies seemed able to take care of the city while they were gone.

The warg told the druids that she had already booked two rooms at the inn for them and to meet her in the town hall in the morning before she went to reunite the children with their parents. Virgil also wondered which one was the healer

Valgorna had summoned to help. Maybe he could learn from them.

As they entered the village, a notification appeared.

Quest Complete!
Raid the Raiders
You have successfully recovered 2 out of the 3 kidnapped from the village of Ginterbacher. You shall be rewarded accordingly.

Reward:
+3000 Experience
+10 Gold
1 new spell
Increase in Relationship with the villagers of Ginterbacher. Current Relationship: Trusted.

Virgil dismissed the notification and wondered how he was going to get his new spell. His question was quickly answered when he heard a familiar shrill cackle from his left that sent shivers up his spine.

"Hehehehe, hello, my pupil," the voice of an old elf woman called out.

Virgil sighed as he turned to see a small dawn elf female with shriveled skin leaning on a cane, standing on the porch of the home. "Hello, master Lucille," he said with forced calm. Lucille Boquar was a legendary healer in the Yggdra Timberland. She was Virgil's trainer. The old elf also had a quick temper, propensity for violence, and repeatedly tried to get into Virgil's pants.

The dark elf had been able to deny the dawn elf, but she was persistent, and it definitely made him uncomfortable. Despite her small form, he knew that she was a *very* capable killer and could crush him in seconds. He *did not* want to get on her bad side. Beside Lucille was a very fat cat with blue eyes, a brown face, and a cream-colored body—Mr. Bigglesworth.

The cat had previously not been a fan of the druid during

his training and repeatedly attacked him unprovoked. After talking with Lucille, Virgil figured out that the cat had severe dental disease which was causing him pain and affecting his eating and attitude. So, Virgil had sedated the cat and was able to remove the broken and infected teeth. Ever since, the dark elf had gone from foe to friend.

Upon seeing the cat, Splinter let out a defensive hiss. The obese cat returned the gesture in kind. "Now be good, you." Lucille looked down to her cat and tapped him on the head with her cane. The cat closed his mouth and sat down, giving a very good Grumpy Cat impression.

The old healer's focus returned to Virgil. "Well well well, it looks like you've collected some good gear and become a good bit stronger since last we met, my pupil," she said as she walked down the stairs. "And you've kept up your good physique. You must really want to tempt all the ladies here, walking around flaunting your shirtless body." She promptly gave him an exaggerated wink.

"I assure you, it's not intentional," Virgil said, quickly bowing to the elder elf and blushing profusely. Gwen put a fist to her mouth, chuckling at Virgil's discomfort. "I don't know why, but apparently Yggdrasil is insistent that I not wear a shirt. Honestly, I think the great tree may have a cruel sense of humor. She gave me this pauldron," he said pointing to the silverbark pauldron on his right shoulder that was part of the silverbark armor set that Yggdrasil granted him. "It has a requirement that I don't wear a shirt with it."

Lucille squinted at the piece of armor, giving the impression that she was analyzing it. She started laughing. "I can't believe it, you're right." She wiped a tear from one of her eyes. "Well, if you don't want a fun night with me as a reward, let me teach you another spell. I heard that Valgorna offered you a new spell with her quest, and I will be the one to grant it. What's your Life Magic level?"

"It's Restoration Magic, which is a mix of both Life and Earth Magic."

"Yeah yeah, whatever. What's your level?"

"Twenty-four."

Lucille put a hand on her chin and looked to be thinking. "Hmm, good, that is much improved. There are quite a few spells that I could teach you. Is there a certain type of spell you're looking for in particular?"

Virgil thought about it. There were a few kinds of spells he could find beneficial. Having a more rapid or instantaneous healing spell versus his healing over time spell, Restore, or Nature Bolt that could only heal druids could be good. Despite now having both Leeching Vines and Nature Bolt, it still wouldn't hurt for him to have another offensive spell. There was something, though, which had really bothered him.

When he stared into the possessed elf's third eye, he literally felt his body being controlled as if the demonic presence was somehow invading and dominating his very being. The idea of being trapped in his own body while another controlled his actions terrified him. If Virgil was going to face this Zinthos again—and it was very likely that he would—he needed some sort of mental protection.

"Do you have some sort of magical protection from one trying to take control of your mind or body? We recently dealt with an opponent that tried to invade my mind, and it scares the shit out of me if I have to face it again."

Lucille pursed her face as she contemplated Virgil's words. She then snapped her finger, and her expression lightened. "I've got just the thing," she said and, without any ceremony, she jumped up and put each of her hands around Virgil's head, pulling it down to her level. She pressed her thumbs to his forehead, closed her eyes, and before Virgil could protest, began imparting a spell onto the dark elf.

Virgil's eyes widened and his vision went white as he took in the spell's information. As he absorbed the knowledge of the Life Magic spell, the essence of Yggdrasil inside him transformed the spell from its Life Magic form into a unique

Restoration Magic version. After thirty seconds, he had gained a new spell.

Purifying Aura
Cost: 50 MP
Effect: Causes an aura to emanate from the caster. The aura removes all debuffs on the caster and all friendlies within the aura. Lasts for 10 minutes.
Cooldown: 10 seconds.
Range: n feet, where n = Restoration Magic Level/3

"Thank you," Virgil said to Lucille as he blinked the spell's info clear from his vision.

She let go of his head, and he began to fall forward. Virgil felt a familiar form grab him, keeping him from falling to his knees from the effects of learning a spell directly from another person. This was the first time Virgil had learned a spell not directly through a spell book, and it was definitely more intense on his system. If given a choice, he would use a tome any day of the week compared to direct transfer. He would also bet that ten out of ten veterinarians recommended it.

"Are you okay?" Gwen asked as she held onto him, concerned.

"I'm good, it was just a lot," he said as she helped him stand back up.

"Oh, so you actually did find someone to appreciate your body, eh?" Lucille asked with a wry smile.

Both Gwen and Virgil looked at each other then quickly separated and looked away, blushing a deep shade of red. Both of them were definitely interested in each other, but the status of their relationship had not been ever fully addressed and it was still new.

"Hehehe, well I'm always here in case it doesn't work out, young whippersnapper," Lucille said, then pinched Virgil's butt, cackling as she walked toward the town hall, Mr. Bigglesworth trailing close by.

Now, without any urgent need for them, the druids and their animal companions felt the weight of exhaustion beat down on their bodies. They were tired and hungry.

Virgil had Baphomet change back into its smaller form as they made their way to the inn. The barkeep seemed to disapprove of having animals inside, but when the druids stared at him, daring him to force them to separate from their pets, he quickly changed his mind.

Thick soup with chunks of meat and vegetables was served. The barkeep had a look of disgust as he gave the last bowl to Splinter, but a quick look from Virgil was all it took to see the deal done.

Both druids were given a room for the night.

"You did really great out there. Though, I'm surprised."

"Surprised by what?"

"I didn't know you were into such older women."

Virgil rolled his eyes and chuckled.

Before he could retort, Gwen kissed him. She broke the kiss with a wink. "Goodnight… whippersnapper."

Virgil had a big stupid grin plastered on his face as he went to his room for the night.

CHAPTER FIVE

Lessons

The next morning, both druids slept in. Despite being elves and not needing as much sleep as a typical human, they were still both tired and exhausted from the three fights the day before. Fortunately, no one woke them up, and they both made it out of their rooms by around ten in the morning. Well, no person woke them up. A talking skull *did* wake Virgil up.

"Lad, it be time to get up. Quit dreamin' 'bout yer new girl, and hop up outta bed."

"Mmm, go away, Grief," Virgil said half-awake as he put a pillow over his head.

"GET UP NOW LAD!" the skull yelled through their mental link.

Virgil shot up out of bed from the sudden verbal assault on his psyche. He grabbed the skull that was on the desk by his bed. "What was that for?" he asked through gritted teeth, putting his face threateningly right in front of the skull.

Before Grief could answer, he felt something tug at his pant leg. Virgil looked down to see Splinter tugging with Baphomet in its smaller form hopping from foot-to-foot.

"Yer pets need to drain the main vein, lad, and that purple

puppy of yers has been lookin' at me funny fer the past hour. I don't know 'bout you, lad, but I ain't interested in havin' some beastie pee in me eye socket again. I not be a toilet."

"Again?" Virgil cocked his head to the side.

"Do not ask," Grief replied, nonplussed.

Virgil chuckled. Seeing his animals did in fact need to pee, he quickly put on his armor and took them outside. He met up with Gwen in the lobby of the inn afterward and the druids enjoyed a meal of meat, toast, and eggs. Virgil decided to inquire what Grief knew about this Zinthos. "So, Grief, what kind of demon are we dealing with exactly? I've never dealt with something that had such mental powers before," he said after he swallowed a mouthful of food.

"I've been thinkin' bout that, lad, and I have some ideas. The devil be using some sort of mind control power. There be only a few kinds of foul pieces of filth who have that kind of skill. The first be a little, ugly, scaled imp called a quisik. The next be a chained devil who like to sadistically torture their prey. The last I know of be called Nawfuls. They be a bunch of fat, deceptive manipulators, much like me Aunt Thelma. Haha! We called her 'Aunt Awful Nawful.' Hehehe, good times."

Virgil and Gwen looked at each other at the joke. "Soooo, do you think Zinthos is one of those demons?" Virgil asked.

"Truth be told, lad, eh, prolly not," he said, clearly unsure, but explained his reasoning. "Quisiks be dumb little shites that prefer mischief over mass control. Chained devils use chains, not fiery tentacles. It could be a Nawful, cuz the thing seemed to manipulate others and wanted to consume things. Nawfuls are pretty fat... just like Thelma."

"Grief!"

"Sorry, lad, I was just reminiscin' me childhood memories. What I was gettin' to was, even though Nawfuls are gluttons, they're lazy. Controlling a whole tribe of people is too much work for 'em. My current idea is some sort of half-breed or hybrid, like yer beastie was before," he said, referencing that Baphomet was previously a half demon-half beast hybrid and the former first demon general. "Maybe it's a half Nawful-half Fiery Horror? That may be the most likely option for now. While I keep thinkin' bout what it could be, ye and the lass need to find a way to protect yer minds when we see this thing in the future."

The druids were disappointed that they didn't have a clear answer as to what kind of demon Zinthos was, but were grateful that Grief was doing his best to help them and for his sound advice. After they finished their meal, they headed towards the town hall.

The citizens were already busy making repairs and preparations for a burial ceremony for those that hadn't survived the orc attacks. The hooded rangers were still patrolling the village. It was easy to detect the beastkin among the rangers as all of them seemed to have tails, whether mammalian or reptilian, sticking out from their cloaks.

They made it to the large central building that served as the town hall and were led inside by a couple of rangers. There they saw Valgorna speaking with Lucille, her mate, and a reptil ranger that looked to be an iguana man.

"I see you have fully recovered? Good, now please sit. We have much to discuss," Valgorna said, gesturing to the two chairs.

The druids sat with their animals beside them.

The old white warg continued, "First off, thank you for your aid in protecting the village and rescuing the children. Without your aid, many more lives would've been lost. As you have already discovered, firebrand orcs are not a common occurrence in Ginterbacher. In truth, they shouldn't ever be able to have made it this far at all."

"You said that there is a barrier that keeps the orcs out. What kind of barrier is it? Clearly, it's not working right now," Virgil said.

"As said before, the firebrands are isolated to stay in the Scorched Lands which is by Mount Brandios to the northwest of here. The entire area surrounding the volcano is surrounded by a set of magic totems. Now, I do not possess magic, so I cannot tell you how they work exactly. Somehow, they manage to prevent the firebrands from crossing."

"Who put up these totems?" Gwen asked.

"The Mage College, located in the independent city of Amthoon. As we had discussed before, though Ginterbacher is technically part of the Rubasal Kingdom, it is that, just off of a technicality. So, the founders of this village made a secret deal with Amthoon. We would pay the city a fee, and they would provide protection from the firebrands in turn. They had the college install the protective totems, and also have provided a contingent of guards to patrol the totem border weekly."

"So, why are the firebrands getting through?" Virgil asked.

"That is the question," Valgorna replied. "We have been paying our fee of coin, honey, and lumber on time, without any delay or missed payment. That makes it confusing as to why the firebrands have been able to travel so far from their homes. I suspect this Zinthos you encountered is to blame."

"I agree," Virgil said. "My druidic senses really gave me the impression that the thing was a demon. If that is the case, it is definitely concerning."

"I felt it too," Gwen added. "If there is a demon leading the orcs, the village is at greater risk of more attacks."

"Indeed, Gwendolyn," the warg agreed. "If the firebrands have been able to make it through both the protective wards from the totems and the patrols from the college, they definitely had help. I suspect that the malevolent totem we encountered may actually be some sort of corrupted version of one of the protective totems. I also suspect that the elf we fought was one of those 'helpers.' Still, even if they made it through, they should have been intercepted by Amthoon guards. Either the firebrands killed the guards, or there weren't any guards at all. Both options are disturbing."

The village leader gave the druids a more serious expression. "That brings us to why we asked you here. With my ranger allies and Lucille here, the village should be relatively safe for the time being, but we need to discover as to how they are getting through. Please, we ask that you travel to Amthoon, show the king the corrupted totem, and have them rectify the problem."

Quest Unlocked
A Call For Aid 1

Valgorna, leader of the village of Ginterbacher, has offered you a quest. Her village has recently been under attack from orcs of the firebrand tribe. She has asked that you deliver a message to the king of Amthoon, asking for aid to solve the problem which they had previously agreed to handle.

Requirements:

Meet with the jarl of Amthoon and show him the Zinthos totem.

Have the jarl send forth patrols.

Reward:

2000 Experience.

Do you accept?

Yes or No

"We accept," Virgil said. In truth, it actually worked out well with their plans anyway, as they were already heading towards the independent city.

The party rested another day before leaving. They took time to restock supplies and do some training since both their teachers were there. Gwen did approach Lucille to ask if the old elf could teach her any new spells like Virgil, but was unfortunately told no as her Predator Magic was a mix of Air and Earth Magic. Lucille knew Life Magic, and Gwen did not have the capability to learn that particular branch of magic. That didn't mean that Gwen went away empty handed.

"Since my pupil favors you, I do have something that can be of benefit," the old elf said and pulled out a small ring. It was made of silver and had a weird pink item adorned on the top that looked like a brain.

Name: Ring of Sound Mind
Item Type: Accessory
Durability: 50/50
Item Class: Rare
Effect: +5 Intelligence, +15% resistance to mind-altering effects.
Description: A ring enchanted with Life Magic and adorned with a crystalized fragment of a Mind Flayer brain. This ring increases both the Intelligence statistic and defense of the mind.

Grateful, the Hunter Druid gave Lucille a hug and ran off to go practice archery with Valgorna. When they were not busy helping the injured people and pets, Lucille and Virgil were working on Manna Manipulation. He repeatedly cast Barkskin and Lucille guided him on how to direct his flow of manna. Apparently, with his mind, he could target a particular part of the body with the spell. It was a concept he was familiar with as he had been able to focus his Restore spell on certain injured parts of the body to allow them to heal quicker.

What was different about this spell, though, was that it didn't provide a physical effect. It affected the mind instead. When he first cast the spell, he just targeted himself. Lucille noticed, and, with her usual exuberance, helped him to direct the flow of manna from his staff to go straight to his brain instead.

To his surprise, after an hour of repeatedly casting, he actually felt a difference and not just from Lucille's vigorous use of pain. Virgil was now able to easily target his own mind with the spell. He also gained the Manna Manipulation skill, which allowed him to more easily direct the flow of manna and target his spells.

After training with their teachers, the party shopped around town to restock their supplies. Gwen didn't have self-repairing armor like Virgil had, so she went to a leather worker and had her gear repaired. Virgil was interested in utilizing his Herbology and Alchemy strengths, and went over to the local apothecary. There was a 'No Animals Allowed' sign on the building, so Virgil had Splinter and Baphomet stay outside. The stego rat was rather excited when Virgil gave her permission to go around and eat any scraps of food she could find. He did make the caveat that she couldn't actively steal from the villagers though.

Virgil read the sign with the shop's name on it. It was called the 'Serpent's Surprise.' As Virgil opened the wooden door to the small shack, he could tell the hinges needed help as they groaned with a creak. Inside was a dark store with no windows. It was illuminated by spaced-out wall sconces adorned with orbs of magical white light. They provided just enough illumination to highlight the different potions and ingredients spread out along shelves, both on the walls and aligned in rows of what looked to be repurposed wooden bookshelves.

There was a large counter to the left of the store with a reptil merchant standing behind it, looking at Virgil expectantly. The reptil had a humanoid body, but the head of a purple and black cobra. "Welcome, sssir, to Serpent'ssss Surprisssse. I am Rassss. How may I ssserve you, druid champion of Yggdrass-sil?" the reptil asked as he bowed to Virgil in a courtly manner, tongue still flicking out of his mouth. Ras wore a black sleeve-less tunic that was not so ornate that he would fit in with royalty, but he was definitely not impoverished. That or he just knew how to dress well.

"Hello Ras, you can just call me Virgil. I've come to see your shop and check its wares. I'm also interested in any recipes you may be willing to sell."

"Ah, a fellow alchemisssst I sssee, hmm? It'sss nice to see that the great tree appreciatesss my profession. Pleasssse, Virgil, take your time to perussse my ssshop. I will go fetch some of my recipessss I'm willing to sssell. May I asssssk, what is your current Alchemy Level?"

"If I may ask, why do you want to know?" Virgil asked cautiously. Though he knew the reptil man was an ally, Virgil was not keen on divulging too much information about himself.

"Hehehe, a fair question," Ras admitted. "I asssk because basssed on your level, there are only certain recipessss you can learn. Although, I may be able to help increassse your level for a priccce," the snake man said with a grin that admittedly made Virgil nervous at what exactly the alchemist meant by 'price.'

"Twenty-three," Virgil said, finally relenting.

"Very good. At your current level, there are a variety of concoctionsssss I can teach you to make. I can also sssshow you the sssspecific methodsss instead of just handing you instructionsss. That way, you will more actively increassse your Alchemy sssskill. As for priccce, I can take my paymentsss in many formsss, but there isss sssomething you possssessss that none of my other customers have," the alchemist hissed, smiling an even bigger grin.

Virgil gulped. "And what is that?"

The reptil continued. "Assss you can guessss, my storessss of healing potionsss have been drained due to the recent attack. Even though you healed a majority of the victimssss, my creationsssss helped to sssstablize a good many of the town. While I have been working diligently to replenish my sssupply, I have not been able to meet the demand. I am happy to help my fellow villagerssss, but the constant work on the same potions hassss been… taxing on me. Due to my frequent and repeated usage of the sssame recipe, I no longer gain any experience towardssss my Alchemy sssskill as well. In order to increase it, I need to add new and unique ingredientssss to my healing spell, and that is where you come in, sssir. I need," he paused and licked his serpentine lips, "your blood."

Quest Unlocked!
A Bloody Price

Ras, the reptil alchemist in Ginterbacher, has made so many healing potions using the same recipe that he can no longer level his Alchemy skill by using that formula. In order to remedy this, he needs new ingredients. As the Healer Druid Champion of Yggdrasil, your blood has natural healing and regenerative capabilities. Ras realizes this and wishes to collect some of your blood for a new batch of healing potions.

Requirements:

Donate 300 milliliters of your blood to Ras.

Rewards:

Increase in Alchemy skill.

Permanent 10% discount at The Serpent's Surprise.

Training Under Ras the Alchemist.

5 new recipes.

Do You Accept?

Yes or No

Virgil sighed. He was not sure how much blood was 'safe' for his dark elf physiology to lose. The average for humans back on Earth was actually five-hundred milliliters, from what he recalled. Despite that, he was genuinely concerned about giving his blood to someone he just met and the… collection methods the alchemist had in store. Even though he liked working with snakes back on Earth, that didn't mean he was a fan of getting bit by one.

After some more discussion and a little bit of negotiating with the Ras, Virgil pushed those concerns away. Ras was an ally, a citizen of Ginterbacher who was looking out for both Virgil and seeking to grow his own abilities.

Virgil respected that. The dark elf wanted to grow his abilities too. That was why he came to the alchemist shop. If a bit of pain and some blood loss were what was required to get stronger and keep his party safe, he would do it. "I'll do it as long as you don't bite me," Virgil said and accepted the prompt.

Ras's smile quickly turned into a pout. "Oh, you're no fun," he whined. "Very well, I accept your termsss, but I will sssample ssome after it'ss collected. I'm ssso very intrigued as to what effectsss it may contain!" he said, clapping his hands like an excited schoolgirl. The serpentine man took a few steps back and pulled open a large hidden door on the floor leading to some sort of cellar. "Come along then," he said, waving for Virgil to follow.

The dark elf walked around the large wooden desk and did just that.

The room below appeared to be both the alchemist's laboratory and living quarters. The walls, unlike the building above, were made entirely of solid stone. The floor was made of wood of much better quality than that above. Instead of creaky boards, the wood was perfectly aligned so that it flowed like it was all one smooth surface. There were multiple bright-white orbs of light that illuminated the room much better than the storefront.

All along the walls were multiple shelves, drawers, and storage units. The ones that were open and exposed had rows of ingredients placed in a neat and orderly fashion. They also appeared to be color-coded. One wall had a single twin bed with a small night table by it. The bed was made, and there wasn't a single wrinkle. In the center of the medieval laboratory was a large cauldron flanked by two circular tables adorned with beakers and vials of liquids of various colors. There wasn't a speck of dust that Virgil noticed... except for a small glass vial labeled 'Dust,' but you get the picture. It was a dream lab for a scientist with OCD. Virgil could think of a few of his colleagues back on Earth who would've loved this!

"Impressive" the druid said. "So, this is where you do your experiments. You do a great job keeping it clean."

"Thank you, ssir," Ras replied. "While many alchemistsss do not mind a bit of mustinessss, dirt, or debris in their labssss, I find that the fewer impuritiesss lead to better quality creationsssss."

Virgil nodded, as the reptil's logic made sense. If someone was making medication for him back on Earth, you best believe he'd want there to be as few impurities as possible!

Ras pulled out a chair from under one of the tables. "Pleasse, ssssit."

Virgil complied. The alchemist pulled out a large needle,

some tubing, and a large beaker from his stores. Ras stroked a rune on one of his tables and it began to glow red, then quickly, a small gout of red flame erupted from the rune and burned lowly, like the flame from a Bunsen burner in a high-school chemistry lab.

"Lad, ye be sure 'bout this? This fella seems a few sandwiches short of a picnic," Grief asked through their mental link. Virgil watched as Ras dipped the needle over the flame and realized the man was sanitizing the needle. Virgil was impressed at the alchemist's knowledge and cleanliness. At least the dark elf shouldn't get an infection.

"I think we should be fine," he replied back to the skull. After Ras activated another ward, a small upward burst of freezing air emerged from it. He stuck the hot and recently sanitized needle over it, and it rapidly cooled.

The reptil came over to Virgil, applied a wet cloth to the inner side of the elf's right elbow, then said, "Now, count to three."

Virgil breathed and closed his eyes. "One, two, mmm." Virgil groaned as the man stuck the large needle right in his vein before the count finished. He opened his eyes indignantly and saw his blood quickly drain from the needle, through the tubing, and into the beaker.

After only a couple of minutes, Ras took out the needle and placed a clean cloth to Virgil's arm. "Place pressure on this."

Virgil complied, then cast Restore on himself. Fortunately, he did not receive any 'blood loss' debuff, so the three-hundred milliliters was indeed a safe amount to donate, as he'd thought. Ras took the beaker full of Virgil's blood excitedly and giggled. "Hehehe, yesssss!" he exclaimed and quickly poured Virgil's blood into small glass vials and corked them. A notification then showed up before Virgil.

Quest Complete!
A Bloody Price
Despite his outwardly appearance, you trusted the snake man

alchemist Ras and allowed him to collect your blood. You have also learned about the importance of cleanliness towards potion effectiveness, plus your blood can serve as an ingredient for healing potions.

Reward:

+2 to Alchemy Skill.

Permanent 10% discount at The Serpent's Surprise.

Speak to Ras to receive the rest of your rewards.

After Virgil's spell healed all his damage, he stood up and walked over to Ras, who was organizing multiple different ingredients, eager to use Virgil's blood in new recipes. "Er hem, I'm glad I could help, but I believe I'm owed some training and some recipes."

Ras turned back to Virgil and was startled, showing that the reptil had completely forgotten the elf was there. "Oh! Of coursssse, ssir. With your blood, I believe we both can increassse our skillsssss. Essssspecially if you're interested in donating more blood? Perhapsss a finger? Oooh! Your bonesssss could provide a permanent buff!" Virgil just pushed up his round glasses and stared at the alchemist clearly unamused. "Oh fine! Sssssstill no fun," Ras grumbled.

For the next five hours, Ras and Virgil brewed and concocted various potions, poultices, and powders. The reptilian snake man was a fount of knowledge. After Virgil gave the man his blood, Ras was practically ecstatic to use the new ingredient. He was so grateful, he taught Virgil many tips and trade-secrets. The dark elf was able to gain six levels in the skill in just five hours! Even Lucille, who was a master healer, was not able to teach Virgil in the skill so fast or effectively!

Congratulations! Your skill, Alchemy, has reached Advanced Rank!

Due to your increasing in rank of Alchemy, particularly with using your blood, all created items using your blood as one of their ingredients are now 10% more effective, and you will have a 20% increased chance to succeed in crafting new brews when using your blood as one of the ingredients.

That was an… interesting perk. He wasn't going to advertise that particular one any time soon. Virgil was also able to increase his Trade skill multiple times by bartering with the reptil for different unique ingredients that he possessed. The alchemist valued them very greatly, and readily traded with the druid. By the end of the training and negotiating, Virgil had learned ten new recipes, learned more about fifteen different herbs, and had acquired six unique potions. The new recipes ranged from poisons and paralytics to antidotes and invisibility brews to Darkvision boosts. Four of the new unique potions acquired were created during Virgil's training with Ras.

One of the things Virgil was reminded of during his negotiations for blood donation was his Manna Restoration Potion. Ras expressed some discomfort at the idea of parting with such a rare recipe, but when Virgil promised to give more blood at his next visit, the alchemist didn't hesitate. Apparently, the dark elf's blood plus crushed and boiled termite bodies could actually improve the Manna Restoration Potion! Unfortunately, it took a long time to make, and the ingredients were very expensive, so Virgil wasn't going to be able to mass-produce them any time soon. In addition to that recipe and the ten others promised to him, Virgil had discovered three new ones, since he had brewed them during his training with Ras.

You have found Analgesic Sleep Powder.
Item Type: Potion
Durability: 20/20
Item Class: Great
Effect: When inhaled, the powder will cause the target to fall into a pleasant sleep that will last 1 hour. Target cannot be awoken unless they take 100 points of damage or receive some sort of electrical shock. During the sleep, the powder will also

target the pain receptors in the body, dulling them and reducing overall pain felt by the target after they awaken by 50%.

You have found Potion of True Taunt.
Item Type: Potion
Durability: 15/15
Item Class: Epic
Effect: Instantly improves or worsens your Taunt skill to a score of 50 for 5 minutes. Makes all enemies within a 50-foot radius immediately hostile toward you for the potion's duration. All attacks made against you deal double damage for the potion's duration.

You have found Metallic Acid.
Item Type: Potion
Durability: 5/10
Item Class: Exceptional
Effect: This acid was made from the body of a Black Slime that was harassing dwarven miners and subsequently killed by the Furyfire Mercenary Guild. After some experimentation, the alchemist working on the slime enhanced the corrosive abilities. Now it is a deadly acid that will degrade any metal it touches by 25 durability/second for 20 seconds. In exchange for the increased metal degrading capabilities, it cannot dissolve any other substance.

You have found Liquid Light Flash.
Item Type: Potion
Durability: 10/10
Item Class: Great
Effect: Break vial to cause a burst of light that will last for 3 seconds. Will cause blindness to all exposed to its light within 50 feet of it.

You have found Potion of Snake Hands.
Item Type: Potion

Durability: 20/20

Item Class: Exceptional

Effect: An accidental creation by Ras the Alchemist after he spilled some ingredients together when he unintentionally added his blood. The reptil's blood mixed together with the random ingredients to cause a random effect. Whoever drinks this will have both their hands turn into cobras for 2 hours. The cobras will follow the commands of whoever imbibes the potion, but will have minds and desires of their own.

You have found Potion of Icy Essence.

Item Type: Potion

Durability: 10/10

Item Class: Uncommon

Effect: Causes an icy aura to exude from the drinker for 5 hours. The aura will cause the temperature around the drinker to decrease and will also reduce all heat-based damage or debuffs by 50% while in effect.

He had learned the Analgesic Sleep Powder, Liquid Light Flash, and Potion of Icy Essence. All-in-all, it was a *very* beneficial training session. Virgil was satisfied.

————

That afternoon, the village held a burial ceremony in honor of the five dead. It was a somber time, but the families of those who passed showed strength despite their loss. They said kind words in remembrance of the dead, and expressed gratitude toward both the village and the druids for their part in keeping them safe. After that was done and the bodies were buried at the base of a large tree, a feast was held. The beastkin called it a 'Celebration of Life.' Apparently, the beastkin way was that after the dead were buried, the time to mourn was over. Though still sad, the beastkin chose to honor the dead by trying to live life to the fullest, and that was done with a large feast.

The entire village took part and they provided a large amount of well-cooked food. Even the rangers grabbed some food in between guard shifts. It was just as good as any large Thanksgiving meal either druid had ever had back on Earth. To be fair, Gwen only had a few Thanksgivings since she didn't grow up in the United States.

Virgil and Gwen were seated next to Valgorna, who honored the two with a toast. People were laughing, drinking, eating, and even singing despite the grim happenings of the night before. Virgil was extremely impressed at the people's hardiness to go through what they just did and be able to celebrate life the next night.

He noted that he was also happy to be in a place where he didn't have to hide his dark elf identity. Not one person, even the other elves or dwarves that called Ginterbacher home, treated him with discrimination. This was a place he could frequent on his travels! Even the animals were treated well and were each given their own bowls of food to eat out of. The beasts still weren't allowed in most buildings, but that didn't seem to bother them as they still had and readily ate their bowls full of tasty treats on the ground

Virgil wanted to revisit last night's kiss with Gwen, but Lucille's flirtiness went to a whole new level as she became tipsy. The elderly elf, now with a flushed face, chased Virgil around the large central table, very eager to pinch his butt, drawing a good bout of laughter from the townsfolk. He eventually managed to ward off the elf, but by the time that was done, he was tired, and Gwen had already gone to sleep. She left a message that Virgil needed to be up by six that morning, as she wanted to get an early start to make it to Amthoon before dark. Hoping that Lucille wouldn't wake up by that time either, Virgil was okay with the plan.

CHAPTER SIX

On the Trail

Virgil promptly woke up at six. This time, Grief did not yell directly into his mind, almost causing him a heart attack. Virgil did have to go find Splinter. He was concerned that something bad had happened to her, before he found the rat laying atop a pile of garbage with a very distended belly. There wasn't a spot of food mixed in with the waste. Her Survivalist trait was something else allowing her to eat anything and not be poisoned. Apparently, the rat went out for a late-night snack and was very efficient in finding food. He stored Splinter inside his satchel to sleep off her food coma. Baphomet was not too fond of sharing its space inside the bag and transformed into its large beastking form. Now ready to go, the party headed out.

Gwen showed Virgil a map of the continent that she and the other druids were originally given by the elf king Darcassan. Valgorna took the time to add more detail to the map in the area they were in, on the western side of the Kygora continent. Virgil was both impressed and grateful for the information. Looking at the map, they decided to go to the Scorched Lands border to the northwest, then go directly west towards Amthoon.

Their trek from Ginterbacher was definitely more eventful than their journey to the village. The first trek of their journey was deep and wild jungle. The party did eventually make it to the border of the firebrands' territory. It was easy to notice the Scorched Lands; it looked like someone had carved a literal line in the ground. On one side was a dense jungle. On the other was a land of hard blackened rock, with boiling geysers, streams of lava, and whittled dead trees. Many plants were black and burnt husks of their former selves. Yggdrasil's influence was still strong here, just a day after damage vegetation was already starting to return.

As the party traveled along the border, they noticed the totems spread out miles apart in an even pattern. The totems each looked the same, possessing an exaggerated carved face of an orc on them. It reminded Virgil of carved tikis back on Earth.

As they traveled along the border, they noticed some gaps in the spacing of the totems. Where those gaps were, the bordering jungle was much more burnt and damaged, signaling those orcs had utilized the gaps to travel. The party only happened upon one more contingent of firebrands, but this time was different. Instead of a demonic shaman, the orcs had an ogre with them. Apparently, orcs and ogres were cousins and would often join together in tribes. The Firebrands were no different.

The ogre made the fight more challenging as the large brute towered eight feet tall and wielded a large tree as a makeshift club. Thankfully Baphomet was able to keep the ogre distracted long enough for the party to handle the orcs. The beastking even managed to slap the ogre straight across the cheek with its giant clawed hands, knocking out some of the giant's teeth. After the battle, there were two bits of interesting loot the ogre dropped.

Name: Firebrand Ogre Teeth x4
Item Type: Alchemical Ingredient

Durability: 50/50
Item Class: Great
Effect: Variable fire-based effects.
Description: 4 teeth dislodged from the jaw of a firebrand ogre.

Name: Firebrand Ogre Eye x2
Item Type: Alchemical Ingredient
Durability: 50/50
Item Class: Great
Effect: Can provide strength-boosting effects.
Description: 2 eyes removed from the skull of a firebrand ogre.

The Alchemist inside Virgil was excited about the possibilities of experimenting with the new ingredients. He was hoping their blood would provide some sort of benefit, but his Alchemy skill did not notify him of any use. They did take a stop to rest, and to Virgil's surprise, Grief spoke to him through their mental link. The skull had a tone of concern in his voice. *"Hey lad, can I have a chat with ye?"*

"Sure, Grief. Everything okay?"

"Yes... well, no, not everythin'."

"What's going on?"

"Well, I know I'm just a skull now, but I can't help but want to help ye in yer fightin'. I was a warrior in my past life, and the warrior spirit be callin' me recently. Ye reckon there be anything I can do to help ye? Well, besides getting swallowed by some foul creature again."

Virgil chuckled at that, thinking of when his soulbound companion was swallowed whole by a giant mutated rat and was summoned back to Virgil via the Soulbound Recall skill. It was... admittedly gross, but it worked to kill the giant rat creature.

"Hm, well, let's see what skills you have." Virgil looked to see that the skull had four skills; Soulbound Communication, Soulbound Recall, Ancient Lore, and Storage. They were useful in

terms of utility, but for combat, they weren't that useful in a direct manner. Grief's Ancient Lore skill contained a plethora of information in regards to demons and it had helped Virgil in numerous battles. Still though, Grief was a warrior on the inside; he didn't want to be just on the sidelines, but Virgil was unsure how the immobile skull could be anything but. He didn't want to disappoint his friend and companion, however, so he tried to give him something to focus on to potentially help.

"Tell you what, bud, when we're in Amthoon, I'll see if there is someone at the Mage College who could help you somehow participate in combat. In the meantime, the only two things that could be of use is if Soulbound Recall could work the opposite way. If I could place you some-where and have you pull me away from an enemy attack, it could save my life. The other thing is your Storage skill. You have a literal pocket of space in the back of your head. Could you, I don't know, use it as a vacuum to suck things into it?"

That idea actually excited Grief. *"Ye know, that be soundin' pretty great, lad! Think 'bout it, I could be strapped on yer shield and absorb all arrows and projectiles headin' yer way!"*

"That sounds great, Grief. I don't know how to train you in those skills, so why don't you focus on that then. Feel the connection you have to the pocket of space and try to suck something into it?"

"What should I try to absorb, lad?"

"I don't know," Virgil sent, then looked around the ground. He picked up a fallen leaf and set it inside the foramen magnum of Grief, making sure not to activate the storage abil-ity. *"See if you can bring this into your Storage ability on your own."*

There was silence. Then a straining noise in his head. It sounded like someone was straining to lift too much weight at the gym. The skull was literally straining trying to suck the leaf into the pocket of extradimensional space he had inside of him.

Grief spoke again, sounding a little tired despite not having a physical body. *"Well, that be tougher than expected. It be strange not having ye activate the Storage skill fer me. Don't ye worry, ye long eared bastard lad. I'll figure out how to bring things into me storage space in no time."*

Virgil smiled at the skull's confidence and rested while his companion continued to train.

As the group continued on their journey, they realized they were getting closer to the coastal city, as the smell of saltwater started to permeate their nostrils. They did have to break away from the Scorched Lands border to go more in the direction of the independent city.

As they estimated, they were around thirty minutes away from Amthoon. A large elk-like creature with the coloring of a zebra came running at full tilt from across a small open valley. As Gwen pulled up her bow to aim, eager to use her Hunter Druid skill, Virgil stayed her shot. Something was off, yet he couldn't place it. Not long after the elk emerged, three large wolves with fur that were a camouflaged mix of gray and green followed and quickly surrounded the cervid.

"Should we help the elk?" Gwen asked.

Virgil felt a tug at his heart, but he shook his head. "No, we need to let nature take its course. Whatever animal wins, we'll help it." The veterinarian wanted so badly to intervene and save the elk from the chance at death, but this was as nature intended. Herbivores keep the plant life in check to prevent it from choking out animal life, and carnivores keep their prey populations in check to prevent deforestation and resulting mass animal death from occurring. Like it or not, that is why hunting is sometimes needed in highly-populated countries as there are not enough predators to keep the prey population in check. This life and death battle for survival happening before them needed to play out for the good of the entire Timberland.

The party watched as the elk shifted its head frantically, trying to keep an eye on its three attackers. One of the green wolves to the buck's right jumped in the air and lunged at the elk when he was looking the other way. Faster than the airborne wolf realized, the elk buck swung his head violently back towards it. Both gravity and the elk's momentum caused the wolf to fall right on the sharp point of one of the buck's antlers, impaling the canine straight through the chest.

Dark green blood surged out of the wolf's back and mouth as it let out a high-pitched cry of pain and swiftly went limp. The other two wolves took the opportunity of their brethren's demise and charged.

The elk swung his head to the left and flung the dead wolf's body at one of the two charging wolves. The body hit its mark and stopped the wolf completely. Though fast, the cervid was not fast enough to deal with both attackers, and the last wolf was able to bite straight down on its left hindlimb.

The elk cried out from his sudden pain and tried to kick the wolf off. The green wolf held on tight with its jaws, determined to not let go now that they finally caught their quarry. The buck tried to run again, but the weight of the wolf biting down on his limb and pulling back caused the buck's pace to slow dramatically. That gave the other wolf enough time to shake off its daze and return to the fight. Fully distracted with the wolf on his leg, the buck did not notice its companion charging at him. The buck let out a cry of surprise as the charging green and gray wolf jumped and bit down on his neck.

The buck halted his running and began trying to shake off the wolf, dangling off his neck and biting down on the windpipe, before he suffocated from the crushing of his windpipe.

It was a brutal way for an animal to go, but Virgil had seen this kind of death many times. Though it was unpleasant, surviving in the wild was tough, and the veterinarian didn't blame animals for using whatever effective means they had. He had seen a lioness bite down on the muzzle of a wildebeest and slowly suffocate it by clamping its jaws shut and biting down on its nose hard enough that it literally couldn't breathe out of any orifice. It looked like the black and white striped elk buck was going to suffer the same fate. Then something happened Virgil had never seen before back on Earth.

The elk, instead of shaking from side-to-side, threw his head up causing the wolf's body to move upwards. The head throw caused the wolf's bushy tail to be visible to the elk, right in front of his face. The elk then opened his mouth and bit down on the tail. The wolf unhinged its jaws and let out a whine of pain as the elk lifted the canine upwards and slammed the wolf hard to the ground with a thud.

Virgil was pretty sure he even heard some bones crack from the impact. The elk, still with the wolf's tail in his mouth, pressed a hooved foot on the wolf's body. Its tremendous weight caused the foot to crash through the wolf's ribcage and bury itself into its chest. A surge of bright green blood sprayed from the wolf as the elk tossed his head one more time, ripping the tail off its body.

The wolf did not cry, as it was already dead from its chest being caved in. The last wolf, still latched onto the elk's leg, finally wised up after seeing its two buddies get killed and quickly let go of the elk and ran back into the woods. The buck did not chase the final wolf, just watched as he heaved his chest with rapid breaths and flared his nostrils, staring daggers at the fleeing predator. About fifteen seconds after the wolf had disappeared, the adrenaline started to leave the buck's system, and it collapsed to the ground.

"Okay, now we'll help the buck," Virgil whispered. "The elk has an injury by his left calcaneus and may have a tracheal puncture based on the dyspnea he's exhibiting."

"Ya realize we can't understand what yer blabberin' 'bout, lad," Grief said, trying to gently remind the veterinarian that the others weren't trained in medical knowledge like him, thus were unfamiliar with the jargon.

"Oh, right. Sorry," Virgil apologized. "Essentially, the buck has hurt his lower left hindlimb, affecting his movement, and has a serious injury to his throat which may be making it difficult for him to breathe. It could be bleeding into his trachea. If we don't address these injuries, the creature may very well die from bleeding into his lungs. We need to find a way to subdue him and address his wounds."

"Can't you just, you know, use your healing magic on him?" Gwen asked.

"I can, but there's no guarantee that it won't startle the buck and cause him to run off. Also, my Restore spell isn't perfect. It does not heal every type of injury. At least... not immediately," the dark elf explained. "We need to find a way to sedate and subdue him, and I have just the thing."

He then pulled out one of his newly acquired alchemic creations. It was a small glass vial containing a dark green powder called Analgesic Sleep Powder. Essentially, it was a magical equivalent to surgical premedication he would've used back on Earth. "Do you think you can hit the buck's face with this?" he asked Gwen as he handed her the vial.

Gwen gave a confident smile as she took the vial. "Who do you think I am?" she asked with surety. She then pitched the vial toward the elk. As the vial descended towards the buck, the high elf nocked an iron arrow and fired. The arrow struck and shattered the vial just as it was above the elk's head. The sound of the glass shattering startled the elk, and he raised his head, causing him to put his nose straight in the airborne green powder and inhale. The buck's eyes went wide and his neck went stiff. Then his body went limp, and his head fell to the ground, completely asleep.

"Nice shot, lass!" Grief complimented enthusiastically.

"I know," Gwen replied with a smile.

The party quickly ran over to the injured striped elk buck. As Virgil closed in, he used Analyze.

Name: Shrelken Buck
Level: 10
Race: Cervid **Type:** Shrelken
Health: 100/400 **Manna:** 0 **Stamina:** 125/500
Resistances: Piercing Damage 10%
Debuffs: Bleeding, Partial Tendon Tear, Tracheal Damage, Blood Aspiration.

Shrelken are a large species of cervids known for their thick hides and ability to camouflage. This buck has recently survived an attack from predators and is currently injured.

Virgil took that information in, grateful for the lists of debuffs, as they told him what needed to be addressed. His objective veterinarian mindset took over. "Okay, ABC. Airway, Breathing, Cardiac. Baphomet, lift up the buck by its hind end. Gwen, apply this poultice to its injured leg," he said, handing her a small jar containing the healing ointment.

The beastking grabbed the shrelken by the hips and lifted him upward having only the buck's body angle in a downward slope. An outside observer would be curious as to why Virgil would have the buck be in that position, but there was a sound reason. In vet school, he learned in critical care medicine you needed to establish that the airway was viable. Then you made sure the patient was breathing okay. Finally, then you assess the cardiac state.

When he saw the Blood Aspiration and Tracheal Damage debuffs, his concerns were proven true. The shrelken's trachea had torn open, and blood was going down the airway into the lungs. As the buck was elevated, he reflexively coughed as blood left his lungs and traveled downward due to the pull of gravity. As Virgil looked at the tear in the beast's throat, he saw that blood was indeed flowing out of the wound onto the ground at a small constant trickle. Virgil felt the hot air push out of the wound as the buck exhaled. The buck's chest was rising and falling at a much calmer rate than earlier.

With the breathing seeming to be alright, Virgil pulled out one of the few items that had actually made it with him, his stethoscope. Despite his new giant dark elf ears, they still fit like a glove. The veterinarian started auscultating the heart. "Heart rate is at sixty beats per minute. Lungs sound clear on both sides and respiratory rate is at twenty-five breaths per minute," he said to himself as he collected data on the sedated beast. Virgil didn't know what the average vitals of shrelken were, but he had an idea about elk vitals back at home. He extrapolated based on that information, and the normal vitals seemed to match, at least for a cervid being sedated.

Now that the patient was both sedated and appeared to be stable, he got to healing. Virgil stored his stethoscope and channeled his Restoration Magic using Manna Manipulation to focus the healing on the shrelken's neck. The restorative powers of the spell visibly worked wonders as Virgil channeled it.

Even though he had now spent weeks on this new world, Virgil was still fascinated by the healing capabilities of magic in this new world. He watched in wonder as his magic helped to literally repair cartilage, restore muscle, reconnect vessels, and reknit skin before his very eyes. After a few minutes, the wound was completely repaired. There wasn't even a scar. The only evidence of an injury was the uneven section of hairless skin. Virgil's spell could replenish health and remedy damage, but apparently hair growth was not one of its abilities.

Virgil then used Analyze again and saw that all of the debuffs were gone. Gwen had done a good job applying the poultice for him. "You can set him down now, Baphomet." The beastking complied.

"He's all better now?" Gwen asked.

"Yep, great job. Thanks for your help."

"Not a problem. Isn't that what we druids are supposed to do anyway—help nature?"

"Good point," Virgil agreed.

"So, do you have an antidote for your sleep powder?" she asked.

Virgil opened his mouth to answer but then realized that he actually didn't have a reversal. He pulled up the powder's info, and realized that either damage or some form of electrocution was the only known way of reversal. Not really the best options when he thought about it, to hurt an animal after they had worked hard to heal it. They couldn't afford to stay and watch over the creature though. The jungle was dangerous, and they needed to get to Amthoon so they could find out why the people of Ginterbacher were no longer being protected.

An idea did strike him though. "I don't have one exactly, but I know our second-best option. Gather up any loot of value from those green wolves first using your Harvest skill. Then, we can wake up the buck." Gwen had a unique skill called Harvest which allowed her to cause the body of the deceased target to fade, leaving only the lootable bits behind just like a video game. It only took a few seconds, and it was much less gruesome than having to actually acquire the items himself. Any hunter could tell you that cutting into dead animal bodies can be a nasty business.

When Gwen first started to use Harvest, she had to force their three animal companions off the dead body of one of the wolves. All three of the beasts were very opportunistic eaters, Splinter most of all, and while the druids were busy healing, they were busy snacking. They looked rather gruesome with blood coating all their muzzles. Fortunately, Virgil cleaned them off with water from his Everfull Canteen. After Gwen was finished harvesting the dead wolves and looting what remained, she came back to Virgil and said, "Done. Now how are we going to wake the buck?"

Virgil took the rest of the party to the other side of the clearing in the direction they were going, so they were out of sight. "Use your Lighting Arrows spell, and hit him barely with just one of them. Yes, it will do some damage, but it is our best option. Hopefully it will be minimal, and besides, the sleep powder also has a pain numbing effect."

Gwen sighed, not seeing a better option, and did just that. She conjured a ring of five small arrows made of lightning around her wrist. She aimed slightly away from the buck and released. The Hunter Druid's aim was true, and only one of the arrows struck the buck on his thick rear end. The shrelken let out a pained shriek as he suddenly returned to consciousness. The buck quickly stood up and scanned his surroundings, breathing heavily in nervous concern. After about ten seconds, the shrelken buck decided standing out in the open was not a good life choice and sprinted into the thick jungle on the clearing opposite from the druids.

"Nice job, lads! That be some good carin' fer nature there! The great tree would be proud," Grief said. The druids thanked him and continued on their way to Amthoon.

CHAPTER SEVEN

Amthoon

On their final leg of the journey, Gwen handed Virgil the looted body parts for him to use in his alchemical experiments later.

Name: Jungle Envirowolf Heart x2
Item Type: Alchemical Ingredient
Durability: 10/10
Item Class: Uncommon
Effect: Can be used to help provide either tracking or camouflage-based effects
Description: 2 hearts from the bodies of dead jungle envirowolves. Envirowolves are stealthy predators found all over the continent of Kygora, known for their abilities to blend into their environment and hunting prowess.

There was also a pelt and some meat from the wolves. Gwen elected to hold onto the pelt, stating that she had a use for it. Virgil stored the strange-looking wolf meat inside Grief's storage compartment to prevent degradation. As they continued west, the jungle became less dense. It was no longer as dark, and the air was notably less humid. A nice breeze blew against them, cooling off their bodies.

They crested the jungle's edge and saw their destination. The party was on a large hill overlooking the city, which gave them a bird's eye view to see the grand scale of it. Amthoon was a large port city against two cliffs separated by a river that fed into the ocean. The city was divided into three sections all connected by bridges.

The large section by the right cliff face contained the docks and a lighthouse atop the cliff. Most of the buildings on that side were at most three stories high with the exception of a large long open-air structure that had the vibe of some sort of bazaar or market.

Across the river on the left side, the buildings were much larger, ornate, and grandiose. That wasn't the only difference; the cliff face, instead of being uneven jagged stone, had multiple ornate carvings of stocky men with large beards. The statues surrounded a large, open black door directly in the center of the wall.

The final section of the city was unlike the other two. It was an island a little farther out into the ocean and only connected to the left section of the city by a bridge. A large central tower flanked by a few smaller buildings on both sides dominated the island. There was an open grassy courtyard out front; even from this distance it was very green. Virgil assumed that it was the Mage Academy.

The party descended the hill towards the city.

Virgil made sure to pull his hood up over his sensitive dark elf eyes, as he no longer had the shade of the forest for protection. A few people adorned in simple roughspun garb worked the fields, which resembled corn, on both sides of the trail, with hoes collecting crops into baskets.

Virgil had to pause for a moment as he saw a human woman who looked to be in her forties with skin tanned from working under the sun, an actual human being, for the first time since getting transported to a new world. She didn't pay him any mind. Virgil smiled upon seeing that this world did have humans in it after all.

The farmers were not the only people present. Guards were occasionally posted along the trail. They were not dressed like the guards from the elven capital, but instead wore tanned red and brown leather armor with sickles strapped to their hips and simple bows on their backs. Clearly, these guards were built for speed and not durability. When a pair of guards saw the druids approaching, they tensed and walked toward them. "Halt and state your business," a bulky wood elf male ordered.

"We are the druid champions of Yggdrasil," Gwen answered. "We have come to investigate why the firebrands have been able to break free of the protective wards the city had put in place."

"The druids?" the guard said in awe. His face returned to its stern visage. "No disrespect, but we're going to need proof. Just because you have a massive beast with you, doesn't prove that you're the druids. You could be a couple of rangers, for all we know."

Virgil pulled off his hood. "I take it that my presence is enough proof." Virgil knew he was a wanted man and presumed that even though Amthoon was not subject to King Darcassan's rule, they'd probably heard about it. He was the only dark elf anyone had seen with glasses. So, hopefully that would be distinguishable enough.

As the guards looked at Virgil's face, the awe returned. "A dark elf with glasses and a pet rat? Haha! You weren't joking! You are Yggdrasil's champions!" They released their grips on their weapons. "Well, it's a good thing you came here. We do not abide by the hateful decrees of the Rubasal Kingdom, and we have need of your aid. I'm Grekko, and this is Halba," the male guard said, sticking out his hand.

Virgil matched the gesture, and the two clasped wrists. "I'm Virgil, and this is Gwen."

"Oh, we've heard about you, Healer Druid and Hunter Druid. Your defiance against the king has already made you famous here," Grekko said. "Now, come this way, I'm sure the jarl is eager to meet you."

Grateful for the warm welcome, the party followed.

On occasion, Grekko made quick glances back and whispered to Halba. After a couple of minutes, he finally spoke again. "I am not sure that beast will be allowed in the city, due to its massive size."

Virgil had the beastking shrink back into its small form and hop back into his satchel, which caused another look of surprise to plaster the guards' faces before continuing to walk. Following Baphomet's action since he also did not want to garner too much attention, Virgil put the hood of his cloak back on. "So, can you tell us why the firebrands have made it through the barrier or why we haven't seen any guard patrols?" Virgil asked.

"I don't know as to the first," Grekko answered. "As to your second question, I'm... not allowed to disclose much about our city's troops," he answered uncomfortably. "The jarl can answer more of your questions when you see him, though." The guard then leaned in conspiratorially. "What I can say is that it's a good thing for both you and our city that you're here," he whispered cryptically before turning to continue their escort of the druids.

Not long after that, they made it to the front gate of the city at the rightmost section. The wall was maybe twenty feet tall and ten feet thick, much less massive than Kygor's towering walls. The inner part of the gate was broken into two sections. There were murder holes on both sides where archers could fire freely without fear of retaliation. It looked to be an effective kill box despite its notably smaller size.

The guards, seeing Grekko and his silent comrade, Halba, leading Virgil's party, let them by without difficulty. When they finally entered Amthoon, they were greeted with cobblestone streets and an underlying fish smell. Unlike Kygor, there were no large trees intermixed throughout the city or nature-based constructs. All the buildings were made of wood and stone, reminding him of a classic medieval setting. Some buildings appeared to be carved into the stone of the rightmost cliff this section of the city was built by. A small human boy with a blue bandanna tied over his head stood over a stack of newspapers yelling, "Extra, extra, read all about it!"

Grekko and Halba helped the party navigate through the densely populated streets, zigging and zagging until they were deep in the heart of this section of Amthoon. Finally, they led the group down the cobblestone street which ended at a large central building. It had the appearance of a town hall, which was confirmed by the sign above the door.

Inside was a central chamber with a large fire pit. Sitting on a tall stone throne was a pudgy high elf wearing a thin silver crown on top of his short brown hair, adorned in fine blue and brown attire. He wore a cape made entirely of thick brown fur. Virgil noticed the man's ears were pointed but were not as long as any other elf's ears he had seen.

Standing beside the regal elf was a dark elf female in dark red samurai-esque armor to his right. To his left was a thin, older human man with just a ring of gray hair around his temples, wearing a well-kept black tuxedo and writing on a clipboard.

On the wall behind the trio was the mounted head of a giant worm. It was as large as the front of a semi-truck and had its round mouth open, displaying multiple concentric, intimidating rows of teeth. It looked like it could have swallowed an entire elf whole when it was alive; nightmare fuel for sure…

In front of the regal elf whom Virgil presumed was the jarl, were three elves and one human. They looked battle-hardened, having muscles and scars covering their exposed flesh. What was not exposed was covered in matching sets of iron and leather armor. All four of them had a black three-clawed foot branded on their chest pieces. It was clear that these were some sort of gilded fighters. Maybe mercenaries?

Virgil decided to use Analyze on the jarl.

Name: Claus Stableborn

Level: 16
Race: Half-Elf **Type:** Half High Elf, Half Human
Health: 200/200 **Manna:** 50 **Stamina:** 150/150
Resistances: Charms 100%.
Debuffs: None.

Half-Elves are born from the mating of a human and an elf. Humans are very adaptable beings and so can produce half-born offspring from almost any race. Claus was the bastard son of the last jarl, who was a high elf of pure lineage who was a distant cousin to the king of Kygor. Due to that, he was often discriminated against by the jarl's family, but still served by working in the stables for the royal family like his mother.

After a deadly case of Pointpox spread throughout the city and killed the royal family, Claus was the heir to the throne. Since being on the throne, Claus has dedicated his life to serving all peoples equally, no matter their heritage, and to not repeat the discrimination he experienced in his youth. Due to his policy changes, Amthoon was once at war with Kygor, but they are now at a tenuous peace. The jarl's open acceptance of all peoples has caused the economy and peoples of his city to thrive under his leadership, making him a beloved and popular leader.

Virgil was impressed with the information he took in. He could tell he already liked this ruler much more than that jerk Darcassan Rubasal.

"Come on, jarl," a wiry high elf male said in a slimy, cockney accent. "Your guards haven't proved capable. Why not let us Blackfoots have a crack at 'em, eh? We can do it for, say, ten-thousand gold."

"Ha! And they said you weren't funny, Slivell," the jarl replied. "Ten-thousand is a ridiculous price. The only reason I am taking an audience with you is that none of the other guilds are willing to take up the task so far."

"They know it's dangerous," Slivell replied. "Me crew and I know it too. That's why the price is so high. Unlike them cowards though, we're willin' to take on the job. We might be willin' to do it for less pay… on one condition."

"That is?" the jarl asked.

"You give ownership of the mine to the Blackfoot Company once we clear it out."

"That is an even more absurd price!" the dark elf female belted out. She had a deep, commanding voice.

She wanted to say more, but the jarl put a hand out to stop her. "The captain is right. Your request is too much. The mine is one of the main sources of income in the city. I cannot give you that. The city appreciates your… willingness to help, but right now, your offer is denied. Now go," Claus ordered.

The roguish elf just shrugged. "Suit yourself. My crew is willin' to do the hard job, but only if you'll pay up one of those prices, jarl. In the meantime, ask yourself, how many more lives are you willin' to sacrifice until you've had enough?"

"Now!" the jarl yelled.

The elf put his hands up placatingly, still not seeming to be bothered by the anger he was receiving and the Blackfoot crew promptly left. Slivell stared at Virgil on his way by, with his eyes lingering on Grief a little longer than was comfortable before winking at Gwen. He looked like he was about to flirt more with Gwen, but some angry grunting from her protective terror boar caused the rogue to have a look of concern on his face and quickly leave with his crew in tow.

"Thanks, love," she said as she leaned down and patted her pet on the head. Christopher snorted happily, closed his eyes, and wagged his tail like a dog at his master's praise.

"That boar's a good judge of character," the jarl called out from the other side of the chamber. The party turned to see the half-elf smiling at them. "You did well choosing it as your companion. Keep it close."

"Eh, Jarl Stableborn," Grekko said in surprise and stepped in front of the druids. "May I present Virgil the Healer Druid,

Gwen the Hunter Druid, and their animal companions," the guard said as he bowed and gestured to the party.

"Druids? Great tree be praised!" the jarl said. "Welcome to Amthoon, champions of Yggdrasil! What brings you to our fine city?"

"Thank you, jarl," Gwen answered. "Unfortunately, it is not for pleasant reasons that we've come today. We have come from the village Ginterbacher to the east of here. It seems that the barrier to the Scorched Lands has been deteriorating and the villagers have been under attack by orcs of the Firebrand Tribe. We have come to investigate as to why that is, as we were informed that their village had an agreement with Amthoon to help keep the marauders at bay."

The jarl had a sad look on his face. "I know of this village of which you speak. It is a small, pleasant place settled deep in the jungle and populated by various beastkin. I have received no word of Firebrand incursions. What proof do you have that the village is under attack?"

Gwen gave Virgil a nod, and he pulled out the Zinthos totem from inside Grief's storage compartment. "This is one of the totems that was previously used as one of the wards to keep the Firebrands in check. It has been corrupted and was being used by some sort of shaman cultist," Virgil said.

All the others' eyes widened in surprise, even the jarl's. "I admit, I do not possess much in the ways of magic, but even with my limited capabilities, I can sense the malevolence from that item. Now please, remove it from this place. I'll not risk it being present any longer," the jarl ordered, and Virgil stored it back in Grief.

"What you say is true, young druid. Amthoon does have an agreement with Ginterbacher. They are to pay us in lumber, coin, and their delicious honey, and we are to ensure their borders are protected as long as we are able to spare the labor. Unfortunately, we currently cannot spare a single soldier to leave the city or its surrounding farmland."

"Why is that?" Virgil asked, stepping up.

"Because, young man, our fair city has been under siege."

Virgil had a confused look on his face. The city that they had seen so far had seemed fine. There were no signs of death, damage, or battle at all.

The jarl noticed Virgil's look and put his hand up to stop the druid. "I shall explain. At the left section of the city, built into the rock wall, is an ancient and abandoned high dwarf city. They were called the Dwemdurians, and they were known to be one of the most technologically advanced races in all of Imeria."

"And where are they now?" Virgil asked.

"No one knows," the jarl answered. "Hundreds of years ago, they all locked themselves in their hidden cities and never returned. Scholars have speculated as to why. Civil war, disease, interplanar travel has even been suggested, but none have borne fruit. That is beside the point, though. The abandoned city has been a boon for our people. It was just twenty-five years ago that a citizen accidentally leaned against a hidden button which dispelled the enchantment covering the mechanical city, and ever since, it has served as a mine that has provided numerous resources and income for Amthoon. Everything was going smoothly until recently, when our miners found a hidden catacomb of some sort. Ever since then, the dormant mechanical automatons placed throughout the abandoned city have reactivated. Instead of just keeping miners out of the city, they occasionally make raids into Amthoon." He then nodded to the female dark elf guard.

She nodded in response and continued for the jarl. "The constructs are tough and mobile fighters that do not act or move as one would expect. They are composed of a rare and extremely durable metal that is resistant to most physical attacks. For every one of them, it can take ten to fifteen of our warriors to bring it down. As to why they are attacking, we are not sure. All the automatons seem to want is to kill." Her look turned from serious to somber. "They murdered numerous civilians the first time they raided. They also do not seem to speak or have any obvious consciousness, so they cannot be reasoned with."

"Do they have any weaknesses?" Virgil asked.

The dark elf guard nodded. "Aye, the constructs' tough metal exoskeletons appear to have one major weakness, and that's magic."

"Indeed," Jarl Claus added. "Fortunately, the monstrous metal creatures seem to have distinct issues with magical attacks. It may be due to the fact that most dwarves possess no magic. There are a few, of course, but dwarven mages are rare."

"I'm confused then," Gwen said. "You have a whole Mage College in this city. Why not just hire them to take out these automatons?"

"Aye, the Mage College is in this city, but it is a separate entity all together. It is just a branch of the main college who governs it. Centuries ago, they made a binding deal with my grandfather that they could build their college on our land, and in exchange, they provide us with various magic items as payment, their 'rent,' you could call it. Unfortunately, they have refused to work with us on this matter due to one of their professors being in the mine during the initial attack."

"The headmaster, Ramsay the twenty-second, blames our jarl for the awakening of the automatons and death of the professor inside the mine at the time, blaming Jarl Stableborn for reckless digging. As such, they have shut off all contact outside of the required magical goods they pay in service to the city," the thin, well-dressed human said.

"Precisely," the jarl added. "So, you can see our predicament. You can also see that your arrival is most opportune for all of us. The citizens of Ginterbacher need our aid to help defend them from the firebrands. We need the college's aid to deal with the automatons. If you will convince the college to address the threat of these constructs, we will reinstate the patrols along the Scorched Land borders."

Quest Unlocked!
Parlay For the People
Claus Stableborn, jarl and leader of Amthoon, has offered you
a quest. Due to the recent incursions by the automatons,
Amthoon has not been able to spare the manpower to patrol the
Scorched Lands border. Jarl Stableborn is asking that you parlay
with Ramsay the 22nd, Headmaster at the local Mage College,
and convince him to help the city deal with the current
construct threat.
Reward if convinced:
500 Experience.
The reinstallation of Amthoon patrols.
Do you accept?
Yes or No

Virgil liked what he saw with the quest, but there was one
thing that troubled him. "Can you also offer to replace any of
the missing or corrupted totems?" he asked.

"Unfortunately not, young man," the jarl answered, shaking
his head. "While the city does have some magic casters, we
are… limited in comparison to the college. What you are asking
will require the college's aid." Satisfied with the answer, the
party accepted the quest. They already had a quest to go to the
college anyway.

"Excellent," the jarl said, clapping his hands together. "I will
have the pair of guards already with you escort you to the island
where the college is. If you have any other questions, I'm
certain they can be of help. Now, if you please, I have other
business to attend to," the large half-elf said, standing up out of
his chair. All others in attendance stood firm with their leader's
rise and kept that way until he left out a back door with his two
advisors in tow.

INTERLUDE

Dirk

Dirk followed Shreez along the forest, hugging the coastline and making sure not to be seen. The druid had joined forces with the dark elf warlock and freed him from imprisonment in return for power from Shreez's master, the archdemon Vozremath. Dirk was tired of this new world. Despite gaining new powers, he had been mocked, disrespected, and abandoned. He didn't get any reward or recognition from defeating one of the demon generals. What was worse was that bitch, Gwen, left him for that punk ass doc, Virgil.

"Virgil," Dirk grunted to himself. He would wipe the floor with that thin piece of shit. "He thinks he's better than me. He thinks he can take what's mine? I'll show you, doc. Just you wait." For the next half hour, the pair continued along the coastline on the eastern edge of the continent.

Dirk was about to threaten Shreez for taking too long when the warlock gestured to a set of black stone ruins. "Hehehe, we're here."

"It's just some fucking ruins. I mean, it matches the whole 'bad guy' vibe and shit, but I put myself out on the line for you. It better be more than just this," Dirk threatened.

"Not to worry, my new ally. Vozremath rewards his follow-ers, and you will certainly receive your reward." Shreez exited the forest and headed toward the ruins. Dirk groaned and followed.

Dirk's druidic senses alerted him to others nearby as they drew nearer to the partially destroyed structure. From atop and behind the crumbled remains, dark, small shadows of creatures emerged.

Dirk could hear coarse, nervous, rapid speaking among them. His Earring of Comprehension allowed him to under-stand what was being said, and what exactly the creatures were. "Goblins," he spat in a low voice.

"Yes, my ally, goblins indeed," Shreez replied.

"Why the fuck are those worthless pieces of shit here?" he asked. At that blatant insult, the goblins let out shrill howls of anger. More emerged brandishing crude weapons.

Shreez's maniacal tone was immediately replaced by one of anger. The warlock turned to the goblins and spoke to them in their language. "He is our ally, scum! I, Shreez, servant of the great defiler, command you to stay back!" A crazed smile returned to his face. "Or I will remind you of your place." All the small half-demons chattered nervously and stepped back, all except one.

An exceptionally big and ugly goblin with a bulbous nose and an empty left eye socket snarled and took another step forward. "You no scare us, Shreez. We also serve great defiler, and that elf is druid, our enemy. You no serve Vozremath. You are traitor, and I will eat your heart. Now di—ugh!" A lance of pure blood punctured its chest, cutting off whatever he was about to say mid-sentence. His eyes went wide as he looked up to see Shreez's crazed smile looking straight at him. Somehow the warlock was able to conjure the long weapon in moments!

"No, you goblin filth, I think I will eat your heart," he said, then clenched his fist. The lance turned into mist and surrounded the goblin in a red aura. The goblin tried to speak but couldn't. His compatriots watched in horror as all of the blood was rapidly drained from the creature, adding to the mist that surrounded it. In a matter of seconds, all that was left of the one-eyed goblin was a mummified husk.

Shreez snapped his fingers and all the blood coalesced into a singular orb the size of an apple and flew back to his hand. The husk fell forward then collapsed into dust as the body hit the ground. The warlock looked at the orb and tsked in disappointment. "Hm, not enough blood for what we need. I was going to spare these fools, but now they've annoyed me. Dirk, would you mind getting some more blood for me? We're going to need it for our ritual."

The Feral Druid let out an evil smile and scraped his claws together, grateful to release some pent-up aggression. "Gladly."

CHAPTER EIGHT

Back to School

The party followed Grekko and Halba back out the way they came. They proceeded back on the cobblestone street toward the large stone bridge. It was now mid-afternoon and there was a nice breeze coming from the ocean. The bridge was wide enough for three carts to be side-by-side and was well-built. Unlike the cobblestone street, it appeared to be made of one solid gray piece of smooth stone. The party stayed to one side, making sure to avoid the carts and animals.

"So, Grekko, who were those people talking to the jarl before us?" Virgil asked.

The guard gave a scowl upon remembering the thugs. "Those were the Blackfoots. Though they are registered as an official mercenary guild, they're more like a crime family. They are thugs who prey on the weak. The only reason why the whole lot of them aren't in prison right now is that no one is willing to testify against them. At least no one willing lives long enough." Grekko's silent companion Halba gave a sullen nod in confirmation. "It's even rumored that they are the city's branch of Thieves' Guild in Kygor," he added as an afterthought.

Hearing that made Virgil's heart skip a beat. Early on in his journey, he had a run-in with a couple of members of the Thieves' Guild. They tried to kill him and take Grief for some unexplained reason. Virgil was able to escape them, but he never did get any clarity as to why they wanted his soulbound companion. Grief was unaware as to the reasoning either. Regardless, it put Virgil on edge. He doubted that the guild would just forget about him, and he wasn't in a hurry to find out. He reactively tugged on his hood a little more, trying to cover more of his dark elf face.

The party crossed the bridge and took in the next section of Amthoon. Unlike the typical medieval fantasy setting the right section had, with humble wood and stone buildings, this one had multiple tall towering structures made almost entirely of stone and metal. They reminded Virgil of apartment structures back on Earth. The humans, dwarves, and elves here were also dressed in finer garb and were notably more well-groomed, indicating that this was a more affluent section of the city. They immediately turned right and started walking along the water's edge of the city going toward the Mage College.

Virgil tried to use his Soulbound Communication to chat with Grief about the Dwemdurians, figuring the centuries-old dwarf spirit may have some useful information, but for some reason the skull was unresponsive. Virgil didn't want to cause a scene in the middle of a city by shouting out loud to a skull, but he was concerned. The only reason he didn't halt their progress and actually shake the skull like a magic eight-ball was that he somehow 'felt' that the skull was present. He chalked it up to them being soulbound companions. Was he ignoring Virgil? Deciding when they were alone, he would have to seriously try to confront the skull.

After about half an hour of walking along the semi-heavy traffic of the city, all of them made it to a small narrow bridge. Whereas the first bridge was made of smooth gray stone, this one was made of a rough black material that looked like hardened lava on the bottom. There was a guardrail on each side that was clearly magical in nature. One was made of solid ice while the other was made of active flame, somehow contained into a solid form. Needless to say, the party wasn't going to touch either of the rails.

Standing in front of the magic bridge was a small, hooded male gnome, standing even smaller than a dwarf and wielding what looked to be a thin wooden wand. His black cloak was a stark contrast to his pale skin and distinct buck teeth. On that cloak was a badge of a red fireball sewn into the fabric. "Stop." The gnome stuck out his hand and ordered the group as they approached. He had a squeaky voice with a lisp.

The guards halted so quickly the druids narrowly avoided running into them. "It's good to see you, Melvin," Grekko stated, trying to calm the on-edge gnome.

The gnome squinted his eyes at the guard. "What do you want, Grekko? I can't go drinking with you right now, and if you're here by order of the jarl, the headmaster doesn't want to speak with him."

The guard coughed and started to blush at mention of his drinking activities, but quickly composed himself. "Um, no, Melvin. We are here today on a different matter entirely. These two here are the druid champions of Yggdrasil and are on a quest to speak with your headmaster. With luck, their coming will be a great boon to both our people. Maybe an extra bonus to your stipend from the college would encourage you to help, eh?" he asked as he flicked a gold piece to the gnome. Grekko didn't lie, but he definitely did not tell the gnome the whole truth either. Still, the party wasn't going to add any more details than necessary.

"*Oh, the* druids of Yggdrasil?" he asked with a wink. He rubbed his chin. "Hmm, technically, my orders were to keep all residents of Amthoon out. Since these are the druids, though, I think we can make an exception. You two will have to stay out, though."

"I think we'll manage," Grekko replied and nodded to the two elves. The party gave their thanks and walked to the gnome. Virgil was almost one-hundred percent sure that they were witness to a blatant bribe, but beggars couldn't be choosers. If this was the best way to reach the headmaster, so be it.

"You first," Melvin said, gesturing for the druids to lead the way across the bridge. "Though I do advise, if you're not Initiate-ranked in either Water or Fire Magic, do not touch the protective railing." Seeing as both druids' versions of Nature Magic possessed neither branch of magic, they weren't going to risk it. Christopher and Splinter kept close to their masters. even more cautious than their masters were of the ice and fire railing. Baphomet peeked out of Virgil's satchel slightly. The oceanic winds had picked up a little and they were getting splashed with bits of saltwater.

As the party neared the island, they noticed a slight distortion surrounding it. There was a semi-translucent dome covering part of the island where the people were located. They hesitated, unsure of what they saw.

"Don't worry about the barrier," Melvin called out from behind them. "Since you're on the bridge with me, it won't bother you."

Virgil gave a cautious nod and walked through the barrier. As he crossed, he was greeted by the sounds of birdsong and a comfortable breeze. Gone was the stronger wind that brought the chilling feel of saltwater against his skin. Immediately, Virgil realized that the barrier was somehow a filter and protected the island, along with the college, from the elements. It was great!

As Virgil inhaled a deep breath of pure clean air, he noticed that the air felt 'denser,' for lack of a better word. It was as if it was giving him power, and it felt invigorating. He wondered what this dense air was exactly when a notification popped up.

Buff Gained!
Breath of Manna

You are in an area highly-saturated with manna. In this particular isolated sphere, it is potent enough that all who reside in it have +20% to their manna pools, + 20% to manna regeneration speed, +20% effectiveness in magical skill effectiveness & success.

So that was what it was! The sphere of air not only filtered out the bad weather, but it also concentrated the manna density like some sort of magical microbiome. Virgil could see why others would want to study and hone their skills here. Speaking of magical skills, there was a sucking noise, then an audible pop to his side.

"Hehehe! By me nonexistent beard, I've done it!" Grief exclaimed via Soulbound Communication.

"Done what?" Virgil asked.

"I brought that damn leaf into the pocket of storage space I have inside me! The buff I gained from this potent manna field we be in gave me the extra boost I needed! Check it out, lad!"

Subskill Gained!
Space Vacuum

You have gained a deeper connection, and therefore a tether of control, to the pocket of storage space inside you. You can now draw in anything that touches you. Literally, you can absorb any item, person, or object you touch.

Current Absorption Rate: 1 inch/second

Note: If you try to absorb anything that is larger than yourself, you will only absorb the section that you touch.

Example: When pressed to a wall, you will just absorb the section you touch.

Virgil's eyes widened in surprise at Grief's new skill's info. *"Damn, Grief. I'm impressed you managed to do this so quickly!"*

"Eh, what can I say? I just be the most impressive sentient dwarf skull ye will ever see."

Virgil chuckled a little at that. *"You're not wrong, bud. Regardless, we'll have to practice your skill's capabilities when we get some free time."* Virgil took in his surroundings. The barrier didn't seem to distort the environment from the outside, just protect it. It was the same as he'd seen from a distance. There was a large, round, grassy courtyard with smooth marble pathways arranged in concentric circles. At the centermost circle, nine columns towered above them.

"Ah, I see you've noticed our sanctuary garden," Melvin said as he went past the barrier. "At the center stand nine columns representing the nine pillars of true magic. Each column is made by a particular branch. Come, I will show you," the gnome said, now taking the lead for the group as he was now back in a more familiar environment.

"What do you mean by true magic?" Virgil asked.

"An understandable question for someone not trained in the magical arts. From what I understand, you druids are brought to this world with no experience of magic. In our world, Imeria, there are set branches of magic granted to us by the gods at the time of the world's creation. They are Air, Water, Earth, Fire, Light, Dark, Life, Death, and Arcane. Arcane is the most unique of the branches as it appears to be more direct manipulation of manna itself. That is represented by the blue crystalline column you see there." Sure enough, as the group got close, there was an uneven column made up of blue semitranslucent crystals.

Seeing it struck a memory in Gwen's mind. "Does the king of Kygor use Arcane magic?" she asked.

"He does, and I was his classmate," a masculine, regal voice answered behind them. They all turned behind them to see a very tall dawn wood elf male wearing a thick black hooded cloak like Melvin looking down on them. He looked to be a middle-aged human, but it was impossible to tell due to how elves aged. The tan wood elf had short, blond, spikey hair that had blue frosted tips as well as a blue soul patch. Virgil noticed there was one distinct difference between his cloak and Melvin's. It was that instead of a badge of a ball of red flames, he had a blue diamond embroidered. It was also of a better quality, too. "Now, why have you disrupted my meditation,

Melvin? And why have you brought trespassers on college property?"

"Professor Tulberkin," the gnome said in fear and respect, bowing his head to the dawn elf. "Mmm, my apologies for the intrusion. I assure you I meant no disrespect—"

"No matter your intentions, Assistant Professor Melvin, my meditation has been disrupted, and you have broken the headmaster's decree. Give me one good reason why I shouldn't throw the lot of you in the dungeon," Tulberkin said confidently, while summoning a wooden wand to his right hand from his sleeve like an assassin would pull out a hidden knife. The gnome's jaw dropped, and a large bead of sweat trailed down his head. Melvin tried to speak, but nothing came out from the fear of his superior's threat.

"Because we're the druids of Yggdrasil!" Gwen blurted out, not wanting it to devolve to violence.

Tulberkin looked at her with a keen, discerning eye. Seeing as he was analyzing her, Virgil decided to use his actual Analyze skill on him.

Name: Maldrakus Tulberkin
Level: 30
Race: Elf **Type:** Wood Elf
Health: N/A **Manna:** N/A **Stamina:** N/A
Resistances: N/A
Debuffs: N/A

Wood Elves are not as graceful as high elves or dark elves, nor as naturally intellectual as dawn elves. They make up for those deficits though in sheer strength and brutish tenacity.

Maldrakus Tulberkin is a great example of that tenacity. Despite his natural magical ability, he has worked hard to become one of the best Arcane Mages in all of Kygor, resulting in becoming one of the top professors at the Mage College. While that tenacity has helped him succeed, it has also led him to have more than a handful of rivals and enemies, one of which is the current king of the Rubasal Kingdom.

It was clear that the professor was powerful. Just by his level, Virgil knew that the mage could handle either druid in a one-on-one fight. Seeing the 'Not Available' information by his stats confused Virgil though. While powerful, Tulberkin's level was not even close to competing with Lucille. When Virgil first met the old Life Mage, he used Analyze to discover that she was level fifty-two and was still able to see her stats. The only other being he hadn't been able to fully Analyze in his experience was the king. Was it a magic item? Skill? Something else? Virgil would have to try to figure that out later.

After Professor Tulberkin scanned Gwen, he looked to Virgil. "Well, you two certainly look the part. Strange nature armor with animal companions. Still could've put on a shirt, though. You're trying too hard to look like savages."

"Hey, my armor prohibits me from wearing a shirt," Virgil replied indignantly.

"Okay, short stuff, sure it does," Tulberkin replied condescendingly. This guy was quickly reminding Virgil of another rude wood elf he knew.

Gwen intervened to cut off the mounting tension between the two men. "As strange as that may sound, Professor, it is true. Please, our mission is of paramount importance. Is there a way we can prove to you that we *are* the druids?"

The tall elf pursed his lips and had a contemplative look. "Hmm, prove to me..." An idea seemed to strike as the elf's face changed. He quickly turned his back to the druids with his hands clasped behind his back. "Go back to your post, Melvin, and thank your lucky stars that I do not report you today. The rest of you, follow me. I will give you a chance to prove yourself."

The gnome bowed feverishly, mumbling thanks, and quickly left the courtyard back across the bridge.

The druids followed the professor across the courtyard

toward the school buildings. Outside the courtyard, arranged in a semi-circle, were three red brick dormitories. Behind them stood a tall gray stone tower with a pointed tile roof that rivaled some skyscrapers on Earth, with two smaller versions flanking it on each side.

The professor led the group behind the cathedral structure to the left small tower. There were a few younger humans, dwarves, gnomes, and elves in bright red robes talking, sharing food, and reading some old tomes. They looked to be the school's students. With the party going by, many stopped and gawked at the strangely-dressed elves. Some of the girls went, "Awww," while looking at Christopher. The boar seemed to smile and snorted at the attention.

When they made it to the small left tower, they saw no door. The professor traced a glowing rune on the stone with his finger and empowered it with manna. The rune glowed blue, and part of the wall collapsed inward, revealing a doorway to a downward spiraling staircase. This screamed 'dungeon' to Virgil. "Where is this going?" he asked, not wanting to go any further.

Professor Tulberkin smirked. "To the arena, young man. There, you will have your chance to prove your abilities to me. If I'm impressed, I will take you to the headmaster."

Quest Unlocked!
Proof in the Pudding
Professor Maldrakus Tulberkin is intrigued but not completely convinced that you are who you say you are. You must prove to him through combat against him.
Requirements: Deal damage to Maldrakus Tulberkin.
Fight Maldrakus Tulberkin without your animal companions.
Reward: A meeting with headmaster Ramsay the 22nd.
Do you accept?
Yes or No

It seemed very reasonable, but the second requirement was a low blow. Virgil could barely fight without Splinter and

Baphomet's aid. He turned to Gwen and asked through party chat, "*What do you think?*"

She gave him a concerned look. "*I don't like fighting without our animals, but I don't think we have a better option. Also, let's kick this guy's ass. He's a cheeky bastard!*" she sent back.

Nodding, Virgil turned back to the professor. "We accept."

"Excellent. Now, follow me," Tulberkin said and started descending down the stairs. Torches sprang to life as they progressed, illuminating the path. After a few minutes, they made it to a door. The professor opened it to reveal a sandy round pit with descending levels of stone seats, reminiscent of a Roman gladiatorial arena. It was well-illuminated by a variety of magical orbs of light and torches.

"Whoa!" both druids said in awe, impressed at the scale and lighting of the underground arena.

"It is indeed impressive," Tulberkin added. "We hold tournaments here every quarter-year for our students. Now, let us enter. Your pets will have to stay on the bleachers."

The druids left their pets on the lowest level of stone seats, all of them looking like fans who showed up too early for the ballgame. Once the companions were situated, Virgil and Gwen followed the professor down to the dirt arena floor where an old gnome with a long gray beard waited.

The gnome guided the professor to the opposite side of the arena, and the druids strategized. Once Tulberkin was in his spot, the gnome left the arena and sat in the mid-section of the lowest level. He lifted his small hand up and said, "Ready... Begin!"

CHAPTER NINE

Pit Fight

At the old gnome's words, the druids took off in different directions. They knew that the mage was strong and wanted to force him to have to focus on one druid at a time. Gwen fired three arrows at the mage in rapid succession.

Tulberkin's palms glowed blue and he said, "Arcane Shell." An orb of translucent blue magic encircled the Arcane Mage, intercepting and blocking the arrows before they could hit their mark. The professor smiled and shot two blots that looked like large blue diamonds at the Hunter Druid from his palms.

The bolts passed harmlessly through the shield and soared at Gwen. Virgil conjured an Yggdrashield in front of Gwen and it managed to block the projectiles from hitting her.

The professor looked at Virgil, put his palms together, and shouted, "Arcane Wave!" Virgil's Danger Sense went off and eyes widened as a six-foot tall vertical line of Arcane Magic soared out at him even faster than the bolts!

The veterinarian's innate dark elf dexterity saved him as he jumped out of the way. The wave of magic struck the stone wall behind him with a boom. Virgil looked back to see that it had actually cut a line into the thick stone. Splinter was nearby, frantically squeaking at her master in concern for his safety.

Virgil's Danger Sense was on the money. That spell was like a flying magic blade. Virgil stood up and fired two Nature Bolts. Gwen took advantage of the mage's focus on Virgil to enact their plan. She stuck out her left palm and cast the spell Silence.

A white glow surrounded Tulberkin. He examined his hands then looked to Gwen, who was standing behind Virgil's Yggdrashield, pointed his finger, and said something; or he would have, but no sound came out. The cocky wood elf's eyes widened in shock as he was caught off-guard. This was the moment that the druids were waiting for. Virgil and Gwen were still new to Imeria, but they knew that every spell they'd seen had a verbal component. So, they decided to make the mage's strength his weakness.

Professor Tulberkin began frantically speaking and going through complicated hand gestures, but to no avail. *"The effect of the Silence spell only lasts for thirty seconds. Hit him with all you've got!"* Gwen frantically sent through party chat.

The druid duo fired on the shielded mage full-force. Virgil's Nature Bolts flew in rapid succession from his staff while Gwen used a bevy of offensive spells followed by her archery subskills. It was after Gwen's Stone Spear spell that the Arcane Shell began to have a noticeable crack along its surface.

"Come on, we just need to hit him once," Virgil uttered. They were so close to achieving their goal. To the druid's surprise, the professor's eyes widened, then his expression seemed to calm. Tulberkin closed his eyes and pressed his hands to the shell's surface. His hands began to glow blue and the shield began to repair itself. *"Shit, I thought he couldn't cast spells right now!"* he frantically sent through Party Chat.

"He still can't," Gwen replied. *"It must be an ability rather than a spell. Fire faster!"* The druids did, but the shell held. Virgil had to stop for a bit to let his manna recharge as his serious attacks were only magical. Both druids knew when the Silence effect

was over though, as the wood elf had a smile on his face that promised retribution.

"Clever girl, but I won't fall for that again."

"Silence!" Gwen shouted, casting the spell once more.

"Refraction!" Tulberkin immediately replied, snapping his fingers and looking at the high elf druid. Gwen glowed momentarily with a bright white aura around her before it quickly faded. She stuck out her hand and attempted to cast another spell, but no sound escaped her. Both druids locked eyes as understanding dawned on them. The professor had just rebounded the spell back on Gwen.

Before either druid could retaliate, the Arcane Mage restarted his assault on them. He began firing bolts of crystallized magic interspersed with his Arcane Waves.

Both elves had a respectable agility stat, so they were able to dodge most of the attacks. Unfortunately, most was not all. Imagine getting hit by a thrown glass mason jar. Now imagine the jar was shaped like a diamond with multiple sharp points. That was what it felt like to get hit by one of the bolts of Arcane Magic. The Arcane Waves hadn't hit them yet, which was a good thing. Virgil was legitimately concerned about possible amputation if that happened.

Virgil chugged three Manna Potions in rapid succession, then cast four Yggdrashields as quickly as possible. Two for him, and two for Gwen. While he cast, Gwen fired her bow, giving him enough cover to erect the spell forms. Though she was still under the Silence effect, it didn't stop her from using her regular bow attacks, or speaking through Party Chat. *"Virgil, I'm running low on arrows. The Silence effect has another ten seconds on me. Any ideas, because if we don't come up with a new plan, he's gonna kick our ass!"*

Virgil contemplated what to do as he hid behind one of his shields, keeping himself from being peppered by the Arcane Bolts. The Healer Druid went through his list of spells, and was struck with inspiration. He crept as near as he could to Gwen while staying behind a shield and without getting in the mage's line of sight. The dark elf tightened the grip on his staff and cast Purifying Aura for the first time. An almost imperceptible clear aura of cleansing Nature Magic rushed out from Virgil's staff, spreading to encompass Gwen. The aura was supposed to remove and prevent debuffs, and he hoped it would work on the Hunter Druid.

Gwen understood Virgil's intentions. She opened her mouth, but no noise left. She bunched her lips and shook her head to him from side to side. It didn't work.

"Crap," Virgil muttered. He hadn't been sure if the Silence spell's effect officially counted as a debuff, but it apparently didn't. They were up a creek without a paddle, while the mage was handling them both with ease. Virgil almost wished that Tulberkin was a demon so that Grief could tell him his weakness. "Huh! That's it!" Virgil exclaimed. *How would you like to test your new skill, Grief?*

"It be 'bout godsdamn time! Let's do it, lad!" Grief sent back excitedly. Virgil then looked back to Gwen. *"I have a plan, but I'm going to have to get close. Cover me,"* Virgil sent, then ran out from his shield cover and towards the shielded professor. Tulberkin, now seeing an open target, turned his attention toward the dark elf and began focusing his Arcane Bolts at him.

With Virgil's ridiculous agility stat of forty-nine, he surprised the Arcane Mage in his ability to dodge the magical attacks for such a prolonged period of time. The ones Virgil couldn't avoid, Gwen shot out of the air with her arrows.

As Virgil neared, the professor started to look more concerned at the druid's reckless charge. The mage changed attack tactics and went back to using his Arcane Slashes.

Virgil's momentum became much slower as he had to utilize more dexterous maneuvers to avoid the sharper and larger magical blades. When Virgil was ten feet away, Tulberkin conjured a vertical slash aimed directly at him. It would've split the dark elf in two had he not conjured an Yggdrashield and slid to the left under its cover.

The slash carved straight through the middle of the magical

barrier, narrowly missing Virgil. Before the wood elf could attack again, Virgil unlatched Grief from his belt loop, stood up, and chucked the skull at the mage like he was throwing a fast-ball yelling, "Now!"

"Good Grriiiiiiieeeeeeeef!" Grief yelled as he flew toward the magical shell and mage behind it. Like a knife through butter, the skull went through the shell, absorbing a skull-sized hole as it made contact. Grief continued his trajectory until he hit Tulberkin straight in the head. There was an audible 'crack' as both skulls made impact. The wood elf's eyes rolled to the back of his head, and he fell backwards, landing on his back.

"Winner, the druid duo!" the arena master declared.

Quest Complete!
Proof in the Pudding
You have managed to deal damage to Professor Maldrakus Tulberkin. You also managed to do so without your animal companions! Good things he didn't say you couldn't use *all* of your companions!

Reward: A meeting with headmaster Ramsay the 22nd.
Bonus Reward: 500 Experience.

"Yes!" Virgil celebrated with a fist-pump. They were able to show the cocky professor that they could take him! He then used his Soulbound Recall skill and summoned Grief back to his palm, the skull using the vacuum skill to create another hole in the magic barrier.

"Good thing I don't count as an animal companion, eh? Hahaha!" Grief laughed.

"Indeed," Virgil sent back and re-equipped the skull.

"That was a stupid plan. I can't believe that worked, and since when has Grief been able to go through magic barriers like that?" Gwen asked as she walked up to Virgil, her Silence debuff clearly done. Though she sounded angry, Virgil knew she was just venting her frustrations and relieving the tension after that dangerous bout.

"I'll tell you about it later. Great shooting, by the way," Virgil said. Before he said anything else, a groan arose from inside the shell. The druids turned to see the professor clutching his head. As he slowly stood up, his shell dispelled.

He then turned to face the druids, face stern. "I said you couldn't use your companions."

"No, you said we couldn't use our animal companions," Gwen responded.

Tulberkin's lips bunched in frustration. He looked like he was about to yell at the druids, but then exhaled. "Shit… You're right. Congratulations. It seems you are the druids and are worthy to meet—"

"Me," a deep voice interrupted from behind Tulberkin. All of them looked behind him to see an elder male dwarf. He wore a hat made of what looked to be an envirowolf skull, but instead of green, it was red with antlers fixed on its head. He had long, braided, gray mutton chops. Instead of a robe, he wore a black sleeveless leather vest adorned with bones, and simple brown pants. He wore no shoes, and both feet and arms were adorned in multiple tattoos. A purple cloak topped off his outfit that seemed very out of place with the tribal attire.

"Headmaster Ramsay," Tulberkin said in respect and bowed his head to the shorter man.

"I see you have been roughing up our guests," the headmaster said. He had a smooth tone to his voice that, while not outwardly hostile, made his intent felt.

"I was merely ascertaining if they were truly who they claimed to be," the professor explained. There was a pleading, nervous tone to his voice. "You said yourself that we needed to prevent all trespassers from entering the main tower."

"You did not have to fight them to determine who they were, and we both know that, Maldrakus. Honestly, just because you're in charge of security does not mean you get to fight anyone who enters our borders. Or do you want to end up like the Darcassan boy ruling over the Rubasal Kingdom?" Tulberkin's eyes bulged at the mention of his rival.

"I assure you, headmaster, I would never act so hostile to outsiders as he does," the professor stated with grim determination.

"See to it that you don't, Maldrakus," the headmaster said, then finally looked to the druids. "So, you two are the druid champions of Yggdrasil? I'm headmaster Ramsay, the twenty-second of the Kygoran branch of the Mage College. I heard that we had unexpected newcomers on our island, so I thought I'd investigate the matter myself. What are your names?"

"It's nice to meet you, sir," Gwen said. "I'm Gwen, the Hunter Druid, and this is my companion Virgil, the Healer Druid. We are here to discuss multiple urgent matters with you. Please, is there somewhere we can talk in private?"

A look of understanding crossed the dwarf's face. "Ah, I see. Of course. You may follow me. I presume those animals on the bleachers are with you? If so, they may join us *only* if they do not urinate or defecate in my office," the old dwarf said, then turned away and began walking out of the arena.

CHAPTER TEN

Disciplinary Action

The party followed the headmaster out of the small tower they were in, back outside, then into the tallest central tower. When they entered the tower, they saw that there were now two spiraling sets of staircases going up the tower, crossing by each other like a double helix. The headmaster led them to the center of the tower to a large stone circle. In the center of the circle was a podium. The headmaster pressed some sort of button on the podium, and the edges of the circle glowed blue.

"Don't worry, you'll be fine as long as you stay within the circle," the headmaster stated, then the circle lifted off the ground. The druids braced themselves as the stone floor began rising up at a quick but not concerning pace. They quickly realized that this was a magical elevator. The animals, not knowing what an elevator was, were definitely huddled close to their masters, concerned they might fall out of the sky. The headmaster didn't look bothered at all by the elevator and smiled at the party with his hands behind his back.

Virgil took the time to use Analyze on the dwarf and discovered that the headmaster was a particular type of mage called a Shaman. Shamans were elemental-based mages who focused their powers, like druids, through nature, but did not have the unique Nature Magic that druids possessed. Oftentimes, they would employ totems to channel their magic or leave as a constant beacon of power. Virgil wondered if this headmaster could actually repair the border to the Scorched Lands, or if he even made it in the first place.

In just thirty seconds, the party had arrived at the top level of the tower. There was only one door with a small ledge and two sets of stone stairs connected to it. Virgil assumed it was the end of the staircases they saw at ground level. He was definitely glad they hadn't walked all the way up.

"Come," Ramsay said as he walked to the door. "This is my office. We can rest assured our conversation won't be overheard here."

The party, comforted by the information, followed the old dwarf into his office. Ramsay closed the door behind them, uttered a few words to the door, and the multiple locks on it began activating on their own. "There, the door is now magically sealed; this room is warded, and now we can talk openly. Now, what can I do for you druids?" he asked as he sat in a thick wooden chair behind his desk.

Both druids sat down on the leather seats on the other side. Knowing that Gwen had a much higher Charisma score, she led the conversation. "There are a couple of reasons we've come here today, headmaster. The first is that we are here in regards to the village of Ginterbacher."

The headmaster stroked one of his braided mutton chops. "Ginterbacher? Oh, yes, I remember it. It is a small lumber village across the jungle east of here. Why is that place my concern?"

Gwen went on to explain the situation with the Scorched Lands and the lack of guard contingents to patrol the border. "And the jarl said he would send his troops back there once the automaton threat was handled," she finished.

"I'm sorry for their circumstances, but I am still not seeing how that has to do with me," the headmaster said.

"Because the automatons are weak to magic. If only just a few of your mages—"

"Young lady, I appreciate what you're saying. I know what it is you wish. You want our mages to solve the problem that jarl and his people started. Because of that man's greed, he enacted lax policies to ensure the safety of not only his workers, but *my* people," Ramsay interrupted with clear anger in his voice at the situation.

The shaman then noticed his rising anger. He closed his eyes and took a deep inhalation. "I'm sorry. It... is hard to deal with. One of our professors, a close friend of mine ever since we were students here, was lost when the automatons awoke."

"I'm sorry for your loss," Virgil said, truly feeling bad for the dwarf. "What was her name?"

"Thank you, young man. Her name was Talia, Talia Ogrul." That name sounded vaguely familiar to Virgil for some reason. He couldn't quite put his finger on it as to why. The universe answered for him.

Quest Update!
A Student's Treachery

You have discovered 1 of the 3 professors at the mage academy who were replaced by a demonic clone. Talia Ogrul is one of the people presumably lost to the automaton incursion. Probably should tell somebody about that...

Virgil groaned inwardly at the uncomfortable conversation to come. "That... brings us to the other reason we're here," he said. "When I was in Kygor, I stumbled upon a secret underground lab. Upon some investigation, I found it once belonged to a warlock named Weylan Forsworn."

The shaman's face went into a scowl. The former student's name must have truly angered the dwarf, as Virgil's Danger Sense went off. "I know of the man of which you speak. He is an escaped traitor and criminal. Did you find him?"

"No, but I discovered that he died. I also discovered this,"

Virgil said as he pulled out and handed the warlock's journal to the headmaster. "His crimes may be even worse than you know. The warlock somehow replaced three people in the college with demonic clones in some grand scheme. I don't know who the other two are, but the third is—"

"Talia Ogrul," Ramsay said, reading the journal and finishing Virgil's statement. His voice and face both expressed a sad disappointment to them. "I cannot believe we've been housing a demon for centuries right under our very noses." The dwarf shaman sighed. "I was much younger when Weylan was exposed as a warlock. The two others on this list were caught at the time his crimes were discovered, but it seems that Talia was able to evade detection. Even after wiping their names from our history, our college's tainted past has reared its ugly head once more. I'll be honest with you both, I do not want to believe you, but the evidence is irrefutable."

A look of shock and realization then crossed the shaman's face as he gasped. "Oh no! That means," he said, frantically scanning the journal.

"Means what?" Gwen asked.

"Talia, I mean the demon, was a professor here at the college specializing in the studies of ancient magic. She was brilliant but also rash, and I feared she would be tempted to study forbidden magics. Nevertheless, she made great contributions to the college. For the past twenty years, she had been obsessed with golem crafting, an art that has been lost to the world for centuries. She thought that the Dwemdurian ruins may hold some kind of key to helping her work. When the metal automatons rose up and started attacking, I blamed the jarl for reckless greed. Now, I think something much more sinister has occurred."

Virgil's analytical mind put the pieces together. "It no longer seems to be a coincidence that she was studying golem crafting and now there are occasional raids by metal golems into the city."

"Precisely," the headmaster said. "Struck by grief and anger,

I was blinded to evidence in front of me. Now with this information, young druids, I realize that the error was mine, not the jarl's. Thank you for bringing this information to me. Both I and the college are in your debt."

Quest Complete!
A Student's Treachery
You have informed the headmaster of the school of the 3 demon imposters at the mage college. Unfortunately, you've been alerted by Ramsay, Talia is the only remaining threat at large.
Reward:
Esteemed Student status at the Mage College.
2 new spells (1 to each druid).
1000 Experience (500 to each druid).
2 magic rings (1 to each druid).

Virgil clicked his tongue at the prompt, a little upset that his rewards were halved since he added Gwen to the quest. Beggars couldn't be choosers, though. He'd rather have her around versus not, and was still happy with the rewards he was getting. "Now, please let me reward you as a show of thanks," the dwarf said. He got out of his chair and went to a bookcase set against the wall behind him.

The headmaster grabbed a couple of books then went over to his desk. He reached inside a desk drawer and retrieved two rings. He set the two books on the desk then set one ring on top of each. "There. For you, Virgil, and you, Gwen, I give you a new spell and magic item that were all crafted here at our fine institution as thanks for your service to us."

The druids gratefully took the items, looking at each other with gleeful anticipation before opening the books. They absorbed the spells' information without even looking at what the spells were.

Both druids and tomes glowed as the spells' information was transferred to their minds. The essence of Yggdrasil inside them changed the spells from just Life and Earth Magic spells into two unique Nature Magic spells. Soon enough, each druid had learned one unique spell.

Your connection with Yggdrasil has changed the Life Magic spell: Healing Flame to the Restoration Magic spell: Phoenix Fire!

Phoenix Fire: Channel flames from a nearby source of fire into a renewing source of healing energy. The stronger the flames, the stronger the healing.

Cost: 100 MP

Cooldown: 100 seconds

Range: 40 feet

Effect: Gain +1HP to target for every 1 degree Celsius of heat the flame provides.

Gwen's spell was also powerful.

Your connection with Yggdrasil has changed the Earth Magic spell: Stone Stride to the Predator Magic spell: Spider Climb!

Spider Climb: Your hands and feet gain the ability to walk up surfaces and ceilings as if gravity is not affecting you.

Cost: 50 MP

Cooldown: 2 minutes

Range: Touch

Effect: Target can walk on walls and ceilings without any negative effects for 60 seconds.

"Thank you so much!" Virgil said, truly grateful.

The headmaster nodded. "I'm glad they are satisfactory to you. The rings are not as impressive but are still useful, especially to elves such as yourself, seeing as the strength statistic is not your strong suit."

The druids examined the rings and found that they were identical silver rings with dark red rubies in their centers. They were aptly called 'Ruby Rings of Strength' and gave the wearer plus two to their strength stat, which also resulted in plus twenty to their health pools. With only ten points in strength and one-hundred-and-two points in health, one attack from a tough opponent could one-shot Virgil. Well, it would bring him down to one hit point due to his other ring, the Ring of the Bound Warrior which kept him alive always. It didn't, however, remove any pain, as Virgil had already experienced, and in the wrong hands could be a terrible torture device. The druids still accepted the rings with gratitude.

"Now, it seems that this automaton incursion may very well not be the jarl's fault. I will send word to him that our college will aid him. Maldrakus is an experienced battle mage, and shall serve to eradicate the automaton threat. Though I will have some difficulty finding others willing to accompany him, as he is rather hard-headed."

Both druids smiled as they both received more notifications for the completion of two different quests. With the headmaster's words, they finished the quest for the jarl and for Valgorna. For Virgil in particular, the twenty-five-hundred experience rewarded from the two quests was enough to bump him up to level fourteen!

"I know the jarl will be very pleased, as well as the citizens of Ginterbacher," Gwen said. "There is still one more issue, though."

"What is that?" Ramsay asked.

"While the village may have guards to protect them from the dangers of the Scorched Lands, some of the defensive totems are no longer working. Some were even corrupted by some sort of demonic influence. I was wondering if you would be willing to accompany the guards to fix the totems? I assume as a shaman that you work with them?"

"I do indeed, miss," Ramsay answered, stroking his mutton chops. "Hm, it seems that we are both in need, and that we both can help each other. I need people to join Maldrakus in the mine, and you need a competent shaman to restore the Scorched Lands defensive wall. So, here is what I propose: join my professor in the Dwemdurian ruins, and eradicate the automaton threat. Also, you must make sure to eliminate the accursed demon impersonating my friend, if the thing is still alive in there. If you do this, then I and Melvin Boomflame, our school's assistant professor and second-best shaman, will address the totem issue personally."

Quest Unlocked
A Call For Aid 2

Ramsay the 22nd, Headmaster of the Mage College, is in need of aid to help address the violent automatons and the demonic professor roaming inside the Dwemdurian ruins. He also wants it handled discreetly. Will you join forces with Professor Maldrakus Tulberkin and deal with both the metal and fiendish threats?

Requirements:
Find the source of the automaton threat and subdue it. Eliminate the demon impersonating Talia Ogrul inside the ruins if still alive.

Reward:
Ramsay the 22nd will personally address the totems along the Scorched Lands border.

Do you accept?
Yes or No

The druids looked at each other and activated party chat.

"You're the analytical one. What do you think?" Gwen asked.

"Well, that Tulberkin guy is kind of a jerk, but he is strong. I'm pretty sure that the thing influencing the firebrands is another demon general, so we're going to have to go to the Scorched Lands after this. It's probably a good idea to secure the border so more of them can't escape."

"Good point. It's probably a smart idea to take care of the demon inside the mine too, if there still is one. That's what we're summoned here for anyway, to kill demons," Gwen sent back. She turned to the shaman and said, "We accept."

"Wonderful. I'll have a magic message sent to Maldrakus

right away. He'll meet you in the courtyard," Ramsay said, standing back up out of his chair.

Both druids stood and went to shake the dwarf's hand, but the shaman visibly recoiled. "I'm... sorry. Physical touch is not my strong suit."

The druids shrugged, understanding that and not wanting to press the issue.

They turned to leave and the headmaster said, "Press the button on the bottom of the podium. It will take you back down. Now, take care and be safe."

The druids nodded their thanks and left the headmaster's stone office. After they closed the door, they walked over to the elevator and pressed the button. Just like before, it started moving at a good pace but now downward.

That was where Grief started speaking out loud to both druids. "I'm goin' on record here that I don't like that dwarf."

"What? Why?" Virgil asked.

"Did ye see him? He be a dwarf that can use magic. Almost no dwarf can use magic, and most of the ones that do tend to have a screw loose in the noggin'. Them Dwemdurians disappeared nigh almost a millennia ago, centuries before I was born, and those magical dwarfs were 'bout the most reclusive, jealous, and prideful kind of people that ever claimed the title 'dwarf,' according to me pappy. Also, that shaman wouldn't shake yer hands. I get it, some people don't like touchin' another, but we dwarves *never* be like that. In all my years, no dwarf has ever been afraid of contact. Why, many times, people prefer to head-butt versus shaking hands."

"You said it yourself, Grief, it's been five-hundred years since you've been out in the world. Maybe, like the orcs, dwarves have changed as well, but hopefully for the better," Virgil suggested.

"While that be a good point fer other races lad, we dwarves be *not* the biggest fans of change. Why, some dwarven lore suggests that some of our first ancestors almost died because they refused to leave their underground dwellings and go outside, despite poison fumes coursin' through their homes. I be skeptical that my folk have changed *that* much that no touchin' be an acceptable thing."

"Well, your feelings are noted, but we are still taking the quest," Virgil said, finishing that branch of discussion. "Also, if you knew stuff about the Dwemdurians, why didn't you answer my questions about them earlier when we were walking through Amthoon?"

"Ye were askin' me questions in the city?"

"Yes, and you wouldn't respond. I was concerned, man," Virgil said, emphasizing his annoyance.

"I be sorry, lad. I was so busy focusin' on trying to absorb that damn leaf that I must've tuned out all other noise," Grief apologized.

"It's okay. Nothing super serious happened during our walk, so it worked out fine. Just don't do it again, because it could end up with us dying."

"Understood, lad," Grief said begrudgingly as the magical elevator landed on the ground level.

The party left the tower, moving towards the stone and grass courtyard. They didn't see any more of the students they'd previously noticed. Maybe they were all in class?

The party examined each of the columns in the courtyard with fascination, something they didn't do before the professor took them away. One was made of pure light, while another was made of shadow. One was like a tall shrub adorned with much plant life, while another was made entirely of bone. There was one made of fire, ice, condensed electricity, and one of stone, along with the crystalline Arcane column. It was truly a wonder to see such magic on display.

Soon enough, the party saw the professor walking his way toward them. Instead of his loose-fitting black robes that they had seen him in earlier, the tan wood elf wore a set of black cloth armor with golden trimmings. The blue diamond patch indicating his Arcane Mage status at the academy was still there, embroidered by his left shoulder. He had on a set of golden metallic wrist guards as well as gold-trimmed boots. The Arcane Mage wore a large golden necklace with an onyx jewel in its center and three rings on each hand. Slung over his shoulder was a brown satchel.

Virgil presumed the satchel was some kind of special storage device like how Grief was. This guy looked to have a set of valuable equipment! The only thing that seemed out of place was a large white bandage on his left temple. Virgil remembered that was where Grief had struck him, and a small smile curled up as he recognized that was the reason for the bandage.

The mage had a stern look to his face as he approached. "Now listen here. I can handle this threat myself, but the headmaster has insisted that you accompany me. So, I will bring you along. Now, as the highest level among us, it is only proper that I should lead."

"Whoa now. We won't just let you walk all over us just because you're higher level. You may be the best choice as leader, but we're not your students. We won't just do whatever you say because you say it. If we're going to work as a team, we're going to work *as a team*," Virgil said, emphasizing his last words. Splinter added a snarl as she stared at the mage while on her master's shoulder.

The professor looked at Virgil at first with anger before he got his look under control. He even gave a small smile as he nodded slightly to the dark elf. "Wise words. I concede your point, druid. I promise that I will work with you as a team and not, as you said, walk all over you." The mage's smile grew a little, and he said, "Besides, if I did, it looks like your strange dire rat would have no issues biting me. I've been bitten by one before, and I'm not too keen on it happening again."

"You're right about that, their bites really do hurt," Virgil said, remembering the time he had to fight dire rats inside Kygor's sewers. "I still think that I'm actually the better choice to assign as leader."

The wood elf's eyebrow raised. "Oh, and why do you think that you're more suited than a trained battle mage like myself?"

"I have a special trait that allows me to have my animal companions inside my party. That way I can track their statuses and send them commands through party chat. They can't do too much communication back, but they can send basic messages," Virgil explained.

The mage put his hand to his chin. "Hm, that is a useful tool, but can your rat and small dog thing really do that much? They don't look that intimidating to me." At that, Baphomet's head popped out of the satchel, the beastking in its small form growled at the mage for his words.

Virgil put a hand on and pet in between the beastking's antlers. "Trust me, when it comes time, there's no animal more intimidating than Baphomet here."

Maldrakus did not look entirely convinced, but shrugged. "Very well, if you say so. I will voice my opinion if I do think we need to change though."

"Entirely reasonable," Virgil replied, glad they didn't have to prove their point further with the bullheaded elf. With that, the professor joined the group and the party made their way to the Dwemdurian ruins.

INTERLUDE

Dirk

Dirk was cleaning off the blood that was caked on his claw weapons. "You done yet, Shreez?" he asked. The warlock was busy doing some gruesome ritual, drawing a large pentagram taller than the dark elf on one of the stone walls of the ruins using the aforementioned goblin blood. At each point of the pentagram was one goblin body part impaled using their own weapons; two legs, two arms, and a head at the top with a spear driven straight through the forehead.

"Almost done," Shreez replied to Dirk in between his ritual chanting. After a few more minutes, the warlock shouted some word in the infernal tongue and clapped his hands that radiated with the red-colored power of blood magic. The pentagram glowed and then a round portal emerged from it. The eyes of both men widened, Dirk's with surprised fear and Shreez with mad glee.

The world on the other side of the portal was anathema to the one they were on. The sky was gray with rolling thunder clouds, accompanied with regular flashes of lightning. The ground, instead of being full of life, was a flowing desert of red sand. Occasional withered husks of trees dotted the landscape.

Way off in the distance, an orange light shone, indicating a city of some sort. Dirk could make out towers of black and red at the source, a city of some sort.

"This it?" he asked.

"Hehehe, yes," Shreez cackled. "Welcome, Dirk, to the infernal realm, home to my master. While he cannot move from his realm, we can." He then pointed to the city across the distance. "That is Unseogal, the infernal capital where he resides." The warlock snapped his head to the Feral Druid. "Now, do you still want power? Power to crush all who stand before you?"

Dirk clenched his fist and gritted his teeth. "Yes. I want power and the respect that I deserve. The respect that's been taken from me by that punk doc!"

"Good, then follow me, but know that if you do, you will never be the same," the warlock said before stepping into the portal to the infernal realm.

Dirk flared his nostrils in anger, but also in fear, though he wouldn't admit it. He wanted power, but he didn't want to end up like the crazed dark elf to get it. He wanted to go home, to go where he was famous, handsome, and strong; where he could use his money, looks, and body to win over or intimidate others into giving him what he wanted.

As he thought about Earth, and how he couldn't go back to that life, Dirk scowled. His desire to go home, no matter how strong, was impossible right now, and he wouldn't—no, couldn't—work with those losers back in Kygor, or those so-called worthless champions he'd been summoned with. No, Dirk was a winner, and he would join the winning side. He wasn't going to die for some dipshits who brought him here to save some dumb talking tree. Instead, he would do what he always did, he would take power however he could, and use it to gain more and get what he wanted.

With that, Dirk nodded to himself and stepped through the portal.

CHAPTER ELEVEN

Ruins

As they walked through the nicer parts of Amthoon to make it to the entrance of the ruins, Virgil allocated his new points from his leveling up. One point each in agility, intelligence, and endurance. That also brought his endurance and stamina pools up by ten points too.

He still had two free points to allocate, though. It didn't take him much thought on where to put them. He had learned two new spells in as many days, pushing him further into the caster role. He put the remaining two into intelligence, bumping his total manna pool to three-hundred-and-sixty. Virgil was happy to have reached level fourteen, but his current level also reminded him about his Attunement.

Each of the five druid champions had a rare ability unique to each one of them called an Attunement. Attunements were extremely powerful, and could help separate the druid champions' capabilities from others. The catch: they were dormant when the druids first arrived. Druids could not forcibly awaken them either. They could only awaken them in a moment of extreme choice between two options, typically between life and death.

Virgil had actually awakened his Attunement rather early. It was a life and death decision, though. His was called 'A Veterinarian's Pact,' and it allowed him to evolve and tame any creature that was considered a 'Beast' after petting it continuously for sixty seconds. He could only use it once every ten levels though, so he needed to get to level twenty to be able to use it again.

Thinking about his Attunement also reminded Virgil about the other druids. So far, that he knew of, only Dirk had awakened his. The Feral Druid's attunement allowed him to shift any body part of his into a concurrent part of an animal he had killed before. Dirk could also transform into an entire animal, but Virgil could appreciate somehow combining the best or deadliest parts of creatures to become a more lethal hybrid.

The dark elf realized he should probably help Gwen awaken hers as well. Maybe he should put himself in a life-threatening situation? He had done so when they had fought Baphomet when it was still under the archdemon's influence as a demon general. It shouldn't be too hard to put himself in danger again where they were going. As they continued, Virgil was also struck by the realization that he could now access Tulberkin's information since they were in the same party. Wanting to know his new party member's capabilities, he pulled up some of the mage's information.

Name: Maldrakus Tulberkin
Level: 30
Race: Elf **Type:** Wood Elf
Health: 600 **Manna:** 400 **Stamina:** 300
Resistances: Arcane Magic 50%.
Debuffs: None.
Profession: Battle Mage.

Virgil liked the information he saw, but was first confused as to why he couldn't see the mage's stats earlier. Secondly, he was also confused as to the mage's stat allocation. As a true and dedicated mage, the wood elf's health and stamina seemed *way* too high in comparison to his manna pool. Virgil had played dedicated mages in games back at home himself, and he knew that while min-maxing did sometimes inhibit creativity, it really could help you survive in the long run.

Emboldened by the fact he was the official party leader, Virgil tapped on the wood elf's shoulder. Maldrakus turned back slightly, giving Virgil an expectant look. "Now that we're on a team, I do have some questions."

"In regards to what?" the mage asked, trying and failing to keep the annoyance from his voice.

Virgil continued undeterred. "Well, the first thing is, how couldn't I see information on you when I used my Analyze skill, but I could on someone else who is a higher level?"

The mage gave a confident smirk and turned back to continue walking. "It is because I use Arcane Magic. We Arcanomancers have the unique ability to modify pure manna, as well as magical abilities. That not only helps us be expert mages, but the best battle mages. We can use our skills to attack as well as defend from mages in particular."

"I don't know too much 'bout magic lad, but I think he be tellin' the truth. I know that Arcanomancers are also called Magehunters. That seems to fit the cocky bastard's explanation," Grief sent Virgil through their Soulbound Communication and not Party Chat so that the mage couldn't hear him.

The professor continued, "One of the key skills we learn is called Aura Shroud. We set up a thin magical field around our bodies that hides us from magical detection, as well as keeps others from ascertaining our information. One can overcome it, if they have a high enough Detection or Analyze skill, but they are few and far between."

Virgil nodded, happy to finally have an answer as to why both Maldrakus and the king repelled his Analyze skill. He was about to ask another question, when the party made it past the last set of large buildings and into the open area in front of the mine.

The druid's eyes widened as they saw the stone wall where the dwarf ruins-turned-mine was set into. What Virgil saw when they first spotted the city was correct: there were carvings of bearded people. Seeing it up close revealed that the people were indeed dwarves. Their proximity also revealed the fine craftsmanship and grandiose nature of the carvings. The large square holes carved into sections of the rock he saw earlier gave off the impression that they were vents of some sort. Around the large open doorway at the center was another large carving of a dwarf, but only the man's face. The massive set of doors underneath made it look as if you had to go inside the dwarf's mouth to find the entrance.

The level of skill to make just this wall of the ruins was remarkable and challenged any other that Virgil had seen yet.

Grief spoke in party chat. *"I tell ye, if I could cry, tears would be flowin' down me right now. It be beautiful."* The skull choked out in joy upon observing his ancient kin's work.

Maldrakus looked back, obviously surprised by the talking skull in group chat, but turned away and said nothing. Well, he said nothing out loud.

"Let me do the talking, and please, don't let the damn chatty skull speak. The people here, while appreciative of magic, have been warier of mages as of recent, due to our leaders'… disagreements. Let's not give them any extra ammunition for paranoia, shall we?" the professor asked rhetorically through Party Chat.

Grief grumbled angrily in Virgil's mind at the wood elf's call out, but the group complied. As the party walked toward the mine entrance, they saw a semi-circular ring of armored guards surrounding the mine entrance with wooden spiked barricades pointing toward it.

As the party approached the guards, Virgil's Danger Sense triggered slightly. He gripped his staff lightly and scanned the guards. No one showed open hostility towards them as they came, but Virgil knew that didn't mean some would not try to harm them. He wondered if it was actually behind them. Virgil pushed his glasses up and quickly looked back into the city streets. It almost looked like he saw someone hide, but he couldn't be sure.

"*He's right. Stay quiet and keep your guard up,*" Virgil sent. The party did for the most part. Since Christopher was not one of Virgil's animal companions, the terror boar could not officially be in the party. Therefore, he did not have access to Party Chat. He was taking some louder sniffs of the open air, snorting like… well, like a pig.

A thin human male Amthoon guard garbed in customary leather armor and wielding a circle shield and a slightly chipped long spear noticed the incoming party and approached them. "Halt. You lot can't be here. It's too dangerous for the common folk of the city to be by the mine, not with those constructs about," he said.

Maldrakus put on a warm smile. "Not to worry, friend. As you can tell, we are not mere common folk. I am Maldrakus Tulberkin, professor at the Mage College and professional Battle Mage. I have come to deal with your metallic menaces."

The guard pursed his lips. "From the college, eh? 'Bout time you lot came out here and helped us. I've lost two of my sword brothers because your master was too proud to get his hands dirty with us 'non-magical' people," he said, jabbing his finger in the mage's chest. He then looked behind Maldrakus. "Who're these two with you? Students and their science experiments?"

Maldrakus bunched his lips and forcibly restrained himself at the guard's physical taunt. "I'm sorry for your loss, sir. I'm glad that I'm able to help now." Then added in a whisper so low that only Virgil's enhanced dark elf hearing perked up, "As your people are clearly incapable."

"What was that?"

"Oh, nothing for you to worry about," he answered, brushing off the guard's suspicion. "As for your question, these are two of the druid champions of Yggdrasil," Maldrakus answered.

"The druid champions?" the guard asked as his eyes

widened in awe. "But, but, you lot should be out fighting the demons! Why are you here helping folks like us?"

"Well, we happened to be in town, and what kind of champions would we be if we don't help those in need?" Gwen asked with a wink, her high charisma score on clear display.

The human blushed and stood there slack-jawed for a couple of moments before regaining his composure. "Oh... yes, yes! Of course! Thank you both so very much! If you and your mage companion wish to follow me, I shall tell my men to allow you past the barricade," the guard said, slightly bowing to the druids.

"Though they may not be a fan of mages, they don't seem to mind druids," Gwen sent and followed the guard.

The men gave each other a look that communicated, "How'd she win him over so easily?" Then they shrugged and followed. The guard stopped a few feet back from the entrance. He looked spooked, clearly concerned about the threat of these machines the group had not seen yet. Noticing the group looking back at him, the guard scratched his head and chuckled nervously. He then stated that only a small fraction of the guards would remain outside since they were going in, then promptly walked away from the group at a notably quicker pace than when he approached. The party then turned and entered into the ancient dwarven ruins.

A notification flashed in their visions.

Warning: As there is now an active conglomeration of hostile creatures congregated inside, the Dwemdurian Ruins of Amthoon have been changed from the classification "Ruins" to the classification "Dungeon." As such, there are creatures that will reward you with experience if defeated. Defeat the boss of this dungeon to once again make it safe for others to enter and receive bonus experience!

Hm, this was the second dungeon that Virgil had ever entered before, the first being the sewers under Kygor that had a mutated rat warlock inhabiting it. Apparently, having a boss monster with servants hidden in a place classified it as an official 'Dungeon' according to the mechanics of this world. Virgil, possessing high stealth capabilities and Darkvision, took the lead.

A dark, narrow hallway greeted them as they entered. They didn't need a light source, as there was some sort of blue-green glow emanating from the end of their path. As they crept forward, they came to the room where the glow came from. Their eyes widened as they took in a large central cavern.

The cavern was maybe two-hundred feet tall with a stone ceiling with veins of glowing crystal running along it. The glow from the crystals illuminated the chamber in a soft hue of sky blue. As they came out of the hallway, there was a small stone bridge stretching over a steadily flowing shallow river. The river emerged from one hole in a stone wall and disappeared in the wall on the other side of the cavern.

A central pillar made of a rust-colored metal in the middle of the chamber looked to be keeping the room from collapsing. There were multitudes of mining carts with railways on the ground. Random pieces of mining equipment were scattered about as well, showing the hastily abandoned nature of the work stations of the miners. Oh, and there was also blood. Random splatters of blood were plastered throughout different spots in the cavern. Some even had an occasional amputated rotting limb by them as well. It was... not comforting.

"Stay close," Virgil sent, then began to slowly move forward. He activated his Danger Sense subskill Detect Hostile Intent to make sure there weren't any enemies waiting in ambush. Fortunately, the skill showed that was not the case. Nevertheless, they moved forward carefully, as there could be traps. As they moved around the pillar to the other side of the room, they saw three different exits.

All three had a steel metal border and a unique dwarven carving atop. The one on the left had a female dwarf adorned with a helmet, wielding a sword in one hand and a smith's hammer in the other. The center had a male dwarf with a wild beard raising a mug of foamy ale with a pickaxe resting on his shoulder, and the third had a stern-looking bald male dwarf with a short, well-groomed beard and wielding a staff. All three exits were dark and at least twenty feet tall, giving the party an ominous feeling when looking at them.

"*Does your talking dwarf skull have any ideas where to go, oh fearless leader?*" Maldrakus asked sarcastically through Party Chat, which Grief happened to be on too.

"Hey, how do ye know that I be a dwarf? Are ye be usin' some sort of mind readin' spell or something?" Grief sent back.

"Your forehead is disproportionately large compared to other skulls, and only dwarves say… 'Ye be.'"

There was a pregnant pause for a few moments, until Grief gave the equivalent of a mental shrug. "Eh, yer not wrong there," he admitted. "Lad, let me examine them doors." Virgil complied and showed the skull each of them. "Hm, I think I know what these stand fer. In dwarven culture, while we have many talented and skilled workers, there be four great crafts revered by me folk. They be battle, blacksmithin', brewing, and mining. The left and middle doors show two of the four great crafts. The right one be… different. I think it represents—"

"Magic," Virgil said, finishing his companion's thought out loud. "You said that the Dwemdurians were rare because they had more magical capabilities than most dwarven races, right?"

"Aye, lad," Grief replied. "If ye had any suspicion about some magic metal fighters, that be the direction I'd reckon."

"I agree," Gwen added. "Not because of what he said, but because my love Christopher here found a trail of blood leading inside the tunnel. Let's go," she said before creeping forward slowly in the dark, following her boar sniffing the ground like a bloodhound.

Virgil let out a small, irritated groan after his deduction skills were just proven pointless, but followed. While the tunnel was dark, it wasn't completely black. There were occasional sconces along the tunnel walls with a magical orb of light above them where a flame would be if they were just regular torches.

Virgil let his race's natural senses take over. Dark elves were literally made for the dark, and had both Darkvision and ridiculously large ears with increased hearing as adaptations to thrive in darkness. Those developed senses proved to be beneficial to the party as they began to twitch, picking up on a subtle scuttling sound right before his Danger Sense began sending alarms to his head.

"Above you!" Virgil shouted to Gwen before firing a Nature Bolt at the ceiling. The sound of breaking metal and whirling gears met their ears as a six-legged creature fell from the ceiling and landed on the ground between Gwen and the others. It was roughly one foot tall with six metal legs spread out from a central body. Atop the body was a large red jewel that had a very subtle glow to it. One of the legs was partially broken at the joint from where Virgil presumably hit it, and sparks were coming from the wounded limb. Immediately, two more fell down in front of Gwen and behind the rest of the party.

The spider-like creatures let out a shriek that sounded like two rusted gears rubbing against each other and lunged at the party. Virgil conjured an Yggdrashield in front of Gwen, protecting her from the two in front, while Maldrakus fired Arcane Bolts at the two behind them. The injured creature in the middle went after Virgil, but Christopher ran up behind it and flung the metal construct in the air with his snout. Splinter took advantage of the airborne creature's current position and leapt off Virgil's shoulder at it and tackled it to the ground.

The stego rat was an evolved version of a dire rat and had one of the most painful bites in all of Imeria, and she bit down on one of its uninjured legs. To everyone's surprise, her powerful bite did not break through the thick metal, only dented it. The small automaton flung Splinter off of it and stabbed the rat in the stomach.

Virgil's eyes widened in horror at that. "Splinter, no!" he shouted in fear, then fired two more Nature Bolts at the creature. Both hit its central body and caused it to crash into the wall, cracking the red jewel atop it. There was a slow winding sound as the creature died, and its body went limp. Virgil didn't give it too much mind; he was more focused on his animal companion.

Splinter was curled in a ball, with blood and stomach contents flowing out from her wound. Virgil immediately cast Restore on his pet and ran over to her, ignoring the rest of the fighting. Fortunately, he was fast enough and his magic was strong enough to repair the damage, though his companion looked both tired and pale from the blood loss. He heard another metallic shriek and was reminded of the battle, so he put her back on his shoulder and ordered her to stay close.

When Virgil looked back, he saw that there was only one creature left alive. It had climbed up his magic shield and leapt off of it, sharp metallic legs pointed straight at Gwen. The Hunter Druid was ready for it. She quickly turned to it and cast her Air Strike Arrow spell while Maldrakus also fired an Arcane Bolt. The arrow of air seemed to wrap around the magic bolt, causing it to accelerate even faster. Both struck the metallic creature with deadly force, slamming it into the wall of the tunnel and shattering it into multiple small bits.

Virgil looked around and cast Restore to heal all the minor wounds the rest of the party sustained. "I take it those were the automatons we were warned about?" he asked.

"Yes," Maldrakus replied. "And I have the feeling that these were just the pawns."

"I agree," Virgil said. "It looks like they weren't kidding. These things are weak to magic, but I've never seen a material as tough as the metal these things were made of. I mean, even Splinter's bite couldn't break through it in one chomp."

"Indeed, it looks like you should have kept your animals at the college. They may be more hindrance than help here. If we come across bigger threats, a boar and a rat will likely not be able to do a thing."

Splinter did not like the mage's words and turned to face him baring her teeth.

Virgil calmed down his animal companion then looked at Maldrakus. "You are right in that the animals' fighting style is not well-suited for fighting these things, but do not underestimate them, especially the big one. You'll want its help when the time's right."

"The big one?" the blue-haired elf asked.

"*You'll see,*" Virgil replied via party chat while turning and heading forward through the tunnel. The party examined the remains of the creatures. They were able to discover that the creatures were called 'Dwarvum Hexatons,' and that they were indeed more of a sacrificial vanguard when it came to the automatons, based on their information gleaned from Analyze. There wasn't any obvious loot of value from them either. None of the party had the mining skill or knew how to work with the metal they were made from.

Each of the five Hexatons had a small container of something called 'Dwemdurian Oil' in it. Virgil's Alchemy skill registered it as an 'Exceptional' level ingredient, so he stored them inside Grief, figuring that it being labeled 'Exceptional' had to mean there was something of worth about the liquid.

Virgil did try to take a look at the jewels embedded at the top of the dead creatures, but they all had broken post-death. When Virgil tried Analyze on it, all he received was a name, Anchor Gem-Depleted. He asked the rest of the party if they knew, but they did not. Something wasn't quite right about it. The druid wasn't sure exactly what, but the gem's presence didn't sit well with him. He decided to store one of them to see if he could learn anything about it later.

Virgil wanted to lead the group since he had Darkvision and Danger Sense, but he knew that Gwen had a Master-ranked Tracking skill plus great instincts. He just wished that she had Darkvision. Then he remembered, he had both the Alchemy and a Master-Ranked Herbology skill, in addition to freaking treasure-trove of ingredients and potions stored inside Grief!

One of which was a dry flower called Thiefsbane. When ingested, it granted the person Darkvision for a short period of time. From his training with Ras, Virgil knew how to extend the effectiveness of the plant by making it into a potion.

"*Guard both the exits,*" Virgil sent to the other elves as he took a knee and pulled out his Alchemy set.

"*We're in the middle of hostile territory, and you want to play with your chemistry set?!*" Maldrakus sent back in both shock and anger.

"*Trust Virgil. His analytical mind helps him understand situations better than I ever could. If he feels he needs to make a potion here, I know it's for a good reason. So, shut up, and watch out for enemies,*" Gwen sent and turned to face one of the tunnel's exits.

The mage pursed his lips and flared his nostrils but complied, muttering under his breath. Virgil was grateful to have Gwen with him and her trust as well. It may have seemed strange, but he genuinely thought the tunnel was actually a good spot to craft, as it wasn't very wide. So, they couldn't be taken by overwhelming numbers if any more automatons appeared.

Virgil first pricked his finger with his nail, putting ten drops of blood into the mortar. Though it kind of freaked him out to use his own blood, Ras did show that the druidic powers laden in his blood provided potent abilities. Then he took out two Termite Bodies he had previously collected and used the pestle to crush the insects' bodies into a heterogeneous liquid. Virgil had discovered that using Termite Bodies helped increase the efficacy of a potion as long as it was used in conjunction with something that came from a living body, such as his blood. Lastly, he took out the Thiefsbane. Once again, he used the pestle to crush the plant, petals and stem, in with the bloody mixture.

Once he was done, the concoction let out one subtle purple glowing pulse before a notification filled Virgil's vision.

You have found Druidic Darkvision Potion.
Item Type: Potion

Durability: 13/13
Item Class: Rare
Effect: Utilizing the blood of a dark elf druid, enhanced by the body of two termites, and combined with a Thiefsbane plant, this potion provides increased Darkvision capabilities more than just ingesting the plant ever could. Provides 60 feet of Darkvision to the drinker for 12 hours.

Congratulations! Alchemy has reached Level 32!

The substance was almost like a gel. With distinct chunks of termite exoskeleton, it looked like a toddler's attempt at making jelly. Nevertheless, it worked! Virgil filled four vials with the substance, then handed one to each of his elven companions. Both of them gave a disgusted look when checking out the potions through the glass vial, but when Virgil told them what it did, they both begrudgingly tossed them back like a shot of tequila.

Both mage and druid had their pupils dilate and their faces had wide grins plastered on them, but not as demonic as the firebrand orcs. It was... kind of creepy, but they soon expressed their gratitude and desire to continue forward. So that's what they did.

With Gwen in the lead, Virgil in the middle, and Maldrakus pulling up the rear, the party ventured deeper into the ruins-turned-mine. They pushed on for hours. Despite the blood trail almost running cold, they discovered a good bit of the abandoned city and encountered a number of different automatons as well.

Though the Hexatons were like six-legged spiders, the rest were all bipedal. Most stood around six feet tall with helmets for faces that possessed carved mouths and noses. There were two sockets containing glowing red eyes. They said no words, just attacked on sight. Their Anchor Gems broke just like their brethren's when the creatures were defeated.

There were three versions of the bipedal automatons that they encountered. One had a sword and shield. The other wielded a two-handed greataxe, and the third had a crossbow instead of its left hand and a dagger in its other. Based off using Analyze on them, they were called Shielders, Berserkers, and Archers respectively. The dwarvum metal they were made of was even thicker than the Hexatons' and was less vulnerable to magical attacks, making them more difficult foes to overcome. The party still managed to overcome them with their strategy and magic.

Maldrakus was definitely surprised when he was introduced to 'the big one.' In fact, the elf fell on his ass when Baphomet transformed in front of him. The ever-confident Battle Mage quickly composed himself after the druids had a good laugh. Their strategy consisted of Baphomet primarily tanking for the group. The beastking's physical attacks couldn't do too much to the automatons, but it could take a good hit. After a few fights, they found a solid battle plan.

After Virgil refreshed Barkskin on the beast, Baphomet would charge in, drawing aggro from all hostiles. It was ordered to try to primarily focus on shoving, throwing, and forcing the metal constructs away from it to grant some distance. Meanwhile, Virgil would focus all his healing onto the beastking while Gwen and Maldrakus used their ranged offensive spells to fire at the automatons that Baphomet put some distance between. They went with this strategy to lessen the chance of friendly fire, and it worked wonderfully.

Occasionally, Gwen and Maldrakus would accidentally cause one of the constructs they fired upon to focus on them instead. Virgil would then intervene with a Leeching Vines spell to stop them and give the other two elves more time to eliminate them.

Virgil was proud of his team. Maldrakus sometimes tried to challenge his authority, sometimes ignoring his warnings, but the Arcane Mage had been reliable for the most part. He was curious as to how the blue-haired elf could regenerate his manna so quickly for all these fights, but Virgil had put that curiosity to the side, as it wasn't imperative to know for now.

Many sections of the city actually had wide open spaces despite being underground. Though multiple spaces were in various stages of destruction from Amthoon's mining efforts, they found plenty of places that were still untouched by the excavators. Many rooms had large gears and cogs spaced throughout. Virgil and Gwen were surprised to see some of them were even still moving at a slow pace. In addition to turning gears, there were many pipes placed throughout with occasional vents that shot out bursts of steam and beams of electrical currents crackling across the ceilings of some rooms.

The ruins had a very steampunk-esque vibe that exhibited technological capabilities far beyond anything else seen in Imeria. Most rooms were lit, some with the glowing crystal, others with motion sensing torches, or magic orbs. They saw multiple laboratories, a mausoleum, an apparent tiny jailhouse with beds carved out of the stone floor in the cells, and what looked to be a small library filled with desiccated books no longer legible.

This place seemed like it would be Indiana Jones's dream to explore the secrets of these ruins. Maybe the archaeologist would've been better at finding valuable loot than the party did. Despite the weapons and remains from the automatons, there wasn't too much.

Virgil wondered if the city had sent scouting parties when the mine first opened to take any and all valuable material that didn't need to be mined. They did find a couple of bars of gold and some more Dwemdurian Oil.

Virgil's Herbology skill allowed him to find a unique moss growing under one of the pipes utilizing the moisture that leaked from its vent. It was called Psylum, and it shriveled in sunlight. The moss was apparently loaded with fluid; ingesting a certain amount of it could adequately rehydrate a dehydrated individual. In case they ever lost the Everfull Canteen, the moss would come in handy!

Virgil was concerned the party would get lost due to the nonlinear path they had taken. He couldn't tell where they were in regards to the entrance.

When he voiced his opinion, Gwen reassured him her Master-ranked Tracking skill helped her know just where they were.

Virgil knew they were going in the right direction as they fought automatons more regularly, but, more importantly, the foulness of demonic influence grew stronger. If it was not the professor, then there was some other demon behind what was going on.

CHAPTER TWELVE

Group Bonding

They came across a small prison room in a secluded hallway off the main path. Since the demonic influence and feeling of danger was growing more potent, they decided it to be the safe call to rest in the prison and recover their lost resources. Deciding that the small prison with thick barred windows and only one way in or out was the safest place they could be, the party decided to make camp for the night. Despite there being no sun to tell time in the deep, they still had internal clocks in their vision. It was around eight at night.

Maldrakus produced a stone from his bag.

"What are you going to do with a stone in a mine?" Virgil asked, watching as it started to glow.

"It's a flame stone. They are made to give heat and light to travelers." Maldrakus placed the stone on the ground. It illuminated the room a little more than the torches did and sent off pleasant waves of heat. The party ate in relative silence, munching on the travel rations they each had brought. The well-dressed Battle Mage's food consisted of some delicious-smelling dried meats wrapped in a leaf green vegetable, much better than the hard tack that the druids had. Splinter stared at the Arcane Mage with a thick glob of saliva hanging off her mouth. Virgil had to order his voracious rat to not leap over and steal the food for herself.

Now that they were in relative safety, Virgil relaxed some, closing his eyes, took some deep breaths, and let the day's tension fall off of him. They had been through a lot in the past twenty-four hours, and the stress was taking a toll. After a few minutes, he felt notably lighter.

He turned to their mage companion. They were likely going to face this demon tomorrow, and the party needed to know more about the wood elf to come up with the best strategy possible, as their opponent would likely be more... unique in comparison to the foes they'd faced so far. "So, Maldrakus, I wanted to ask you; how come your stats are so strange for a mage? I would think you'd want to have more points into intelligence to boost your manna pool."

The wood elf's form stiffened and he scowled. His face went from scowl to frustration, and finally, he got himself under control and calmed his expression. This was clearly a sore subject. "Yes, as you saw, despite my rare ability in possessing Arcane Magic, my statistics are not... ideal. That is due to me being a wood elf."

"What does that have to do with it?" Gwen asked.

"Much," he replied. "As you know, when we level, we are awarded five statistic points. Depending on your race, the gods have already allocated a few of those points for you. Wood elves, like myself, have two automatically put into strength and another put into endurance. That leaves me with only two to put into agility, intelligence, or charisma. We wood elves are strong, but not natural mages such as high elves like you, druid," he said to Gwen.

The professor continued. "It was a handicap that many of my classmates, including Darcassan Rubasal, never failed to remind me of. I was determined to become a Battle Mage, though. It had been my dream since childhood. So, I worked longer and harder than any of my privileged classmates, carefully allocating my statistics and making friends with the Enchanters' Guild in the city. What I could not make up for with natural talent, I made up for in effort and equipment." He then wriggled the fingers on one hand, causing the rings on them to gently rub against each other. "Each of these rings possesses an enchantment. Most are minor, but a few are major. They augment my statistics and my spellcasting capabilities. With them, I am the most formidable Battle Mage on the continent."

"Even better than the king?" Virgil asked with a sly smile.

"Pfft, Darcassan may be good, abyss, he may even be a great Arcanomancers, but he is no match for me," Maldrakus replied with no hint of doubt in his voice.

"Well, I'm glad to have you on our side then," Virgil said. "Now, how much can you tell us about this imposter who's been pretending to be Talia Ogrul? Whatever we can learn about the demon before we have to fight it, the better chance we have of coming out the other side of the battle alive."

"I wouldn't have believed it, but with your appearance as the druid champions summoned to fight the demons and hearing from the headmaster himself, I've come to accept that my colleague was an imposter the whole time. Still, it's hard to swallow that I've been working with a demon for decades." The mage realized he'd gone off-topic. "Oh, my apologies. Er hem, Talia, or the fiend pretending to be her, was a professor of magical history, bit of a dull subject for my liking. She was quiet and appeared as a reclusive human woman who kept mostly to herself. When she wasn't teaching, she was researching. Numerous times, I would see her in the school's library searching through dozens of old scrolls and tomes regarding lost and ancient magics. Whenever I would see her there, she'd give me a kind nod and a subtle wave before going back to her research. Not a great beauty, or a great conversationalist for that matter, but for all intents and purposes, seemed like a pleasant woman. We even became good friends. Despite her going on and on about ancient magics, we were actually very close."

He looked around, slightly melancholy. "Now I see that her studies haven't gone to waste. She's somehow corrupted the ancient magics of the Dwemdurians to make herself a metal army."

"What type of magic did she use?" Virgil asked.

"Honestly, I'm not sure. I never saw the woman cast a single spell in my entire life."

"Er hem, I think I have a better answer fer that question, lad," Grief spoke up.

Virgil unlatched his skull companion, and held him up so that the skull could face everyone. "Go on."

"Well, we of the Devilslayer clan know much about the fiends that be tryin' ta overcome this world. If the lass we're looking fer be a demon and can use magic, then she automatically be a warlock. Warlocks can only use a few types of magic. The first be blood magic, which we've experienced firsthand. The second be Corruption Magic. It be magic that spreads the influence of the infernal realm, overriding, contaminatin', and corruptin' everything in its path. The rotwood imps possess a small form of that magic. The final form be the vilest of all." The skull's tone turned ominous. "It be Soul Magic."

"Pfft, Soul Magic," Maldrakus replied in disbelief. "That is just a fairy tale meant to keep children from leaving their beds at night."

"I'm sorry, do ye know more 'bout demons than someone whose whole bloody clan hunts them?" Grief asked with obvious venom. "Soul Magic be real, ya blue bastard, and I should know, I seen it the last time the demon generals invaded."

The mage gave a begrudging shrug, but still didn't seem entirely convinced.

Grief continued, "Soul magic be having two separate ways to be used. The first be channeling yer anger. The magic changes it into a physical flame that can burn enemies to a crisp. Good grief, I even lost a sizable chunk of me beard one time to one of the flames back when I had me body. We experienced it before with that Zinthos devil. Next be channeling yer will. This is prolly the scariest version."

"Why is that?" asked Gwen.

"Because of what it can do, lass. Soul domination magic can literally attack and suppress the will and soul of something recently dead or near-death. If ye kill a creature with it, you can steal their souls and use it as fuel and a power source. If ye use it on a living creature, ye can attack their very minds. I've seen plenty of demon hunters go mad from the spellcraft of those damn domination mages. We best hope we don't run into any of 'em here."

Hearing Grief's explanation made Virgil wonder about his recent encounters, both with Zinthos and the automatons. He remembered the demon speaking through the totem somehow pushing its will into him. Was that soul domination magic? Maybe it was. He thought about his new Purifying Aura spell that he learned from Lucille. He hadn't used it yet aside from their 'trial battle' with Maldrakus, but when he encountered the Zinthos again, Virgil definitely would cast it again, as his master had gifted him the spell specifically to help protect him from the fiend's manipulation. Thinking about the soul domination magic Grief had elaborated on, Virgil was also reminded about the glowing anchor gems that the automatons had inside them that would be 'depleted' when they died. It reminded him of a concept called soul gems from his gaming experience.

"Do you think that this demon could be using soul domination magic to force souls to power the automatons?" he asked.

There was a heavy silence, as no one in the group immediately responded while they processed the grave possibility of that being true. Eventually, Grief did say something. "Lad, I not be sure. But if yer right, that be a terrifyin' thing."

"Indeed," Gwen added. "Now that we know more about our quarry, why don't we strategize our plan of attack for tomorrow?" The group nodded and went over their abilities, strengths, and weaknesses for the upcoming battle over the next couple of hours while the three animals they had with them ran around and played as if they were in an animal sanctuary and not an underground death trap. Splinter was curious and put her head in a small hole at ankle height and almost electrocuted herself had Virgil's Danger Sense not warned him. He quickly pulled the stego rat away from the hole, and a beam of electricity shot across the room from one divot in the wall to the other. The beasts quickly tempered down their playing after that.

The three elves came up with two solid plans from their brainstorming efforts. One was under the condition that the animals couldn't do much damage, while the other was the opposite. The group agreed that if the animals could help, their chances of success would go up dramatically.

"What if we coat the animals' claws and teeth in some kind of substance that could break through or destroy the dwarvum metal?" Gwen suggested.

That reminded Virgil of a particular acid he had received from Ras, and exclaimed as he produced a vial from Grief's storage space, "Gwen you're a genius." She blushed at the compliment. "With enough time, both Gwen's arrows and the beasts' attacks should work on the automatons," he told the other two elves in the party. The primary objective, though, was rest, and he needed to do some Alchemy.

CHAPTER THIRTEEN

Experimentation

Virgil stood up, went over to one of the raised stone beds, and excitedly pulled out his Alchemy set, placing it on the bed as a makeshift table. Given that the bed was made of stone, flat, even, and without any cushion at all, it basically was a table. He then pulled up the list of items stored in Grief and organized the list into just the alchemical ingredients and potions with basic summaries as to what they did.

- **X5 Minor Health Potions** – +25 Health
- **X5 Minor Manna Potions** – +25 Manna
- **X5 Minor Stamina Potions** – + 25 Stamina
- **X2 Enhanced Druidic Darkvision Potion** – 12 Hour Darkvision
- **X7 Poison Cure** – (Ingested or Inhaled)
- **X1 Manna Restoration Potion** – Restores Manna Pool to 100%
- **X10 Healing Poultices** – Replenishes Health
- **X4 Enhanced Scatter Scat Paste** – Increases Agility by 15% for 15 minutes

- **X2 Enhanced Demonic Fury Paste** – Causes Berserk status
- **X1 Enhanced Beast Sense Potion** – Increases senses
- **X1 Enhanced Potion of Cackling Stiffness** – Causes laughter and movement debuff
- **X1 Nightmare Powder** – Causes nightmare-laden sleep, if killed while in nightmare will become wraith
- **X1 Liquid Light Flash** – Causes flash of light
- **X1 True Taunt Potion** – Brings Taunt skill temporarily to 50
- **X1 Metallic Acid** – Breaks down only metals
- **X1 Potion of Snake Hands** – Causes hands to turn into snakes temporarily
- **X1 Potion of Icy Essence** – Gives icy protective layer
- **X1 Analgesic Sleep Powder** – Causes sleep and removes pain
- **X2 Termite Bodies** – Enhances properties of ingredients taken from living things
- **X1 Dragonberry** – Causes firebreath
- **X3 Amphigray** – Allows for underwater breathing
- **X1 Shimmerleaf** – Causes temporary invisibility
- **X15 Psylum** – Keeps hydrated
- **X1 Mummified Fire Sprite** – Variable fire-based effects
- **X1 Sageweed** – Manna Restoration
- **X10 Healing Herbs** – Replenishes Health
- **X4 Tulitan** – Can be made into a lubricant
- **X2 Deep Sleep Lichen** – Helps sleep
- **X4 Firebrand Ogre Teeth** – Variable fire-based effects
- **X2 Firebrand Ogre Eyes** – Strength booster
- **X4 Stamina Herbs** – Replenishes Stamina

- **X2 Vile Stalker Venom** – Poison, if dies from venom will come back as a demon
- **X6 Jungle Envirowolf Heart** – Various tracking or camouflage-based effects
- **X10 Dwemdurian Oil** – Unknown properties

Besides the general love and gratitude that Grief had an unlimited amount of storage slots, Virgil had two thoughts after he had organized his list. First was, "*Crap, I need to use more of my herbs and potions.*" Second was, "*If I wasn't fighting demons right now, I could possibly start an alchemical monopoly.*" Nevertheless, he needed to focus and work on finding an ideal way to apply, and possibly improve, the Metallic Acid. First though, he needed to hand out some of these potions to the other two elves in preparation for the upcoming fight.

Virgil set out two of each of the three types of Minor Health, Stamina, and Manna potions for both Maldrakus and Gwen. He also set out the last Druidic Darkvision potion for each of them. None of the automatons utilized poison so far, so he held onto the poison cures he had, as well as the Manna Restoration Potion. As the group's dedicated healer, he needed to make sure he never bottomed out on manna or it could spell death for them all. He gave each of them four out of his ten Healing Poultices, as well.

Virgil lastly gave each of his elven party members one portion of Enhanced Scatter Scat Paste. It was a rather gross but effective concoction he made and happened upon by chance by using Jackalope feces as one of the ingredients. By taking a deep inhalation of the dry paste, it increased your Agility by fifteen percent for fifteen minutes. Now that may not sound that impressive, but if you already had a high Agility like Virgil did, you could possibly become too fast for the eye to see!

None of Virgil's other items seemed too relevant for him to give out to his party. Next, it was time to experiment. Virgil knew well that while his Herbology skill listed ingredient uses, it did not always give *every* possible use. So, he used the tried-and-true way of testing ingredients to determine any unknown properties: he ingested them. It was a calculated risk, but Virgil did have poison cures and could likely heal himself to compete with any negative health effects of a potentially poisonous item.

Virgil found that the Psylum had a rather bland taste and that it could reduce the rate of Stamina depletion. Tulitan was bitter and the flower, in addition to being an ingredient for a lubricant, provided cold resistance and could be used to turn liquids into gels and pastes. Virgil then cut off a tiny piece of Jungle Envirowolf heart. It increased his sense of smell and, when ingested raw, led to vomiting. It was *very fun* to have an increased sense of smell of your own vomit... At least he leveled up his Herbology skill once and gained the Culinary Skill from his endeavors.

After concerned looks from his animal companions and the rest of his party, Virgil rinsed out his mouth and continued. Finally, the last test ingredient was the Dwemdurian Oil. Virgil took a deep breath, dipped his finger in the oil, and touched his tongue. The oil was a level of bitter that far surpassed the Tulitan flower. It reminded him of the final cup of coffee from the bottom of a pot that had been on all day. Fortunately, he received a notification listing off some of its uses for his efforts.

Dwemdurian Oil uses discovered!

- Amplification: Amplifies all magic it comes into contact with.
- Lubricant: You feel this could be used to make a salve to ease joint aches and pains
- Alchemical Synergizer: When coming into contact with a liquid alchemical substance for 5 minutes continuously, the oil will synergize with and turn into the substance.

Alchemy has reached Level 33!

The dark elf's eyes widened. The oil was like an alchemical miracle! It could amplify magic *and* it could turn into any liquid alchemical substance it came into contact with, which included potions or, in his case, acid! With this, he could make more portions of the Metallic Acid, and with more acid, they could beat the automatons more handily!

Virgil cackled to himself and channeled his inner Sith. "Hehehehe, good, good." After more concerned looks from his allies, he quit acting like a madman and continued his work, muttering that they were no fun and didn't appreciate sci-fi cinema classics. He then took out seven of the ten portions of oil and began having them synergize with the metallic acid. After that was done, he took one more container of oil, synergized, and turned into another of his super rare Manna Restoration Potions.

Once that was complete, he called Splinter over to him. The stego hopped onto the stone bed and waited for the next command. Virgil had her dip her claw into a container of Metallic Acid. As she raised her claw out of it, Virgil noticed how it rolled off the claw, not sticking to it as he wanted it to. In fact, none of it stuck at all, and it all rolled down back into the bowl. Splinter looked back at her master and cocked her head, confused as to why he asked her to do that.

Virgil pushed up his glasses then stroked his chin. "Hmm," he muttered to himself then let his analytical nature take over, "Our problem is that our animals cannot penetrate the tough metal exteriors of the automaton. The Metallic acid can destroy any metal, but doesn't do damage to any other substance. It also won't stick to items like Splinter's claws. So, how do I make the acid more viscous like a protective coating of paint?" He asked himself.

After a half a minute of pondering, an idea clicked in his head, "That's it! Instead of a coating like paint, it can be a paste or stick like hair gel!" Virgil took out one of the portions of the newly created Metallic Acids and took out the common Tulitan flower. He placed the flower into the mortar, then poured the Metallic Acid over it.

As expected, it did nothing to the plant, and it just floated in the dark liquid. Virgil took out his pestle and began crushing the plant. The flower broke apart inside the acid and the liquid began to subtly bubble. The longer Virgil kept crushing the more the bubbles spread and the liquid became more viscous. Suddenly, the bubbling stopped and began disappearing.

Virgil looked down at the acid and noticed the liquid was no longer moving. He lifted his pestle and felt a distinct sucking sensation. He tipped the tool up to look at the bottom and saw the acid no longer ran right off. It was stuck like a thick paste. The Healer Druid looked down with a big crap-eating grin at his new creation. He had done it!

You have discovered a recipe! Metallic Acid Paste.
Ingredients: 10 oz of Metallic Acid + 1 Tulitan Flower
Description: An inspired creation discovered by the Healer Druid champion of Yggdrasil. Doing something no one else would think of, risking losing an extremely rare alchemical compound by combining an extremely rare acid with a very common flower, he has made the acid into an applicable paste. You are either really intuitive or ridiculously lucky!
Effect: For as long as the paste makes contact with metal, it will dissolve away and break down the material as if it was thin paper. Can be used to coat weapons, but will only last 20 minutes when applied.

For discovering a working recipe never created before, Alchemy has reached Level 35, and you have gained the following Trait: Alchemically Inspired – You now have a +10% chance of succeeding when creating alchemical creations and an extra +5% when attempting to create a brand-new recipe never seen before in Imeria.

Virgil was pumped by the notifications, and they inspired him to continue experimenting. First, though, he applied a small amount of the acid paste onto one of Splinter's claws and ordered her to attack one of the metal prison bars. There was the usual grating sound of bone against metal, but there was also a distinct ring of metal breaking as the rat's claw passed through the bar. All the elves looked in awe as the thin bar of Dwemdurian metal had been cleaved in two by the stego rat's claw.

"By the gods!" Maldrakus exclaimed. "I didn't think your plan to break the metal was possible!"

"I knew you could do it," Gwen said to Virgil with a smile and a sly wink that made him blush.

Virgil smiled back, feeling pretty dang proud of himself. "Of course, with this paste I've made, the animals should be able to help us in fighting the automatons tomorrow."

"That's great!" Gwen went over to Christopher and kneeled down, rubbing the hair on the top of the terror boar's head. "You hear that, love? You'll be able to fight back against those metal baddies."

The boar snorted happily, closing his eyes and leaning his head against the elf's hand. The beautiful high elf then stood back up and walked over to Virgil, leaning against one of his large ears. "I'm proud of you, babe," she whispered and kissed him on the cheek, sending shivers of glee up his spine.

"Babe?" Virgil asked in surprise. "I mean, don't get me wrong, that sounds like it could be really great, but we've only had one date so far."

Gwen bit down on her lower lip. "Yeah, well, if we survive here, I'll let you take me out on date number two," she said with another wink and went back over to lay down on her bedroll by the heat from the enchanted flame stone.

With much more motivation to survive after that, Virgil went back to his alchemical work. For the other two portions of oil, he had an idea how best to use them, but he needed to test it out first. He was curious as to what exactly the 'Amplification' use meant.

He poured a small amount onto the ground, took a few steps back, then cast Leeching Vines from that exact spot on the ground. To his surprise, larger and thicker barbed vines erupted from the spot, flailing out to find a target.

Excited and knowing what he wanted to use his potions and items for, Virgil stored them back in Grief and went to sleep. Tomorrow, the Dwemdurian Oil used to power or fuel the automatons would now be the source of their demise.

CHAPTER FOURTEEN

Heart and Soul of the Issue

In the morning, the party discussed their plans, had their potions and items ready, equipped and stored their gear, and continued their trek to find the demonic imposter of Professor Talia Ogrul. They would try to use their items sparingly until the final battle, but wouldn't hoard the items to the point of unintentionally leading to a party member's death. Maldrakus had a slight reluctance to use his items on the animals if need be, but a firm glare from both Gwen and Virgil convinced him otherwise.

Virgil had also given the other two mages a container of Dwemdurian Oil each and told them to use it on his signal. Both Maldrakus and Gwen drank their Druidic Darkvision Potions.

The party reopened the door they had sealed that had kept them safe in the ward of cells and continued their pursuit of the demon. It had been surprisingly easy to seal the room as the small collection of prison cells locked from the inside. It was potentially the safest place in the whole dungeon, like a safe room where he could save in his games.

Gwen led the way; her Tracking skill was still able to find a small amount of blood occasionally splotched against a wall or on the ground, as if a body was brushed against them. It was a grim reminder of the dangerous foes they were up against.

For the next few hours, the party continued their trek in pursuit of the demon and the likely cause of the automatons' attacks. The party did encounter a few more automaton contingents. Virgil used a few of the Metallic Acid Pastes on the animals, and sure enough, the beasts were able to tear right through the metallic creations!

Finally, as they rounded a corner, Virgil felt a presence in a room up ahead. His Danger Sense started sending alarms in his mind. The presence felt... wrong. It was disgusting to Virgil's druidic senses, making it clear it was some sort of demon. Virgil could sense dread and pain coming from the room as well. It seemed like there were multiple people in that room, silently crying out for help.

He turned to Gwen. She looked at him with a serious expression, and through Party Chat she sent, "*I felt it too. We're close.*"

Virgil eyed the Arcane Mage. "*We need to go in quietly and carefully. We don't know what's up ahead, but it isn't good,*" he sent.

Maldrakus rolled his eyes. "I know we're supposed to, but why does it matter? With our magic, these dwarvum constructs are no match against us," he whispered aloud. Though he wasn't loud, with the empty stillness of the dungeon, it felt more like screaming to the druids.

Virgil quickly put a hand on the wood elf's mouth. "*Dude, Party Chat please,*" he mentally sent, clearly frustrated with the mage's laissez faire attitude. He then removed his hand and continued. "*Because, if this follows the pattern of a typical dungeon, we're likely to encounter a boss ahead. Plus, there's likely a demon too, not an automaton. That means our magic may not be as powerful. So please, let's continue on this winning plan of being stealthy. It's kept us alive so far, and I really like living,*" he explained.

Maldrakus groaned a little, rolling his eyes even more dramatically like some disgruntled teenager, but relented to the game plan. The party then even more carefully stealthed their way to the room at the end of the hallway. As they got closer, they saw that the doorway was unlike the other well-carved ones they had seen throughout the ruins. This one was rough, uneven, jagged, and didn't possess any doors at all. It looked like someone had either dug or blown their way through the wall and into some room.

As the party made it to the entrance, hugging the two walls, they peeked into the room. There was a descending stairway from the entrance that led down to the room, which meant that the party had the advantage of having the high-ground, another one of Master Kenobi's valuable lessons.

The room was a vast open chamber with torches ensconced throughout, giving plenty of illuminating light outside of the dark ceiling. Like the first chamber in the ruins, there was a stream of water that emerged from a small hole in the stone wall to the left and fed into another section of the same wall just a few feet away from it.

The room also looked like it was going to be turned into some dwemdurian room, but was left mid-construction, as one small section in the back of the chamber had both a smoothed-out floor and walls with carved out slots on them. There was a small altar in the middle with an unconscious male dwarf laid prone across it. Large cables of wires were strewn about the room, along the floor, walls, and ceiling. They all seemed to originate from the altar area with the dwarf.

While the room itself was interesting, what really kept the party's attention were its occupants. Outside of the unconscious dwarf on his back, piles of dead human, elf, and dwarven corpses were in another corner, like a pile of garbage. All of them were practically skeletons with gray and shriveled skin with hollowed-out eyes. Two automatons bigger than the party had ever seen, standing around twelve feet tall, were standing guard. One was a Shielder and the other was an Archer. The arrows locked in its crossbow arm were big enough to be ballista bolts to the party. They both had their backs turned to the party and were looking at the one ornate section of the room.

There, standing over the altar with the prone dwarf, was a pale human woman with jet black hair. She wore the thick black robes of the Mage College as well, and was muttering some incantation Virgil couldn't discern the meaning of. He just knew that it wasn't good. Her back was also turned away from the entrance, giving the party an amazing opportunity for a sneak attack. Then something happened that Virgil did not expect.

"No, no, no, this can't be right," Maldrakus whispered, immediately walking into the room.

Virgil's eyes widened. He tried to grab the Arcane Mage's elbow, but Maldrakus shoved him off.

"Talia!" the wood elf shouted.

The two automatons turned to face the intruder, locking their weapons onto him.

"Shit!" Virgil spat, entering the room with the others on his heels, with their weapons focused on the automatons. Talia didn't respond to Maldrakus, she just continued focusing on her ritual and moving her hands in a particular pattern. The professor fired an Arcane Bolt at her but was blocked by the Shielder's massive and thick round shield.

Though the dwarvum metal was susceptible to magic, it still only left a minor dent. The professor didn't stop though. He fired again, but at a stalactite hanging above her. A chunk of it broke off and descended toward her.

Talia was posed with her hand in a claw ready to rip the dwarf's heart out when the stalactite fragment hit her in the head, causing her to stumble backward and land on her rear. "Noo!" she shouted. The dwarf opened his eyes and let out a gasp before streaks of blood leaked out from his mouth and eyes. He died right there on the spot. Unlike the other corpses, though, he did not shrivel.

Talia quickly stood back up, looked at the dead dwarf, then looked at Maldrakus. A small streak of blood ran down her temple. The two large automatons had not moved to attack, still keeping her protected. "Grr, you've interrupted my ritual, you fool," she spat.

"Talia... please, it's not too late. End this madness. We're friends," the Arcane Mage gently pleaded as he made it to the bottom of the stairs.

Talia cackled, "Hahaha! Friends?! Fool, we're not friends! You're simply a tool, fuel for my master's fire. Why, I'm not even Talia. I killed her decades ago and have been wearing her disgusting meat suit since." She then took in Maldrakus' form, licking her upper teeth. "You know, now that you're here, I think it's time for an upgrade," she said and snapped her fingers. Her body began to change. Her legs fused together, morphing into one large serpentine tail. The light human skin turned into a shade of dark red with two curling horns erupting from her head. Finally, her eyes turned yellow with vertical slits to match elongated yellow fangs from her mouth.

"Now that's better," she cooed.

Maldrakus' saddened expression turned to anger. "What is the point of all this, you wretch?!"

The demon angrily snapped back at the mage, "Careful now, Maldrakus. Unlike poor little Talia, I, Erogg, won't hesitate to rip your soul from your body." She composed herself. "The point of all this is to build an army."

"An army for what, demon?" Gwen asked, an arrow pointed at Erogg.

The demon hissed at Gwen before answering. "Druid!" she shouted with venom. "You know well for what, scum. I serve the general, one who will burn all. With him leading us, we will finally free our master from the bonds that keep him restrained. We will overwhelm with numbers, numbers not from the infernal plane, but from your own world. And your people will not be able to stop us or see it coming, starting right here in Amthoon."

That caused the druids' hearts to race. There were more traitors? More warlocks? They were making armies? From where? Virgil wanted to get more information, so he Analyzed her.

Name: Erogg
Level: 34
Race: Demon **Type:** Sorlith
Health: 250 **Manna:** 700 **Stamina:** 250
Resistances: Nature Magic -50%, Corruption Magic 50%.
Debuffs: None.
Profession: None.
Sorliths are called the "changeling" or "shapeshifter" demons. Infernal magic runs deep throughout their blood, permeating their bodies and allowing them to be dangerous warlocks. They can take the form of a being they eat, hiding in plain sight.

Well, that description was terrifying.

"That demon be a sorlith," Grief sent through Party Chat. *"Many of 'em be spies due to their shapeshiftin' skills. Unlike most demons, though, these things be susceptible to fire fer some reason or 'nother."*

Virgil wanted to try to get more information out of the demon before they fought, trying to capitalize on the fact that villains seemed to enjoy monologuing. "Why here, though? We haven't seen any evidence of Yggdrasil's roots in Amthoon. What's the point?"

Erogg shook her head and tsked. "Foolish druid, you claim to have such a deep connection with the world tree, and yet you don't even realize her presence. Well, I suppose it won't hurt to let you know, since you're going to die here. There is a reason the Mage College is on the island right outside the city. You noticed the strong magical ambience there. Did you ever think to question *why* it was there?"

Understanding dawned on Virgil. "The world tree is there," he said in realization.

"Ah, so you're not as foolish as you look, wearing no shirt to cover your torso in the midst of battle, how idiotic."

Virgil glared at the sorlith. He now *really* wished his armor allowed him a shirt.

"Oh, did my words hurt your feelings? Poor baby druid," she said sarcastically, then cackled. "Yes, a piece of Yggdrasil, precisely one of her roots, is in the ground under the island, permeating the area with her accursed magic. For years, we researched a way to reach the root hidden somewhere on the school grounds, but the tree seemed to sense our true presence and the root always appeared to evade our attempts to bring it out or dig it up. So, if we couldn't find it covertly, we'd find it overtly instead. The general has ordered us to build an army to raze the city and college to the ground until we find the root and finally free Vozremath."

She gestured to the giant automatons. "That's where these beauties come in. The Dwemdurians were trying to make themselves immortal, but they ended up destroying themselves in the process." She held up an intact Anchor Gem. It was dull and gray. "They had made mechanical bodies, but they needed to find a way to put their souls into them. I discovered that, in their experiments, they succeeded, but... it worked too well, and they accidentally turned every single one of their people's souls into magical gems."

She looked directly at the gem. "Those fools managed to store their souls all at once, but had no one to put them into their bodies just feet away. With no one here for centuries, their souls managed to slip out through minute cracks, leaving perfect containers for new souls to go into. When I discovered what the Dwemdurians had created, I knew I could use my Corruption Magic to capitalize on it. Instead of free-minded people of metal, I have been killing and taking the souls of my victims one-by-one—whether they be miner, warrior, or child—and making an army of slave soldiers completely obedient to my will."

That statement finally made everything click together, why the automatons were attacking, why people were getting kidnapped, why there were piles of dead, desiccated bodies. This woman, this fiend, was literally stealing the souls of innocents and forcing them to fight against their will, all in order to bring more death and suffering to all in this world.

Those souls would only find freedom when someone would 'kill' them and destroy the stone imprisoning them. Everyone's eyes widened in shock at the pure malice of the demon's plan. Virgil, even though he was typically a calm and calculated person, had his jaw tightened in a scowl at the pure evil of what had transpired.

"You're going to die here," he said to Erogg.

She laughed in a spine-chilling manner. "Hahaha, oh no, I think you will be the ones dying here," she said and spoke in the infernal tongue. Virgil's Earring of Comprehension helped him understand what was said and heard the demon say, "Pure Dread." Her palm glowed green, signaling that what she said was a spell name. Before the group could respond, the ground underneath glowed green and all six party members, animal and elven, were struck by some invisible force.

All of them fell to their knees and felt a force atop them, as if gravity had been increased three times its normal effect. A notification appeared in the group's vision.

Debuff Gained! Dread

You have been struck by the spell Pure Dread.

You feel the burden of dread inside your very being. Feeling as if all hope is lost, you have an extreme lack of motivation to do anything but collapse in a pile of your own uselessness. Woe to the one who succumbs to suffering, for if you break through, you'll come out stronger.

-300% movement penalty for 60 seconds. -50% to spellcasting power for 60 seconds.

Virgil fell to his knees. One palm landed on the uneven, stony ground while the other still held onto his staff. He saw the notification, but he… didn't care about it. He didn't care about anything, really. He had failed so many times. He couldn't save the dwarf on the altar. The people of Kygor wouldn't accept him because they saw how useless he was. Even the notification from the universe confirmed how pitiful he was. He might as well just drop his staff and give up…

Virgil looked to his left, noticing Splinter. He saw his pet, his loyal and faithful companion, quivering, crying, and laying on the ground. She looked up at her master, extreme sadness evident in her eyes. Virgil saw the suffering, the pain inside the rat's very being that he was experiencing. It helped him realize that the thoughts that he was experiencing weren't his thoughts. They were lies from a malicious bitch, and she made his pet suffer. As a veterinarian, he made an oath to prevent that suffering. He *would not* let this demon get away with this!

Virgil glared up at the cackling Erogg, who was taking pleasure in their suffering. She wasn't even letting her metal slaves attack in order to prolong the party's pain. He gritted his teeth, tightened the grip on his staff, and forced out the words, "Purifying Aura!" Virgil slammed the butt of his staff on the ground as the top of the staff glowed white as a veil erupted from it. The veil spread out just far enough to cover the whole party. It felt like a breath of oxygen to someone who had been underwater for too long. All of the party inhaled and immediately stood up, free from the terrible debuff.

Erogg's cocky smirk was quickly replaced by one of fear. Before the demon could say anything, Gwen took out one of her special Ignitum arrows and fired it at the sorlith. It struck the demon in the chest, the heat from the friction of the impact triggering the arrow's special properties, and both it and the demon erupted into flame. She yelled in pain and began rolling on the ground. The two giant automatons, triggered by the harm to their master, charged at the party.

The Shielder swung his gigantic sword at Maldrakus.

A semi-transparent blue shell of Arcane Magic surrounded the mage and blocked the swing.

The Archer fired its massive crossbow bolts at Virgil. His Danger Sense triggered and he managed to roll out of the way of one, then conjured an Yggdrashield. Though tough, the shield barely managed to block the shot, as the head of the bolt managed to puncture through, thankfully not far enough to hit Virgil.

"Air Strike Arrow," Gwen said, and her conjured arrow of Nature Magic struck the Archer automaton in the side of the head. The massive construct turned its head at the Hunter Druid, its attention adequately drawn away from Virgil. "Put on the damn acid! We can kite them for a little bit!"

Virgil quickly complied. He grabbed three containers of Metallic Acid Paste and slammed them in the ground to make a large puddle. He stuck his hands in it and began rapidly applying it to Splinter's boney spikes, claws, and large incisor teeth. Then he applied them to both Christopher's ram horns and protruding tusks. Virgil had cut his hands multiple times applying the paste to the sharp protuberances, but didn't give it any mind as they were in a life-and-death battle against two giants.

Virgil sent the two animals to join the fighting, then stuck his sticky hands into his bag and pulled out the group's trump card. They were finally in an area where Baphomet's larger form wouldn't be encumbered. "It's time, Baphomet. Let's show them what you got," Virgil said, throwing the small creature in the air.

The beastking then activated its shapeshifter ability, transforming into its massive form. The purple beastking landed on the ground right in front of its master with a boom, now at least ten feet tall and looking like a bear-moose hybrid with sharp antlers; Baphomet was ready.

Virgil quickly coated Baphomet's antlers with the Metallic Acid Paste while the beastking dipped its paws into the puddle of the substance still on the ground.

"I could use some help here!" Maldrakus yelled. Virgil turned to see the mage's Arcane Shell break under the pressure from another swing. The mage managed to dodge the large weapon, but was not fast enough to evade the following kick and was knocked back.

Virgil could see a streak of blood from the mage's mouth. The Shielder stomped over to the downed mage. The other two animals were helping Gwen with fighting the Archer.

Virgil hopped on top of his beastking companion and said, "Baphomet, let's go kick some ass." The beastking roared in agreement and charged. Virgil lowered his staff and fired two Nature Bolts at the Shielder. It blocked the first one with its massive shield, but the second one hit its mark, striking it square in the face.

The Shielder stumbled backward, causing its shield to move away from its body. The charging beastking took advantage and jumped over Maldrakus, impaling the automaton with its paste-covered antlers. The alchemical creation did its job, and the antlers pierced through the thick metallic torso as if it was merely flesh.

The Shielder let out a grinding metallic groan as it was tackled to the ground. Baphomet reared its antlers back, tearing out chunks of the protective metal, and began clawing at the Shielder recklessly.

Virgil took the opportunity to cast Restore on the mage. Maldrakus was quickly back on his feet.

With Virgil focused on healing, and the beastking focused on the enemy in front of him, neither of them noticed that the giant Archer automaton took aim at the large animal. It fired a large bolt, striking Baphomet in the upper right arm. The animal reared back on its two hindlimbs and roared in pain. The injured Shielder took the opportunity to smash Baphomet in the face with its massive shield. Virgil flew off Baphomet's back as they sailed through the air. Maldrakus dove to the right, narrowly managing to avoid the crashing animal.

Virgil hopped to his feet and adjusted his glasses. He saw

the Shielder, now heavily injured, slowly stand up. Its torso had a massive hole in it, exposing its glowing red soul gem, various wires, and moving gears with occasional sparks shooting out. He also saw that the Archer's attack on Baphomet was not wise on its part, as its distraction freed Virgil's allies to attack unencumbered. Splinter had activated her Spike Wheel skill and cut straight through one of the automaton's arms at the elbow. Christopher used his tusks and dragged them along the heel of the automaton, causing it to fall to one knee.

Gwen was walking along the wire-laden wall, clearly using her new Spider Climb spell, and threw a clay container at the construct. Unbeknownst to Virgil, she had siphoned a small bit of the Dwemdurian Oil into another container for her own use aside from when he gave the signal. It struck the being on its back, spilling Dwemdurian Oil on its body. "Lightning Arrows," she shouted as she stuck her right arm out. Five arrows made of pure lightning appeared around her forearm and shot out toward the automaton.

All of them struck the construct, and the magic amplifying ability of the oil kicked in. The lightning coursed through the automaton's body much more quickly and violently than Virgil had ever seen it.

A deep, sad noise came from the Archer as its glowing red eyes dulled, and it collapsed dead. One down, one to go. Maldrakus threw his arm in a vertical arc and conjured an Arcane Slash at the Shielder. The Shielder moved its massive shield and used it to block the spell. The pure thickness of the shield prevented it from getting destroyed and only left a small gash in the armor.

"*Use the oil,*" Virgil sent to the mage through Party Chat then went to pull the arrow out of Baphomet's arm.

The mage pulled the clay container from his bag and chucked it at the automaton. As expected, it blocked the container with its shield, and the oil splashed over it. The Shielder lumbered toward the wood elf. Maldrakus conjured another Arcane Slash, and this time, it cut straight through the shield and hit the metal construct square in the chest.

Virgil had just finished removing the bolt from Baphomet and looked up. He had just enough time to see the Shielder break in two and slide into two parts.

He turned to verify Erogg was down. Flames still covered her, but she was still trying to stand.

Finally, she made it to her feet and raised her left hand up, converting the orange flames into a sickly shade of green. Most of her robes were destroyed, revealing various burns, streaks of dark blood still leaking from both sides of her mouth, and the fire was being pulled into a compressed orb of green flame floating above her head.

"Haha, fools! You think you've won? Those things were just grunts in an army. Allow me to show you what true monsters I've awoken," the demon spat, then fired a beam of her green infernal flame at Maldrakus.

Virgil instinctively conjured an Yggdrashield, but the Nature Magic spell of vines and wood lasted just seconds against the flames it was naturally susceptible to. Fortunately, that gave the Arcane Mage just enough time to down a Manna Potion and cast another Arcane Shell around himself. The demonic fire struck the shell with violent intensity and the hastily produced protective layer already started showing cracks.

Gwen loosed another two arrows at Erogg, but the sorlith demon was ready this time and produced a green forcefield of her vile Corruption Magic to block the shots. As the arrows made contact, the magic shield caused both the wood and metal of the projectiles to degrade and rot completely away before the druid's very eyes.

While Gwen was focusing on the demon, Virgil racked his brain for potential ways to help Maldrakus. He had a potion of Icy Essence, but there was no way to get it past the mage's Arcane Shell to him. Fire was the one element that Virgil's magic was naturally weak to. He had no spells to deal with fire... but wait, that wasn't the case anymore!

Virgil cast his newest spell, Phoenix Fire. Virgil focused and channeled a large amount of manna through his staff. The top of his staff glowed white, and after one-hundred manna was invested, the flames glowed white as well. Virgil's spell took effect and the spell the demon was casting at the Arcane Mage was halted. Virgil took control of the remaining glowing, transformed white flame and directed it at Baphomet. The healing flame struck the beastking, curing its wounds and recovering its health with its healing warmth.

The demon grunted. "Fine, druids. It matters not. One way or another, you will die here! If I can't use the dwarf to finish my ritual, I will use myself!" she proclaimed from behind her green shield. The demon then did something... unexpected. She took her right hand and buried it in the center of her chest, breaking through skin and muscle. More blood shot out of her mouth, and her body lurched in response to the trauma.

Virgil's Danger Sense kicked into high gear, giving him major heebie jeebies. Whatever the demon was doing it was *not* good! "Destroy the shield! We can't let her finish!" he shouted, but it was too late.

Erogg ripped something from inside her chest cavity. It was not her heart or any organ, though. No, it looked like a small, round orb. It was dark red just like her skin. Instinctively, Virgil realized it was the demon's soul!

The sorlith gave the party a smug look as she pushed the dead dwarf's body off the altar. Gwen, Virgil, and Maldrakus were firing spells at the Corruption Magic barrier, but it was still holding. They watched as the demon's body began to shrivel and mummify before their very eyes! The demon cackled once more, her voice much coarser than before. "Hehehe, now you die!" She hissed and slammed her soul into the altar. The demon's body collapsed into a pile of dry, dead remains as the stone altar absorbed her soul and began lighting up with the green of Corruption Magic.

The Corruption Magic shield dissipated at the same time, but it was too late. The wires coming from the altar began glowing with the same sickly green hue. The party watched in horror as the glow and sparks continued and traveled up and into the dark ceiling. All eyes widened as the green glow illuminated the darkness, revealing what was hiding above them the whole time.

All three elves said the exact same words in unison.

"Oh… shit."

CHAPTER FIFTEEN

Hydra

The party looked up to see a monstrous automaton like they'd never seen before. One, two, then three sets of red reptilian eyes appeared out of the darkness. As the wires around the dark ceiling glowed, the body of the metallic creature's silhouette appeared to the party's view. It had two large legs tipped with three sharp claws. The torso had a large, hollow, crystalline center; a green anchor gem was embedded in the center. Veins of green power spread out from the gem. Instead of a humanoid form with a head and two arms, it had three reptilian heads atop long metallic necks, with a large serpentine tail.

Virgil quickly activated Analyze.

Name: Dwemdurian Automaton – Hydra Monarch
Level: 35
Race: Golem **Type:** Advanced Automaton
Health: 1000 **Manna:** 750 **Stamina:** 500
Resistances: Magic -50%, Piercing Damage 75%, Slashing Damage 75%, Blunt Damage 75%.
Debuffs: None.

Profession: None.

An experimental prototype automaton built by the Dwem-durians to be a literal machine of war that could easily bring about the genocide of many of the races that rivaled them. This construct is powered by the soul of a demon warlock, infusing it with infernal powers and giving it a higher awareness.

Right after Virgil digested the information, the hydra began to move, breaking itself free from the clamps keeping it attached to the ceiling like it was Frankenstein's monster.

"Move!" he shouted, and the party quickly dispersed to the edges of the room. The giant mechanical monster landed with a boom, shaking the entire cavern and causing rocks to fall from the ceiling. A large boulder crashed down in front of where the party entered the chamber, trapping them with the monstrosity.

"Hahaha! Fools!" the hydra said. Unlike all the others, it actually spoke! It had the voice of Erogg, but now with some mechanical filter to it. "Zinthos will be pleased that I will have eliminated two of the world tree's champions. Now, die!" All three heads dipped down, and a gout of green lightning erupted from each of their mouths.

The lightning streaked across the ground, tearing through it to the party.

They dodged out of the way, narrowly avoiding being electrocuted. All except Maldrakus, who was too exhausted from his rapid expenditure of manna to move quick enough.

"Shit," Virgil spat. *"Gwen, keep it busy. The mage has been hit,"* he sent through Party Chat as he ran to the wood elf.

Gwen barrel rolled out of the way of one beam. *"Fine,"* she grunted in clear frustration back through the chat, and cast Stone Spear as she stood back up. A lance of Earth Magic erupted out from the ground and pierced the hydra's left leg. The dwarvum metal of the construct was layered like dragon's scales, and was able to resist some of the penetration effects of the spell.

The hydra's leftmost head flung itself at the Hunter Druid

with jaws open to bite, but Christopher saw the incoming attack on his master. The terror boar ran and collided his thick ram horns into the side of the hydra's head, the tips of his acid-covered horns shallowly piercing the metal hide. The head let out a metallic shriek as the concussive force knocked it off-course and into the stone wall of the cavern.

The head quickly dislodged itself and recoiled back to the main body. All three heads focused on Gwen. "You burned my old body, you cur!"

"Bring it, bitch," Gwen said back with a smile.

Angered by the response, the hydra roared and charged at the Hunter Druid, easily breaking the stone spear off and leaving a piece still embedded in its leg. Even though it had three heads, the anger of the construct blinded it to focus onto Gwen. It was a good thing too, because it kept it from noticing the large beastking Virgil had sent to flank it.

Baphomet charged at the hydra monarch automaton, lowering its head and piercing the construct's side. The Metallic Acid Paste on the beastking's antlers allowed them to pierce deep into the metal, shredding through it as if it was flesh.

The hydra was knocked to the side but kept its footing. Its right head then launched down and bit Baphomet in the right shoulder as its tail wrapped around the beast's body. The other two heads now focused on the large creature. Two quick Imp horn arrows shot out from Gwen, hitting them and causing them to groan in pain.

As the titanic figures fought, Virgil focused on healing Maldrakus. Splinter had run up to protect her master as he was busy healing. Her body was still covered in the Metallic Acid Paste, as the rodent hadn't been able to get a clean attack against the hydra when she was helping Gwen. Virgil cast Restore on the Arcane Mage, who had a burn scar from the lightning that tore through his robes and left a vertical scar that ran up from abdomen to head. Though Virgil's magic was healing the wood elf, Maldrakus would still have a scar from his contact with raw Corruption Magic. The mage's eyes widened as if he'd taken a gulp of strong coffee and sat up quickly, coughing.

"Easy, man," Virgil said. "Are you okay?"

"I'm alive, but I can't fight anymore," the mage said between heavy breaths. "Damn! I've practically run out of all my manna."

Virgil pursed his lips as he really didn't want to part with his rare items, but now was not the time for frugality. "Take this," he said, handing one of his two Manna Restoration Potions to the mage.

Maldrakus' eyes widened in surprise, but quickly took the potion and gulped it down without a word. "Thank you, friend," he said, panting. "I admit that you might be a better leader than me."

Virgil rolled his eyes. Of course he was a better leader. The overconfident mage was the very reason they were in this situation right now! Virgil suppressed his anger. Getting upset at a situation that had already happened was fruitless right now. They needed to focus on surviving!

The wood elf groaned as he slowly stood back up with Virgil's help.

Virgil realized he couldn't still have the mage be a standing target again, though, so he took matters into his own hands— literally. Virgil pulled out one of his Scatter Scat Pastes, applied it to two fingers, and shoved it up Maldrakus' nostrils. If the healing magic was coffee, this thing was an espresso as the mage visibly recoiled from Virgil.

"What in the abyss was that? Ugh, it smells awful," he said as he shook his head in a pointless attempt to get it out.

"Quit whining. It'll help you move quicker," Virgil said sharply before casting Barkskin on him, then turning away from the mage. "Now, let's rejoin the fight." Both elves moved in opposite directions, firing magic bolts, and Splinter bravely charged in to fight the metal giant. The hydra tried to wrap its tail tighter around Baphomet, but Christopher bit into it. The construct let go of the beastking in response, and flung the boar into a nearby boulder. Virgil immediately began healing the boar with Restore.

Gwen fired two more shots at the hydra, but the construct was ready and flung its newly freed tail at her.

Virgil was able to see what was happening and quickly cast an Yggdrashield in the tail's path. It slammed into the wooden shield, causing splinters to fly, but the shield held. Gwen used the opportunity to use Spider Climb to get away.

Baphomet, finally released from the tail's grip, broke free of the right head that was biting down on its shoulder.

The hydra turned to face the beastking again, and roared with all three reptilian heads.

Baphomet roared a challenge back, activating Instill Fear, but the metallic monster resisted.

Maldrakus fired an Arcane Slash at the hydra, but the creature blocked it with its thickened scaly metal tail. The tail did not have oil on it like the Shielder's shield did, so it couldn't cut all the way through. It did leave a shallow wound, though. Baphomet took that opportunity to charge again. The hydra swung its body around to slam into the beastking's side. Baphomet was charging recklessly. Virgil inhaled to shout a warning.

Splinter saved the day. Having climbed up a larger boulder beside the hydra, she jumped in the air and activated her Spike Wheel skill as the tail came near. Like a buzzsaw through a piece of lumber, the stego rat cut straight through the appendage, utilizing the gash that the Arcane Mage had created.

Oil shot out of the amputated tail like arterial blood, as the tail continued its swing and missed Baphomet.

The beastking was able to tackle the hydra to the ground and began fighting it tooth and nail like some sort of kaiju Krav Maga match.

Virgil finished healing Christopher back into fighting shape and downed a Manna Potion, as he was feeling a manna headache come on from his frequent and rapid use of spells.

He looked back up to see that all of the paste had worn off of Baphomet and the beastking was no longer penetrating the tough metal hide of the automaton, but it was still holding its own. No one was firing at the hydra for fear that they would hit Baphomet.

"Virgil, what do we do? The paste worked great, but we don't have time to get Baphomet out of the fight to reapply it. Do you have any more Dwemdurian Oil?" Gwen asked.

"No," Virgil sent back since he used the other containers of oil to synergize and enhance his other alchemical concoctions. He then noticed the broken tail laying a pool of oil nearby. *"Scratch that, I do, and I have a plan."*

CHAPTER SIXTEEN

Resurgence

"You sure about this?" Gwen asked as she stored the potions Virgil had given her.

Virgil shook his head as he finished ingesting his True Taunt Potion. His face made a scowl as he gulped down the foul-tasting liquid. "No, but it's the best plan we've got." The dark elf took in a deep breath and yelled, "Baphomet, change form!"

The beastking, standing face-to-face with the automaton, obedient to its master, activated its unique Trait and shifted back into its smaller form right as the hydra's three heads shot out three more streaks of Corruption Magic lightning. All three missed completely as they were aiming at where the beastking was, not where it was going, which was at the bottom of their feet.

The hydra monarch lifted its right foot to stomp at the beastking, who was growling up at it, looking like an angry puppy, when it heard a horrible, terrible noise. The hydra's heads looked up to see the dark elf druid banging his shield and shouting in some terrible tone that hurt its mechanical auditory receptors. It hurt the hydra monarch's senses. It annoyed the hydra. The noise *needed* to stop. It *had* to stop, and the hydra would make sure of that. The three-headed construct glared at the dark elf and took a step forward, missing Baphomet. With all its focus on Virgil, the hydra roared and charged at the Healer Druid.

Virgil gulped. His Enhanced Taunt worked well. He kind of wished it hadn't. The veterinarian quickly pulled out and inhaled the last of his Scatter Scat Paste. The malodorous paste sent a shock through his system but increased Virgil's agility by fifteen percent for the next fifteen minutes. Seeing as his agility was already at fifty points, it sent him almost to sixty just right there. He'd need it too, as the druid needed to get the fuck away!

Virgil began bolting away from the hydra, running along the large chamber and doing his best to keep away from the metal monster chasing him. *"Hurry up! I can't keep kiting this thing forever!"* Virgil frantically sent through Party Chat.

"Don't get your knickers in a twist, you're plenty fast," Gwen sent back, sounding *way* too relaxed for the current situation. Virgil was pretty sure he may have heard her laugh as well, but maybe that was just his imagination.

"To yer left, lad!" Grief shouted aloud.

Virgil immediately jumped to his left, just avoiding the jaws of the right head clamping down.

"Gweeeen?!" Virgil sent back in clear concern. He hadn't forgotten the other effect of the potion in that it caused him to receive double damage for its five-minute duration. Seeing as Virgil was already an extra-squishy healer, he was pretty sure that one well-placed attack would end him.

"We're hurrying!" she sent back, now sounding more concerned given the close call. As Virgil rolled back up, he cast Leeching Vines on the hydra to slow it down. Thorn-laden vines emerged from the stone floor and up to the hydra, wrapping around both its legs. The right leg easily broke free, but the left leg, weakened from the stone spear still embedded in it, was

not as strong. The vines held it in place, keeping the hydra from moving, and providing Virgil some much-needed extra distance.

"*We're ready!*" Gwen sent.

Virgil smiled despite the hydra releasing itself from the vines after a few seconds. The rest of the party had all hidden in one isolated corner of the room and had given Baphomet enough simple Manna Potions that the beastking could turn back into its larger form and given even more Manna Potions after that for what else Virgil had planned.

Virgil ran past the detached mechanical tail of the hydra, now in a small pond of Dwemdurian Oil from its tail wound, the oil still pulsing out. "*Baphomet, change form,*" Virgil sent to the beastking through party chat.

Baphomet complied. Virgil kept running with the hydra still chasing him due to the Enhanced Taunt. He turned back to see it nearing the oil puddle, and stopped to entice it to move further. As soon as one of its feet made contact with the puddle, Virgil yelled, "Demon-Beast Flame!"

The beastking stood up on its two hindfeet, took a large inhalation and released a gout of magic blue flame at the hydra. It struck true, and the flames hit the crystalline chest of the automaton. Quickly, the magic fire descended the metal legs and made contact with the oil puddle underneath the three-headed monstrosity. The blue flame erupted from the ground like a volcano, encompassing the entire form of the massive hydra.

The monster screamed and fell on its back. Baphomet continued the flame breath attack, and the hydra flailed in panic, trying to get rid of the magically-enhanced flames engulfing its body. After a few more seconds, Baphomet had used up too much manna, and the beastking stopped its attack and reverted back into its small form.

Finally free from the constant source of fire, the hydra rolled away. The three metallic reptilian heads were heavily melted, its six eyes glaring at the druids, promising vengeance. It tried to stand, but as soon as its previously injured left leg bore the weight of the heavy metal body, it broke off completely above the knee. The hydra collapsed to one limb, no longer able to fully stand. Virgil Analyzed it once more to see that the automaton was on its last leg... pun intended.

The hydra, finally realizing its dire situation, had its eyes widen in surprise. It then glared at Virgil. "Fools! If I go down, then I will take you with me!" Bright green light began to shine out from the wounds in its body, then its eyes, then the large crystal in its center emitted the same green light.

Virgil's Danger Sense started sending warnings again in his mind. The party was trapped, though. There was no place to escape. Quickly, Maldrakus cast an enhanced version of his Arcane Shell spell that covered the entire group. Virgil added onto that by casting an Yggdrashield just before the hydra imploded.

There was the sound of a dying engine giving one last burst of power, as the lights went out in the hydra, and it collapsed. As soon as the automaton hit the ground, a wave of green gas rushed out of it from its many wounds, spreading throughout the chamber quickly as if it was alive.

Grief was able to see the noxious fumes and began to panic. "Shite! That be infernal exhaust! There be no time! We need to get out of here now!"

"Crap! What does it do, Grief? If you hadn't noticed, our exit is blocked!" Virgil responded.

"It be one of the worst poisons ever created, lad! One whiff, and ye can kiss yer arse goodbye! Its weakness be it not too long-acting out in the open. Now, get yerselves in gear and run back to the entrance! I'll use me skill to make a hole through the stone blocking yer path."

Understanding the severity of their current situation, the party did just that. Virgil downed a Stamina replenishing potion as they ran, to make up for the effort he had just put in kiting the hydra.

They quickly made it back up the stairway to the large—no,

gigantic—boulder that had embedded itself in front of the entrance. Virgil detached Grief and pressed the skull to the stone.

Grief activated his Space Vacuum skill, and the skull began absorbing the stone into the pocket of space inside him. Virgil at first smiled, but then remembered that the skill only worked at a rate of one-half inch a second. The stone was too thick, and they needed more time!

"Gwen, you and Maldrakus use any magic you have to try to keep the gas away from us for as long as you can," Virgil said, desperate for anything they could do to keep the deadly gas at bay. Maldrakus fired a few Arcane Slashes, but the magic did nothing to the encroaching poisonous gas. Gwen fired a few more Air Strike Arrows. They pushed the gas back slightly, but the spell was not enough to completely halt its momentum.

The Hunter Druid, realizing they were all going to die, gave a sad smile. Virgil looked back at her and stopped pressing Grief to the boulder, realizing it too. He smiled back at the beautiful elf he had real, genuine feelings for.

"Guess I won't get that second date, huh?" she asked.

Virgil sighed. "Guess so, but there's one thing left I want to do."

"What's tha—" Gwen attempted to ask but was interrupted by a kiss.

Virgil had taken a hand to the high elf's cheek and given her the most passionate kiss he could muster. If he was going to die, he would put it all on the line. To his great joy, she kissed him back. The two just stood there, closing their eyes and enjoying this last, blissful moment of their lives.

The kiss was wonderful. It seemed to transcend time. That was when, Virgil noticed, it had actually been a good bit of time. In fact, they had been kissing for half a minute straight! He opened his eyes and saw the poisonous Infernal Exhaust gas, but it wasn't in their midst. Instead, it had completely surrounded them.

A clear aura, his Purifying Aura, provided a protective dome for the party! Virgil began laughing wholeheartedly. Tears ran down his cheeks as he laughed.

"What in the abyss is going on?" Maldrakus asked, perplexed at their unexpected safety. Gwen also seemed confused. Virgil explained his Purifying Aura spell that he had activated before when the warlock had cast Infernal Dread. The spell lasted for ten minutes and prevented any debuffs from affecting anyone inside the aura's zone of influence which emanated from Virgil's body. Not only did it prevent the Dread debuff, it looked to prevent poisons too!

Maldrakus looked mad at first that Virgil was fully unaware of his spell's effects, but then collapsed against the boulder and began laughing, joining in the revelry of surviving a near-death experience. Gwen gave Virgil another kiss and smiled warmly as she hugged him tight.

"Er hem, I don't want to be the party pooper here, but need I remind ye folks that the spell only lasts for a certain period? We need to get ye out of here before it runs out," Grief said. The party members all then made 'oh' faces.

Virgil checked the spell's timer, and saw that it only had a couple minutes left. He quickly let go of Gwen and began to press Grief back into the partially absorbed section of boulder. Grief activated his subskill again and began sucking in the section of stone into the space pocket. The rest of the party stayed close by, making sure to stay within the protection of Virgil's Purifying Aura. Splinter and Baphomet, wanting to help their master, began digging into the boulder as well, in an attempt to make another tunnel. Virgil was impressed that the duo was actually making good progress compared to the magical skill.

With only half a minute still left on the aura's timer, Grief managed to puncture a skull-sized hole through the boulder. Immediately, physics took its effect, and the gas rapidly exited through the hole to spread out as much as possible. Splinter continued digging and was eventually able to claw completely

through as well to make a four-foot tall by four inch wide opening. With the larger hole, more gas began exiting even faster. It
was a vacuum-like effect, as if they were astronauts that had
opened a door into space.

The party celebrated, as they were now truly free of the
deadly vapors. Virgil took the time to use his healing magic and
potions to mend all the injuries and replenish any manna and
stamina of the party as best he could. Finally, now that they
were safe, Virgil examined the notifications flashing in the
corner of his vision.

Congratulations! You have defeated 3 giant Dwemdurian
automatons: 1 Shielder, 1 Archer, and 1 Hydra Monarch! In
addition to that, you defeated the boss of the dungeon, Erogg
the warlock, whose soul was empowering the hydra. Dwemdurian Ruins of Amthoon has now been reclassified back to
"Ruins."

Rewards:
+2,563 Experience from giant automaton Shielder.
+2,563 Experience from giant automaton Archer.
+15,000 Experience from giant automaton Hydra Monarch.
+40,000 Experience from clearing dungeon.

Congratulations! You have gained enough experience to reach
level 16!
Current Experience: 22,319/33,210
As you have leveled twice, you have gained +2 to Agility, +2 to
Intelligence, and + 2 to Endurance. You also have 4 unused Stat
Points.

Congratulations! Using your companion's abilities to the fullest
and your unique skill sets, you were able to find an unorthodox
way to overcome your foe. As such, you have gained levels in
multiple skills!
+3 to Alchemy

+10 to Taunt
+3 to Danger Sense
+8 to Restoration Magic
+5 to Stealth
+2 to Analyze
+1 to Medicine

Congratulations! Your use of the Potion of True Taunt has allowed you to increase your Taunt skill from Novice to Beginner rank!
You can now use your Taunt skill on up to 3 opponents at once if desired!

Congratulations! Your frequent use of Stealth throughout the dungeon has caused you to increase the skill's rank from Beginner to Initiate rank!
+25% chance of being undetected while stealthed.
+25% chance of detecting stealthed opponents.
+25% extra bonus of going undetected while in the dark due to your dark elf heritage.

Congratulations! Your quick thinking and clever use of your Restoration Magic spells not only helped to restore health, but quite literally saved you and your allies' lives on more than one occasion! Restoration Magic has increased from Initiate to Advanced rank!
The manna cost and cooldowns for both Phoenix Fire and Purifying Aura have been reduced by half!
Phoenix Fire: Cost – 50 MP Cooldown: 50 seconds
Purifying Aura: Cost – 25 MP Cooldown: 5 seconds

"Crap!" Virgil said aloud in surprise. He just gained a lot of experience! In fact, it was the most he'd ever received! The Healer Druid had leveled up twice and was close to leveling again, which was saying something, as it had become harder and harder to level the higher he went!

Virgil also increased the rank of three of his skills as well! Both Purifying Aura and Phoenix Fire were amazing spells, but the cooldown and cost made Phoenix Fire hard to use. Now, though, he wouldn't have to invest as much manna and had more opportunity to use the life-saving spell! When he had to confront Zinthos, who was all about burning, the spell could prove *very* handy!

"Did all of you get a lot of experience from that?" he asked.

"Yeah, I got sixty-five thousand experience just for helping clear the dungeon!" Gwen replied. Virgil's eyes bulged. Sixty-five thousand experience?! He thought the forty-thousand he gained was impressive. He then remembered that, as the healer, he did not contribute to the actual damage aspect of combat that much, and the world of Imeria rewarded experience in conjunction with damage dealt. Despite it making sense, it still sucked…

After they all discussed their rewards and laughed in celebration, the party decided to check the remains of the hydra and giant automatons. Both the automatons had a container of Dwemdurian Oil inside them. However, the Shielder that Maldrakus had bisected with his Arcane Slash had its container slashed in two as well.

Gwen was able to collect a whole quiver of the ballistae bolts from the giant Archer. Somehow, she was able to handle the giant bolts with ease. Virgil also noticed that they seemed to shrink down and fit into the quiver on her back. He figured it was some sort of special ability, as her soulbound weapon was the bow given to her by Yggdrasil.

Next, they examined the ruined remains of the hydra. The metal scales were severely melted, and droplets of re-solidified metal were hanging off its heads and neck, appearing like the melted wax off a candle that had once again hardened. They found another two containers of Dwemdurian Oil again, but the most interesting was the large crystal at its center.

You have found Greater Crystal Core.

Item Type: Accessory
Durability: 555/555
Item Class: Mythic
Description: A rare artifact crafted by the dead subrace of dwarves, the Dwemdurians, this item is considered the highest form of an advanced Anchor Gem and is one of the pinnacles of golem crafting, allowing the constructs to use magic abilities.
Effect: Can bind and tether to an unbound soul or energy source to make an advanced golem capable of using magic.

Virgil's eyes widened. This thing was the core of the dead golem, what held the demon's soul. It looked like a giant donut with small rivulets carved out from the center. All the party could feel the magic power oozing out from this.

Maldrakus' s eyes widened. "This... is astounding! Do you... think I could have it?" the professor asked nervously. "The study of golems is a rare craft, and much information about it has been lost since the Dwemdurians' disappearance."

Virgil shrugged. "Sure, go ahead. The thing is amazing, but I have no golem crafting skill."

The professor, without a second glance, hurriedly added the core to his Satchel of Holding. "Thanks... for everything," he said, scratching the back of his head uncomfortably.

Virgil raised his eyebrows.

"I... admit, I could have been more... compliant as your party member."

"You think?" Gwen asked, walking up and joining the conversation.

Maldrakus sighed. "I was an asshole when we first met, and was stubborn during our time down here. For that, I'm sorry. It's been an honor to fight alongside you, chosen of Yggdrasil, and I do hope to count you as friends and allies in the future. If you'll allow it," the mage said as he bowed to the pair.

Virgil and Gwen looked at each other. Did the arrogant mage just give a genuine apology?! The druids didn't exchange words, but communicated with each other with just their expressions, understanding each other's intentions. They both gave a sigh and a slight smile as they turned back to face Maldrakus. "Apology accepted. Just try not to be such an asshat in the future, and treat people with more respect. If you do that, we'll be fine."

The Arcane Mage raised his head. "That I can do." He then shrugged and had his confident smirk return. "Just like all my other abilities, I excel at my people skills."

The druids suppressed a groan, but they took the W where they could get it.

Looking back to the exit, Virgil said, "Guess it's time we head back out. Hopefully the gas has dissipated, since it doesn't have a long time to be effective and the dungeon is huge." Virgil's ears then twitched slightly as he heard a whistle to his right. He turned to see Gwen waving at him by the small stream that emerged out of the left wall.

"What's up?" he asked as he came up to her.

The woman tsked as she smiled, waving her finger and head side-to-side. "Oh my sweet, sweet druid, you forget your time on Earth. You know how the game developers would *always* give the players a way to skip going through the entire dungeon after the boss fight."

"Yeah, but this isn't one of those games. I don't think that logic works here."

She then gave him a shit-eating grin that he was pretty sure she stole from his playbook. "You think wrong then," she said, pressing her palm against the wall. There was an audible 'click' as a hand-sized section of the wall sunk in a few inches. Gwen removed her hand to reveal a small, shallow carving of a staff, easily missed if not actively looking for it.

The sound of stone rubbing against stone greeted the party's ears as a section of stone raised upward, revealing an open doorway from where the stream emerged. Both Virgil and Maldrakus gawked as they looked to where it led, and saw it was the large open chamber with the metal pillar at the very start of the dungeon!

Virgil had a flurry of mixed emotions. On one hand, he was elated to not have to trek back through the entire dungeon over another day and a half. On the other, the boss had been right by the entrance the entire fucking time! He sighed, though. He couldn't change the past, might as well embrace their present situation.

CHAPTER SEVENTEEN

Crime

When Virgil entered the chamber fully, his newly leveled Danger Sense went off in his mind again. Acting on instinct, he activated the subskill Detect Hostile Intent. Immediately, he felt four malignant forces in the chamber with the party, two behind the large pillar and two—

"Huh! Behind us!" Virgil shouted and fired a Nature Bolt above the doorway they just exited. The magic missile crashed into the stone, sending out pebbles and dust. Two forms darted to the right of the bolt and landed on the ground next to the party as two more emerged from each side of the pillar, one firing a crossbow while the other threw a dagger. Gwen shot the bolt out of the air with one of her arrows while Christopher tackled Virgil to the ground, knocking him on his ass and helping him avoid the dagger. "Thanks, buddy," he said as he petted the boar and quickly stood up to face their attackers.

They were two wood elves, a high elf, and a human. All were male and had the same three-toed foot insignia on the chest of their armor. These were the Blackfoots, the mercenary guild that the group encountered at the town hall when they met the jarl. "Well, well, well, looks like I was right, boys," the greasy high elf rogue Virgil remembered was named Slivell said, then turned to Virgil's party. "I figured that if you lot survived those metal monsters, you'd have to come back this way. Though I have to say, I wasn't expectin' you to notice us so quickly," he said, spinning a dagger lackadaisically and leaning against a tall and bulky human brandishing a crossbow in one hand and a shortsword in the other.

Virgil squinted at the thugs. "What do you want?" he asked, already having an idea as to the answer.

"Straight to business I see, fine with me. We just want one thing. That," the rogue said, pointing his knife at Grief.

"Do not say anything, Grief," Virgil ordered his companion through their Soulbound Communication so as not to be heard by the mercenaries. "You want the skull? Why?" Virgil asked Slivell.

"That's not really your concern, is it? Just give me the skull, and we'll be on our merry way. I'd prefer not to get me hands dirty with yer blood if I don't have to."

Virgil took his Druid's Staff in his left hand and pointed it at Slivell. "It'll be your blood dirtying your hands if you don't tell me," he said. The rest of the Blackfoots all tensed at that, noticeably tightening their grips on their weapons.

Slivell put his hands up. "Alright, alright, fine, if you must know, our boss has been looking for that skull for a long time. Technically, it's his property. We just want to return it."

"There are plenty of skulls in this world. How does 'your boss,'" Virgil said in quotations, "know that this one is his?"

"Because that's Grief, the warrior whose spirit has been stuck inside that skull, and before you say it isn't, don't. Because you in particular, blackheart, stand out like a sore thumb. Not many elves wear glasses unless they're so old they've got one foot in the grave, and I've never seen a dark elf wear glasses in me life, let alone one walking around with no shirt. It's pretty obvious that you're that dark elf druid fellow it's rumored can't fight worth shit." The rogue then put a hand to his chin in a contemplative look. "Strange, really. If you can't really fight for shit, why don't you wear some armor over your body, or at least a damn shirt? It's not like you're a barbarian, and the winters here can get a bit nipple-y."

Virgil groaned subtly, annoyed at the fact that despite having awesome druidic powers, a simple shirt was denied to him due to his unique upgraded items. "Just like you said, it's not really your concern, but you're right. This is Grief."

"I know," Slivell said confidently. "So why don't you be a good lad and just hand him over? Unlike you blackhearts, we Blackfoots prefer to get some sunlight, eh?"

Virgil was trying to rack his brain for potential ways to gain an advantage on their foes, when Slivell's last sentence gave him an idea. He, in a deliberate and slow manner, began unlatching Grief from the belt attachment at his side. As he did so, he activated Party Chat to communicate with all but Christopher since the boar was Gwen's pet, and could not gain access to Party Chat via Virgil's special Trait, Beast Commander. Virgil's plan was going to suck for the boar, but it was the party's best option. *"Grief, do you remember that 'special' phrase I taught you?"*

"The one ye say when yer 'bout to kick a lot of ass? Course I do, lad!"

"Good. On my cue, you're going to shout it, then activate Space Vacuum. Everybody else, I want you to cover your eyes for three seconds, then attack. Got it?"

"Got it," everyone sent back in unison. While the elves sent back audible consent through Party Chat, the animals' equivalent was a line of text from each of them in Virgil's vision notifying of their understanding.

"Any day now," Slivell said with his hand out and his foot tapping rapidly, annoyance at Virgil's slowness clear in his tone.

Virgil quickly finished unlatching the skull, stealthily removing a potion stored inside Grief, then tossed the skull over to the rogue, who exhibited a high dexterity as he gently caught the skull and didn't cause any noise from his palm smacking the bone.

The rogue then put both hands on the skull to look at it

more thoroughly. Satisfied, he gave the party a smug smile. "You see, that wasn't so hard, was it?"

Virgil's Danger Sense started going off again, and felt it from the rogue's group members. Clearly, the Blackfoots were about to double-cross the party.

Virgil was onto them, though. He sent the signal to Grief through Party Chat with a simple, "*Now!*"

"Yippee-ki-yay, motherfucker!" Grief shouted out loud, startling the Blackfoots. On that cue, Virgil threw the glass vial of Liquid Light Flash on the ground and slammed his eyes shut.

A strong source of blinding white light shot out from the site of impact and spread out, blinding all in range. There were shouts of pain and surprise coming from the Blackfoots as the light caused them to recoil. It also sounded like Slivell gave a shrill yell of pure agony that Virgil had not expected.

Virgil couldn't blame them. Even with his eyes closed, he could still feel the intensity of the light. Christopher let out a snort of surprise but no more than that. Virgil figured that Gwen had kneeled down to cover her pet's eyes instinctively, like a protective mother. After he counted to three, Virgil reopened his eyes. There were a few dots he had to clear out, but nothing more.

The Blackfoots, though, were much worse. Three out of the four brutes were squinting their eyes shut and moaning in discomfort. The large, armor-clad human thug had his shield up reflexively, but still took a few steps back.

The worst was Slivell. The high elf was on his knees and screaming in pain. Where his hands were supposed to be, there was nothing, replaced by bleeding stumps that spurted out blood. Grief was on the ground and Virgil could hear the skull chuckling inside his mind.

Virgil quickly activated Soulbound Recall and summoned Grief back to him. As soon as the skull flew back to his hands, he lowered his staff at the thugs and said, "Sic 'em." Immediately, the party attacked.

Gwen activated her Multi-Shot subskill and fired two arrows in rapid succession, landing both in the eye sockets of one thug, downing him instantly.

Maldrakus activated an Arcane Slash, bisecting another thug.

Virgil activated Leeching Vines on the human thug. The vines erupted out from the ground underneath and wrapped around his shield arm and right leg.

Splinter and Christopher had charged on Virgil's command. Splinter jumped at the human. The thug tried to raise his shield to block, but Virgil's vines kept his arm in place. Somehow, he caught her with his free hand mid-air.

He gave a smug smile at catching her, but it quickly went away as the stego rat bit into his hand. He grunted and let go reactively. Splinter ran up the guy's arm and flung her tail at the man. The spikes of her tail struck into his temple, and his body went limp in a matter of moments.

Christopher went after Slivell. The greasy elf was too focused on his missing hands, distressed by the pain and sudden loss, and by the time he processed that the terror boar was coming at him, it was too late. The elf's damaged vision cleared up just enough to see mister Chris P. Bacon just two feet away from him with his head lowered, the curled horns at face level. In less than a second, the horns made contact with Slivell's face. There was a sickening crunch of bone and a cry of pain as the elf's face caved in, flinging him backward, and bringing death upon him milliseconds after impact.

As soon as the last rogue died, there was an eerie silence in the cavern as the party just breathed. All three elves were impressed and a little disturbed at how quickly and efficiently they killed the Blackfoots. Guess that was what going through a dungeon with a bunch of constructs that wanted to kill you would do... Nevertheless, they searched the bodies for any loot or evidence. They found gold, four minor healing potions, some daggers, two crossbows, and plenty of bolts. Maldrakus was fine with leaving the loot with the druids. Virgil took all but the crossbow bolts, which Gwen happily took.

"Why do you take all the arrows of various sizes? I didn't think you could fire crossbow bolts with your bow," Virgil said.

Gwen gave Virgil a surprised look. "Oh, I didn't tell you? During our time in the mine, I reached level twenty! Yggdrasil thought to give me a reward for reaching that level by granting me a new Trait! It's called 'Utility Improviser,' and it allows me to use arrows of *any* kind with my bow!" she said excitedly.

"That's awesome! Is it your Attunement?" Virgil asked.

She gave him a sad look. "Eh, no. I haven't discovered mine yet..."

"Don't beat yourself up," Virgil said as he put a comforting hand on Gwen's shoulder. "It's still an awesome Trait. Also, you did get another reward."

"What?"

"You get to go on another date with this guy," Virgil said, being cheesy and pointing a thumb to himself.

She giggled and shook her head at the bad attempt at humor.

"Er hem," Maldrakus coughed loudly, clearly trying to interrupt the conversation. When the elves looked back at him, he continued, "If you two are done flirting, I'd like to get out of here. While I've enjoyed your company, I'd like to see the sky again."

"Agreed," Virgil said. They began to walk to the exit when Christopher ran up in front of Gwen. He had something in his mouth and was trying to give it to his master.

"What is it, love?" she asked as she kneeled down to take it. "It's a letter," she said, opening it. Her eyes widened as she read, then she gave it to Virgil. "I think you should read this."

Virgil took the letter and complied.

Slivell,

From what you have described, that does sound like the magic skull that the Thieves' Guild has been after. If possible, capture it and bring it back to the Blackfoot headquarters intact. Once in our possession, we will bring the skull back to the leader of the Thieves' Guild, Chaos, in Kygor. One of their sergeants named Havoc tried to take it but wasn't up to snuff.

Chaos has put up a ridiculous bounty on the skull and we can improve our relations with his guild with this gesture. Apparently, the man's grandmother dated the dwarf when he was still alive and broke her heart. I met her once, she was battier than a pile of guano. Her grandson seems to share her crazed nature, and the maniac actually has sworn to destroy the skull to uphold vengeance. I trust in your crew's capabilities and expect the skull within the week.

Remember, no witnesses.

Anduin Blackfoot

Virgil squinted as the puzzle pieces went together in his head. So, he was right, he realized. The Blackfoots were connected to the Thieves' Guild. While Virgil was happy to prevent the thugs from getting his companion, he felt other emotions as well. First was concern that more thieves would come after Grief. The second was frustration that it looked like his companion's amorous activities in life had caused another woman to become a jilted lover that wanted vengeance years later. Jeez, couldn't Grief have dated some more short-lived species versus these elves who lived for multiple centuries?!

"Grriief?" Virgil asked, annoyance clear in his voice.

"What, lad?" the skull replied. The dark elf lowered the note for the skull to read. "Oooh, shite," the skull said with a bit of trepidation.

"What did you do?"

"Eh, well, ye know—"

"Spit it out."

The skull sighed then explained, "Well, before I met me Katarina, I was workin' with a beautiful wood elf lass named Filaurel. She was a rogue and had an affinity for daggers and short blades, though at night, she was particularly good at handlin' me own long blade, if ye know what I'm sayin'? Haha."

"Ew, gross," Gwen said.

"Foul-mouthed dwarf," Maldrakus said.

Virgil just rolled his eyes, but did give a small smirk at the pun. "Go on, Grief."

"So, Filaurel was a deadly rogue, but she be right crazy, lad. Those roguish types, the prettier they are, the more somethin' ain't right with their noggin, I tell ye. And Filaurel be the most beautiful thief I ever laid eyes on. She had an alias under the name "Chaotic" back in the day, and she wanted to rob the king of Kygor of his damn crown! So, I turned her in to the royal guard, because if I just up and left her, she'd try to kill me. Guess she's still kind of bitter..."

"You think?" Virgil asked sarcastically.

"Lad, I know ye have a lot on yer plate, but I need yer help. Will ye help stop Filaurel and her grandson? Cause she won't stop until either I'm dead, like really dead, or she's apprehended, or ye know, dead."

Quest Unlocked!
Bitter End
It's clear that your companion Grief would've thrived as a bard as he trekked across the continent, winning and then breaking the hearts of numerous women. He wasn't the best in his taste though, as one of his jilted lovers is the grandmother of the current leader of the Kygoran Thieves' Guild. Grief asks that you find a way to either detain or eliminate Filaurel's grandson Chaos in order to remove the current bounty on his literal head.
Reward:
+10,000 Experience
Removal of bounty on Grief

Unknown
Do You Accept?
Yes or No

Seeing Grief's safety as a reward, Virgil begrudgingly accepted the quest. "I'll do it, *if* we run into more Blackfoots or Thieves' Guild members. We have more pressing matters. Saving Yggdrasil and the world takes precedence," he said.

"Thank ye, lad," Grief replied. "I knew ye were a good one. Ye make this dwarf proud to be yer companion," the skull said, sounding like he was about to cry if he actually had eyes.

"No worries, Grief. You're my companion, we look out for each other," Virgil said. After that moment of bonding, the party reset and prepared their way to leave. They piled up the bodies for the authorities to see and use for evidence or as some food for some lingering monstrous creatures.

When they exited the ruins, there were a few guards present, much less than before. In fact, there were only two, and they both were sleeping. Easy to figure out how the Blackfoots were able to make it inside the mine without detection. It honestly made Virgil a little angry. The guards' lackadaisical nature put him and his friends' lives at risk. Maldrakus went over to the sleeping guards and nudged one in the shoulder before Virgil could say or do anything.

The guard, a slender human male, slowly opened his eyes then quickly realized he was sleeping at his post and quickly stood up. "Er, um, sir mage," he said, tapping the head of his snoring companion, a burly dwarf with a brown beard. The dwarf quickly rose to attention and wiped the drool from his mouth. "Have you been able to clear the dungeon?" the human guard asked.

"Indeed," the blue-haired mage answered. "Go and let the jarl know that mining operations can resume." He leaned down and whispered to them. Virgil's Increased Hearing Trait picked up what he said, though. "Also, inform the jarl that there were Blackfoot thugs inside, and that my druidic companions would like to speak with him soon." Both guards' eyes widened in fear. The dwarf was about to say something, when Maldrakus put a finger up. "Shh, don't say a word of this to anyone but the jarl. Clear?" The two guards nodded emphatically.

They turned to leave, when an idea struck Virgil. "Guards, what are your names?"

The two stopped in the tracks nervously and turned back to Virgil. "I'm Rikon, and this is Hamil," the human guard said.

Virgil smiled. "Good. Well, Rikon and Hamil, I don't want to be rude, but I'm pretty sure that the Blackfoots we fought were only there because *you two* were sleeping on the job. In the long-run, I'm okay, but putting my friends and those that I care for at risk is inexcusable. Now, you can understand how that would make someone unhappy. We're friends with both the jarl and the mage college headmaster. It's not a good idea to make us unhappy," he said, glaring at them. The veterinarian fancied himself a collected and objective person, but when he was angry, he made his anger known. These two goobers of guards endangered both the lives of his friends and pets with their poor handling of their jobs

Upon hearing Virgil's words, the human gulped. "W-w-we're sorry, sir," he sputtered.

"Sorry, sir," the dwarf added.

Virgil sighed. The saps were scared shitless. Though he was still angry, he wasn't actually going to do anything to them, but a prudent part of his mind realized that he could turn this to his benefit. "I tell you what, we won't tell the jarl of your error, and you will owe us a favor. Let's say… you let us know of any threats to us, and promise to do your best to try to keep any other druids from entering Amthoon, agreed?" Both of the guards looked at each other, confused as to why one druid champion would try to malign himself with his other compatriots, but they then shrugged and nodded at Virgil emphatically again. "Swear it on Yggdrasil's name."

The two guards gulped, but slowly complied. Virgil received a notification that Rikon and Hamil had made a binding vow on the holy tree's name, and would receive divine retribution if they broke it. Virgil nodded, feeling comfortable that his party was now safer and that they would hopefully be notified of any of the other druids showing up. Those three seemed to cause more problems than good.

INTERLUDE

Pierre and Marianna

It had been about a week since Pierre, the Moon Druid, and Marianna, the Plant Druid, had their most recent encounter with Virgil and Gwen. Despite their advanced numbers, location, and equipment, the dark elf and his companions were able to escape. Marianna was still bitter about how the veterinarian had managed to outmaneuver her and Pierre in particular. Both she and Pierre had cornered the party in a dead end in one of the many streets of the large capital of the Rubasal Kingdom, Kygor.

Virgil had somehow managed to defeat and tame the demon general they fought, claiming he somehow 'cleansed' it, and rode atop it as a mount. Marianna and Pierre were astride their drakes, rewards given by King Darcassan Rubasal for their service. Before they could take down the Healer Druid though, he had managed to get some sort of sticky material on Marianna's plant-based Spriggan Drake. Whatever that substance was sent Pierre's male drake into hormonal overload, and it attacked Marianna's drake.

When they had finally broken up the lovefest, Virgil's party had made their escape. They also learned that Dirk had disappeared not long after with the warlock prisoner. It appeared that *he* was actually a traitor all along.

Pierre was devastated, while Marianna was not too shocked. Dirk was rude and narcissistic. She wasn't surprised the pendejo had gone turncoat on them when things didn't completely go his way.

Despite that though, both druids were berated by the king when they gave their report. He even threatened to take their drakes and magic draconic armor away for their failure.

Even though Dirk had escaped with the warlock, King Darcassan Rubasal was still completely convinced it was all Virgil's doing. The royal elf's bigoted outlook toward dark elves was completely blinding him to the truth right in front of his face. Marianna didn't care much. She knew that the one the druids actually served was Yggdrasil, not the king. The king had apparently forgotten that, which played to Marianna's advantage. She wanted power, as much as she could get, and people overtaken by emotion could be easily manipulated into helping her attain more.

That was one of the reasons she liked to keep Pierre around. The man had become focused on becoming the epitome of an honorable knight, and had unintentionally hidden himself from the terrible truths in front of him to obtain that goal. She had just played on his feelings, mainly his crush on her and his knightly dream, and he'd become a loyal and unquestioning dog. When Gwen had revealed that the king had given her, Marianna, and Dirk a secret quest to kill Virgil's pet, even if it was no longer a demon, Pierre almost left the capital on the spot with his drake to join Virgil. Fortunately, with a few white lies and fake tears, she had manipulated him into trusting her once again before that could happen.

She convinced the king to let her and Pierre leave the capital once more, promising to come back with Virgil, Dirk, or proof of the death of the next demon general. Of course, she also negotiated for more power upon their successful return, namely the position of general of the entire Rubasal Kingdom army.

"My lord, you can't be serious!" King Darcassan's current general, Tiberius, called out in outrage at the proposal.

The king was still on edge emotionally after Virgil's escape. "I am serious, Tiberius!" he shouted back. "If it wasn't for your incompetence in managing our city's defenses, those two criminals wouldn't have escaped. You may be married to my sister, but *I am the king!*" he emphasized. "My word is law," he said, then turned to the druids. "Go and bring me those traitors. When I have that dark elf here in my dungeon, you shall receive your reward, Plant Druid." With that, he officially agreed to her terms. The Plant Druid had to work hard not to let a malicious smile show at the king's decree.

After a couple of days of recovery for her Spriggan Drake, both Marianna and Pierre left the capital atop their draconic mounts, and began scouting and traveling across the thick forest of the Yggdra Timberland. They had been able to fly over and see many of the dense and varied forest types within the timberland. The duo also discovered rare fauna and flora, fought some demons and monsters, and visited a few smaller villages and cities. They never found any sign of Virgil or his party, though, nor had they found any evidence of Dirk or the next demon general. That was the case... until they stopped at a moderately-sized duchy to the northwest.

They first met with the local lord and lady and explained the purpose of their visit. "Druids?! What brings you to our humble home?" the ruling noble asked. Marianna squinted her eyes at him. He was a dawn elf like her, but ugly with a crooked nose, which made her feel slightly superior. "Could it be that you've come to help us with the goblin incursions?" he asked, looking genuinely hopeful. "We've been able to fight them off for now, but we could certainly use your aid."

Pierre puffed out his chest and gave a warm smile. "Why, of course, sir! As the champions of Yggdrasil, we—"

"We have to deal with even more serious matters," Marianna interrupted.

Pierre looked slightly aghast. His ridiculous code of honor made him want to help anyone and everyone, but Marianna knew better. She had a goal, and she would make sure the gullible fool would help her. She brought up a fake, kind smile at the Moon Druid, then to the noble. "While we would certainly love to help, Yggdrasil has brought us here for a more urgent reason. We are looking for our fellow druids. We fear that they may have turned traitorous to the world tree. One is a high elf with a bow, and the other is a dark elf with spectacles. Have you seen them?"

The noble had a shocked expression and was noticeably disturbed at the news of his goddess's heroes going turncoat. "That is... grave news indeed. I can see why that is a priority. We were concerned when we heard news of a dark elf being a druid champion. It seems their people truly are irredeemable." He sighed. "Unfortunately, they've not come across here, but the traveling merchants below may have word as to their where-abouts. I could send one of my servants to—"

"No need for that," Marianna cut off the noble, suppressing her smile at asserting her power to make the pompous idiota shut up. "We can go and check for ourselves. Thank you for your... attempt at helping us," she said sarcastically, and gave a slight bow to the noble before turning. Pierre had a confused look, gave a hasty full bow at the now-scowling noble dawn elf, and jogged to catch up to Marianna.

"Are you sure we cannot help them? Perhaps if we defeat these goblins they've been fighting, we could gain some more information as to the next general's location," he suggested.

Marianna clicked her tongue as she shook her head. "Ah, Pierre, you're thinking too small. Who do you think will provide us with more valuable information: a goblin grunt or a druid traitor high up in ranks?" she asked, intentionally twisting her words to make her point sound obviously more reasonable. "Unlike hobs, goblins are small, stupid, and weak. An incursion of those little piss stains is nothing that their local militia can't handle."

"If you say so, Marianna," Pierre begrudgingly submitted, clearly not fully comfortable with the idea, but trusting the woman who had been his constant companion since the beginning. Also, if he was honest, he definitely had a crush on her too.

They began questioning the traveling merchants and barkeeps. It was when they left a dirty little bar at the edge of town that they actually found a viable source. They left the tavern and noticed an oddly well-shaded area despite it being mid-afternoon. In a nearby alley, by a shabby-looking fruit vendor cart, was a man wearing a thick shirt with a hood. Though he acted like a beggar, both druids easily picked up that he wasn't by the assortment of knives that were mostly hidden in his sleeves and pants.

When the pair walked by, the man started speaking. "That's some good armor you blokes got on. Reckon that you were the ones flyin' on those dragons earlier, aye?" he asked. He had a thick and gravelly accent that was similar to an English Cockney accent. The elves turned to see that the man was a human. He was well-muscled but not overly bulky, with a dirt-smeared face. He was missing one eye, multiple teeth, and sported a good five o'clock shadow. Marianna's eyes narrowed as she noticed a small tattoo on the man's left cheek. It was a skull with two daggers embedded in it in an x-formation. It was the symbol of the Thieves' Guild.

Pierre noticed it too. The honorable elf quickly pulled out one of his glaives and pointed it at the man. "You are a member of the Thieves' Guild. By the power given to me by Yggdrasil and his majesty, Darcassan Rubasal, I place you under arrest," he said with righteous confidence.

For his part, the thief didn't seem bothered by the deadly weapon not far from his neck. He just shook his head as if he was disappointed. "The reports were right. You are a straight-laced one," he said under his breath. The man lifted his hands up in a placating gesture. "Take it easy there, friend. I mean you no harm. In fact, I've come to help."

"Friend? I am no friend to the likes of you, stealing from good, innocent folk," Pierre replied indignantly.

He was about to shove the thief out of the alley and toward the local prison when Marianna stopped him. "Wait," she said as she put a hand on one of Pierre's draconic shoulder armor pieces. "What do you mean, you've come to help us?"

"I've heard that you two may be lookin' 'round for a particular couple of elves, a blackheart who wears glasses, and a she-elf with a bow. Sound right?"

"Go on," Marianna replied.

"Well, you see, my organization is also looking for the dark elf. We don't really care 'bout him, mind you, we just want the skull he has. Turns out, we know where he's at. So, I'm thinkin' we could help each other. We tell you where he is, and when you capture him, you leave the skull with us."

"You foul wretch! Do you think we woul—"

"Hush, Pierre," Marianna interrupted her compatriot in a firm but gentle manner. It was the tone she had found was best at putting the Frenchman at ease. She then activated Party Chat between the two of them. *"He may be a criminal, but we may have to work with their guild currently. What's the bigger threat, a group of thieves, or a potential druid-turned-warlock?"*

Pierre bunched his lips as he took her words in. He then nodded and looked back at the thief. "Fine, the enemy of my enemy is my friend," he said. *"For now,"* he added mentally so that only Marianna would notice. She was okay with that attitude though. The dawn elf Plant Druid would happily turn on the thieves when it was convenient.

"So, do we have a deal?" the thief asked, revealing a gap-toothed smile and extending his hand.

"We do," Marianna replied, shaking the man's grimy hand. "Now, where is that pendejo who hurt my drake?"

CHAPTER EIGHTEEN

Recovery

The party first went back to the Mage College to report to Ramsay what had happened. When they met with and gave the dwarf shaman the news, the headmaster of the college expressed sadness that his suspicions were correct and relief that the demon imposter was taken care of. Both Virgil and Gwen also received notifications that they had completed the 'Parlay for the People 2' quest.

The shaman then gave a large sniff and scowled. "Oh, you lot certainly smell the part of those who had just returned from dungeon delving."

The elves, taking in their appearance for the first time, apologized.

"Not to worry," Ramsay said. "I have just the thing for that." The dwarf opened a drawer in his desk and pulled out a scroll and a ring. "This is a scroll of Prestidigitation. If you don't mind… all of you could use it right now."

Virgil casually smelled his armpit and couldn't help but agree. The party stood together as the headmaster opened the scroll and cast the one-time spell written on it. A cleansing aura fell on the group like light rain, and the sweat, odor, and grime left their bodies and items in a matter of moments, as if they had never been there. Even the three animals looked immaculate, with hair that looked like it had been freshly bathed and combed.

"Thank you," Gwen said. "You don't know how bad I've been wanting a bath since we've come here. This is much better now!"

"Of course, young druid," Ramsay replied. "It was the least I could do. You druids have done this college a great service. As promised, I myself will go out to the Scorched Lands and fix the broken totemic barrier. I think a Master-ranked Shaman spell-caster and his gnome pupil will suffice for your purposes?" he asked knowingly, with a wink.

"I think it will," Gwen replied, chuckling at the question.

"One more thing, though," the headmaster said, and tossed a ring to Virgil. Virgil caught it and examined the ring. It was silver with an opal adorned on top. Small, intricate runes were carved on its sides. He then triggered Analyze.

You have found Ring of Prestidigitation.
Item Type: Accessory
Durability: 20/20
Item Class: Exceptional
Description: A ring finely runecrafted to obtain the unique Prestidigitation spell.
Effect: Channel 5 manna into the ring to activate the spell, Prestidigitation, on a target within 10 feet, removing all debris from the target's form. The well-cut opal on top has enhanced the ring's capabilities to allow it to recharge the spell and allow the spell be used twice in a 24-hour period.

"Wow! Thank you, Ramsay!" Virgil said as he put on the ring. He reached a hand out to shake the dwarf's.

The shaman became notably uncomfortable and took a step back. "No need for that," he said, clearly put off by the thought of physical contact. Quickly changing the subject, he turned back to his desk and heaved a massive green backpack onto it. "I better get on with it then." Not only was the backpack as tall as the dwarf, it was filled to the brim. "Setting up totems is a costly task. It requires many supplies and not a small amount of manna."

"Do you need a bag of holding?" Gwen asked. "Surely the college can spare you one."

The dwarf waved off the question. "No need, young lady. We dwarves like to keep our bodies strong as well as our minds. This bag should help strengthen my body during the journey." The shaman heaved the large bag onto his back with only mild effort. The party joined the headmaster and headed out of his office. Once they took the magic elevator and descended to the bottom of the tower they walked with the headmaster out of the college grounds.

After they crossed the bridge, they were met by two guards. It was Grekko and Halba. Both guards had wide grins on their faces. "Grekko, Halba, did something happen?" Virgil asked.

"No, but something will," Grekko replied good-naturedly and handed him a sealed scroll. Virgil broke the seal and read the small parchment. It was a letter from the jarl. The half-elf congratulated the party for their heroics and personally thanked them for finally presenting irrefutable evidence of the Blackfoots' wrongdoing. The jarl had already sent the guard to their headquarters and arrested most of their known members. He also had requested that the party come to the town hall later that night, as the city was having a festival in honor of the druids and the mines being reopened.

Virgil handed the scroll to Gwen then looked at Grekko. "So, what kind of festival is happening?"

Both guards' smiles turned into even wider, toothy grins. "Alefest," Grekko replied. Both druids smiled back at the wood elf guard and nodded appreciatively.

Virgil looked back to Gwen. "Would you care to be my date for the festival?"

Gwen smirked a little. "Of course, as long as you're

buying," she said, then winked at the dark elf, causing him to blush.

"*A festival dedicated to ale? Now that's what I be talking 'bout! Count me in!*" Grief exclaimed through the party chat.

"*Can you, you know, even drink beer anymore? I think you need a mouth to drink,*" Virgil replied.

The skull seemed to remember his current predicament with that question. "*Ah... shite, lad! Ye just had to go and ruin the fun now, didn't ye?*"

Virgil chuckled then turned back to Grekko. "Count us in," he said.

"Excellent!" Grekko replied. "The festival is set to start at sunset."

"That fast?" Virgil asked in surprise.

"Most assuredly! The city is *very* motivated to have a good time, given our recent hardships. Of course, the Mage College is invited as well," he said to Ramsay.

"I'm certain that the students and staff will be delighted at that news," Ramsay replied, patting the pack on his back a couple of times. "I, however, need to prepare for a mission to the Scorched Lands, and besides, I don't drink. I'm going to find Melvin. The gnome is probably off gambling again."

Grekko promptly looked away at the dwarf's statement.

"We can help you find him," Gwen offered.

"No, no." Ramsay waved off her offer, but then it looked as if an idea struck. "You know, if you are so insistent on helping me, I suppose we could use an escort to the Scorched Lands tomorrow. There is safety in numbers."

"We'd be honored," Virgil said.

Ramsay clapped his hands together. "Wonderful, meet us outside the front gate of the city at midday tomorrow. That should allow you to recover from the night's festivities." He winked knowingly as he stroked his beard. "Besides, that should allow Melvin and I to better prepare. See you on the morrow, druids," he said, then waved goodbye to the elves and left them.

"*I still don't like him,*" Grief sent just to Virgil.

"*Why? He's been nothing but helpful,*" Virgil asked.

"*He don't like physical touch, which be the number one love language of all dwarves, and he don't like to drink!*" he replied exasperatedly. "*Ye saw it fer yerself, even the Dwemdurians, as different as those dwarves may have been, still held to the tenets of dwarven culture and appreciated their drinks. Ye know, I wonder if the shaman even be a dwarf at all. Maybe he just be a really short human or a very hairy gnome?*"

Virgil rolled his eyes at Grief, discarding it as crazy talk. Who cared if Ramsay was not a 'typical' dwarf? Virgil wasn't going to judge someone just because they didn't fit a stereotype. Still, he couldn't completely ignore the skull's concern, as there had been demonic imposters roaming about. It was smart to stay too cautious versus too trusting. Virgil could hopefully ease Grief's suspicion tomorrow when they traveled with Ramsay. Maybe Melvin would be able to shed more light as to the headmaster's eccentricities. "Is there anything else you two need?" he asked Grekko.

The guard shook his head. "No, sir. We are just appointed to escort you wherever you'd like to go in the city until the time of the festival. The jarl figured you could benefit from having people who know the city guide you in the most efficient and safest manner possible."

Virgil pursed his lips. "That's... great! Thanks!" he said. "Actually, we used a lot of our potions and herbs on that dungeon dive. Do you know where the best alchemist shop is?"

For the next couple of hours, the party walked across the city and did some shopping and even some relaxing. First, they went to an alchemist shop. Actually, it was a spa that had multiple stores within it. It was manned by a rather plump gnome who happily traded with the party. Apparently, news had already spread throughout the city and caused the party to get a twenty-percent discount in all shops in Amthoon for the next seven days. Virgil could get used to that!

Virgil showed some of the items he had to trade. One potion in particular he was wanting to get rid of was the Potion of Snake Hands. While it was definitely one of the most interesting potions he'd ever encountered, the dark elf couldn't think of a single valid use for it.

The gnome's eyes widened looking at that potion in particular, and to Virgil's surprise, he offered him two-hundred gold just for that one by itself. When asked why, the gnome informed him that one of the chiropractors inside the spa did some competitive fighting on the side, and he was looking for a potion to give him a particular advantage in hand-to-hand combat. This potion seemed to be a perfect option.

Virgil shrugged and accepted the deal as long as they could get tickets to the next fight. The gnome happily complied and gave Virgil the gold as well as two tickets for the fight, scheduled for that night during the festival. Apparently the chiropractor was some guy named Jaxon. Virgil felt like he'd heard of this guy somewhere, but couldn't quite place exactly where…

After some more haggling, Virgil purchased three, fifty-point replenishing Stamina, Health, and Manna Potions as well as traded some of his recipes for a variety of alchemical ingredients. Virgil also had a number of items that had variable fire-based effects. Seeing he had a professed alchemist in front of him, he asked if the gnome could make some potions of fire-resistance at a discount if Virgil supplied some items to help. The gnome happily agreed at a rate of nine silver per potion and said they would be ready in an hour. Virgil was tempted to negotiate for some training, but he had a date tonight. It could wait.

During Virgil's shopping to restock supplies, Gwen was not paying attention to the dark elf's trading. Instead, she was focused on the fact that they were in an actual spa. It had been weeks since she'd had a proper bath and not just cleaned herself off in some stream. Despite their recently clean forms, Gwen could use some time to just soak and relax. If fighting a giant metal demon-possessed hydra didn't earn you a spa day, what did? So, when Virgil was done, she did her best pouty face and puppy dog eyes and asked if she could use the bathhouse.

Virgil tried to protest, but quickly conceded to the beautiful elf. Gwen jumped up and down in glee like a schoolgirl and gave him a peck on the cheek before running off. As she left, she turned back to the dark elf. "I'll be done in an hour. If you're still going to shop, go get me some arrows, please. Bye!" she said as she waved and went down a hallway, Christopher happily trekking behind her. Virgil thought that the place probably didn't allow animals, but he wasn't going to be the one to get in Gwen's way and doubted anyone else in the spa would either.

Halba stayed behind to keep guard of Gwen while Grekko escorted Virgil to the nearest smith. He was able to trade the three daggers and two crossbows looted from the Blackfoots for a total of three gold, the crossbows bringing in a majority of the profit. Most of that profit was immediately lost when Virgil purchased the arrows Gwen had requested. He was able to get her fifty steel arrows, twenty-five iron arrows, and even three silver arrows after Virgil analyzed and discovered they did extra damage to infernal creatures.

Next up, Virgil had Grekko take him to a tailor that had experience in dealing with magic wearable items. He had an idea for a gift for Gwen. To Virgil's surprise, the guard took him to a shop at the bottom of a tall stone building. That part wasn't surprising, there were many multilevel buildings in Amthoon.

No, it was that it was owned and operated by the Mage College, an outlet of sorts. There was a female gnome with bright pink hair sitting on a high stool behind the desk. She wore thick black robes indicating she was indeed a part of the college. Apparently, gnomes and dwarves were popular shopkeepers in the city.

"Welcome to Just Like Magic, where we can meet all your magical needs. My name is Julie, how can I help you?" she asked in a squeaky voice.

Virgil was a little thrown-off by the surprisingly ordinary name of Julie, but he quickly regained his composure. "Ah, yes, hi there. My name is Virgil and—"

"Let me guess, hon, you need a shirt? What'd ya do, burn it

off in a fireball experiment with the college? I thought all first years were supposed to have fireproof cloaks on at all times..."

"Haha! She got ye there, lad! Glad someone else can give ye crap 'bout goin' 'round acting like some strange human clothing model with yer muscles and no shirt. Honestly, why do humans do that? If yer going to have someone advertise clothing, have the models actually wear all the clothes, not just strollin' round in their britches."

Virgil ignored his companion's jab at what sounded like the fantasy equivalent of an Abercrombie model and blushed at the gnome's quips. He cleared his throat before continuing. "Er hem, I'm not actually part of the college. I'm a druid champion of Yggdrasil..." he said, letting the words sink in.

It was Julie's turn to blush. "Oh... um, well forget I said that," she said, brushing some of her pink hair out of her face. "Wait, *you* are one of the legendary champions?!" she asked in realization.

"Indeed," Virgil replied.

"Wow! So, the rumors are true," she said to herself. "Wait, that still doesn't explain why you don't have a shirt. I know druids are supposed to be all tough and 'nature-y,'" she said in quotations, "but that still doesn't explain why you're going around with your body just exposed like that. I mean, you're not bad to look at, but you don't strike me as the beefy 'tank' type. Even the robes provided by the mage college gives an innate magic armor boost. Wait... Are you flirting with me...?"

Virgil just stared at the fast-talking gnome, mouth agape for a few moments. "No," he said matter-of-factly, then pulled his cloak more over his form. "I'm not here to flirt. I'm here to do business, but if you're just going to gawk at me, I can go elsewhere," he said and turned to leave.

"I'm sorry!" Julie said as he turned. "I was just curious. I'm curious in general, and sometimes I think out loud without knowing. Please, sir, I'm sorry. If you'll stay, I'll give a ten percent discount."

Virgil turned around and pushed his glasses up the bridge of his nose. "As long as that is added onto the already twenty percent discount I have this week, then I'll stay," he said with a wolfish grin.

The gnome's eyes widened, realizing that she'd been had. "Ah… fine," she said defeatedly. A notification flashed in Virgil's vision.

Your quick thinking, turning an awkward situation into an advantageous one, has increased your Trade skill to Level 9!

"Excellent," Virgil said, dismissing the notification. "I have an item I was wondering if you could tailor for me," he said and pulled out the Elemental Mage Robes. The item they had taken from the demonic shaman working with the firebrands decreased the manna cost of Fire, Air, Earth, and Water Magic spells. And it happened to be that Gwen's unique version of Nature Magic, Predator Magic, was a combination of both Air and Earth Magic. He had hoped to customize the robes so that it could become more of a cloak for Gwen. Currently, the robes were too bulky and provided too much of an encumbrance for her highly mobile fight style. Hopefully, he could get it 'trimmed down' and gift it to her.

Julie's eyes widened at the robe quickly then returned to practiced neutrality. "Impressive. Do you have any more?"

Virgil shook his head. "I do not," he said, then looked at the badge on her robe. It was a solid brown square. Knowing that the badges indicated what branch of magic the mages of the college practiced, he presumed that the gnome was an Earth Mage. It made more sense as to why she was interested in the Earth Magic-enhancing robes. It did give him an idea though.

"I'm looking to get it thinner and have it become more of a cloak, like what I'm wearing. Do you think you could do that?"

"Oh, I can, but it's going to take a lot of time and a lot of gold, *even* taking in your thirty percent discount," she added.

"How long we talking?"

"Probably a week."

"What's the fastest you could do it?"

The gnome chuckled at the question. "If I had all my coworkers help me... an hour, *but* it would be four times as expensive to account for the expedited work, and the contributions of four different mages on the item."

"How expensive would that be?"

Julie looked up and tapped her chin, doing some mental math. "Well, even with your discount, it would cost five-hundred gold with just me. That times four is two-thousand. Then taking the expedited rush into the schedule... It would be two-thousand three-hundred fifty gold."

Virgil coughed reflexively at the cost. Over two-thousand gold?! That was ridiculous! Virgil had less than three-hundred gold in total, and that amount wasn't something to scoff at. That cost helped enforce that magic items and working on them was a rare and expensive commodity. It also showed the value of the college that someone with ability but not a lot of inherent money could gain knowledge and ability there despite their financial status.

His thoughts must have shown on his face as Julie had a saddened tone to her voice. "Yeah... I know. Only nobles can really afford that. So, just the regular time then?"

"Actually, do you do trade?" Virgil asked.

"Of course, what do you have to offer?"

He pulled out the Shaman's Staff they had also looted from the corpse. This particular item provided an increase to damage and a decrease to cost of all elemental-based spells. If the robes were powerful and expensive, this thing had to be even more so.

"You just keep pulling out surprises, don't you?" Julie asked, her eyes looking at the staff longingly.

Virgil shrugged nonchalantly. "I figured a certain Earth Mage could benefit from an item like this." He then leaned in conspiratorially. "Tell you what, instead of trading this to the shop, I trade this to you personally for tailoring the robe. Fair trade?"

"Ssseriously?" she asked in disbelief.

Virgil nodded. Neither he nor Gwen could use the item

anyway, given their restrictions to their soulbound weapons. So, he might as well make use of it.

"Deal!" Julie said, and the two shook hands.

After perusing a few more shops and finding a couple of rooms to rent for the night in a well-kept inn, Virgil went back to the spa.

There, standing outside of the building, were Gwen and Halba. The two were talking amicably. Virgil was impressed that Gwen was able to get the quiet guard to talk at all. The high elf's high charisma was certainly kicking in. Though she had Prestidigitation cast on her earlier, she looked cleaner, brighter, healthier, and even had better posture. Even Christopher looked to have more energy, wagging his curled tail like a dog. The terror boar's curled ram's horns were shining and looked like they had been buffed too.

"You look great!" Virgil said, taking in the beautiful elf he had grown to care for.

"Trying to butter me up before our date?" she asked playfully, then took his hand. "This place provides so many buffs. They only last for twenty-four hours, but they can be really beneficial," she said, then handed him a small leather bag. "This is from the alchemist inside."

Excited to see what the gnome had come up with, Virgil quickly examined the bag's contents. In it were three separate small glass jars, all varying shades of red. Virgil Analyzed them.

Name: Potion of Flame Armor
Item Type: Potion
Durability: 10/10
Item Class: Rare
Effect: Shrouds the form of the imbiber in pure flame for 5 minutes. The flames will not harm the imbiber or any part of their body, but will do damage to any equipped items or to anyone that makes contact with them.
Description: A unique item made from combining the ground-up remains of a Mummified Fire Sprite with melted

Firebrand Ogre Teeth and other ingredients, such as a Jungle Envirowolf Heart. While providing protection to the imbiber, the elemental nature of the dead sprite caused the potion to destroy anything else on contact. So, you shouldn't be too attached to your clothing when you drink this...

Name: Fiery Strength Potion
Item Type: Potion
Durability: 12/12
Item Class: Great
Effect: Doubles the Strength stat of the imbiber for 60 seconds.
Description: A potion using 2 Firebrand Ogre Eyes as the main body of the recipe. Once consumed, there is a 50% chance that the imbiber will gain temporary access to the Rage skill for the next 60 minutes.

Name: Gelatin of the Flame Eater
Item Type: Potion
Durability: 10/10
Item Class: Exceptional
Effect: Grants the consumer the skill: Flame Dragon's Hunger.
Description: An accidental success. This potion enhances the effect of the rare Dragonberry and will grant the consumer a new skill permanently! Flame Dragon's Hunger is a skill typically reserved for draconic beings who are closely aligned with the element of fire. It allows the creatures to literally eat flames and convert them into Health.

Virgil was impressed! All three of the potions could come in handy. It did suck that the flame armor potion would burn your clothes off, but fortunately, they had animal companions too. They could consume them and not worry because, well... no clothes. Also, the flame eater gelatin gave a new permanent skill!

He didn't have time to contemplate who to give the new skill to though, as Gwen grabbed his hand and led him back into the spa. "Come on, I have a surprise for you," she said. She then took him to a door labeled Jaxon.

"The chiropractor?" he asked.

"I know it sounds strange, but his work gave me a permanent buff! So, I booked you an appointment. I will watch Splinter and Baphomet. Have fun!" she said and quickly left with his animal companions. Virgil shrugged. He could use a little 'me time' to help improve himself and do self-care.

Besides, how bad could it be?

CHAPTER NINETEEN

Second Date

Virgil walked out of the spa, both energized and terrified from his experience. Jaxon the chiropractor was one strange dude. He was a human who was oddly obsessed with bones. When Virgil received his 'adjustments,' they kind of hurt and the man did his adjusting of the elf with quick strikes to his body like the guy was some kind of kung fu master. After a moment or two, though, Virgil's joints felt notably better, and after his appointment was over, Virgil did stand with better posture, had more energy, and received a permanent 1% boost to Stamina regeneration. Though one percent wasn't much, Virgil would take any permanent buff he could get!

"That was... interesting," he said.

Both Gwen and the guards chuckled. "Yeah, his appointments are kind of like a rite of passage here. I was weirded out too, but hey, I feel great now. How about you?" she asked.

"I... do, actually," Virgil said with a smile.

"We have about thirty minutes left before we need to escort you to the festival," Grekko reminded them. The sky was darkening and had changed to a purple-pinkish hue. Lamp posts holding orbs of Light Magic in them began to illuminate the large metropolis. Virgil checked his time, and smiled as he realized his gift was ready.

He then took Gwen's hand. "Come on, I have a surprise for you, too," he said and led the Hunter Druid to Just Like Magic. Fortunately, Virgil made it just before closing.

Julie was at the door, clearly about to go lock up. She looked tired and had a layer of sweat on her face. "I was wondering if you were going to show up," she said, then led the party to the counter. She reached under it and pulled out the robe. "Voila, one elemental cloak, ready to go."

Virgil picked it up, noticing the heavy robes were much lighter. The thick material felt like it had been compressed in some way like a vacuum seal. The runes inscribed on the black cloak gave a subtle glow of four different colors, likely indicating the branches of magic they were connected to. Virgil then handed it to Gwen. "*This* is how I'm trying to butter you up before our date," he said.

The high elf's eyes widened in joy. She quickly equipped the item, replacing her other cloak, and looked at herself in the mirror. "I feel... stronger. Thank you, Virgil," she said with a warm smile. "Consider me buttered up." She then put her arm around his. "Now we have a festival to enjoy," she said, and the couple left the shop.

The party trekked over to the other side of the city where the Alefest was to be held. There was a large main tent set up by the jarl's home. Both druids were seated near the jarl at the end of a long, large table. After they arrived, the jarl gave a rousing toast to the druids, praising them for their courage and heroics. He then informed the crowd of both nobles and common folk alike what they did for the city, informing them of their ability to bring about cooperation between the city and mage college once more and their uncovering of the Blackfoots' wrongdoings. The last bit caused a number of gasps and murmurs.

The jarl was a good speaker, though, bringing the crowd's attention back to him instead of their murmurings by using the

Blackfoots' exposure and arrests to motivate the crowd that with the druids' arrival, a new era of peace and prosperity was headed for Amthoon. At that, the crowd raised their mugs of ale in cheers, and the festivities began. It first began with a feast of a delicious variety of seafood, which Virgil loved, and Splinter, the always-hungry rat, loved even more.

There were many different varieties of ale as well. Virgil was more of a sour ale kind of guy, and he discovered Gwen was more of an IPA-style woman. Next, there were games. An entire street of vendors were replaced with different styles of carnival games. It was eerily reminiscent of small-town carnivals back on Earth, which gave both druids a bit of comfort at its familiarity.

Virgil was able to win a ring toss game, while Gwen, the expert archer, won a game throwing balls at targets to knock them off. Virgil was pretty sure these games were rigged, as most of them were in some sort or fashion back on Earth, but the games didn't have enough precaution to account for the power and accuracy of a level twenty-one Hunter Druid.

Both druids were having a fun time, enjoying their momentary reprieve from all the stress they'd undergone these past couple of weeks. They each won a stuffed animal and gave them to each other.

The druids proceeded to give the toys to their pets. Both Baphomet and Christopher happily chewed and shook their new toys, quickly destroying them like overactive dogs. Splinter had a good case of food coma, and the stego rat was asleep in Virgil's satchel and he had Baphomet atop his shoulder where the rat typically perched.

After their games were done, Virgil and Gwen went to go see the fight that Jaxon was scheduled to be in. To the druids' surprise, the fight was scheduled outside of Amthoon proper in a small arena about a half mile outside near a place called Glassy Cliff.

After asking one of the townsfolk joining them on their way to the arena, they learned that the cliff gained its name because a giant worm creature once made its home inside the rocky outcropping. It stayed there for so long and grew so big that most of the stone composing the cliff had been eaten away by the large invertebrate before it was vanquished by a group of adventurers who wanted to use it for fishing bait.

The cliff was deemed unsafe to tread, and was too dangerous for anyone to traverse for risk of the entire cliff collapsing and someone falling to a watery grave, as apparently the deep waters around the cliff were claimed to be one of the deepest spots in all of Imeria, according to the citizens of Amthoon.

Virgil wondered if it was the mounted, taxidermied worm that was displayed above where the jarl sat when they had first met him in the town hall. If it was that creature, or one related to it, Virgil could believe in that story. It made him wonder though, if a worm was as monstrous as the one he saw, or even larger, how big was the monstrous fish they were trying to catch that they needed to use it as bait?!

Not too long after that conversation, they made it to the arena. It reminded Virgil of some sort of small gladiatorial arena with a round dusty arena floor with rising concentric circular stone bleachers around it. The arena was quickly packed, but the druids were given great seats on the third row. This competition was reminiscent of boxing matches back on Earth, and plenty of humans, elves, dwarves, and even some gnomes were placing bets. Apparently Jaxon was the underdog in this competition, facing some sort of bulky human kickboxer named Jean Claude.

Wanting to have some fun and knowing the chiropractor's capabilities, Virgil placed a five-gold bet on the man. Soon enough, the announcer came out. It was the same bald human that the party had seen with the jarl. He was still in the tuxedo, and Virgil was pretty sure he had his clipboard behind his back. He cleared his throat and addressed the crowd, who had already gone silent when he entered the stage. "Er hem, good people of Amthoon. We gather here tonight, this first night of

Alefest, only because of the heroics of the two druid champions of Yggdrasil that have aided us in our time of great need. Please join me in applauding these two heroes and their animal companions for their bravery." The multitude of Light Magic orbs then turned and shone on the two druids. Virgil squinted instinctively due to his race's natural disposition for bright light.

The crowd loudly applauded the elves and creatures, which caused both Virgil and Gwen to blush then wave back at the crowd in appreciation. Fortunately, the lights turned back to their normal positions, and the old man continued speaking. "Yes, thank you again, brave heroes. Now, let's get onto tonight's main event. Who will be crowned the best hand-to-hand fighter in all of Amthoon? Who will gain the title of this year's Alefist?!" The crowd roared in anticipation. Both Virgil and Gwen let out a small chuckle at the punny title.

"Before we begin the bout, let me explain the ground rules," the proper man continued. "Each fighter can use magical skills, but cannot use any magical spells. Also, each fighter is allowed to bring one, and only one, potion to help them in their fight. Now, let's introduce our contestants. We have last year's champion, 'Jean Claude The Kickboxer,' and his challenger 'Jaxon The Adjuster'!" The crowd roared in response as the two men entered the arena, sizing each other up. "Ready? Begin!"

CHAPTER TWENTY

Resurgence

"Wow!" Virgil said as he and Gwen were walking back from the fight. "That snake hands potion was crazy! I didn't expect it to be *that good*," he said.

"I know," Gwen agreed. "That other guy didn't stand a chance! Did you hear what he called them? T-rex hands? Did they look like t-rexes to you?"

Virgil shrugged his shoulders. "Maybe?" he said, not really sure what type of reptilian creatures the potions turned the chiropractor's hands into during the fight. The crowd was so loud it was hard to make out, but it sounded like he said that's what his hands were turned into. "Either way, I don't think I'm going to let him do any more adjustments on me anytime soon," he joked.

"I see you were enjoying the fight as well," a familiar voice brimming with too much confidence said from behind them. Both druids turned to see Maldrakus, the wood elf Arcane Mage once again back in his thick black academy robes they had first met him in.

"I didn't expect you to be a fan of physical combat fights," Virgil said.

"I can appreciate those who do their best to excel in their chosen craft. You saw it yourself, the one who claims the title of Alefist is a proven fighter. Also," he said, producing a large bag of jingling coins from his belt. "Unlike Melvin, I'm a pretty good gambler."

"At five-to-one odds, it looked like you chose wisely," Virgil said. "I should've put more down on the guy, but at least I made some money back," he said, producing a much smaller bag of coins.

"Ha! You should've seen our headmaster back in the day. Before he was elected to be the next Ramsay, he was an even more tenacious risk-taker!"

A squeaky voice called out from behind them, "Hey, I'm an excellent gambler!"

The elves turned back to see Melvin in his thick robes, walking toward them. That was strange. Where was Ramsay?

"Ha! Then where's your winnings?" Maldrakus asked.

The gnome's face reddened in embarrassment as he walked up to the group.

Maldrakus put a hand on the gnome shaman's shoulder. "No matter, Melvin, you're still good company," he said, being notably nicer to Melvin than when they first met him. Guess he was serious about not being an asshole.

Virgil shrugged off the mage's change in demeanor. Something that the Arcane Mage said threw Virgil off. Did he say the *next* Ramsay? "Wait, what do you mean, 'elected to be the next Ramsay'? Isn't that his name? And you, Melvin, shouldn't you be with Ramsay right now?"

Melvin had a confused look on his face. "Why would I be with the headmaster?"

Before he could say more, Maldrakus interrupted, chuckling, "Oh, that's right, you druids are not naturally from here. Yes, Ramsay is our headmaster's name. It is the name that every headmaster takes on when they are elected to lead." Virgil was getting a sinking feeling in his gut, but let the mage continue. "Let's see here, what was his name beforehand? I know he was involved in helping remove a traitor decades ago, and there was a report on it... Ah! Yes, I remember now, his name was Mikael, Mikael Brandeen."

Virgil was about to pull up his already completed 'Student's Treachery' quest info, but the world of Imeria already connected the dots for him and sent both him and Gwen notifications.

Alert! You have just discovered that one of the 3 demonic clone imposters, Mikael Brandeen, is still alive and has escaped under your very noses. Probably should do something about that. I know, how about a quest?

Quest Unlocked!
Runaway Imposter
You have discovered that the headmaster of the mage college, Ramsay the 22nd, was actually a demonic clone of the dead dwarf shaman, Mikael Brandeen. The demon has left the city of Amthoon and is now likely regrouping with his allies. Find him and put him down before he can do more damage to the world of Imeria.
Requirements:
Find and kill the sorlith demon pretending to be Mikael Brandeen within the next 7 days.
Reward:
20,000 Experience
Countless Lives Saved
Unknown
Do You Accept?
Yes or No
"If you don't accept, you know a lot of people are going to die horrible deaths, right?"

Both druids' eyes bulged, and they readily accepted the quest. Gwen turned to the mage who was looking confused at the two druids' sudden surprised expressions. "Maldrakus,

Melvin, you're not going to believe us, but the headmaster is an imposter." The mage and shaman gave her an incredulous look. "Show him the quest information," she said to Virgil.

Virgil added the mage to the party and sent him the quest's info.

The mage stopped in his tracks and his eyes went distant as he read the information displayed in both of their visions. Quickly, both of their faces went sullen. "By the gods, I... no, this cannot stand!" he pronounced loudly, standing up straighter.

"Shh," Gwen quickly hushed him, bringing both him and the gnome in close to make sure to look around at the others nearby. They gave the mage curious looks, but none of the other citizens fully stopped to investigate what was going on. "No one else knows this," she whispered. "We don't want the city or the college to erupt in a panic."

"Especially so quickly after they had been freed of one threat terrorizing their city," Virgil added.

Melvin's face went pale in utter shock. "I... saw him leave the front gates of the city earlier. I thought he was helping with the festival, but then he went into the jungle," he said, sounding detached, still in shock.

The Arcane Mage took a few angry breaths then looked around, noticing the others, and nodded in agreement with the druids. "I'm sorry. You're right. We need to get back to the college as quickly as possible. There, we will enable our defenses, I will equip my gear, and together we will end this abomination that has been infesting my college." Both Virgil and Gwen nodded, grateful for the skilled Battle Mage's help. "Good, I'm glad that's settled. At least things can't get any worse," Maldrakus said.

Both druids just looked at the mage, dumbfounded.

"What?" he asked.

"Hey blueboy, I know ye be a smart lad, but that be the stupidest thing I've ever heard someone say in a long time," Grief said.

"What are you talking about, skull?" Maldrakus asked.

"You broke the cardinal rule," Virgil answered.

"Exactly," Gwen added. "One of the biggest rules of adventuring is that you never, *never* say things can't get worse."

"Pfft," the mage said, waving off their comments. "Are you really going to tell me that you believe—"

"Sir Druid!" A voice called out from ahead of the trio of elves, interrupting the mage. They were now by the downward slope about one-hundred yards from the city gate. The party turned to see a pair of guards sprinting to them, a thin human and a chunky dwarf in leather armor. It was Rikon and Hamil, the two lackluster guards Virgil had scared... and forced them into a promise to warn them of danger.

There was another pit in Virgil's stomach. "You just had to say that, didn't you?" he asked the mage before the guards came up to them.

Both guards were breathing heavily and had to rest their hands on their knees to catch their breaths before they could speak. "We came to warn you. We promised on Yggdrasil that we would warn you of the other druids' arrival. The captain of the guard had just informed us that—"

"RAAWWWRRR!" A loud bellow echoed from the sky.

Virgil's Danger Sense sent shivers up his spine. He and Gwen knew what that sound was. That was an ocean drake, and they knew someone who had one as a mount.

"Crap," Virgil muttered as the crowd began to panic. The walking group turned into a sprinting one, coming close to a mob heading toward the city gates. "Where are they coming from?" he asked.

"From the east, sir," Rikon answered nervously.

"Shit," he said. They needed to go east to get to the Scorched Lands. Virgil wasn't one-hundred percent sure that was where the demon masking as Ramsay had gone, but Virgil had a pretty good hunch that he was indeed heading there. Now that he thought about it, Ramsay may have been the one who perverted the deformed totems, keeping the firebrands back in the first place. "Is there a secret passage that is not well known to the public to the east? We have to head there, and we *do not* need whatever made that noise to follow us."

The two guards exchanged nervous glances before Rikon looked back. "There is, sir, we can take you there."

"Absolutely not," Maldrakus said. "I'm coming with you. Though I'm a capable Battle Mage on my own, I will need my gear."

"No," Virgil said. "The situation has changed, and we need you and Melvin here. That sound was an ocean drake, and I bet there's another drake with it. Two of the other druids that were summoned with us have them as mounts."

Maldrakus looked confused at Virgil's statement. "Other druids? If those are other druids then, why are you hiding from them?"

"We don't have a good relationship with them," Gwen answered. "They have been actively hunting us on orders of the king of Kygor."

"That's right," Virgil added. "Pierre is a nice guy, but super gullible. Marianna is the one you have to watch out for, and you don't want to mess with Dirk! Whatever you do, do not let them into the city, or people will likely die. You are one of the few people who could probably hold them off, Maldrakus." He then put a hand on the mage and shaman's shoulders. "Please, we need you here. I promise, by Yggdrasil's power inside of me, we will take down the imposter." The world of Imeria and Yggdrasil herself heard Virgil's words and accepted them with the gravity he meant them.

You have made a binding vow on Yggdrasil's name. She has accepted your words and will honor them, whether you fail or succeed. You must find and kill the demon impersonating the shaman Mikael Brandeen within 7 days or else...

Reward for success: Enough experience to reach your next level.

Penalty for failure: Regressing back to level 10.

Greattt, Virgil thought sarcastically to himself. Like Maldrakus, he also needed to choose his words carefully, as there were clear and quantifiable consequences.

The mage and shaman both took a breath of relief, seemingly satisfied with Virgil's promise, "Very well. I know you are capable, and I trust in your abilities, druids. I will do my best to keep the others out of the city, but please, hurry. I do not think we will be able to repel a force of dragons for a week straight," Maldrakus said.

"We'll do our best," Virgil said, smiling at his friend. He then dismissed him from the party as Maldrakus and Melvin took off in a jog to join the crowd running for the city gates. "Lead on," Virgil said to Rikon, and the guards began taking the druids off the main path. They lead the party into the thicket of tall thick crops that looked like corn. Eventually, they made it to a small clearing in the crops. There were a couple of bedrolls and awnings made of palm fronds over them. It also looked like there was a sewer drain in the center of the clearing...

"Hamil and I like to come here when we're posted on outer guard duty over the farmland. We... usually just sleep and slack off during our shifts..." Rikon admitted slowly with his head held down. "There's a drain there. It is connected to a series of drains that channels overflowing waters from the forest above and guides the waters to the river down below to help prevent flooding. The pipe should lead you to a secluded section of the jungle way off the beaten path."

While Virgil was upset at the guards' clear disregard for the duty to protect the people, he was immensely grateful for the 'get out of jail free' card that they had just provided them. "Thank you. You have really done us a great service," he said.

"Does that mean we have upheld our vows?" Rikon asked.

"Help us open the grate, close it back up when we're in, and tell no one we're here, and we'll say you're good, chaps," Gwen said.

The two guards looked at each other then helped open the

grate. The two elves and animals squeezed it. The pipeway was pretty cramped, about six feet tall and just wide enough to force the party to travel single file. There was a steady stream of water flowing down the center of the path, but it was very shallow and easily traversable. It reminded Virgil of the Kygor sewers, but notably cleaner with no waste in sight! Instead of the odor of excrement, the compressed air had the scents of water and decaying plant debris. Hopefully there weren't any alligators here either!

"Good luck," Rikon said before placing the grate back on top, sealing the druids inside and removing the main source of light. While Gwen had some trouble, this was Virgil's element. His Darkvision took over, illuminating the place in shades of green. Carefully, he led the party with the exception of Splinter. The area was like her previous home, and the evolved stego rat confidently guided the party out of the tunnels, sniffing the ground like a bloodhound and eating the occasional insect that had managed to crawl into the piping.

"We safe here, lad?" Grief asked.

"Yeah, at least relatively. What's up?"

"Well, I want to take this moment to say… I… told… ye! I told ye, lad, there was something wrong with that dwarf, but nooo, I was just blown off like my opinions didn't matter. I mean, good grief, what kind of dwarf doesn't like to drink?! Even the younglings get a little mixed in with their milk."

"Seriously? I'm pretty sure that would cause developmental issues in any other race."

"Bah!" Grief said, blowing off that concern. "We dwarves be a sturdy race, sturdier than any fancy elf and thin human. We can take the alcohol. In fact, it makes us stronger!"

Virgil rolled his eyes at the statement then spoke, "Yeah, I thought you were an expert on demons, not dwarven child rearing."

"Did it ever occur to that pointy-eared head of yers that I may be knowledgeable in more than one thing?" the skull asked with more than a bit of edge in his voice. "If there be anything

I know well, it be dwarven culture, killin' demons, and women-folk. Of *all* those things, I'm considered an *expert*."

Virgil pushed up his glasses back up the bridge of his nose and nodded in concession. While Virgil had no doubt that he was an intelligent guy, he wasn't too proud to admit he was wrong. Also, it made sense when he thought about it. Grief was a dwarf, at least in spirit. Even though he'd been gone for centuries, dwarves were a long-lived race, and he would be much more knowledgeable about them than Virgil would likely ever be. Though based on how many angry ex-lovers Grief had managed to accumulate when he still had his body, Virgil wasn't convinced that his soulbound companion was truly an expert on women, maybe an expert on pissing them off though...?

"I'm sorry, Grief. You were right. Clearly Ramsay was not who we thought he was. From now on, I will take your wisdom more seriously when it comes to dwarven culture."

"And womenfolk too, right?"

"Ha! No, I'm not interested in becoming a talking skull anytime soon."

"Hm, point taken," the skull conceded and the party continued their trek up the piping. After twenty minutes, they crawled out of the pipe to be greeted with a secluded and shaded section of the jungle. The sky above was almost completely covered by the thick brush. There was a large pond right beside the pipe that fed the small stream that went down the descending pipe with occasional splashing from the waves. Apparently this body of water was one of the things that was a flood risk for the coastal city. Virgil was surprised by the thought, but shrugged. He hadn't been in Imeria too long, and maybe they had extreme torrential downpours or something?

The party all carefully emerged along the shoreline of the water. "It's so dark here," Gwen said. "Do you have any more of those Darkvision potions?"

Virgil shook his head but then remembered that she couldn't see him. "Uh, no. Not right now, at least. I bought a bunch of ingredients to make more potions, but I haven't had enough time to make anything."

"Well, I'll just light a torch then, at least until we get to a section of forest that has more exposure to the night sky," she said and reached into her bag.

Virgil grabbed her wrist before she could pull out the torch, though. "Wait, my Danger Sense just slightly went off," he said, then scanned around and activated the subskill Detect Hostile Intent. Virgil's awareness spread out, scanning for any lifeforms that meant his party ill-will. He felt nothing in the immediate forest, but then his senses went upward to the sky through the small gaps in between the foliage. There he felt... something!

He gasped. "Duck," he whispered and brought Gwen down to the jungle floor right before a large form flew over the sky. The currents of air it brought flew across the top layer of the forest, exposing more of it to the night sky above, illuminating the water below with the light from the twin moons. Fortunately, the party was outside of the illuminated area. Despite that, they backed up a little more to stay in the safety of the darkness and activated Stealth.

The large creature that flew by made another pass but higher above the forest, so it did not affect the trees. That allowed the party to get a good look at what it was. The flying creature was a large dragon made entirely of plant material. Atop the creature was a small figure wearing glistening metallic armor.

It was a *very good* call that they didn't light the torch! That was Marianna, and unlike Pierre, the party had no trust in the woman. Like Dirk, the female dawn elf was out for herself, and right now, taking them down was her way of doing so. Her and her Spriggan Drake had set off more alarms through Virgil's Detect Hostile Intent, indicating she was very much hostile to them. The party stayed in Stealth for the next five minutes until they were satisfied that Marianna had left. Both Virgil's Danger Sense and Detect Hostile Intent had not given any more sensations of danger, so they used that as a good sign and began their trek back toward the Scorched Lands.

They decided not to use a torch for the first hour to play it safe… just in case. They had to fight a couple of jungle envirowolves, which they handled easily, but the flashes of light from Virgil's magic seemed to attract more creatures. It also didn't help that Baphomet kept wanting to join the fight despite Virgil trying to keep the beastking hidden. Baphomet had a Trait called Alpha Predator, and it had a fifty-percent chance to cause any non-allied beast within sight to either run or attack it for dominance. The damn beast was persistent enough that Virgil finally let it hop out and join the fight in its larger form. There was definitely more fighting, but it was also easier, too, when you had a giant bear-like creature with antlers helping.

All in all, they fought around a dozen demons and beasts in total. Every single one of the beasts were predators. Most of them were ambush predators, and all of them were tough, even tougher than their counterparts the party had faced in daylight. It truly gave credence to the forest being dangerous at night. By the time they had traveled four hours into the humid jungle section of the Yggdra Timberland, the party was tired, sweaty, and hungry. Well, that last one was just Splinter and Christopher—those two could eat!

It was a little after midnight when the party finally found a small cave to make camp in. It was well-hidden in the thick jungle and by a small stream. Feeling relatively safe, they decided to start a campfire to help give Gwen some aiding light. Despite the jungle being a warm place, the heat from the fire was comforting.

"Man, talk about bad timing for our dates, huh?" Virgil asked.

Gwen gave a slight chuckle. "You're telling me," she said, smiling. "Still, though, I had a great time! That Jaxon guy is bonkers, but he sure can fight!"

"No joke!" Virgil agreed. "Well… hopefully date number three won't get interrupted by a chaotic clusterfuck like the other two. That is, if number three is on the table?" he asked, trying his absolute best to be cool for once in his life.

She nodded. "Smooth. I'll make you a deal. I'll do it, *only if* we finish off this Zinthos and that Ramsay chap first. What do you say?"

"I've never been more motivated to kill demons in my life," Virgil said. "You got yourself a deal. Now why don't you get some rest? I'll take first watch."

Gwen let out a yawn, nodding in agreement. "Good call, I could definitely use some sleep." She then laid down next to her curled-up terror boar companion. "So, how do you think they found us?"

"Dirk and his posse? Not sure. Likely the king has spies throughout the continent looking for us," Virgil reasoned. "Though I'm not certain that Dirk is with them. When we last saw him, he wasn't exactly on the best of terms with the other two," Virgil said, recalling how essentially Pierre and Marianna left Dirk and the party for dead when fighting Baphomet, and left to go play lackey to the king. Dirk was *very* unhappy with that...

"True," Gwen said. "Dirk has a particular skill at pissing people off. I wouldn't be surprised if they aren't working together anymore. I wouldn't be surprised if the git was planning his revenge on everyone right now. Dude knows how to hold a grudge."

"That's comforting," Virgil said, remembering that he was also on the Feral Druid's shit list.

"Don't worry, chap. If he comes after you, I'll protect you," Gwen said with a wink.

Virgil rolled his eyes then pushed up his glasses back up his nose. "Ha-ha, get some sleep. I'll wake you up when it's your shift." He chuckled, then left to go work on his potions.

CHAPTER TWENTY-ONE

Progress So Far

Virgil tapped Grief. "Keep an eye out for any threats, okay?"

"Ye realize that placing watch responsibilities on a skull who can't move may be considered an unwise choice, right, lad?" the skull asked.

Virgil unlatched the skull then placed Grief on a stone ledge looking out the cave's exit, "There's only one way in or out of here, and you're looking right at it. Also, my Danger Sense will help alert me of any threats," he retorted.

Grief grunted something unintelligible before agreeing to the assignment. "What're ye going to be doin' then, lad?"

"There's a saying back where I'm from, 'Proper preparation prevents poor performance.' I need to prepare, not only for myself but for the party."

"Ye going to be makin' those weird concoctions with jacka-lope shite again, aren't ye? Good grief, lad! Those things smell worse than a fart in a shower!"

Virgil sighed. "I'm not just going to be working with the jackalope scat, and what are you complaining about? You don't even have a nose," he said indignantly.

"Maybe so, lad, but that don't mean I'm not right."

Virgil rolled his eyes at his companion's antics, then began emptying and working on creating more of the potions, pastes, and poultices that had helped his party in the past. Before he started in earnest, though, he checked the auto-minimized pending notifications in his vision.

Your constant fighting in a nighttime jungle environment has awarded you not only experience, but advancement in multiple skills and your Stamina Pool. You have been awarded:
+1 to Restoration Magic
+2 to Detect Hostile Intent
+2 to Stealth
+1 to Analyze
+10 to Stamina

From the Harvest skill of your party member, Gwen, you have gained the following loot from your opponents' bodies:
x4 Panthera Eyes
x2 Jungle Envirowolf Hearts
x5 Dark Imp Horns
X5 Giant Python Meat
X1 Giant Python Skin
X2 Imp Hearts
X1 Tattered Zhroherz Hide
X1 Nocturnal Eagle Gizzard
X1 Nocturnal Eagle Liver

Virgil was happy with his skill progression just from these few hours of fighting. He was also happy with Gwen's unique skill Harvest. Instead of taking the arduous time and effort to do the gory work of cutting open dead bodies, the skill allowed her to forcefully dissolve the dead opponents and leave only the remaining lootable items of value.

With the multitude of alchemical items he had, Virgil began crafting the potions that would help his party with the fights to come.

First, he crafted four Fortify Alchemy potions. Each potion lasted for thirty minutes and would increase the potency of his creations during the time it was in effect by ten percent. He hadn't crafted the recipe he had learned from Ras yet, because of the time it took to craft it. Now though, they were not in some foreign dungeon and in relative safety. It took an hour to just make the four potions, but Virgil knew it was worth it as it would help his other creations.

Before continuing, he consumed one and began crafting other magic brews. Every thirty minutes, he drank another of the surprisingly tart mixtures to keep the efficiency bonus going contiguously. After two hours, Virgil fell flat on his back, exhausted by the focused, tedious, and draining work.

As he lay there, he thought about pharmacists before factories and mass-production were things, and had a greater respect for them after the work he just did. All in all, he had crafted sixty-three potions and gained two whole skill points in Alchemy in that two-hour grind session of potion making. He was pretty pleased with his work. While not his most glorious task, Virgil knew firsthand that Alchemy could literally mean the difference between life and death.

He had crafted five Enhanced Beast Sense Potions, two Druidic Darkvision Potions, one Enhanced Demonic Fury Potion, fifteen Enhanced Scatter Scat Pastes, three Liquid Light Flashes, four Potions of Icy Essence, six Minor Health Potions, nine of both Minor Stamina and Manna Potions, two Analgesic Sleep Powders, and seven unique poisons for Gwen to coat her arrows with.

Turned out, after further examining the Vile Stalker Venom he had collected days ago, that the effect of turning a creature it kills into a demon didn't work on things that were already demons. Virgil was concerned that if they used the venom on a demon, the demon would revive back after being killed. Virgil had also used the Nocturnal Eagle remains to create a couple of unique potions for the Hunter Druid to use, too. After he rested for the next ten minutes, he then decided to allocate his four unused stat points.

Initially, he wanted to put more points into strength so as to increase his total health pool, but he knew that wasn't the best choice. Having a high health pool was not his strong point. No, Virgil's advantages came from both his speed and spellcasting ability. So, he put two points into intelligence, bumping him up to a total of forty and increasing his manna pool to four-hundred. He then divided the other two points into agility and endurance. Sure, he could've put both points into agility, but what good was having a high speed if you didn't have enough stamina to use it for long?

After that was done, Virgil decided to look at his Status.

Name: Virgil
Level: 16 (30519/33210 experience to next level.)
Unallocated Stat Points: 0
Race: Elf **Subrace:** Dark Elf
Class: Druid
Specialization: Healer Druid
Attunement: A Veterinarian's Pact
Languages: Common, Elven
Companions: Grief (Soulbound), Splinter, Baphomet

Pools & Resistances
Health: 122 (+2)
Manna: 400
Stamina: 260
Armor: 119 (+10)
Life Magic: 50%
Earth Magic: 50%
Nature Magic: 50%
Light Magic: -50%

Statistics
Strength: 12

Agility: 53 (+10)
Intelligence: 40
Endurance: 31
Charisma: 13 (+2)

Traits
True Healer
Darkvision
Increased Hearing
Ally of Darkness
Beast Commander
Alchemically Inspired

Skills
Medicine Level 53
Herbology Level 54
Nature Magic (Restoration) Level 33
Spells:
- Restore, Leeching Vines, Yggdrashield, Nature Bolt, Barkskin,
Purifying Aura, Phoenix Fire
Stealth Level 23 – Subskill: Sneak Attack Level 3
Analyze Level 13
Danger Sense Level 15 – Subskill: Detect Hostile Intent
Level 7
Skinning Level 4
Trade Level 9
Soulbound Recall
Alchemy Level 40
Skinning Level 4
Taunt Level 13
Culinary Level 1
Manna Manipulation

Not bad, Virgil thought, definitely satisfied with his progress, especially when compared to when he first arrived on the continent of Kygora with barely any valuable equipment or offensive capability. Next up, he looked at some basic information regarding the rest of his party.

Name: Gwendolyn
Level: 21 (21/252,188 experience to next level.)
Unallocated Stat Points: 0
Race: Elf **Subrace:** High Elf
Class: Druid
Specialization: Hunter Druid
Attunement: Unknown
Languages: Common, Elven
Companions: Christopher P. Bacon

Pools & Resistances
Health: 165
Manna: 400
Stamina: 310 (+105)
Armor: 150
Air Magic: 50%
Earth Magic: 50%
Nature Magic: 50%

Statistics
Strength: 14
Agility: 41
Intelligence: 40 (+5)
Endurance: 21
Charisma: 31

Name: Splinter
Level: 24
Race: Beast – Rodent **Subrace:** Stego Rat
Class: N/A

Pools & Resistances
Health: 145

Manna: 5
Stamina: 250
Poisons: 100%

Statistics
Strength: 11
Agility: 43
Intelligence: 7
Endurance: 35
Charisma: 7

Name: Baphomet
Level: 25
Race: Beast **Subrace:** Beastking
Class: N/A

Pools & Resistances
Health: Current: 50 Enlarged: 1150
Manna: Current: 230 Enlarged: 230
Stamina: Current: 50 Enlarged: 750
Fire 50%
Cold 50%
Piercing Damage 25%
Slashing Damage 25%

Statistics
Strength: Current: 3 Enlarged: 115
Agility: Current: 8 Enlarged: 50
Intelligence: Current: 9 Enlarged: 9
Endurance: Current: 7 Enlarged: 75
Charisma: Current: 7 Enlarged: 7

Next up, he Analyzed Christopher. Since the terror boar was Gwen's animal companion and not his, Virgil's Beast Commander Trait wouldn't allow the pig to officially join the party, hence the need to Analyze.

Name: Christopher P. Bacon
Level: 18
Race: Beast – Pig **Subrace:** Terror Boar
Class: N/A

Pools & Resistances
Health: 250
Manna: 5
Stamina: 300
Blunt Damage: 50%

Statistics
Strength: 25
Agility: 30
Intelligence: 6
Endurance: 30
Charisma: 6

Virgil was happy with the rest of the group's leveling and progression. The information also revealed a massive difference in stats when Baphomet was in its smaller form. Virgil also wasn't surprised that everyone was a higher level than him, given their ability to deal damage resulting in higher experience being gained from combat. He was, however, happy that he wasn't too far behind the rest of the party.

The veterinarian was impressed with Gwen's leveling too. The Hunter Druid had already made it past level twenty. He then looked over to his one other companion, thinking about the skull's new power. Virgil was both thrown-off and grateful that Grief could actually gain a new skill. It did make Virgil wonder though. "Hey, Grief."

"Yes, lad?"

"Where does all the stuff you suck in through your Space Vacuum skill go?"

"Oh, that be simple, lad. All those things go into the pocket of space I have inside me."

"How come I couldn't access them when I looked inside the items you had stored inside you?"

"Hmm, ye bring up a good question, lad. I not be sure, honestly."

"Can you access the stuff you absorbed?" There was silence in response. Virgil could tell through their soulbound link that the skull was checking himself to see that if he could. Quickly, they discovered their answer. Grief made a noise like he was about to vomit, then, like a geyser, a stream of rocky debris shot out from both of the skull's eye sockets and his nasal cavity. For three seconds, the debris flew out while Grief made a clear vomiting noise. The rocky debris then stopped and was followed by a lone green leaf that shot out of Grief's left eye then floated on down.

"Uugh, it turns out... I can, lad... Good grief," Grief groaned.

The loud crashing of rocky debris woke up the rest of the party. "What's going on?" Gwen asked.

"Sorry, lass," Grief said. "It turns out my vacuum skill goes in reverse, too," he said, not enthused by the fact.

Gwen rolled her eyes at the skull then sighed. "Well, please be quiet next time. Remember, we're not alone in this jungle," she said before falling back to sleep against Christopher.

Deciding not to accidentally stir up any more trouble, Virgil leaned against the cave wall and closed his eyes too. He chewed on a leaf of a nearby budding plant that his Herbology skill said would help aid him in getting some sleep without any interruptions from Grief's bantering. It definitely helped, as unconsciousness quickly took him.

CHAPTER TWENTY-TWO

The Scorched Lands

Virgil awoke to a throbbing pain in his forehead. "Ow, what, what happened?" he asked, rubbing his aching skull.

"Well..." Grief said, trailing off, sounding like a kid trying to explain away the mistake they've done to their parents.

"Spit it out, Grief," Virgil said, in no mood for games as he massaged his temples.

"So, ye know how ye were workin' on yer skills last night to help the party? Well, I thought to do the same. I be able to absorb and vomit out the things from my Space Vacuum. I thought if that skill can go both ways, why not the Soulbound Recall skill?"

Virgil closed his eyes, trying to piece together what the skull was saying. "So you're saying—"

"That we both can recall each other away from danger, lad," Grief interrupted to answer. "Now that I've got a taste of action from fighting that Mage and saving yer sorry asses from the poison, I wanted to contribute even more. So, you're welcome," he said, sounding rather pleased with himself.

"And the reason my head hurts?" Virgil asked in clear irritation.

The skull's confidence quickly faded away. "Ah... well... I was a little... overzealous when I finally figured out how to use the skill, and yer unconscious body went flyin' toward me, giving me a good ol' fashioned dwarven head crack that would have made me ancestors proud. I give credit, lad, yer skull's almost as thick as mine. I'm surprised ye didn't wake up, really."

Virgil sighed and opened his eyes to see that Grief was no longer in the place the druid had originally put him at. Grief was now on the ground against an exposed tree root. Guess Virgil was able to knock the literal thick head back a bit from that interaction too. He now regretted eating that leaf that helped him sleep more. If he hadn't, maybe he wouldn't feel like he had a hangover. Virgil's big ears twitched as he heard Gwen chuckling and the sounds of sizzling meat. He turned to see her cooking some of the python meat they had collected from last night's fighting on a small skillet over a small fire.

"You okay, thick skull?" she asked with a smile.

"I'll make it," Virgil replied.

"Good, now go get something to help your head from Grief. He's a literal pharmacy at your fingertips. You should have something to help with the headache."

Virgil nodded, conceding to her logic, and retrieved a minor healing herb from Grief. As he reattached Grief to his belt and chewed, the throbbing inside his skull started to notably lessen and he gave a contented sigh of relief.

For the next hour, the party cleaned up, had a breakfast of tasty giant python meat that Gwen only semi-burned, re-equipped their gear, and continued to the northeast toward the Scorched Lands' border. While the animals cleaned up in the stream, both druids used the new handy Ring of Prestidigitation to remove the grime from their forms. Both elves had to admit, there was simply a good feeling to starting a journey fresh and clean versus grimy. It helped them feel more vitalized and ready for the day.

Virgil gave Gwen the five poison vials and two special potions he had made for her, too.

Name: Fortify Archery Potion
Item Type: Potion
Durability: 15/15
Item Class: Great
Effect: Increases Archery skill by 10% for 60 minutes.
Description: A unique potion created by the Healer Druid and utilizing a Nocturnal Eagle Gizzard. The aerial hunter favors stealthily attacking opponents, diving from a distance. The long-range nature of their attacks provide a benefit to someone who uses the Archery skill.

Name: Increase Stealth Potion
Item Type: Potion
Durability: 9/9
Item Class: Great
Effect: Increases Stealth skill by 10% for 65 minutes.
Description: A unique potion created by the Healer Druid and utilizing a Nocturnal Eagle Liver. The aerial hunter favors stealthily attacking opponents, diving from a distance. The ambush attacker's organ provides a benefit to someone who utilizes the Stealth skill.

Virgil explained the potions and their uses to her. She did not have the Alchemy skill like him, so she couldn't retrieve any information about the potions and their contents. Virgil thought that was a good idea, as she may not like knowing that the potions used the boiled organs of a giant bird... That logic seemed valid as she gratefully accepted the potions.

The party then continued their trek along the jungle. As they went eastward, the topography transitioned from coastal woods back to thickened massive oaks, showing that the trees further inland were both older and larger than their counterparts. They made sure to keep Baphomet inside his bag so as to not provoke any nearby neutral animals. After a couple of hours, they found a distinct, well-traveled dirt path. Gwen's high Tracking skill identified some recent footprints that matched the thick sandals that the Amthoon guards wore. It looked like the patrols were indeed reinstituted. Maybe the party could give them a warning about Ramsay.

Unfortunately, they were too late. They found a spot to see the border to the Scorched Lands distinctly. Lying on the ground by the border were the burnt husks of three Amthoon guards, their bodies unrecognizable outside the almost completely destroyed armor and weapons. Standing by the dead bodies were two female Firebrand Orcs. One was scanning the environment for intruders, while the other was chewing the remains of a dead guard's detached humerus like it was a buffalo wing. Fortunately, the scanning orc hadn't noticed the party hiding behind a thick tree and dense foliage.

What was even more concerning was what was behind the two. There, erected scanning the environment like the eye of Sauron, was a terrifying totem. It was made of wood and stood five feet tall. It was a solid beam except for the top; that part had ornate carvings on it. Oh, and it had a flame-wreathed eyeball with four wriggling small flame tentacles at the very top. Clearly, this was another one of the Zinthos totems.

If Virgil had any doubts that Zinthos was a demon general, they faded away when he saw a floating crown of flame over the totem. When they had fought Baphomet, who was originally a beast that had been corrupted into a demon general, it had the exact same floating crown of flame atop it. It seemed to be some sort of calling card for the generals. It also strongly indicated that the Ramsay imposter was apparently in this general's service.

It was easy to tell the border outside of just the totem; the landscape was vastly different! On one side was lush and thick rainforest. On the other, a charred and blackened land. The ground was rock hard, rigid, and firm. It looked like it was made of hardened lava. Where the ground wasn't blackened, there were rolling dunes of sand. In regards to plant life, there were dry bushes with sparse clusters of palm trees and weeds. It was truly a barren land.

The party crept a few feet back and formulated a plan of attack through Party Chat. After a few minutes of discussion, they spread out and readied themselves.

On Virgil's command, they enacted their plan. Virgil first walked out in the open, fifteen feet away from the orcs and totem and in their clear line of vision. Zinthos was the first to see Virgil through the totem. "Ah, so you've returned, dark elf. Good, I've been hoping to add you to fuel my fire. Go, my minions, bring me his body to burn!" the demon ordered.

The red-skinned orcs focused on Virgil, giving the druid manic grins before charging at the veterinarian. That was what the party was waiting for. From the orcs' flank, Christopher and Splinter emerged, the rat riding atop the pig like they were Timon and Pumbaa. The terror boar charged, then headbutted the left orc in her leg, shattering her kneecap into pieces. Splinter used the momentum from the impact to fly off Christopher and attacked the other orc, spinning right into her face.

Still hiding in cover, Gwen fired an arrow using a sturdy dark imp horn at the totem. To her surprise, two of the flame tentacles reactively reached out and caught the arrow, quickly incinerating the projectile with their heat. The eye turned to look at the woman in its periphery. The pupil widened as it caught sight of the Hunter Druid. "Come here, elf," Zinthos said as the demon locked eyes with her.

Gwen felt some supernatural pull at her psyche. She tried to resist, but couldn't. She then silently berated herself. Virgil had warned her that the demon had some sort of mind control powers and *not* to look it in the eye, which was exactly what she did. Her body then let go of her bow and began walking out of the thick forest cover she had been using. The demonic totem cooed in anticipation of its next meal as Gwen continued to walk toward it, its tentacles writhing in anticipation. "Good, come now, elf, and become part of my consuming fire."

Gwen looked in fear at the flamebound creature as it lured her in like a spider in its web. She knew that one of these totems had caught Virgil in the same type of trap. Fortunately, she had been able to break line of sight to save the dark elf.

Virgil hadn't forgotten about that either, and he was ready to return the favor. The Healer Druid quickly ran past the two orcs fighting his bestial allies to get near Gwen. Once he was close enough to her, he cast Purifying Aura. Immediately, a clear dome of Nature Magic erupted from and surrounded Virgil, encompassing all within eleven feet based off of his current Restoration Magic level. Gwen was within that range, and the spell freed her from the mind-altering effect of the totem, returning her body's control back to her.

The one-eyed totem stared in shock at the Healer Druid's new spell. "No!" it screamed. "You will pay for your insolence!" it said, shooting out its tentacles at Virgil. Though fast, the dark elf was not ready for the sudden attack, as the fiery appendages appeared to stretch out at him with violent intentions.

Luckily, Baphomet was ready. As soon as Baphomet saw the totem attempt to attack its master, the beastking jumped out of the bag it was peeking out of and transformed into giant form, placing itself between the totem and its master. The tentacles wrapped themselves around Baphomet's right forearm. There was a sizzling sound, and the smell of burnt flesh hit the elves' nostrils.

Baphomet's sudden appearance only seemed to enrage the totem more. "Grr, traitor! Vozremath gave you his power, and this is how you repay him?! You will burn!" Zinthos said, and wrapped its tentacles around the beastking's forearm tighter, causing a stream of smoke to come from the wound. The beast somehow gave the totem a grin. Though it was hurting, it was now in control. It had saved its master, and now, it would put an end to the threat.

Baphomet let out a savage roar and swiped its free claw downward at the Zinthos totem. Its massive paw easily cut into the totem and quickly shattered it into shredded wood chunks, dispelling the flames surrounding it. Without the totem's influence, the orcs weakened, and the boar-rat team were able to overcome them in seconds. Virgil immediately began casting Restore on Baphomet. Though a tough SOB, it had managed to get some serious burns from the demonic totem.

"You okay, buddy?" he asked.

The large beastking nodded, then licked Virgil's face like a large dog.

"Thank you both," Gwen said. "I'm sorry. I was stupid for not being more cautious," she apologized.

"Mistakes happen," Virgil said. "In the end, we're all okay. Also, now you really know how deadly those totems can be."

She nodded in agreement and smiled at Virgil, then went to go use Harvest on the dead orcs.

Virgil used a couple healing poultices on Baphomet's burn wounds. While Restore was amazing, the salves would help with the healing process and hopefully help hair to regrow in the burn spots. As he applied the poultices, he wondered how to deal with the fire more effectively, as they were likely going to encounter more of it. His Phoenix Fire spell was useful, but it still couldn't be used frequently, despite the spell's halved cooldown time.

He thought about his potion and promptly smacked himself in the forehead. He had forgotten about the Gelatin of the Flame Eater! The potion would give whoever ingested it a permanent new skill that allowed them to literally gain health from eating fire. It was dumb that he hadn't used it yet. He just needed to decide who would get it. Looking up at his loyal and massive animal companion, it was obvious who should have it.

The veterinarian pulled out the gelatin and fed it to Baphomet. The beastking gulped down the concoction readily, like a dog scarfing down some Jell-O it had stolen from a kid's high chair. Once Baphomet was done, it licked its lips in satisfaction and then its eyes glowed red for just a moment. Understanding seemed to cross the beastking's face, then it looked down at Virgil. The two just stared at each other for a few seconds before the large beast licked Virgil's face in thanks.

Virgil promptly wiped the large amount of saliva from his face, then was greeted by a notification.

Congratulations! You have given your animal companion, Baphomet the beastking, a new skill!
Skill Learned: Flame Dragon's Hunger Level 1
Effect: Can consume any source of fire and convert it into Health Points at a rate of n/second, where n is the skill's level.

Virgil smiled upon reading the new skill. It worked differently than his Phoenix Fire spell. His spell converted a flame into a source of warm healing and provided more healing based on the level of heat the flame provided. This skill seemed to be more time-related, restoring the same amount of health no matter how hot the flames were, but could be used continuously as long as there was a source of flame feeding it.

Gwen then came back and gave Virgil a glass dagger, and a greatsword to store inside Grief from the orc bodies. After they made sure that all of the party was fine, they crossed the border into the Scorched Lands.

Just crossing over into the Scorched Lands, the party felt an increase by at least ten degrees Fahrenheit. The sun's rays seemed to beat down brighter as well, without the thicker forest cover. Virgil pulled his hood on tight, making sure to cover his sensitive eyes. This was also one of the few times Virgil was grateful to be not wearing a shirt. Having a case of sweaty back sucked when it stuck to your shirt.

Grief felt the heat too. "Shite, lad! This place be hotter than me legs when I chaffed them too hard!"

Off in the distance was the Brandios volcano. Virgil remembered that the Firebrands worshipped the volcano and made camp at its base. He figured that if Zinthos was working with the orcs and Ramsay was working with Zinthos, the volcano was where they needed to be. After discussing his logic with Gwen, they agreed and the party began their way toward Brandios. Gwen took the lead, as she was not as impacted by sunlight and could track.

As they went on, Virgil decided to see if he could possibly get any more information out of Grief. *"Hey, Grief, now that we've seen this Zinthos twice, do you have any better idea of what type of demon it is and its weaknesses?"* he asked through their soulbound link.

"Hmm... well, lad, there be plenty of demons that like fire... Nay, I still can't tell what kind of demon that one be. I'll need to actually see its real body. Whatever it be though, I can tell ye that it be tough. Bein' a demon general ain't no small thing, and havin' the ability to spread its awareness out through them totems shows that it be one strong bastard," the skull explained. *"There be somethin' though that seemed important."*

"What?" Virgil asked.

"That shaman we fought with the firebrands the first time... He said somethin' bout the blasted demon needin' specific sacrifices. I know it's important, and it's on the tip of me tongue as to why. I'll have to think 'bout it. Fer now, we should consider this ugly one-eyed bastard as a Nawful-Fiery Horror hybrid until otherwise disputed."

Virgil agreed and continued on with the party. Baphomet's Alpha Predator Trait did cause them to fight a couple of large scorpions, but also saved them from fighting a pack of desert jackals the size of Great Danes. They were able to collect some scorpion meat and venom from the large arachnids, so it wasn't a complete loss.

For an hour, they trekked across the heat of the desert. Baphomet, being both the largest and hairiest of the group, was having particular trouble with the heat. Christopher would've had more trouble, but the terror boar made sure to walk in the shadow of the large creature to keep cool. Virgil frequently poured water from his Everfull Canteen on the beastking, making sure to pour it over its exposed forearms. Cooling forearms was a quick way to cool off the body. Some animals were even able to grasp that concept on their own. Virgil remembered seeing a Capuchin Monkey at a zoo turn on a water spigot and wipe cold water on its forearms on hot summer days.

Despite Virgil's efforts, the beastking was still not having the best of times trudging through the heat. So, Virgil decided to feed Baphomet one of the Potions of Icy Essence. It was cold to the touch as he poured it down Baphomet's throat. Like Virgil's Purifying Aura, a field of magic energy erupted from the beast-king's body. Unlike the spell, though, this field contained occasional blue sparkles in it.

The temperature inside the potion's AOE dropped by ten to fifteen degrees Fahrenheit, and became much more comfortable. Baphomet audibly groaned in relief, as did the rest of the party. Knowing something conceptually and experiencing it were two completely different things. Virgil knew that the potion would be handy from a logical standpoint. It was hot in the Scorched Lands, so something to help cool off would be helpful. But now, here, actually in this oven-like landscape, Virgil *really* knew how valuable his Potions of Icy Essence were!

After a few more minutes of much comfortable travel, they came across a small little oasis. It was a pond nestled in a small crater and surrounded by a ring of thick grass with tropical trees. There was a small contingent of five firebrand orcs with one ogre. The red-skinned tribe members were not very stealthy, as they were all chanting, "Burn," every few seconds. All five orcs wielded torches and began lighting the grass and trees on fire. The crazed orcs were literally burning away some of the only viable vegetation they had in their barren landscape.

Despite the incredulity of what they were doing, Virgil wasn't going to stop them. He and the party were going to use their distraction to surround and ambush the firebrands who were downhill from them. The party then spread out.

Gwen nocked one of the automaton archer ballista bolts on her bowstring and positioned herself beside her trusty terror boar. She chuckled in amusement at the ridiculousness of her being able to actually arm the massive projectile. Honestly, she reminded herself of a damn anime character being able to fire massive weapons as if physics and gravity didn't exist. But hey, this new world was a magic one, and her Utility Improviser

Trait did allow her to use any sort of arrow; she would take what she could get!

Their plan was solid. The ogre was no doubt their greatest threat. Its back was turned away from the surroundings, so Baphomet would charge down and try to sneak attack the ogre while it was unaware, hopefully causing the behemoth brute to quickly get eliminated by her large arrow and make the remainder of the fight easier.

That was what Gwen planned to do until she saw something in the corner of her vision. Though Virgil had Darkvision, since Gwen was a high elf, she had a different Trait called Sharp Vision. It allowed her to see small details up to two-hundred-fifty feet away in adequate light and with no impeding obstacles. It was only that particular Trait that let her see something unexpected. There, on the other side of the pond opposite from the ogre, were two of the firebrand orcs.

One of them quickly swiped down at the ground with his free hand and picked up a small creature. It was trying to fight tooth-and-nail against the orc who caught it by the scruff, but the other one swung hard with its club. The creature's body curled up defensively in response, not wanting to get hit more. Gwen's eyes widened as she recognized what exactly the creature was. It was a warg, a small one, maybe about as tall as a gnome, but a warg nonetheless.

The two orcs gave malicious smiles at the cowering warg. The one holding it gave his torch to his companion and pulled out one of their tribal black glass daggers.

"Shit," Gwen muttered. Her heart beat furiously as she was given a choice: let the warg die and guarantee the elimination of the firebrands with their ogre tank being killed, or save the warg from immediate death and have a more deadly fight on their hands. Gwen had a split second to decide, but it felt longer in her head. Though both options could have good arguments, in her heart she knew what she *had to do,* deep down. She turned her large arrow on the orcs, and fired.

With power she didn't know she had, the Hunter Druid's

body and weapon flashed white. That energy that caused the flash, her Predator Magic, traveled into the large projectile as it left the bow. It soared at profound speed, going faster than one person could reasonably fire. The large ballista bolt quickly penetrated the chest of the orc holding the small warg, obliterating his upper body. The orc's eyes went cloudy, and he let go of the warg as he collapsed, his body severed into two pieces.

That wasn't all the arrow did, no sir. It continued its path, soaring straight through the heart of the other nearby orc, blowing a hole clean through his chest. The orc just stood there dumbfounded, until his eyes rolled back in his head and he collapsed forward, dead. The arrow still wasn't done. Like the projectile was alive, it bounced off a palm tree that was behind the orc, and launched itself at the ogre across the pond! The large brute barely had time to comprehend what he was seeing before the bolt struck him straight in his open mouth, killing him in one shot!

Gwen stared in shock. "How did I do that?" she asked herself. She not only saved the warg, but killed both orcs and the ogre in one shot? She could somehow curve the bullet like James McAvoy in 'Wanted'! A flashing notification icon appeared in the corner of her vision, but she couldn't look at it. Both her shot and the flash of light it caused alerted the remaining orcs to her position.

The three orcs charged in rage at the one who attacked their comrade. One threw a handaxe. Gwen narrowly dodged the projectile, but it still managed to graze her right cheek. She drew an iron arrow and fired it at the leftmost orc's feet. It struck true and pinned the firebrand to the ground. The one on the right was hit in the face by a Nature Bolt, causing it to stumble. Gwen stole a glance and saw Virgil riding atop Baphomet, charging towards them and having his staff lowered at the orcs.

The center firebrand wielded a large greatsword made out of volcanic glass. The weapon was clearly very sharp and deadly. Christopher charged at the orc threatening his master. He lowered his head, but was struck down by a large downward swing of the greatsword. Blood shot out and the boar squealed in pain as it dropped to the ground. The orc lifted his sword to give Christopher the coup de grace, but he never did finish his attack.

A large spear made of stone erupted from the sand. It launched from behind the injured boar and struck at the exposed abdomen of the orc, impaling him straight through the gut. The orc let out a violent cough of blood, then let go of his sword as his body went limp, dead on the spot. Gwen looked down at the heavily injured boar, then at the remaining two orcs. Both had recovered from their injuries, and the one was able to remove the arrow embedded in his foot. Virgil was still too far away to do too much in regards to offense.

In that split moment, Gwen knew what she needed to do. Despite being a ranged fighter, she charged forward. *"Christopher's hurt bad. Heal him! I'll deal with the orcs!"* she pleaded through Party Chat as she sprinted. She ran up the stone spear she conjured and jumped. In the air, she drew one of her dark imp horn arrows and took aim at the right orc. It struck the orc deep in the right shoulder, causing him to drop the dagger in that hand. Landing in between the two firebrands, she swept her bow downward and tripped the other orc.

In his prone position, the orc was exposed. Gwen took advantage of that, pulling out three iron arrows at once and activating her Multi-Shot subskill. The three arrows fired all at once at the orc. He was able to deflect one with his shortsword, but the other two hit their mark, striking him in the neck and heart. She turned to face the other orc, but she was too late.

The remaining firebrand swiped at her and cut into her right arm with his axe. He then kicked her in the chest, knocking her on her back, stunning her, and forcing all the air from her lungs. It stood over and looked down on her with malicious glee as it ripped out the arrow she had embedded in his shoulder. Despite the pain, the orc didn't lose his manic grin and quickly pulled out the arrow, causing a fount of blood to flow out of the wound.

"You will pay for that, she-elf. Once I'm done with you, our master will make all that you love *burn!*" the orc shouted as he grabbed his axe with both hands and lifted it up in the air. Before he could bring his weapon down, there was an audible 'Thwack!' sound and the orc's vision went distant. He had a confused look on his face as he fell on his face right beside Gwen.

Gwen was able to overcome her stun at that moment and quickly rolled away and stood up, pointing a nocked arrow at the orc. Gwen's tension lessened slightly as she saw Splinter on top of the back of the orc's head, the stego rat's horn lodged in the back of the firebrand's skull. Splinter pulled back and there was a wet 'schlunk' noise as the rat's horn removed a section of skull and chunk of brain tissue. Gwen was both thankful for the rat's help and grossed out at the gory remains skewered on her horn like a kabob.

Gwen's musings were interrupted when the flames burning the plants in the oasis turned a supernatural white. All of the flames then left the plants and coalesced together in the air, looking like a living torrent of flame. She then saw the flame move over and past her. She followed it with her vision and saw the flames strike Christopher. Virgil was right by the boar and directing the magic flames, using his Phoenix Fire spell.

Christopher's grievous head wound immediately healed and the boar's eyes widened with newfound vitality. Christopher sprang up in the air, back at one-hundred percent. He saw Gwen and ran over and nuzzled his head against her leg. She knelt down. "Thank you for protecting me, love. Who's my brave piggy? You are," she said, praising the boar as she was scratching behind his right ear, to which he grunted appreciatively.

"What happened, Gwen?" Virgil asked. "We were supposed to let Baphomet ambush the ogre. How did you do that crazy shot? I mean, I'm not upset by it. I just wish you would've told me you could do that."

Gwen chuckled slightly. "I didn't even know I could do that.

Honestly, I'm not sure what that was. Here, let me check my pending notifications. They may tell me something." She opened them, and they certainly did!

Congratulations, Druid of Yggdrasil!
You have discovered your Attunement! – Impossible Shot
In a time of serious decision with dire consequences, you acted and made a choice based on your true nature. You chose to save the life of an innocent over a better chance at defeating your enemies, putting yourself at personal risk.
Effect: Infuse your will into an arrow you are about to shoot, specifically, your will to deal death to your enemies. Doing so will not only instill your intentions, but Yggdrasil's magic as well. You may target up to 3 opponents within your vision, and the arrow will seek out all of them with the intention to bring them a swift death.
Time to recharge Attunement: 12 hours

Subskill Gained! Pinning Shot Level 1
Your focused shot has awakened a new Archery subskill. Fire an arrow at the foot of an opponent. Depending on the grade of the arrow, dexterity of opponent, and armor of opponent, you will have varying degrees of success. If the shot does succeed, you will pin your opponent in place for 1 second/10 levels of your Archery skill.

Archery has reached Level 56!

Your discovery of your Attunement and battle prowess despite fighting at close-range, which is not ideal for archers, has allowed you to gain +20 to your Stamina Pool.

Gwen excitedly told Virgil about her attunement. He was both happy and impressed with the ability and its recharge time. He was a little sore that his Veterinarian's Pact attunement could be used only once every ten levels, but then looked at the hulking behemoth of a beast beside him that the attunement had tamed and thought it wasn't actually that bad.

Their celebration was cut short by Grief. "Er hem, this be nice and all, but ye might want to know that we're not alone," he said, without any panic in his voice. Despite that, both elves quickly looked behind Gwen. There, standing not ten feet away from them, were a pair of small wargs. They both looked like tiny, bipedal fennec foxes with brown fur, dark eyes, and large pointed ears.

One was slightly larger with more wild hair and appeared to be male. The other was more well-groomed with one of her ears pierced with a couple of rings. She appeared to be female. "My thanks to you elves for saving me and my wife from those firebrands. Without your aid, we would have surely perished. Please, tell us your names and what brings you to the Scorched Lands?" the male asked with a squeaky voice.

Virgil used Analyze.

Name: Zemeepo
Level: 10
Race: Beastkin **Type:** Warg
Health: 90/100 **Manna:** 10/10 **Stamina:** 85/100
Resistances: Heat 50%, Poisons 25%.
Debuffs: None.
Profession: Alchemist.

Zemeepo is a smaller desert fox warg. Though not outwardly tough, he is both resilient and crafty in order to survive in the harsh environment of the Scorched Lands. One particular strength is his affinity for poisons, which have allowed him to defeat foes much stronger than he.

So the warg was an alchemist? Virgil could work with that! "I'm Virgil and this is Gwen," he said. "We are druid champions of Yggdrasil, and have come to defeat the demon general hiding in these lands."

Both the wargs gave the elves an awestruck look at Virgil's explanation. "W... wow. This is... unexpected," the warg said, clearly surprised that the fabled druids had been resummoned and right in front of him. He then shook himself from his daze and addressed them. "Well druids, I am Zemeepo. This is my wife, Vulpa."

"Thank you for your heroics, druids," she said, giving them a slight curtsy. "Without your efforts, we would have lost our home and our lives." The party then looked at the small oasis behind the wargs. Thanks to Virgil's Phoenix Fire spell, some of the plant life was spared, but not all of it. About half of the tall grass and trees were burnt to a crisp. One tree even collapsed into a pile of ash before their very eyes! There was still a good quarter of the plant life that had been completely spared the fires, but it would take time for the oasis to return to the state it was in before.

"Yeah... sorry for not saving more of it," Virgil said.

Zemeepo waved off the apology, not bothered at all. "It is no trouble, Virgil. Even though our outer oasis is damaged, our home is still completely intact."

"Home? You mean the small section of unburnt grass?" he asked.

Both the wargs chuckled. "Ooh, no, that's not our home. It just covers the entrance. Come, we will show you," Zemeepo said. The warg took a step, then looked back uncomfortably. "Uhh, your big pet will have to wait outside. It will be a tight enough fit for you elves."

"Keep guard, buddy," Virgil said to the beastking, who nodded and went off to the pool of freshwater. The party followed the small beastkin duo into the tall grass. Just as Zemeepo had said, there was a small round door in the side of the sandy crater covered by a cluster of tall grass. It was very reminiscent of a desert version of Hobbiton, and sure enough, the door opened to reveal a small, hobbit-sized home just the right size for the small couple. Gwen and Virgil ducked to get in and had to be careful not to hit their heads on the ceiling.

They were led to a large stone living room carved out of the black volcanic rock they had seen earlier. Since no furniture was appropriately sized for the elves, they sat on the ground and leaned their backs against the wall. It was noticeably much cooler inside the underground abode, literally double digits in Fahrenheit less than before!

The room was lit by spaced-out orbs of magic light and had what looked like a fireplace. Unlike a wood-burning fire though, there were a cluster of red heat stones like what Maldrakus had. They gave off a warm glow and did warm the room, but not as effectively as that of a roaring fire. Zemeepo and Vulpa went off to their kitchen and quickly returned with a tray of tea and small 'sandwiches' which were actually two thin dry crackers with a large dried grasshopper in the middle.

Gwen gave a look that said "I ain't eating that," but quickly covered it up and took the tea, not wanting to appear rude or ungrateful. Virgil just shrugged and took one of the sandwiches. When he had worked with large snakes in Southeast Asia, he had been blessed to experience the wonderful and strange assortments of food from that part of Earth. There were plenty of unique options, including skewered and fried bugs on kabobs. It might seem gross at first, but fried grasshopper was good stuff, and it provided a nice source of protein!

Virgil crunched into the sandwich and found that it was even better than on Earth. As both Zemeepo and Vulpa pulled out their pipes and busied themselves with lighting them, Splinter and Christopher looked at the dark elf like begging dogs, eagerly wanting any crumbs from his food. Realizing the wargs were still distracted, Virgil deftly grabbed another sandwich from the tray and gave each section of it to the animals below. Just like on Earth, food was love for animals.

"Ahh," the warg couple said in unison during their first exhalation.

The party used the time to just relax, sitting there in the nice cool room, enjoying the reprieve from the oppressive sun. Virgil felt bad about leaving Baphomet out there, but didn't want to have the animal go back to its small form. It took most of its manna to change forms, and Virgil didn't want to risk not having Baphomet available for a fight if they needed it. After ten minutes of relaxing and enjoying their tea and biscuits, Virgil was ready to go. "Thank you so much for your hospitality, but we do need to be heading out now," he said.

"Wait," Zemeepo said, with a hand out. "Were you serious when you said you were going to stop the firebrands?"

"Yes," Virgil replied.

"Well then, we will aid you."

"That's great but... how?" Virgil asked, a little perplexed at how exactly the small wargs could contribute. Just minutes ago, they were about to be killed by the orcs.

The couple chuckled, seeming to understand Virgil's confusion. "I admit we're not too fierce when it comes to direct fighting. We have survived through more subtle means. I myself am a professed Alchemist, while Vulpa is an Herbalist. Together, we have crafted some very deadly ways to overtake the orcs. What you saw out there was just us getting caught by surprise. If we knew the firebrands were coming, they wouldn't have stood a chance," Zemeepo said with clear confidence.

"Alright, I'll bite, what deadly ways?" Gwen asked.

Zemeepo gave her a sharp-toothed grin. "How else would an Alchemist and Herbalist deal with foes? Poisons."

CHAPTER TWENTY-THREE

Might of the Small

Vulpa and Zemeepo led the party down a few more corridors in their subterranean home. While there were some rooms with wooden elements, Vulpa explained that most of their home was made using the lava channels as they cooled. It made Virgil wonder how far the volcano's influence could spread if it once had channels out this far, miles from its base. Eventually, they came to a dark hallway.

Vulpa turned back to the group and put a finger to her lips in a shushing gesture. "Shh, we're coming up to our garden. It's best that you stay quiet," she whispered.

"Why?" Virgil asked, whispering as well and not liking the sound of this.

"Because it is sensitive to newcomers," she replied, then went off to light a few nearby torches to illuminate the hallway. Gwen and Virgil looked at each other, each showing obvious concern.

"*I think it goes without sayin', lad, but this be a bit... creepy,*" Grief sent telepathically.

"*You're telling me,*" Virgil replied. Nevertheless, they followed the wargs as his Danger Sense was not warning him of any threat. They eventually came upon a large metal door.

"This is our secret garden," Zemeepo whispered. "Vulpa and I have been able to grow special herbs here and use them to make rare poisons. My wife is a great Herbalist and because of that... well, it's better if you just see. Now please, no loud noises or sudden movements," he said, then opened the door.

There was a strong light source that came from the room. Virgil squinted his eyes and recoiled as it felt like sunlight. As their vision adjusted, the druids' blood ran cold. It was a great call for the wargs to have warned them ahead of time because he would have freaked out and possibly shit his pants upon gazing at what was in the center of this artificial garden.

In the center of the large room, in a large pot, was a massive plant, surrounded by splatters of blood, bone, and chunks of red orc flesh. It was no mere shrub or tree, mind you. No, it was a carnivorous Venus fly-trap type plant. Oh, and it was moving! The plant had a massive mouth and seemed to somehow register the elves' presence despite it having no eyes! The large plant also had two squealing vines that seemed to serve as its limbs. It was like some horrible plant abomination from The Little Shop of Horrors!

"*Good grief!*" Grief exclaimed through their soulbound link. "*I think I may have shite myself, and I don't even have an arse to shite out of!*"

Virgil had to agree, the thing was unsettling! "Zemeepo, what... the fuck... is that?" Virgil asked in forced restraint. The towering plant seemed to notice Virgil and let out a subtle roar at the dark elf. Globules of acid dripped out of its mouth, spilling onto the stone ground and burning it with a sizzle.

Vulpa answered for her husband. "Do not be afraid, druids. This is Joaquim."

"Joaquim?" Virgil asked incredulously.

"Indeed," she replied matter-of-factly. "For years, Zemeepo and I have been working to grow a plant that specializes in killing Firebrands."

"That is correct," her husband continued. "Despite the crazed nature of the tribe, they were never too difficult to deal with. They never actively sought the people who lived in the Scorched Lands. They were too busy warring with themselves. That's changed over the past year, however," he said with his tone turning much more ominous.

"Apparently, they found a strong leader to unite them and focus their violence no longer on each other. Since then, all who are not of their tribe have been at risk. We've... both lost friends to the firebrands."

"I'm sorry," Virgil said.

"Thank you, sir druid," Zemeepo said and continued. "We knew that the only way to live truly free and to liberate the Scorched Lands was to get rid of the firebrands. With them gone, our land can thrive again. That's where Joaquim comes in," the warg said, gesturing proudly at the monstrous plant. To Virgil's surprise, it leaned its head down and nuzzled against Zemeepo like a dog with its master.

"Could you elaborate, please?" Gwen asked.

"Oh, of course," Zemeepo said. "Vulpa and I devised a plan to utilize her herbology and my alchemy to overcome the Firebrands. My wife was able to collect one of the more deadly carnivorous plants in the area. She has fed it specialized supplements, while I saturated its soil with unique alchemical components. Eventually, we bred the plant with other carnivorous species while still enhancing them with both special herbs and potions. That process was continued for a few generations, until we came across our masterpiece, Joaquim."

Vulpa continued on for her husband. "He is the only one of his generation to survive, and is the great-grandchild of the first plant I collected. With Zemeepo's help, the plant has gained a mild sentience. Over time, we fed it only dead firebrands. Joaquim is highly adaptable and has gained a unique, er hem, 'taste' for the tribe. We focused our experimentation to specialize a plant into killing the orcs and ogres, but we didn't realize how successful we would be."

"Indeed," Zemeepo added. "I focused on enhancing the degrading aspect of the fluid secreted from the plants' mouths. Through our work, Joaquim now secretes a deadly poison that specializes in degrading flesh. Since we focused on feeding him firebrand corpses we would find, the poison is even more deadly to them."

"So, does that mean you've weaponized the poison for us to use? That would be great! Thank you," Virgil said.

The alchemist gave him a toothy grin. "We have something even better! To my surprise, Joaquim somehow produced a seed."

"Wait, I'm not a plant expert, but don't you need a plant of different genders to reproduce?" Virgil asked, remembering that there were indeed male and female plants from his undergraduate plant biology class. It was one of those difficult classes where the professor didn't round up. Man, those classes could suck! He barely made it out of the class with a B.

Vulpa answered his question, bringing the dark elf out of memory lane. "Typically so, but it seems our... radical experimentation has altered Joaquim's nature so much that he can reproduce on his own." The monstrous plant gave a triumphant screech, as if it was proud of that fact.

"Okay, so you've made a plant that specializes in killing firebrands. It seems like it will take time for the seeds to grow and take effect, time which we don't have," Virgil said.

"That is where you are wrong," Vulpa said. She then reached under a nearby table and pulled out a large seed the size of a softball. It was bright red, round, and had small white dots speckled along the outside. "This is Joaquim's seed. While it technically is a seed, it is more appropriate to call it a fruit, as it actually contains many of his seeds. We've worked to make Joaquim fire-resistant, deadly to firebrands, highly adaptable, and fast-growing. No doubt his progeny will be similar."

Zemeepo then rolled a barrel over by his wife. It was light brown and had a red X painted on it. Virgil quickly realized the dark red 'paint' was actually blood. There was also a sharp, pungent odor to it. "This is a rare barrel of firebrand liquor called Grub. They often drink it before battles or during celebrations. I took a few samples for analysis and discovered that it is actually a dangerous but effective potion. If ingested, it causes the person to go into a rage-like state and take only half damage for twelve hours, but at a cost. The imbiber's intelligence is permanently lowered, and they grow more addicted to both the alcohol and to violence. My theory is that the creation of this brew likely caused the tribe to devolve into their war-like nature. Before they caught me, I overheard the firebrands talking about some ceremony that was going to be had tonight in their city. We ask that you take the barrel, add Joaquim's seed to it, and make sure it reaches the firebrands before their celebration tonight. That will take care of most of the brutes, and you can use your powers to take out whoever's left." Zemeepo said plainly.

A prompt appeared.

Quest Unlocked!
A Tainted Toast!

Zemeepo, the warg alchemist, and his herbalist wife Vulpa, have asked for your assistance. They have used their professions to devise a devious plan to eliminate a large majority of the firebrands threatening not only the Scorched Lands, but the entire continent of Kygora. They have worked to create a plant that specializes in killing those orcs and ogres of the firebrand clan. That plant's seeds are particularly poisonous. They ask that you take the barrel of Grub, taint it with the plant's seeds, and make sure that the firebrands obtain it before their celebration without realizing that you had it. No doubt that a rare barrel of their favorite scarce alcohol will make it to the mouths of many of the tribe tonight.

Reward:

Experience dependent on the number of firebrands killed.
Extinction of the Firebrands.

Acquiring or Increasing the Herbology skill.
Acquiring or Increasing the Alchemy skill.
Do you accept?
Yes or No

Virgil and Gwen blinked as they read the prompt. This plan was devious indeed. Both elves felt trepidation at the request, though, as this seemed like genocide... After a few moments, they realized that the tribe had to be eliminated for the safety of all. They were clearly working with demonic forces and that made them a threat to the entire world. Plus, the poisonous seeds would be the best bet to eliminate much of the enemy with the lowest risk.

Both druids looked at each and gave slight nods, the same thoughts going through their minds, then accepted the quest. "We'll do it," Virgil said.

"Excellent," Zemeepo said happily. "I must warn you though, *do not* drink it. I haven't been able to make an antidote to it yet, and am not sure if I can. Anyway, the lava tunnels lead straight under their fortress. Once we get the barrel ready, I'll take you there."

Joaquim drooled more acidic saliva as the eyeless plant seemed to stare hungrily at the party. None of them took another step forward into the room. While they trusted the wargs, none of them trusted the plant monster. Joaquim made Virgil's Danger Sense continually keep active, as the dark elf knew on a subconscious level that the plant was a threat.

The wargs opened the barrel and dropped the large seed unceremoniously into the alcohol with a wet 'thunk.' Some of the strong, strange-smelling liquor spilled over onto the ground, displaced by the seed. Both wargs resealed the barrel and carted it over to the party. "We have a large wheelbarrow if you'd like to use it to carry the barrel," Zemeepo said.

"That won't be necessary," Virgil said, storing the barrel inside of Grief. Both wargs stared in amazement at the skull and looked like they wanted to know more, but Virgil waved them off. He gave a simple explanation. "The skull works like an enhanced bag of holding. The details are complicated, and I'd rather not get into it. We need to get going."

"Very well," Zemeepo said, then gave his wife a kiss on the cheek before turning back to the party. "I will say it is perplexing to see such an enchanted skull though, especially a dwarven one. Dwarves are not typically very magical or have enough headspace to possess enough room for even a brain! Haha!" He chuckled.

"Ye better watch yer little sharp-toothed mouth, ye furry idgit, or else I'll make ye very familiar with me 'headspace' by crackin' yer skull open with me forehead!" Grief threatened out loud.

Zemeepo's eyes widened and he took a step back in shock. "It... talks?" he asked, unsure, looking at Virgil.

The dark elf sighed. "As I said, it's complicated. Probably best not to insult dwarves from now on, eh?"

The alchemist quickly comprehended. "Oh, certainly. I'm sorry, um, sir dwarf," he apologized to the skull, clearly uncomfortable about talking with a sentient skull.

To his credit, Grief seemed to let it roll off his 'shoulders.' "Ah, ye be fine, lad. Just don't start shite, and there won't be shite."

"Oh, of course, um, now then, we have only one problem. What will you do with your large beast? It obviously won't be able to fit in the lava tunnels," Zemeepo said, clearly wanting to get past that uncomfortable interaction. He was like a teenager that had been caught gossiping about a classmate by their parent. Though he did seem sorry, Virgil wondered if the alchemist truly would have been if he hadn't been caught. Hopefully, that would help prevent bad mouthing others in the future like that from the warg.

"That shouldn't be a problem," Virgil answered. "Just get me back to it, and I'll be able to handle that issue." The warg did just that and brought Virgil back out into the partially burnt oasis. Quickly, Virgil had Baphomet come back to them and change to its smaller form. By that time, Zemeepo had learned to just take these strange wonders in stride, as the Healer Druid appeared to have plenty of them.

The small warg led the party back into their home and to a thick, round, wooden door near the lab. When the warg opened it, it revealed another pathway. Instead of smooth chiseled out stone, however, there was an uneven, dark, rocky tunnel made out of cooled lava. It was about ten feet high. The warg jumped up, beckoning the party to follow.

Gwen was about to light a torch, but Zemeepo stuck a furry hand out. "Ah, I wouldn't do that," he said with obvious concern on his face.

"Why not?" Gwen asked.

"The tunnels that crisscross under the Scorched Lands can be just as dangerous as above ground, but for different reasons. Whereas the firebrands are up top, there are some nocturnal predators down here, and strong sources of light can… attract them. While most will probably not dare to attack, the spiders… can be rather unfriendly…" He trailed off uncomfortably.

Virgil had actually seen the Earth equivalent back in Hawaii. In the cooled lava tunnels there, spiders had evolved to be pale and sightless in order to best adapt to their new environment. Despite the small arachnids not being able to see, they thrived in their new environment as sight was no longer necessary.

While he could appreciate spiders, the thought of giant ones wanting to kill and eat him made his skin crawl. Because of that, he even more actively used his Detect Hostile Intent subskill to make sure the party was safe.

Their progress was slow, as they made sure to not make too much noise on the uneven terrain. Virgil gave Gwen a Darkvision potion, so she would not slow them down. Fortunately, after an hour of travel, none of the infamous spiders were found. A footlong centipede traveled across their path once, from one small crack in the tunnel to another, which made Virgil's heart skip a beat. He almost released a girly squeal at that... Almost. That didn't mean Gwen didn't tease him through Party Chat. *"Heart of a lion you have there,"* she sent.

"And ye sounded like one too! Haha!" Grief added.

"Shut up," Virgil sent back, then grunted in embarrassment as he pressed on. He took the lead, hiding his blushing cheeks.

After another half an hour, the temperature notably changed from cool and damp to humid. As they continued, the heat began to increase. Eventually, even the darkness of the tunnel brightened, as the rocky tube they were in opened into a large cavern filled with multiple criss crossing streams of lava as well as multiple large waterfalls of the molten rock.

Virgil recoiled visibly from the sudden source of light and heat. When his eyes adjusted, he noticed the tunnel had opened up and turned into a bridge over a lava stream one-hundred-plus feet below them.

"We are right by the firebrands' fortress city," Zemeepo said, seeming unbothered by all the liquid death around them. "Continue on this path, and you'll find a ladder. The ladder will lead you up to... Well, you'll find out. Anyway, be careful as you enter the area this is connected to. There may be firebrands using it."

Gwen was tired of the subtleties. "Spit it out, where does the ladder lead us to?"

Zemeepo winced before answering. "Their latrines."

"Are you kidding me? You're saying we're going to crawl up a firebrand toilet. What does that make this place then, their sewers?"

"Essentially," the warg answered.

Virgil shook his head. How did he always end up traveling through sewers? "How did you find this place?"

"Simple, it was by accident. When Vulpa and I were making our home, we came across the tunnel's entrance. I followed it all the way to where you are going. Believe me, I was as shocked as anyone to discover that the orcs use a large hole in the ground connected to one of the volcano's channels as a latrine. You'd

think the backsplash from lava might make them reconsider..."
Zemeepo refocused. "Anyway, this particular latrine is near the
edge of their city. Make sure they get the barrel and that no one
sees you."

"Why can't we just leave the barrel right by the latrines?"
Virgil asked.

"Too suspicious," Zemeepo answered. "The firebrands are
definitely not the sharpest tools in the shed, but they may not
trust that a barrel just suddenly appeared. Also, they can be
greedy. A random grunt may just as likely keep it all for themselves if no one else is around. You need to make sure that
multiple firebrands see it, particularly one of their shamans.
They have staffs and headdress—"

"I know what a shaman looks like," Virgil said, bitterly
remembering the college's headmaster. "Why though?"

"They are their leaders. If one of them spots the barrel,
they will certainly make sure that it is distributed to others, and
their higher-ups."

"Thank you, Zemeepo," Virgil said, putting a hand on the
shoulder of the small warg. "Be safe, and if I get drenched in
orc piss, I expect a barrel of unpoisoned alcohol."

"I may not be able to get you a large amount, but I brew in
my spare time. I'll see what I can do for you. Good luck,
druids. Oh, that reminds me," he said, then reached inside a
pocket and pulled out two small leaves that were multichro-
matic like a rainbow, but looked like a small portion of cilantro.
There was a big rivalry he saw on the internet once about
cilantro. Who knew that a plant could cause so much division?
"These are called Bastard's Lucky Leaves. They will increase
your chances of success in your endeavors for twenty-four
hours. Luck is not a measurable thing in our world, but those
who ingest these leaves remark that they seem to have incredible luck. I myself even met Vulpa after I had one," he said
with a toothy grin.

Both elves took the leaves gratefully and ate them on the
spot, forcing their faces to stay neutral. While they were beau-

tiful to look at, they were dis-gus-ting! "Thank you, Zemeepo. We will do our best to free your land of this threat," Gwen said.

"I trust you will, druids. Now, show those large brutes what the might of the small can do," Zemeepo said, before returning the way they had come.

CHAPTER TWENTY-FOUR

Subterfuge

Virgil and Gwen received a strange notification from eating the leaf.

Buff Gained! Lucky Bastard

You have ingested a Bastard's Lucky Leaf. Those leaves come from Bastard Bush, which is a rare shrub that has been made completely by magic. For the next 24 hours, your chances of success have been increased by an unknown margin. You will notice that things may work out inexplicably, or just seem not as difficult. Be warned, however, Yggdrasil disdains any artificial life that does not have its source from nature. This disdain has caused conflict within your very being. While your chances of success have gone up, the chance of something going horribly wrong has gone up as well. While not a guarantee, there is a definite risk. You have been warned.

The druids looked at each other, completely pissed that they didn't Analyze the plant before they ate it. Virgil was tempted just to wait it out for the next twenty-four hours, but they only had a limited window to get this done.

"Did you know about this?!" Gwen whispered harshly.

"No! Did you? And why do you think I knew?" Virgil asked defensively.

"Uh, I don't know, maybe it's because you spend every bloody night mixing plants and animal guts into potions!"

Virgil opened his mouth to retort, then closed it. She had a point, and he wasn't too proud to admit it. After talking about their circumstances with their current situation, both druids realized they had no choice. They had to continue the mission, despite the increased risk. At least they had an increased chance of success too. Gwen summed it up by saying they were in a high-risk, high-reward situation.

The party continued for another ten minutes, making sure to carefully place their steps so as to not slip and fall into the stream of lava below. Virgil realized that his Ring of the Bound Warrior that he had equipped would be almost like a curse if he fell.

The party made it to the ladder that Zemeepo had mentioned. It led up to a dim light source above. By the ladder was a pit of lava. This structure almost appeared like a well of some sort. Fortunately, it was not too tall, as Christopher couldn't climb, and they would have to use a rope to haul the boar up. Virgil looked up to see the light source was open sky. It was a shade of magenta, indicating that the sun was setting.

Since Virgil had his Danger Sense and was naturally the stealthiest, he went up first. Fortunately, the stone ladder was not hot at all, seeming to not be affected by the residual heat from the lava.

As he began climbing, however, he heard the undeniably loud steps of an ogre approaching. He stayed still on the ladder and activated Stealth, then warned the party to back away from the spot through Party Chat. They quickly backed a few feet to get out of view from the hole.

Virgil didn't see the ogre, but he heard the telltale sign of a man about to take a piss. "Please don't pee on me. Please don't pee on me. Please don't pee on me. Please don't pee on me," he muttered desperately. His pleas were answered... somewhat. While the large, foul-smelling fountain of ogre urine didn't land directly on him, there was some splashing. The stream hit the stone wall by Virgil, giving him a nice misty spray of piss at first. Then, the stream redirected and landed directly in the lava below, causing a font of urine-smelling steam to surge up the entire latrine, covering Virgil completely.

When the ogre was done, Virgil flared his nostrils in disgust and anger, then wiped off his fogged-up glasses as the sound of the ogre walking away hit his large ears. Maybe this was the Lucky Bastard playing against him? He smelt worse than a fart in the shower!

"I guess it be better than the bastard havin' the runs," Grief sent, trying to be comforting.

"I guess. Still though, this is rank. Don't you smell it?" Virgil asked.

"Nay, lad. Along with me body, me Katarina took away me smell. Fer once, I'm glad she did."

Virgil turned to see Gwen looking at him apologetically, her hand held up to her nose. Virgil was very grateful that they had the Ring of Prestidigitation with them. Activating Detect Hostile Intent, and satisfied there were no more firebrands around, Virgil climbed up the ladder using the remaining font of steam for cover. Poking his head above the lip, he saw that they were indeed inside some kind of fortress. There was a large wooden wall behind him with the tops sharpened into menacing spikes; some adorned with the charred husks of different humanoid species. The large latrine hole he crawled out of was surrounded by thick, knee-high grass.

Virgil crouched down and scanned the environment. Virgil could see a few multi-story buildings in the distance in no better shape than the shacks around him.

There were no orcs or ogres nearby, or on the section of the wall behind him, though he could see a few posted as sentries in the distance on the wall, all facing outside. He heard voices off to his right. There was a large black building which did not match the others. It was at least three stories tall and looked like some sort of gothic cathedral. An evil-looking gothic cathedral. That seemed to be the place where the firebrands were going to congregate.

Seeing as they seemed to be relatively safe, Virgil had the others come up. After another five stressful minutes, everyone was up, including Christopher. They quickly hid as Virgil's Danger Sense warned them something was coming. Baphomet was still in Virgil's satchel, as stealth was not its strong suit when in its larger form. Christopher and Splinter hid in the tall grass by the hole.

Like trained assassins, the party quickly took care of the two orcs, the two animals managing to knock the one orc taking a number two into the lava pit, while Gwen used her Silence spell in conjunction with Virgil's Leeching Vines to keep the other orc in place. That orc died in a matter of seconds to an arrow through the temple. After they were done with their grisly work, they looted the one orc before knocking her into the lava pit as well. No need to leave any evidence. Gwen was ecstatic, as the firebrand had a quiver full of glass arrows! Apparently Lucky Bastard was working well for her.

You have found Glass Arrow.
Item Type: Weapon
Damage: +10–20
Durability: 10/10
Item Class: Rare
Description: An arrow adorned with the rare volcanic material, glass. While glass is not the most durable for long fights, it is one of the sharpest materials in all of Imeria.
Effect: +100% to armor-piercing, +200% damage to unarmored foes, + 15% chance to gain a critical hit on unarmored foes.

With Gwen's natural bonuses to damage dealing from her Hunter Druid class, she could do some major damage with her new arrows. It also helped that almost none of the firebrands wore any armor at all, so they could be some easy pickings for the archer.

Carefully, the party approached the large cathedral using back alleys and hiding behind corners to make their way.

The tribal fortress that the firebrands called home reeked of burning flesh and blood. Numerous smokestacks could be seen throughout the city from the pyromaniacs' obsession with fire. More than once, the elves had to restrain themselves from removing a burnt husk of a beastkin or elf skewered near some of the fires. Many of them were missing limbs, presumably ripped off and eaten by the firebrands.

As they moved closer and closer to the cathedral, Virgil noticed that there were fewer firebrands in the back streets and alleys and more in the large central dirt path a few blocks away. All of them were looking at the cathedral. They kept their eyes open for a shaman but didn't see any. As they came closer to the cathedral, an ominous feeling sank in the chests of both elves. They made a slight turn as the semicircular wall angled that way. There, they saw a building that was some sort of mix between the wooden and dirt structures of most of the other buildings and the large cathedral.

It had four walls made of the same obsidian black stone, with a large thatched roof. On the top of the building was another one of the Zinthos totems, a flaming eye fixed on the cathedral. Now that Virgil realized it, the cathedral had one of those totems too.

Gwen quickly grabbed him by his cloak and pulled him back, interrupting his musings. "Keep your wits about you, Virgil," she whispered harshly. "Just because the totem is looking one way, doesn't mean it can't shift its gaze. If it sees us, our sneak attack is done." Her firm visage then went soft. "I don't want to lose you, okay?"

Virgil glanced at the eye, then smiled and nodded, understanding her meaning and grateful for her insight. In truth, he was being careless in examining the totem. He then thought about the strange-looking hybrid building and a plan formed in his mind.

After a few minutes, the two elves nodded in agreement. They sent Splinter into the shoddy hut they were hiding behind through a crack in one of the planks to scope out the situation. She came back after a minute and shook her head no to his question if any firebrands were in there. Using that info, the party quietly broke into the hut so as to not alert any wall guards or the Zinthos totem on the next building over.

It was a simple clay and wooden building that reeked of orc BO. Some of the wood was placed in a mismatched pattern that created a few small gaps perfect for viewing the totem's hut next door.

Virgil and Gwen snuck back out, leaving their animal companions inside. Virgil then took the barrel of poisoned alcohol from inside Grief, and also pulled out the Shimmerleaf herb. When ingested, it would cause temporary invisibility to the user. Virgil watched as his entire body went translucent. With his Herbology level of fifty-four, it augmented the herb's abilities by an extra fifty-four percent. The herb's info didn't give him an exact time of how long it would last, so he knew he had to be quick.

He began to carefully roll the barrel, making sure not to go too fast or be too noisy to not cause any unwanted attention. Gwen nocked one of her new glass arrows and kept an eye out for any potential threats.

None of the firebrands seemed to notice, as they were busy chanting and focusing on the cathedral in the distance, muttering, "Burn," and "Zinthos," between themselves.

Virgil rounded the corner and carefully set the barrel up. Seeing that the invisibility was still up, he slammed his fist on the door of the shamans' hut.

Immediately, a silence fell over the firebrands as a number of them looked directly in Virgil's direction, noticeably bothered by the disturbance at the hut. Two orcs and one ogre started walking toward the hut cautiously.

Virgil's Danger Sense sent him warning bells as he felt Zinthos's eye gazing upon him. The eye shifted left and right, indicating that the totem did not actually *see* Virgil.

Using the knowledge he was still invisible, Virgil turned to make his way around the corner. Before he could make it all the way around, the door slammed open. A firebrand orc shaman emerged. He was seven feet tall with the crazed smile, red skin, and bulging black veins that the other orcs had. He wore a loose vest made of bones and had a feathered headpiece with a human skull as its centerpiece. In his hand, he wielded a bone staff that looked like two fused femurs with an orc skull on top. There was a fire inside the skull, illuminating its orifices as well as the carved eye of Zinthos on its cranium. If this guy wasn't an orc shaman, Virgil didn't know who was!

"Hehaha, who dares disturb me so close to the ceremony?" the shaman asked, somehow both happy and angry.

"We do not know, mighty shaman," one of the incoming orcs replied. "We only heard the noise and came to investigate."

"You dare lie to me in the presence of our master Zinthos's gaze?" the shaman asked, pointing his flaming staff at the orc.

"He does not lie, my shaman," the booming voice of Zinthos rang out from the totem. "This orc did not disturb my chapel which you dwell in. Something else has disturbed me before this ceremony. I sense a presence that offends me... Find me the source of this offense and feed it to my fire," the demon communicated with a menacing tone through the totem.

Virgil's eyes widened in an "Oh shit!" expression, but stayed as still as possible, leaning his still invisible body against the corner of the stone building. He was concerned that if he moved, he may kick up some dust and give away his position.

"*Lad, if ye ever valued my advice, heed me now. Don't move, and don't even breathe if ye can hold it,*" Grief sent through Party Chat. The skull was currently invisible too, as he was equipped to Virgil.

"Yes, master," the shaman said. He was about to walk around the building when he noticed the barrel Virgil had placed. "What's this? Is... is this Grub? We haven't had a good barrel of the stuff in weeks," he said excitedly and quickly walked over to it.

Virgil mentally sent for Gwen to hide back in the shack next door, to keep out of sight, then hugged the wall even tighter as the shaman and the other three firebrands moved over to the barrel of alcohol in wonder. They were now just three feet away from the druid.

"Ooh, this ritual will now be even better with some Grub. Take this to the cathedral and pass it around. This will get our blood going for the sacrifices tonight!"

"Focus, minion!" Zinthos's voice boomed out at the shaman angrily. "Find me the one who has disturbed my chapel. I want whoever has brought this offending aura to burn!"

The shaman bowed his head at the demonic totem. "Yes, master Zinthos," he said apologetically.

The orc made a shocked face and his nostrils flared in disgust. He sniffed once, twice. Three times. "Do you smell that?" he asked, then moved around the barrel. He walked up to where Virgil was, just inches away from the invisible elf leaning against the black stone. The shaman took a few more sniffs followed by one big inhale. "Ogre piss!" He spat, unknowingly, right at Virgil's face. "And not just any ogre piss," he said, turning to the lone ogre in the group. "It smells like yours, Shrok," the shaman pointed his staff accusingly at the ogre.

The large red-skinned ogre took a few steps back. "N..Nnoooo, Shrok no longer pee on buildings. Shrok use fire hole like a good ogre. Shrok no piss on temple of the master," the dumb ogre said defensively.

The shaman looked unconvinced. "Uh huh, then tell me, why does it smell like your nasty ass piss?! Everyone knows you eat too many onions and it makes your piss smell even more rotten than your breath!"

The ogre just stared at the shaman open-mouthed and dumbfounded at the accusations. The two orc companions quickly took a step away from the large dumb brute while the shaman turned back up to the flaming demonic totem. "Master

Zinthos, I have found the source of this offense. This miserable pile of hyena dung had the gall to urinate on your temple," he said, pointing his staff at Shrok. "He is yours to burn!" he said with an evil grin.

"Burn!" the other two firebrands chanted in glee.

Quicker than the ogre's small brain could process, the flame-wreathed totem's four tentacles stretched out and grabbed him. Two tentacles grabbed his arms while the other two forced their way through his mouth and... another orifice. The ogre screamed or tried to as the flames hit his throat and traveled down to his stomach. One flaming tentacle emerged out of the ogre's chest while the other emerged out of his bulbous abdomen like the xenomorphs from *Alien*. The ogre's eyes rolled to the back of his head and he collapsed to his knees, passing out from the pain as his body burned from the inside out. All three orcs and the demonic totem were focused on the burning ogre in glee at his suffering.

"*Now may be a good time to get away, lad.*"

"*Good thinking,*" Virgil sent back, and he quickly made it back to the other building. It was a good thing too, as his invisibility stopped just as he was out of view. Lucky Bastard for the win! He quickly hopped into the shack and activated his Ring of Prestidigitation. "I'd never thought I'd be happy to smell like ogre piss," he said, thinking that somehow his Lucky Bastard buff was truly working out in his favor!

"You're not joking," Gwen said back to him, smiling.

The party then peered out of a crack in the shack's wall, and looked to see that Zinthos had finished his gruesome task and turned the entire ogre to ash. The totem seemed to grunt in frustration. "Grr, I am still not satisfied. I have had ogre, I want something. I need something new to burn," he said.

"Not to worry, master, we have many new things for you. Tonight, you will get to feast with your own body and spread your fires of hate until all burn," the shaman said. "Until then, I give you these two to satisfy your urge."

Both orc grunts looked at the shaman then at each other.

Before either of them made their first step to run, both were ensnared by two flaming tentacles around their heads, muffling their screams. "Good," Zinthos said, seemingly satisfied. "I must now put my focus on the cathedral. Do not tempt my ire again, shaman, *or my anger will burn you too!*" the demon bellowed threateningly before both the totem and two orcs were completely covered in flames and turned to ash.

"Thank you, master," the shaman said to the totem that was no longer present, still showing clear reverence to the demon before carrying the barrel over in the direction of the cathedral. The party took a few moments to rest and catch their breaths from their near-death experience. They were so close to blowing their cover and likely bringing about their deaths. For good or bad, the Lucky Bastard gift Zemeepo had given them had already proven invaluable to their efforts.

The party set off toward the cathedral, stopping at a taller building. After using Splinter to make sure the place was clear, they snuck in and went to the upper level to view the ceremony. With their vantage point, they were able to tell there were about one-hundred firebrand orcs and ogres in the main street looking at the large black cathedral that was partially embedded in the Brandios volcano.

On the steps leading up the ominous building were ten orc and two ogre shamans. At the top stairs, at the base level of the cathedral, was a sight that both infuriated Virgil and made his skin crawl at the same time. There, standing by a massive Zinthos totem, was Ramsay. He was no longer simply a dwarf, his pale skin was now a deep red, his long gray beard was now solid black, and two small curling horns protruded from his forehead. If there were ever any doubts that the headmaster was another sorlith demon, they were now dispelled.

Ramsay slammed his staff on the ground. There was an audible boom that could be heard even from the party's vantage. At that, the crowd turned their focus to the shaman and totem. They began chanting in unison, "Zinthos, Zinthos, Zinthos." A few of the orcs began to move through the crowd toward the cathedral step. Each was carrying small cages with thick metal bars. Virgil's eyes widened as the orcs made it to the steps, revealing that the cages were not empty.

There were five cages in total that were being carried up the steps and set at the traitorous Ramsay's feet. Two cages had some kind of humanoid. One was a human male in the leather armor of the Amthoon guards. The second was a small warg like Zemeepo and Vulpa. The other three had three different animals. One had a panthera, and another had what looked like an envirowolf, but instead of the green leafy fur it was the light brown color of sand and was notably sleeker; a clear desert predator.

The animal in the last cage was a surprise. It was a large opossum with dark red fur. That was one of the rare and endangered blood rhynorns from the beastkin village of Ginter-bacher! Virgil's remembrance was interrupted when all the fire-brand shamans slammed their staffs on the ground as one. The collective boom silenced the chanting of the crowd.

Ramsay looked to the large totem then addressed the crowd. "Firebrands, faithful of Zinthos, the time of our reckoning is at hand!" The crowd roared in response before Ramsay continued. "For the past year, this wonderful year, we have spread our master's influence throughout the Scorched Lands, bringing fire and blood in our wake. Now, his power has allowed me to free our tribe from the bonds that the wretched elves placed on you here. With his fires of hate, we will make them burn!"

The crowd chanted in unison, "Burn, burn, burn!"

The large totem's flames grew brighter and larger, causing the crowd to silence once more. "Yes! Yes, my minions, I will make the world burn! My anger will bring about the destruction of all who have opposed us! You have done well to serve me, and these sacrifices have pleased me," the totem said, looking down at the trapped beings below him. "To grow my strength, I must not only burn... but eat! Every new creature increases my power, which is why I've had you scour the world for new sacrifices to feast upon. With these tasty morsels, I should be strong enough to burn all!" the demon proclaimed, and the crowd cheered in malicious glee.

"Shite, lad."

"What is it, Grief?" Virgil asked.

"I knew that needin' sacrifices was a clue! I can't believe I didn't think of it sooner! I finally figured out what kind of demon that be," the skull replied.

"What is it?" Virgil asked quickly, wanting to know.

"That bloody thing be a damned amalgam."

"What's that?" Gwen asked, taking just a moment to look away from the crowd to look at the skull.

"They are strange demons, starting off lookin' like big maggots. With everythin' they eat, they take in a bit of its power, causing their forms to evolve and change into hideous abomination mish-mash. Needless to say, the longer the gluttonous fiends live, the more dangerous they become. I honestly didn't think of it as an option because they be rare, and I've never seen one older than a juvenile before. We of the Devilslayer clan kill 'em off before they can grow to be a serious threat. If this thing's been 'round fer at least a couple years, ye can bet yer ass that it be strong!"

"What's their weakness?" Gwen asked.

"That be tricky, lass," Grief replied. "Their weakness comes from their strength. Ye see, the first thing that an amalgam eats, the tricky bastards evolve their forms to be the most similar to. They will retain that creature's strengths, and... its weaknesses. Ye get me?"

Gwen nodded. "So, if it ate an ice creature, it would have a weakness to fire."

"Correct, lass. Now that we know what it be, we need to figure out what it ate... whenever we find its actual body. I be surprised to see it able to communicate through those strange totems. No doubt that dwarven imposter had somethin' to do with it," Grief spat.

The crowd's cheering died down and Ramsay continued. "One of our shamans has informed me that he has come across a drink that the firebrands use to increase your thirst for blood. This will no doubt please the master. While we take these sacrifices to him, the shaman will stay behind and allow everyone to partake of this… Grub," Ramsay said, unfamiliar with the term. The demon then turned toward the cathedral and walked his way to its entrance. He was followed by all the other shamans, except the one with the barrel of alcohol, and the five orc cage carriers.

Gwen turned to make her way downstairs to follow, but Virgil grabbed her arm.

"What are you doing? Those people are going to be sacrificed if we don't do anything," she said.

"It sucks, but we have to wait. There's a hundred of those crazed cultists out there. We need for them to either disperse or let the poison take effect. Plus, that massive Zinthos totem is still there," he said, his cool analytical side clearly taking effect. He wanted to save the people as well, but if they weren't careful, they'd end up being dead just like the caged prisoners would be.

Gwen bunched her lips, clearly upset about the decision, but nodded in begrudging agreement. They watched as Ramsay opened the stone doors into the cathedral. It was clearly hot inside the area, as the air coming from the cathedral caused waves of distortion from around the entrance. In a ceremonious nature, the shamans and caged prisoners were escorted in. Once they were all in, the doors were closed with a resounding boom.

With none of his superiors present, outside of Zinthos himself, the shaman walked to the bottom of the cathedral steps and placed the barrel in front of him. There was a smug grin on the orc as he was filled to the brim with pride. "Know that it is I, Reiner, shaman of Zinthos, that gives you this Grub. *I* am responsible for the bloodbath that we will bring. *I* am the one who will help our master *burn*! You owe me your allegiance, and when the time comes, I will assert my claim as the true head shaman our master deserves. If you back my claim, I swear that every one of you will have more Grub than you can even drink! What do you say?!"

The crowd roared in response.

"Yes!"

"Grub, Grub, Grub!"

"If you give us Grub, we will give you blood!"

Both elves stared at the crowd in shock. That shaman was planning a fucking coup and, apparently, it was working! These firebrands must *really* love their booze!

"What do you say, master Zinthos?" Reiner looked back at the large burning totem.

The demonic eye stared at the shaman impartially. After a few tense moments, the demon said, "If you can help me burn, I don't care who serves me. If you hinder my path, my anger will burn you first."

To his credit, the orc shaman was able to keep his composure despite the clear promise of death the demon had given him. Reiner gave a malicious grin then bowed to Zinthos. "Of course, master. I swear that if I weaken your cause, then I offer my body to fuel your fire," he said with a bow.

The orc turned back to the crowd. They were barely containing themselves from turning into a mob to reach the barrel of booze.

Virgil was curious though; the shaman had no cups or way to serve the firebrand horde in front of him. How was he going to make sure that they all were going to get some? The orc quickly answered Virgil's silent question. Reiner slammed his staff to the ground and a large stone column erupted from under the barrel, launching the container of alcohol into the air above the mob. The orc then aimed at the airborne barrel with his staff and fired a small bolt of stone. His aim was true, and the barrel exploded midair, showering the entire group of firebrands with the tainted alcohol like it was rain.

All the crowd had their mouths open like they were kids trying to catch snow. A red aura then showered the mob, and they all roared in unison, their eyes turning almost completely bloodshot.

"Yeeeesssss!"

"Reiner should be lead shaman!"

"He will help us burn all!"

"Burn, burn, burn!" they all shouted in unison.

The orc shaman gave a toothy grin, taking in all the praise of his newly bribed minions. Before he could give them any commands though, their shouting was suddenly cut off. The red aura of rage quickly left their forms. The crowd began clutching their stomachs and moving in jerky motions. The shaman looked at the crowd, puzzled, then wide-eyed as many of them began to either vomit or have explosive diarrhea! More than one of the firebrands did both at the same time. The ogres let loose small waterfalls from their large forms. Many of them collapsed to their hands and knees and began to convulse, some even foaming at the mouth and going into full grand mal seizures.

Both elves stared at the dying crowd wide-eyed. Virgil had dealt with plenty of poisoning cases when working as a veterinarian back on Earth, but he had never seen something so devastatingly deadly so quickly! The druids' disgust turned to horror as something even more unexpected happened. From the various orifices of the convulsing firebrands, branches, roots, and vines emerged! They watched as the plant material coalesced and multiple copies of Joaquim erupted from the dead and dying firebrands, making a small grove of the monstrous plants.

"Virgil, what the fuck did we just do? This... I knew we were poisoning them, but I didn't expect this," Gwen said in horror.

The dark elf pushed his glasses up his nose. "It is horrible, but we know that those firebrands would've done worse to us. I'm not going to lie, what's going on is pretty fucked up, but I don't regret making the world a better place. We can't dwell on our mistakes, either. All we can do is try to be better, and *never* cross Zemeepo."

The high elf first looked hurt at Virgil's words, but then fully absorbed the truth and gravity of them. "You can be one cold son of a bitch, but you're right," she said.

Virgil just nodded. As a vet, his job helped him be empathetic, but he also had to have a degree of separation and logic. That was where his analytical brain thrived. Some may have called him heartless, but he disagreed. Many people struggled when euthanizing an animal, and while it could definitely suck, Virgil took comfort that he helped an animal no longer suffer. He thought it was more heartless to let an animal continue to suffer when there was no way an owner could afford care or its condition was untreatable.

Regardless, there were many difficult parts with being a vet. It wasn't a high-paying job or just playing with puppies and kittens. You had to be a counselor, doctor, investigator, money manager, and janitor, all while dealing with animals that may indeed try to hurt you, and people that could be too emotional to fully comprehend what was happening to their beloved companion. For people that didn't have enough separation in that field, they could be overloaded with compassion fatigue. That, among other factors, has lead to the veterinary profession having a disproportionally high suicide rate in the US. Knowing that, Virgil was grateful for his analytical brain. It had helped him not to become overwhelmed, and it was helping him now.

He grabbed Gwen's hand. "I know it sucks, and it's a lot right now, but we need to go. They are distracted and dying, and we won't get a better shot."

Gwen hesitated for a moment, but quickly joined Virgil and made their way out of the rickety building they'd been hiding in and toward the cathedral. They still kept to the side, making sure not to be seen. As they neared the side of the cathedral, their nostrils were assaulted by the combined scents of the foul bodily excretions the orcs and ogres released.

Stealthily, they made it to the side of the steps and saw the orc shaman, Reiner, being held by the throat by one of the tentacles of the demonic totem. "Master... forgive me, eh, I did not know," he said, choking out his words.

"*How dare you!*" the totem bellowed. "You have the audacity to personally eliminate almost my entire army?! I should have known that one like you, who betrayed my head shaman, would betray me too. You swore that you would not weaken my cause or else you would offer your body to me."

The totem brought the orc closer to its flame-wreathed eye and said menacingly, "I've come to collect. Now, *burn!*" A tentacle pierced straight through the orc's gut and lifted him into the air.

Reiner screamed as his insides burned and gravity pushed his prone body down the tentacles.

The party looked around; outside of the totem and dying orc, all the others were dead. Reiner was still screaming and they could tell that Zinthos was going to take his time with him. The party needed to catch up to Ramsay before it was too late. Virgil nodded to Gwen, and she pulled out one of her ballistae bolts and coated it in some strange, blue, sticky substance which she explained through Party Chat was some sort of fire resistance resin that Zemeepo had given her before they left. It wasn't a bad idea in Virgil's mind, seeing as how one of the smaller totems had burnt one of her arrows to a crisp before.

They counted down, three, two, one, go. On go, they stepped out from their hiding spot and Gwen fired her large arrow while Virgil cast Purifying Aura. The enhanced arrow flew quickly, but the totem was still ready. Fortunately, the resin proved beneficial as it resisted the flame tentacles' grasp and continued forward, going straight through the eye of the totem, striking the wood and shattering it to pieces. The fires around the totem disappeared as its structural integrity went kaput. The impaled shaman suddenly collapsed to the ground. The momentum killed the low-health orc on the spot, causing blood to shoot out in multiple directions.

Notifications appeared in Virgil's vision after that.

Quest Complete!
A Tainted Toast

You had stealthily delivered the poisoned barrel of Grub to the firebrands and made sure that it was given to a large majority of their population, including every last female of the tribe. As such, even if a few survive, the firebrand threat will surely disappear thanks to your efforts. Many innocents will be grateful despite the… grisly means by which the tribe died.

Total number killed: 105 (87 orcs + 18 ogres)
Reward:
55,103 Experience
Extinction of the Firebrands
+1 to Herbology
+1 to Alchemy
Bonus Rewards:
Planting the seeds of the predatory plant Joaquim directly into a suitable source of food (firebrand bodies) has caused the seeds to grow rapidly, bringing about a large cluster of the plant species into the world. You have accidentally introduced a new super predator into the world. That probably won't cause any problems…

Introducing new life into the world has greatly pleased Yggdrasil. The world tree knows, however, that a grove not well-maintained will bring about more harm than good. As such, she has tasked you with a new quest.

Quest Unlocked!
Grove Keeper

You have brought about a new grove of dangerous Joaquim plants into the world. Those plants are both quite unique and quite dangerous. If left alone, they could bring about more harm than good. Yggdrasil herself has tasked you with finding a Herbologist to keep the grove under control.
Reward:
10,000 Experience

Penalty for Failure:
An untamed growth of predatory plants
Unknown

Level up x2! Congratulations! You have gained enough experience to reach Level 18!
You have 4 unallocated stat points. Do you wish to allocate them now? Yes or No

Virgil selected no, and was ecstatic at his progress! He was now level eighteen, and only two levels away from using his attunement again to add another evolved badass creature to their party! That grove keeper quest was definitely ominous sounding, but it seemed to have an easy fix, as Virgil knew of an Herbalist that lived in the Scorched Lands, Vulpa. He dismissed that quest icon for another time. Even though they were in relative safety, the party was still in the middle of hostile territory. They could deal with their stat points later. It was now time to attack the enemy stronghold.

CHAPTER TWENTY-FIVE

Volcanic Temple

There were no other windows or doors for them to sneak into, leaving only the large main entrance. Virgil had Baphomet hop out of the satchel and change back to its large form. Then, on the dark elf's command, the beastking burst through the door.

To their surprise, the large cathedral was empty except for two orc shamans that were standing guard by the altar. "Intruders!" one of them yelled. They both lowered their staffs and were about to conjure spells at the party, but the right one never finished his incantation as Gwen fired one of her glass arrows at his unarmored, tattooed chest. The extra damage properties of the arrow came into effect, and it sank deep under the orc's sternum and pierced his heart.

The other fired a bolt of flames, but to his surprise, instead of hurting them, the giant beast with them caught the flames in its mouth and swallowed them like they were a big treat as it activated the newly acquired Flame Dragon's Hunger skill.

"Baphomet, Instill Fear," Virgil ordered.

The beastking stood on its two hindlimbs and let out a mighty roar at the orc. The orc's eyes went wide and his knees began to buckle. He took a step toward the altar beside him, but was struck in the foot by another one of Gwen's arrows, pinning him to the ground.

Terrified and now unable to flee, the orc shaman fell on his ass, and put his hands up defensively. The smell of urine hit the party's nostrils as he soiled himself. "P-p-please, don't have that beast kill me! Spare me, and... I'll tell you anything you want," he said nervously.

The party approached the downed shaman cautiously, careful for traps. Virgil ordered Baphomet to lean down toward the orc. The beastking did, its muzzle just inches from his face.

The shaman shook in fear and let out a high-pitched squeak as he closed his eyes.

Gwen nodded to Virgil. With her higher charisma, she was the clear choice to get the shaman talking. "Tell us what we want to know, chap, and I promise, we won't let that thing kill you, 'kay?"

The orc opened his eyes slightly, seeming to understand both Orcish and Common. He felt the hot breath of Baphomet right beside his face and quickly nodded in agreement to Gwen.

"That's a good orc," Gwen said before continuing. "Now, where are the rest of your group?"

"There's a secret passage, behind the wall. There's a switch on the altar," he spat out quickly.

"Where does it go to?"

"It leads up the volcano. Our master Zinthos is there. They plan on sacrificing the five in cages. Our master said that's the last he needed to fully transform. Please, that's all I know. You said you wouldn't let it kill me. So please, let me go," he begged.

Gwen gave a quick look to Virgil, a silent message passing between the two elves, and it seemed to help harden the resolve of both of them. "I did say that. You're right. That thing won't kill you," she said.

The pinned shaman put a hand to his chest and sighed in relief. He was about to thank Gwen when she shot an arrow at him at point blank range with blazing speed via her Rapid Fire subskill. The iron arrow sank through the prone orc's left eye, easily penetrating through it and stabbing into his brain and out the backside of his skull. The orc let out a short grunt as his head rocked back and slammed against the ground. It was over in under a second.

Gwen looked at Virgil. "I didn't say that someone else in our party wouldn't do the job, though."

Virgil looked at her with newfound respect and a bit of fear. She may have called him a cold SOB, but she was one badass motherfucker that he didn't want to mess with! He followed her to the altar. Sure enough, there was a small switch carved inside it. She switched it, and a large hidden door opened from the back wall of the cathedral, at least one and a half times the height of an average ogre.

All of them visibly recoiled as a wave of heat emerged from the large door. Fortunately, Baphomet had been fed another Potion of Icy Essence, which immediately helped. As their eyes adjusted to the oppressive heat, they saw what was behind the door. It was the inside of the large volcano, at least a section of it. Apparently, the crazed tribe had actually dug into the active volcano! Inside was a tall hallway with both side walls being flowing lava waterfalls disappearing under large slits in the ground. There was no one in the room that they could see, and another set of doors on the opposite side. As they approached the doorway, a notification appeared in their vision before they entered.

Warning, you are about to enter a dungeon: The Temple of the Cult of Zinthos.
As a dungeon, there are active groups of multiple creatures that will be hostile toward you inside. Once you enter this place, the demon this place is dedicated to will not let you leave the way you came. Take heed.

Well, that certainly wasn't foreboding, but they also didn't have another choice. After confirming with each other that they were ready, the druids and their animal companions entered the volcanic dungeon. As they all fully entered the large hallway, the stone doors slammed shut behind them with a boom. Immediately, they all felt the oppressive heat from the lava flanking them on both sides. It was so intense that they were all hit with a debuff that slowed their stamina regeneration by twenty-five percent!

Virgil cast his Purifying Aura spell in response, causing a field to emerge and surround his allies, bringing about sudden relief from the heat and removal of the stamina debuff. It was still hot, but more like a humid sunny day versus being in the center of an active volcano.

There was a monstrous shriek, and from the other side of the hallway, a large serpent made completely of flame emerged from the lava on the right side. It opened its mouth, hissing at the party. Gwen fired a steel arrow at it, but the projectile passed through its flame body.

The serpent somehow gave a smug look and was about to charge when it saw Virgil's face. It was confused, as the dark elf had a confident smile. It didn't understand why, but that seemed to anger it some more, and it charged at the veterinarian. Virgil gave the incoming creature a shit-eating grin then looked to Baphomet and said, "Dinner time, bud." Those were the last words the serpent heard before the large beastking met its charge and brought it down like the alpha predator Baphomet was.

The serpent's flame body was not only its strength, it was also its weakness, and Virgil figured that out quickly. It proved very beneficial to have a creature on their side that literally ate fire. Despite some burn wounds that Virgil quickly healed faster than they could do damage, Baphomet rapidly took care of the snake, slurping it down like a giant spaghetti noodle.

Splinter was a little disgruntled at that. The stego rat *loved* to eat and was at risk of being a glutton, so she was a little irked that the beastking could eat things that she could not. Virgil seemed to sense his rat's discontent, so he gave her a chunk of wolf meat. The rodent squeaked happily as she chowed down on the meat.

The party encountered no more hostiles in the hallway and continued into the dungeon. For the next few hours, they traversed their way through the heart of the volcano. As they continued forward, they could tell they were actually ascending the volcano. Throughout the dungeon, they encountered a variety of threats, large apes that breathed fire, a terrifying colony of humanoid spiders and, of course, the occasional orc or ogre shaman. While every enemy either had a stone or fire component, the farther the party went into the dungeon, the more demonic elements appeared. There were some altars surrounded by blood and magic pentagram traps carved into the floors.

Virgil was especially grateful to his Danger Sense in regard to the latter, as it saved him from accidentally stepping onto a trap that turned into a large mouth that would have surely cost him a limb if he wasn't careful. Lucky Bastard was still on his side... for now. After the third hour, they had ascended to the top level of the volcano before breaching the outside.

They entered a large round chamber with a pentagram carved in the ground. It was illuminated by a ring of flowing lava around the floor like a moat and various torches placed throughout. There were carved stone statues of the eye of Zinthos with his customary four tentacles on both side walls. It was even painted on the dark ceiling above as if the demon was looking down directly at them. That was not even the most terrifying part of the room; hanging from the ceiling by chains were various dead bodies. All were humanoid, charred to a crisp, hung in painful-looking positions, and somehow had expressions of horrors on their faces permanently stuck in death.

On the other side of the room and pentagram were two figures. One was a large ogre shaman, and the other was another active Zinthos totem. "Ah, druids, so good of you to join us. I've been so looking forward to tasting druids. Ooh, I bet you will burn well. Now, come here," Zinthos beckoned. The entire party felt some unseen pull on their psyches wanting them to actually step toward the demonic totem. They all took a half-step then stopped. A notification appeared in Virgil's vision.

Psychic Domination resisted due to Purifying Aura's effect.

Thank you, Lucille! Virgil cheered internally. He could kiss the senior elf for this spell! Without it, their deaths would have come swiftly due to the demon's control. "Not gonna work this time, you dick!" Virgil spat.

The demon was not bothered. In fact, he seemed to be amused. "Ah, hahahaha! So, you like to struggle? Good. That will make it all the better when I see you burn."

"You think just one shaman is going to stop us?" Gwen asked. "We've handled plenty, and this one should be no different."

Upon being called out, the ogre's distant eyes sharpened and focused on the Hunter, and he gave her a bloodthirsty grin. "I'm not just a shaman, wench! I am a warlock in service to the master, and he will see you burn!" the ogre declared and slammed his staff down, which looked like it was a partially burnt tree he had ripped from the ground.

Virgil's Danger Sense alerted him to a threat above, and he shouted, "Run!" The party, trusting their leader, complied and sprinted toward the round floor in the center of the room, jumping over the small moat of lava around it. When they had made it, they looked back to see that another lavafall had suddenly appeared right above where they had just been standing and was spreading out to cover the entire way they had come through. Its momentum was stopped as it spilled down into the lava moat surrounding the party.

"Subdue them, my minion," Zinthos said. "Bring them to my body. I wish to—" The totem's words were cut short as a spear of stone emerged from in front of it, shattering the totem into multiple pieces and breaking the demon's connection to the room.

"Yeah, yeah, we get it. You want to eat us. Shut up already," Gwen said confidently after she had destroyed the totem.

The ogre notably weakened without the totem's influence, and his massive form shrank down. He was still huge, though, standing at least ten feet tall, though his red skin took on a gray tinge. The ogre scowled and was breathing deeply, as if in pain. "You insolent cur," he growled through clenched teeth, putting a hand to his chest. "Gr, unlike the grunts, I will not be defeated just by severing my totemic connection to the master."

Gwen fired an arrow and Virgil cast a Nature Bolt at the weakened warlock, but the ogre blocked them both with a shield of flame. When the flames went down, the ogre let out a defiant roar, and the sickly green aura transferred from his body to his tree staff.

The green aura then shot out like a beam of energy upward and split off into different directions. To the party's surprise, they struck the burnt husks hanging grotesquely above them.

"Experience the power of a warlock with Corruption Magic!" the ogre bellowed. His eyes flashed the same green aura and he clenched his fist. To the party's horror, the corpses above them let out ghostly gasps and moans. The chains they were wrapped with began to rattle. Virgil's Danger Sense went off again in his mind, warning him of the threat above him.

"Incoming!" Virgil shouted. Immediately, one after another, the corpses dislodged themselves from their chains and fell to the ground. One after another, the bodies hit the floor. Hey, Virgil knew that song! A few broke apart with a sickening crunch, but most of the corpses landed on their feet. One of them, what looked to be made of the remains of a human male, landed in a one-knee superhero pose then looked up at Virgil and gave a screeching roar of anger, both his face and hands erupting in green flame.

Virgil reactively used Analyze.

Name: Corrupted Charred Zombie
Level: 15
Race: Monster **Type:** Undead
Health: 125/125 **Manna:** 100/100 **Stamina:** N/A
Resistances: Fire 50%, Blunt Damage -25%, Corruption
Magic 100%, Nature Magic -50%.
Debuffs: None.
Profession: None.

A corpse whose body was burnt and brutalized in life and now
reanimated to become an undead minion in service to the
infernal powers that brought it to life. These undead, though
not physically strong, enshroud their fists with demonic flames
to burn their enemies. If they are destroyed via magical means,
their bodies also explode on reaching zero hit points.

You probably should just use blunt force to defeat these undead,
unless you like to have things explode right in front of your face.

*"Crap! These things explode upon death if we use magic, but are weak
to blunt damage,"* Virgil communicated through Party Chat.
"Baphomet, the ogre is yours. Go," he ordered aloud, then cast
an Yggdrashield behind them, creating a temporary barrier
between the party and about half of the undead. The beastking
charged forward at the hulking ogre, pushing the undead in
front of the party on their asses. In two quick motions, Virgil
pulled out two different potions then handed one to Gwen. It
was a Potion of Icy Essence.

"For Christopher—give it to him quickly," he said. She
complied without hesitation and fed the terror boar the potion
as Virgil fed the other one to Splinter. A small forcefield of cold
air surrounded the horned pig while a different effect happened
to the stego rat. Virgil had fed his animal companion a Potion
of Flame Armor, and the effect was true to its name as the spiky
rodent's entire body became encased in orange flame, but she
wasn't hurting. In fact, the flames didn't harm her body at all!

Virgil smiled as the undead from behind began to break
through his shield and the ones in front stood back up. "Good.

Gwen, have Christopher engage those in front in close combat. I'll have Splinter fight the others from behind. We'll need to keep our distance." His words were interrupted by the sound of Baphomet clashing in a knockdown brawl with the ogre, followed by a flame-wreathed fist breaking through the thorny wooden shield behind them. The Yggdrashield erupted in green flame and started breaking apart. "Go! Now!" he ordered and the rest of them went into action.

Christopher charged ahead at an incoming zombie. It swung a flame-covered fist at the incoming boar, but it was struck in the chest by an arrow, causing it to step backward, creating an opening for Christopher. The boar lowered his head and charged. His large, curled ram horns easily broke through the weakened limbs of the zombie, breaking through and amputating both of them under the knees.

The zombie landed on its stomach, turned, and began crawling toward the boar. "You've got to destroy the zombie's brain, love!" Gwen shouted to her pet before firing an arrow at a zombie approaching her flank. Chris P. Bacon was a smart pig and understood what his master meant. He stopped his momentum to let the crawling zombie get closer. As it neared, he mule-kicked it in the head with both his hindlimbs, his icy essence dispelling the flames covering the charred zombie's head and aiding him in destroying the zombie's brain. The green light disappeared from the zombie, and its body collapsed to ashes.

While Gwen and Christopher were dealing with the threat in front, Virgil and Splinter were handling the remaining zombie horde behind them. Virgil fired a Nature Bolt at one, then erected an Yggdrashield, blocking a few others from attacking Splinter. The stego rat was tearing through zombies left and right, her flame armor preventing her from receiving any fire-based damage from the undead. She tackled one to the ground and mauled its face with her sharp claws until its body went limp, its face just a bloody mesh of bones and flesh. She then used Tail Whip on another, piercing the dead human's calf and pulling the zombie's body to the ground for her to kill it… Well, kill it again.

Virgil spared a glance over at Baphomet. The beastking and ogre were fighting in a clash of titans. The ogre swung its large staff in a horizontal swing, but Baphomet ducked under the weapon.

The beastking surged upward and bit down on the ogre's exposed right triceps, causing black blood to flow from the injury. They were all doing their part. They just needed to keep this up.

After another minute of fighting, most of the undead horde had been eliminated. There were about ten charred zombies left, and half of them had already been so injured in life that they weren't even as dangerous as their other counterparts had been. Virgil gave the fiery undead a shit-eating grin. They had already killed maybe forty of the zombies. Ten more should be easy-peasy. It was time to finish this.

He wished he hadn't been so cocky. There was a loud cracking sound from the other side of the room. The party turned, but they were too late to react as the large beastking was sent flying toward them! The airborne Baphomet knocked both druids to the ground and squashed a few of the charred zombies behind them.

As the party shook off their daze from nearly getting crushed by Baphomet and stood up, a squealing sound shocked their eardrums. The elves turned quickly back in front of them, fear filling their systems. That fear turned to dread as they saw the source of the squeal.

There, on the other side of the round platform they were on, was the ogre shaman. His body was covered in bleeding cuts and bite wounds, but he still gave them an evil grin. In his massive hand, flailing wildly, was Christopher. The ogre's large hand held the boar by his back like he was scruffing a cat. Desperately, Christopher fought to get free, but he could not reach the ogre's hand where the warlock had him gripped.

"No," Gwen whispered in obvious fear for her pet. In less

than a second, she pulled her bowstring back and cast her Air Strike Arrow spell. The warlock seemed to be ready for that as he used the staff in his free hand to somehow telekinetically force one of the remaining corrupted charred zombies to protect its master. Its frail body flew forward to intervene. It was no match for the spell and it died instantly.

The warlock was counting on that fact as the zombies' unique effect kicked in. As it was destroyed via a spell, its body exploded on the spot, causing a wave of fire to erupt.

The proximity of the explosion caught Gwen off-guard and sent her flying backward. "Baphomet, catch her!" Virgil shouted. Like a skilled outfielder, the beastking jumped up and caught the Hunter Druid in one of its massive forepaws. Virgil immediately cast Phoenix Fire on her, transforming the flames on her body into healing energy before the beast landed on the ground.

He turned back to see the ogre laughing. "Hahaha! Fools!" he bellowed, literally spitting blood from his mouth as he spoke. "You may have been able to defeat me in a fair fight, but we warlocks don't fight fair," he said, then ran through a doorway, still carrying the struggling Christopher.

Virgil growled in frustration. He wanted to chase after the ogre, but he needed to make sure Gwen was okay. "Splinter, take out the remaining zombies," he said to the stego rat still in her flame armor, then turned back to Gwen. Baphomet had laid her body down on the ground and was guarding her protectively from the few undead behind them. Virgil leaned down to examine her. Despite his healing spell, she was still severely burnt and in bad shape. Even the magic of his Purifying Aura didn't dispel her debuffs.

He did a quick exam on her. Fortunately, his two animal companions were easily handling the remaining zombies via non-magical means. Her skin was thick with sweat, very tight against her body, and her lips were chapped. Her pulse was weak and her breathing was rapid. Virgil palpated her ribs and found at least four were broken. It didn't look good for the woman. "Shit, she's going into shock," he said. Shock was a medical emergency where the tissues and organs in one's body were not getting enough blood flow. That led to the deprivation of oxygen that was carried by blood and resulted in the buildup of waste products in the organs. It was a fatal condition if not addressed.

Well... he didn't go to medical school, but he figured the concepts were the same as with animals. The most important thing with shock was to get the patient rehydrated. Virgil cast Restore. He spat in frustration as, even though it healed some of her grotesque wounds, it was still not helping her hydration. He took his Everfull Canteen and tried to force her to drink, but the unconscious Hunter Druid began coughing and gagging after a few gulps.

"Crap," he said after his failed efforts. "Grief, do we have anything that can help rehydrate her?" he shouted in concern at his Soulbound Companion.

"Let's see here... Good grief, lad! Ye bet yer ass I do," he said, then pushed two small pieces of moss out of the foramen magnum. Virgil quickly used Analyze.

You have found Psylum.
Item Type: Alchemical Ingredient
Durability: 4/4
Item Class: Uncommon
Description: A moss commonly found by sources of water, preferably mists. Psylum grows in darkness and is known to frequent many pipes and plumbing.
Effect: This moist moss rehydrates those who ingest it by 50%. It also replenishes 50 Stamina and increases Stamina regeneration by 2 points every 10 seconds.

Virgil was *extremely grateful* for his past efforts scouring for ingredients, as this unassuming moss was incredibly valuable at this moment. He took the two moist pieces of green Psylum and forced them into Gwen's mouth, then made her chew. Like magic, he watched as her skin notably became more soft and not as tight against her skin. Her body seemed to move easier, with more energy, and she regained consciousness.

"Virgil?" she asked as she blinked and gained awareness of her surroundings.

"Easy now," the Healer Druid said. "You nearly died there. Give yourself a few moments."

"What... what happened?" she asked, shaking her head from side to side slightly.

"You tried to kill the warlock with magic, but one of those zombies intercepted your spell and... it blew up in your face."

Her eyes widened in awareness as recollection came back to her just as both Splinter and Baphomet joined them, their work with the remaining zombies finished. She gasped. "Huh! Christopher! Where is he?" she asked. Before Virgil could answer, the undeniable squeal of a pig rang out from the stairway where the ogre exited. "I'm coming, love!" she declared as she sprang up and took off toward the stairway with reckless abandon.

"Gwen!" Virgil called out. "Shit, come on, you two. We have to help her," he said and they all took off after the high elf.

CHAPTER TWENTY-SIX

It's a Trap

The party sprinted after Gwen, who was running headlong in the direction of her pet's cries. They followed her up a set of large stone stairs to a door. It was already hot in the volcanic temple, but they were beset by a new wave of oppressive heat as they opened the door. Virgil's Aura was still in effect, so the negative consequences of the heat were immediately dispelled.

When he saw where the door led, his eyes widened in concern. No longer were they underground. No, they were at the summit of the volcano Brandios and by a large pool of lava near the brim. When Virgil looked down at the lava pool, he saw a chain of flat, rocky islands looking like lily pads in a pond. On the largest island, which was the centermost one, was Ramsay. He had multiple emptied cages by him, and there was a lone orc shaman carrying another caged animal toward him. Not far from the orc was the ogre warlock sprinting with all his might, Gwen around fifty feet behind the bloodied brute. Virgil looked to his right to see another orc shaman who resembled a porcupine with the multitude of arrows in him. The orc was just a dead body on the stony ground, clearly the work of Gwen.

"We have to hurry," Virgil said to the beasts. He was getting a bad feeling about this. As the three descended to the chain of islands, Virgil looked to see what was going on up ahead of them. He saw Gwen take one of her glass arrows and fire at the large ogre as she ran toward him.

The ogre seemed to be aware of the incoming attack, so he picked up the cage-carrying orc by the head with the hand not holding Christopher, and flung the orc as a living shield. The surprised orc dropped the cage he was carrying on the small island he was on and flew toward Gwen. The glass arrow's penetrating properties easily pierced through the orc's unarmored back and the projectile impaled him straight through the lungs.

The orc could have potentially survived, had he not landed in the pool of lava. He screamed in pain as his body erupted in flame. Gwen was too focused on the ogre, but if she had paid attention, she would have noticed that the orc's body was pulled into the lava unnaturally fast, as if something dragged the orc down. That didn't matter to her, though. She was trying to get her pet back.

However, Virgil noticed the orc's death and that didn't make him feel comfortable. He was riding on Baphomet's back, Splinter not too far behind. As they neared the others, Virgil noticed the dropped cage ahead of him. In it was a frantically moving animal. It was the blood rhynorn, and upon closer inspection, Virgil noticed a distended abdomen and developed nipples. The thing was pregnant! He wanted to go warn Gwen, but also his veterinary instincts tugged hard to help this endangered animal carrying the literal future of her species. Virgil sent a mental message to his animals to continue forward, then hopped off Baphomet.

After he landed on the ground, he ran toward the cage and fired a Nature Bolt at it. After two of the spells, the metal door of the cage bent inward. Virgil went up and shook the cage door and was able to get it open after a few seconds. The blood rhynorn burst out of the cage, fueled by her instinctual drive to survive. She took one moment to look back, and Virgil thought the beast gave him a nod before taking off in a full sprint to get off the volcano's summit and into safety.

Satisfied, Virgil turned back and ran toward the large center island. He saw that Gwen just made it there and fired one of the ballistae bolts looted from the automatons at the large ogre. She managed to strike the warlock in his lower back and the bolt lodged itself there, the arrowhead just emerging out of the ogre's bulbous belly. The ogre stumbled to a knee just as he made it to Ramsay. Gwen pulled out another bolt and fired, but this time, Ramsay interfered.

The demonic shaman raised his staff and a wall of unnaturally red flame surrounded both him and the ogre in a semicircle, blocking off all view. Virgil recognized the unnatural-colored flame as the infernal hateflame that Grief had told him about before. The red flames burned the bolt in a matter of milliseconds. Gwen scowled in anger and then began casting Air Strike Arrows repeatedly. The flames gave way partially, but never completely, and the wall refilled right after, as if the flames hadn't been touched.

Not deterred, Gwen cast a volley of Lightning Arrows, vastly depleting her manna just as both Baphomet and Splinter made it to the island. That spell seemed to be more successful, as the small electric arrows seemed to pass through but did not notably damage the wall. There was a groan of pain from behind the flames, and Gwen let out a small smirk.

Then something unexpected happened. From the hateflame wall, two bolts of fire shot back out in retaliation at the Hunter Druid just as Virgil had made it to the island.

"Baphomet, Flame Dragon's Hunger," Virgil commanded right before he cast Yggdrashield for Gwen. The beastking lunged and caught one of the bolts of flame in its mouth and swallowed it like a dog catching a treat. It was a good thing Virgil had made it, as his magic shield emerged just in time to intercept the other bolt of flame. It slammed into the construct with a loud crash, and the Yggdrashield immediately burst into flame. Virgil rolled away from the ignited construct, and the wooden shield disintegrated to ash in a matter of moments.

"Virgil, I need manna potions," she said, looking at the dark elf.

Virgil was about ten feet away from the rest of his party. As he ran toward them, he unlatched Grief and tossed the skull at Gwen. "Give her some potions, bud," he said as he threw Grief. To the skull's credit, he actually took to being tossed without complaint. Virgil looked to the lava around them, getting majorly bad juju from his Danger Sense. That moment of distraction turned out to be a detriment as, to the party's surprise, a glowing red pentagram suddenly appeared under their feet!

In a flash, a translucent box that looked like glass immediately surrounded the entire party! Virgil didn't even need Danger Sense for this! Whatever just happened, this was bad! Baphomet slammed its massive forepaws on the glass, but it didn't crack. It didn't even budge! A notification flashed in both druids' visions.

Warning! You have been caught in an Anti-Magic Box Trap. For the next 20 minutes, all magical effects inside the box and that try to pass through or onto the box are immediately nullified! Does not nullify skills. Know that this trap is extremely durable and will resist most damage.

"Virgil, what do we do?" Gwen asked as she pulled a manna potion from Grief and downed it like a large shot of tequila. Virgil was surprised that she could do so! Before he could say something, the wall of hateflame diminished, revealing Ramsay, the injured ogre, and Christopher, who was now literally hog tied and gagged. The terror boar was trying desperately to get free.

Gwen was overcome with emotion at seeing her distressed pet. "Christopher!" she shouted, then beat against the box wall twice. "Christopher!" She scowled at the two minions of evil who were maliciously smiling back at her. "Release him now! If you do, I'll make your end quick," she threatened in a way that even sent shivers up Virgil's spine.

"Hahaha, oh I'll release your pig, druid, but not yet," Ramsay said, the demon's voice now a deeper malicious version of the dwarven speech they had heard originally from the shaman.

"*Gwen, focus. Please calm down,*" Virgil sent through Party Chat. If she was in an inconsolable rage, that would dramatically lessen their chances of getting out, and an idea was already forming in his head for how to get out. She turned to face Virgil; anger obvious on her face. Like many—if not most —women, telling her to calm down had the opposite effect. Virgil put out a placating hand. "*Christopher's chances are poor right now. He may die, but if we don't focus and keep cool heads right now, he definitely will. So stop, please.*"

The Hunter Druid's jaw tensed, but Virgil's words struck home, and she regained her composure. They turned back to face the demon and warlock. The ogre was still on one knee and coughing up blood. The wound from the arrow in his abdomen was turning black and necrosing before their very eyes. It was clear that Gwen's arrow was covered in one of the poisons Virgil had given her.

Despite his grievous wound, the ogre warlock was still giving a crazed grin that seemed to be the trademark of the firebrand tribe. Even though he was smiling, the ogre was clearly in a great deal of pain. "Er, Head Shaman Ramsay, I have brought another tribute for the master, a rare boar. Please, use the master's power to fix my wounds," he asked the demon.

Ramsay gave the ogre a small, neutral smile. "Of course, fellow servant. The master can most definitely *relieve you* of your pain," he said in a strangely calm manner. The ogre, still on one knee, let out an audible sigh of relief. That was right before Ramsay ran at him and shoved the ogre into the lava pool with supernatural strength.

The ogre fell back and began screaming in pain, "Nooo! You said he'd fix me!" he shouted indignantly at Ramsay.

"I said he'd relieve you of your pain. I never said he'd heal you. Now, let your body serve by burning for the master," he said coldly. He raised both hands in the air. "Master Zinthos, servant of the archdemon Vozremath and general of his army, I give you… a snack before your main course."

The ogre's eyes widened. Before his body sank any further into the lava, a giant worm-like creature surged out from under him, snatched him in its maw and brought him down into the lava completely. It reminded Virgil of underwater predators like great white sharks.

Ramsay gave an evil grin of pleasure before turning back to the trapped party. "That will satisfy him for a bit. Now that we're alone, I think I should explain why I brought you here," he said.

"It's obvious, you git," Gwen spat. "You work for this Zinthos general."

"Indeed I do, druid, but there's more to it than that. Oh, there's much more. I want you to realize the true depths of your mistakes and to understand the grandeur of our plans before I sacrifice you. I want you to suffer as you fully comprehend how your failures will cause the pain and suffering of countless innocents. Ooh, I can just imagine their screaming already," he said, closing his eyes, his body shaking with glee at the thought.

Virgil rolled his eyes. Ramsay apparently was like all the evil pricks in movies. He *had* to start monologuing. Virgil was okay with that, though. It gave him more time for his plan. "*Gwen, press Grief to the wall behind your back. Don't let Ramsay see you. Grief, when you're touching the wall, see if your Space Vacuum skill can break through the barrier. If it can, you and Gwen try to break down as much of it as possible for us to get out of here. I'll keep Ramsay distracted,*" he sent through Party Chat then pushed his glasses up and walked toward the front edge of the box to get Ramsay's attention.

"So tell us this great plan, because from what I'm seeing here, you're just some bitch lackey that is just feeding some sort of lava-dwelling demon," he goaded the demon. It definitely worked, because the shaman turned toward him in anger with nostrils flaring.

"Bitch lackey?! Fool, you've no idea the efforts I've gone through to put this plan into motion," he spat. "Everyone thinks the invasion began just recently, but Vozremath himself entrusted me with growing his general's strength fifty years ago! Do you know what type of demon our general Zinthos is, druid?"

"An amalgam," Virgil answered. He also received a confirmation through Party Chat that Grief was indeed able to break through the barrier and was doing so right now.

Ramsay was taken aback, clearly not expecting Virgil to know. "Why... yes. You're more informed than I realized, druid. A naïve young wizard named Weylan Forsworn desperately sought power, so he made a pact with Zinthos. In exchange for the power he sought, Weylan would serve the demon. He also killed three other mages in his college and summoned we sorliths as their replacements. The fool was supposed to go lay the foundation for our invasion into Kygor, but he disappeared not long after he left Amthoon. But you knew all but the last part; you found his journal, after all."

Ramsay continued. "So, given the bastard had disappeared, I took care to cultivate our master. You see, druid, amalgams can be the most dangerous of demons when strengthened appropriately. They start out as small, insignificant worms, but with every new creature they ingest, they take in a portion of its strength, with the first thing they ever eat being the most important as they take on that being's form and strengths."

Virgil nodded in understanding. What Ramsay was saying matched what Grief had already said. Virgil also noted that Ramsay conveniently left out the fact that amalgams also took on the weaknesses of whatever they ingested. Virgil needed to trick the shaman into telling him what Zinthos ate. So, he thought he'd piss the shaman off again. Virgil began laughing loudly. "You spent fifty years feeding a big worm?! Wow! I knew you demons were dumb and desperate, but a worm? How stupid can you get? Let me guess its first meal, probably a dung beetle or something dumb like that. I always thought you demons smelled funny. If you eat shit, that would explain it."

Ramsay began to shake in anger, his red skin now turning a shade darker. Before he could respond though, the volcano itself began to shake. The lava began to bubble violently. To everyone's shock, a giant shell emerged! It was a horrifying sight as each plate from the shell had a stone face carved into it like Han Solo in carbonite. Each face was from a different creature, but they all had different expressions of pain and horror. From the front of the shell emerged a giant, twenty-foot-tall multicolored neck. At the top of the neck, instead of a typical reptilian head, was a large, single, vertical-slitted eye adorned with a floating crown of flame and possessing two tentacles made of flame on each side. There was no doubt that this was the actual body of Zinthos!

"You insolent scum!" Zinthos blared. "You dare have the audacity to not only insult my servant, but me, the demon general Zinthos the Devourer?! You shall burn!" he said before firing a gout of hateflame from his eye at the party. The party braced themselves reactively, but the anti-magic box trap they were in easily blocked the magic demonic fire. Zinthos growled. "That damn box. Not to worry, though, once it deteriorates, I will burn you all." The general lowered his eye at Virgil in particular. "*Slowly,*" he threatened menacingly at the veterinarian. "I will start with that traitorous general you have with you," he said, turning his gaze toward Baphomet.

The beastking's fur raised defensively and it growled at Zinthos, the former demon general snarling right back at its former counterpart.

Virgil couldn't help it. He shivered slightly and gulped, as the anger and malice the demon projected was so… palpable! "*How's it going over there, you two?*" he sent to Gwen and Grief.

"*We be hurryin', lad!*" Grief sent back. "*Shite, Virgil, try to stall 'em as much as ye can!*"

Virgil gave a very subtle nod then looked at Splinter and Baphomet. Both animals had their back hair flared out like scared housecats and were snarling at Zinthos. Their animal instincts were clearly warning them of the huge threat in front of them. He then looked at the two demons outside the box. Christopher was still there, but had gone completely still, the boar in baby deer mode, and was trying to bring no extra attention to it as there was no way it could escape.

Ramsay's angry glare had changed to a cocky grin. "You see, druid, my master is no worm. I ensured that his first meal would give him unstoppable power! I fed him a rare Psy-Tortoise, a creature that can psionically control others. Combined with the fact that every new type of creature increases my master's strength, Zinthos has truly become an unbeatable force. The great devourer has even been able to use his psychic powers to communicate through my corrupted totems! So, in secret, I fed him dwarf, elf, man, and beast over the years." He sighed. "Eventually, I found that Amthoon no longer could provide the necessary food for him."

"Yes," Zinthos continued for him. "Ramsay has fed me well. It was a good thing too, or else I would have eaten him." Virgil noticed a momentary cringe from the shaman's face that was there and gone in a flash. "My servant brought me here to the Scorched Lands, and I used my powers to infuse those mongrel firebrands with my energy. Those simple pawns easily fell to my influence and have been feeding me well for the past year."

Virgil gave a quick glance back to Gwen and noticed that Grief had almost absorbed an elf-sized hole from the back of the box! He just needed to buy more time! "What's the point? Why keep eating things if you're just going to hide away like a coward?"

"*Coward?!*" Zinthos shouted, his tentacles of flame glowing brighter in his anger. "You dare presume I cower?! I assure you, druid, I am not standing still. I am lying in wait. I have been cultivating my flames of hatred with every new kill. Once this box disappears, I will use my psionic control and make you watch as I burn, then eat, all those you care about, piece by piece!"

"My master is correct," Ramsay said. "As you know, the world tree is resistant to flames." He then put a finger up. "But it is not invulnerable. Zinthos has tasked me with feeding him six-hundred unique beings to fuel his fire to overcome Yggdrasil's resistance, and with the firebrands' help we only need two more. Speaking of..." he said, then looked down to Christopher. "Here is number five ninety-nine."

Both druids, while experiencing a higher amount of luck due to Lucky Bastard, had a pit in their stomach in concern as to if the single moment of bad luck would happen to them or not. What occurred next was Gwen's moment of poor luck. Zinthos looked down to the bound terror boar. The tentacles spread open wider, like the mandibles of an insect, then descended to Christopher. The boar and his master locked eyes for one last time, sharing one last moment of genuine love and care for each other, before Zinthos reached him. In less than a second, the demon's head pounced on the boar with such force that the section of stone underneath Christopher broke and gave way. The boar didn't even let out a scream as he was almost instantly plunged completely into the lava to be eaten by the demon.

CHAPTER TWENTY-SEVEN

Rise of the Devourer

Gwen let out a scream as she watched her beloved pet get plunged into the lava and die before her very eyes. Tears were freely rolling down both cheeks. Ramsay gave her an evil grin as he savored her suffering. She clenched her jaw in anger. He would pay. Zinthos would pay. Each and every warlock bastard would pay! During that whole time, even now during her tears, Gwen hadn't let go of Grief, who was using his Space Vacuum skill to absorb the barrier of the anti-magic box they were stuck in. She looked back to see that the skull had gone into overdrive and had actually made a ten-foot by ten-foot hole.

Gwen turned back to see the beginning of comprehension as to what happened on Ramsay's face, but he was momentarily distracted as Virgil noticed the demon's face too and used his Taunt skill to gain Ramsay's attention. The demon shaman turned and reactively scowled at Virgil. That moment of distraction was just what Gwen needed. She dropped Grief, jumped out of the hole behind her, and grabbed the top edge of the box with just one hand. She then utilized her elven grace to do a backflip onto the top of the anti-magic box trap.

Ramsay's eyes showed true fear as he saw the Hunter Druid

now free from his trap. He raised his staff to cast a defensive shield, but she already had an arrow drawn. She fired and hit the shaman under his left clavicle with an imp horn arrow. The arrow bit deep and lodged itself in the demon's exposed flesh.

Gwen pulled another arrow and fired again, but the shaman was ready this time. He used the blood oozing from his wound to form a kite shield made of blood magic. Zinthos's head was completely submerged in the lava as it ate Christopher, so the general was fortunately too preoccupied to help.

"Baphomet, help me and Splinter up and out. Then press the skull against the box until you can get out," Virgil said aloud, the need for stealth gone. Splinter's flame armor effect had dissipated, so she could accompany him. Baphomet was still in its large form and therefore, too big to get out of the hole at the current size. Though Virgil was an elf like Gwen, her high elven blood gave her a grace that his dark elf heritage did not possess; thus, he couldn't do that awesome parkour move she just performed.

The beastking lifted the two out from the hole in the side then up onto the top of the box. The opening Grief made was big enough for the beastking to reach its arm all the way to the shoulder, but not its whole body completely. Virgil and Splinter looked to see Gwen engaged in one-on-one combat with the warlock. The two appeared to be evenly matched, as Gwen intermixed bow shots with spells from her specific version of Nature Magic—Predator Magic—while Ramsay could utilize both hateflame and Blood Magic. He maintained his blood shield still with a few arrows lodged in it, and from his staff, a whip made of pure red hateflame was attached.

Gwen would fire an arrow, then Ramsay would block it with his shield, following up with a retaliatory whip strike which Gwen would narrowly dodge. It was time for Virgil to even the odds. He and Splinter ran and jumped off the box. Virgil then fired a Nature Bolt at the shaman. Ramsay blocked it with his shield, but that left him open for Gwen to attack. The Hunter Druid was still lower in the manna department than she would like currently, so she just fired another arrow at the shaman and hit him right in the knee. Guess he wouldn't be an adventurer anymore...

Ramsay grunted in pain and was caught by surprise as Splinter charged and bit down on the demon's calf muscle. Ramsay scowled, then slammed his blood shield onto Splinter, dislodging the beast. He went to stomp on the stego rat, but Virgil cast Leeching Vines, binding the raised limb. Virgil cast Restore on Splinter as Gwen used her Pinning Shot subskill on the shaman's foot on the ground, the same leg that still had an arrow sticking out of the knee. Splinter, being close to the demon, readied herself, then jumped at Ramsay. In midair, she activated her Spike Wheel skill, and turned herself into a flying buzzsaw. The large rodent flew forward and up and cleaved straight through Ramsay's left arm, amputating the dwarf-sized demon's limb at the elbow.

Ramsay now screamed in pain as he fell on his ass and lost connection to his staff, as the arm holding it was now severed from his body. The shaman's blood shield also collapsed with his loss of focus. Despite his dire situation, the demon still growled and glared at the party. "Grr, you think you've won! Fools! Look at the fiend behind me!"

As if on cue, Zinthos's neck and head emerged from the lava, the large singular eye looking down like a dinosaur observing its prey. Danger Sense went off on high alert to Virgil. He looked back to see that Baphomet and Grief were still working to get out of the box. "Insects, you will burn!" the demon proclaimed, then shot another gout of hateflame directly at Virgil. Virgil immediately cast Phoenix Fire, transforming the harmful flames of evil into white flames of Restoration Magic. He let himself be hit by the transformed flames, feeling their rejuvenating effects.

That only seemed to make Zinthos even angrier. "Insolent worm!" he yelled, then launched his head at Virgil like a rattlesnake. Virgil had an impressive agility score, so he felt confident he could dodge the attack. He tried to lunge to the left, but something suddenly gripped his right arm.

Virgil groaned as he pulled some muscles and possibly tore his shoulder. He looked at his arm to see that another arm made entirely of blood had emerged from the ground and latched onto his wrist. Pure terror went through Virgil as he saw the blood on the ground was connected to a trail leading to the demonic shaman, who gave the druid an evil smile. It was time for the bad luck of Lucky Bastard to pay its due for him too.

Virgil grabbed his arm and desperately tugged, but he only had moments, and his strength stat was not high enough to break the grip. His analytical brain assessed the situation and he deduced he had only two options. One: Try to cast a shield and either block or deflect the incoming massive demon. Or two: Try to dodge at the last second and likely lose an arm. Given the two terrible options he had, and that he didn't have much time to ponder on it, he went with the option most likely to keep him alive.

As the demon neared, Virgil bunched his body close together, still fighting the grip of blood magic but not winning. At the last second, he leaped to the left with all his might. There was an audible snap as his shoulder most certainly detached, then a flash of scolding heat, followed by a simultaneous pulling, burning, and ripping sensation before Virgil's body rolled free to the side.

He quickly stood up, but noticed something was 'off.' His balance was a little more difficult, and he wondered as to why. Then, he looked to his right. Where his right arm had been, there was now nothing but a charred, burnt, and ugly stump. He went into a cold sweat, then looked up at the giant demon's head rising up from where it had crashed into the ground. In one of his flaming tentacles was Virgil's severed arm, dripping blood. Virgil knew he was in shock. How could he not be?! He just had his arm ripped off! Fortunately, the tentacle's flames seemed to cauterize the wound on the spot.

Virgil's adrenaline gave out and the pain returned when he

saw his arm start to burn. He fell to the ground and started screaming in pain on the spot. It felt like he was burning, like somehow he could actually feel his detached arm boil and char like it was still connected to him! The pain became too much, and Virgil passed out.

———

Gwen watched in horror as Virgil flailed in pain on the ground! She couldn't believe how he had gotten caught. He was usually so fast! It was not the time to stay idle, though. He needed her. Though she lost Chris, there were still others she cared about that needed her, and she would make sure to ensure their hope wasn't in vain.

She watched as Splinter ran over to try her best to comfort her master and protect him from harm. He didn't even notice his stego rat before he passed out. Gwen saw Zinthos toss the burning arm of Virgil into the lava, not caring about it anymore. The fiend's eye was fixed once more on the Healer Druid himself. Ramsay was still on the ground, but had a terrifying grin from ear to ear watching Virgil's suffering. Apparently, the shaman's ability to use Blood Magic kept him from bleeding out! She needed to get Zinthos to focus on another meal source, and she had just the one!

"Hey, you hungry bastard!" she shouted as she drew back on one of her last two ballista bolts. Both Zinthos and Ramsay looked at the druid who dared to insult the general. "Eat this! Impossible Shot!" she said as she activated her Attunement. The large arrow took off with a boom. It struck Ramsay straight in the chest, easily breaking through his bone chest piece. The arrowhead penetrated through the shaman's back but the arrow stayed lodged in his body. The momentum of the projectile sent the shaman flying backward over the large pool of lava then up and toward the eye of Zinthos. The demon gave off a terrifying scream as the arrow hit its eye and pinned the shaman to him as well.

Zinthos lost all focus on Virgil and began flailing about in pain, desperately trying to get the arrow and impaled shaman off of him. Gwen used that chance to run over to Virgil. She also saw that Baphomet and Grief had made it out of their enclosure and were heading this way, the beastking carrying the skull in its mouth.

She ran over and took a knee by Virgil. "Virgil? Virgil, are you there, love?" she asked as she put a cheek to his hand.

"Good grief! What happened to his arm, lass?"

"Not helping right now, Grief!" she shouted back. Gwen closed her eyes and took a couple of deep breaths. Virgil had taught her some rudimentary things in regard to first aid and emergency medical care during some of their nights adventuring. She was nowhere near the medical expert he was, but she needed to try to put his lessons into practice. "Okay, um, the ABCs. Airway," she said, then turned him to his side to ensure that he didn't accidentally aspirate on his own drool or vomit if he threw up. "Breathing," she said next, then looked to see that he was indeed breathing, but only quick and shallow breaths. "Cardiac." Gwen then put two fingers to his neck. His pulse was going rapidly. She didn't know what the normal heart rate for dark elves was, but she assumed that his quick pulse was abnormal. His skin was also covered in a layer of sweat.

Gwen grunted in frustration, as she was truly stumped as to what to do. The only healing capability she possessed was a self-healing passive ability. She couldn't cast healing spells on others like Virgil. The only way she could help would be— "Huh!" She gasped, then looked at Grief. She could heal by administering potions! "Grief, could you give me a Stamina and a Healing Potion?"

"Comin' right up, lass," the skull replied and popped out both green- and red-colored potions from the back of his head. Gwen stole a glance to see that Zinthos was still shaking his head, and trying to dislodge the arrow with his tentacles.

She then grabbed the two potions and cradled Virgil's head.

She uncorked them and fed each of them to the dark elf. Virgil was still unconscious but his form did improve slightly. He seemed to stabilize some, but was still pretty clammy and cold despite the oppressive heat of literally being in an active volcano.

"Shit," she said. "He's still not waking up. Did he teach you anything about healing?" she asked Grief.

"Lass, I be no healer, but the lad be lookin' as bad as ye did when that zombie went boom in yer face. Virgil said ye were in shock and made me give ye two of these," Grief said, then forced out two more of the Psylum. Not seeing any better option, Gwen quickly grabbed the two moist pieces of green moss and force-fed them to Virgil. To her joy, he began to chew on them on his own. His body began to look healthier, his breathing began to slow and stabilize, and the cold sweat seemed to magically disappear from his skin! She was, indeed, one lucky bastard!

"Er, what… what happened?" Virgil asked, blinking his eyes open. As he regained consciousness, reality came rushing back to his mind. "My arm, oh shit, he took my arm," he said, grasping the startling realization of his situation.

"Shshsh, it's okay, we'll figure it out. We can't dwell on that right now. We're not out of danger yet, and we need that big smart brain of yours, yeah?" she said, trying to be as comforting as possible. They could not afford a mental breakdown currently, and she had faith that Virgil's calculating mind could overcome this obstacle.

Virgil took a couple of breaths before he seemed to focus and stabilize. "You're right, help me up," he said. She lifted him up. He was glad that he was holding his staff in his left hand at the time! They looked back at Zinthos just in time to see the massive demon general dislodge the arrow in its eye and Ramsay along with it. Zinthos dropped both into the pool of lava like pieces of trash. Despite Ramsay's fire resistance from his demonic heritage, he was not completely immune. As his body hit the lava, he began screaming in pain. His general did not care, though. No, the Amalgam was focused on Gwen with pure unbridled hatred.

The gargantuan fiend's large limbs began to emerge from the lava, causing the molten rock to sink lower, no longer being displaced. They were the massive legs of a tortoise, but burgundy, and appeared scaled like a serpent's. The gigantic shell of the demon's body began to rise out of the lava, and the party was able to see Zinthos's mouth for the first time. In the same shell hole where the neck emerged out of, there was a massive, sharp-toothed maw. It was under the neck and had just been hidden under the lava earlier. This fiend was truly hideous! A better name would have been abomination, not amalgamation!

Zinthos's eye flashed red as the fifty-foot-tall demon stared down at the party. He cocked his head back like a snake ready to strike again, but then Ramsay called out from the lava pool below. "Master! Please, save me so that I may continue to feed your insatiable hunger!" the burning demon pleaded as the lava covered most of his body.

Zinthos turned his eye down at the demon, a warty and blistering tongue licking his lower lip. "Oh, you may continue to feed me, my minion. In fact, I've never had a sorlith demon before."

Ramsay's eyes widened in fear. "No, no no no no!" he pleaded and raised his hands defensively. The party stared in shock as Zinthos's massive mouth descended on his lead shaman. They thought that with Ramsay out of the picture, Zinthos should be easier to take down. Then the general's words reminded them that he only needed one more new thing to eat before acquiring the capability to kill Yggdrasil. Before they could do anything, Zinthos scooped up Ramsay like the shaman was a small piece of candy and swallowed him whole, globules of lava falling out like bits of drool.

Immediately, Zinthos's body went rigid, and a blood red aura surrounded it. The aura produced a wave of heat and malice that caused waves of concern to the druids' senses. The volcano began to rumble and the lava began to boil. Danger Sense was on overdrive and gave Virgil the feeling that the entire volcano was a dangerous hot spot. Pun intended.

Since Zinthos was stuck, seeming to turn into some sort of demonic Super Saiyan and not attacking, Virgil turned to Gwen. "We have to get out of here!" he said, shouting over the aura wave going against them.

Though Gwen *really* wanted to kill the thing that had eaten Christopher, she agreed. Even without Danger Sense, she could tell that certain doom awaited them if they stayed. Virgil quickly pulled out two of his alchemic creations and administered them to Baphomet. First was a Potion of Fiery Strength; Baphomet was about to need it! Second was the Enhanced Scatter Scat Paste. It wasn't the best smelling creation, but the beastking was about to need as much speed as it could get!

After that, Splinter hopped onto Virgil, then the two elves hopped onto Baphomet. "Run!" Virgil shouted, and the beastking complied. Despite carrying the whole party on its back, with the two alchemic buffs, Baphomet took off with both ease and incredible speed! Virgil gripped tightly with both legs on the beast and closely wrapped his one arm around Gwen, doing his best to stabilize himself. In less than ten seconds, they had made it out of the mouth of the volcano. With the aid of gravity, they descended the rocky face at breakneck speed! It reminded Virgil of a rollercoaster ride!

Once they had made it a quarter of the way down, the volcano erupted! Lava, soot, and ash surged skyward in a violent display of raw power. If the firebrands were still alive, they would have cheered at the sight. Rubble, ash, and bits of lava rained downward, causing the beastking to run in a serpentine pattern. Virgil looked behind them, and his heart sank at what he saw. Besides lava spilling over the top, the giant leg and eye of Zinthos crested as well.

The general's eye was locked onto them as the massive demon, now towering over one-hundred feet, stepped over the volcano's mouth. The eye had a puncture injury on its left side where Gwen had pierced it, but the damage it dealt seemed to be done. Zinthos still had the red aura around his body. "Insects! I can now burn the world tree! Now you and all you care about will burn!" he shouted. Instead of a beam of fire shooting out of his eye, the four tentacles around his eye pointed at the descending party and launched four orbs of flame at them like cannonballs.

"Go right!" Virgil shouted. Baphomet heeded its master's order and made a sharp turn right, dodging the flame orbs as they impacted the ground. Zinthos continued to emerge from the volcano, every footstep shaking the ground. The massive demon followed the party down the volcano. Though it looked like he was moving slowly, the demon wasn't, as each step of his massive foot was the equivalent of thirty of Baphomet's.

The party made it down to the volcano's base right inside the border of the firebrands' fort. The lava was close on their heels, flowing over into the settlement just seconds after they had entered it. The crazed firebrands wanted everything to burn; guess they didn't realize that included them, too…

The demon was still pursuing them. Virgil quickly looked out into the distance past the settlement. There was mainly just sand and molten rock for as far as he could see. There was no cover, and they couldn't survive getting away from the demon in open terrain. They needed a place to hide, and there was only one viable place Virgil could think of.

"Baphomet, run to the large toilet we came out of!"

"What?!" Gwen replied. "Are you serious?!"

"We don't have another option," Virgil said. He squeezed the beastking's body with his legs to signal to continue. "Go, now!" The loyal animal again did as its master commanded. The party began sprinting through the edge of the fortress city towards the pit that served as a firebrand lavatory. Virgil glanced over to see that the large grove of Joaquims were still in the center of town. Their fire-resistant abilities were about to be put to the test with the lava.

After another minute, Zinthos had made it to the base of

the volcano, and the party had made it to the hole. Baphomet was panting heavily, almost completely out of Stamina. Virgil gave the beastking a couple of Stamina restoring herbs and had it change back to its small, antlered puppy form. Ignoring all ceremony, they began to climb down, no longer caring if they accidentally touched a remnant of firebrand excrement. They could focus more on hygiene if they lived through this ordeal.

Virgil climbed down first with Splinter and Baphomet in tow, the rat holding his staff in her mouth. Climbing down a ladder was not as easy without two hands if you didn't have sure footing. He may have taken too long, because as soon as his feet touched ground, Zinthos seemed to notice Gwen standing still up top. Virgil heard the demon's customary, "Burn!" shout above, followed by a curse from Gwen before she jumped down the hole. Right after she jumped down, a giant streak of flame flew over where she was standing.

"Ooooh shiiiit!" she shouted as she descended. She reached for the ladder, but her grip slipped. Her heart skipped a beat as she started to fall backward into the lava pit below. Fortunately, Virgil still had one good arm and he grabbed her forearm, keeping her from a grisly death. Unfortunately, Virgil's strength was already lacking even when he had both arms, so his feet started to slip forward. They both might have died in the lava had they not had Splinter with them. The stego rat grabbed Virgil's cloak and pulled with all her might, and was able to pull both the druids and beastking in Virgil's satchel to safety.

All of the party laid on the rocky tunnel floor, breathing heavily. Virgil looked over at his first animal companion since becoming the Healer Druid with loving affection. "Splinter, I tell you what, after that, I'm getting you an all-you-can-eat buffet! You deserve it!"

The large rodent closed her eyes, squeaked happily, and wagged her bony spiked tail like a dog from side to side. The rat loved to eat, and she seemed to comprehend what her master had promised.

Virgil felt a new wave of heat behind him and saw that the

lava from the volcano had reached the hole and was pouring in readily, completely covering the opening.

"We have to move," Gwen said, then got everyone to stand up.

They began sprinting across the dark tunnel that was occasionally illuminated by exposed streaks of lava. The tunnel began to shake with an angry roar. *"Insolent worms!"* Zinthos yelled, but through his psionic powers, as the party was multiple feet underground. *"I know not where you went, but I assure you I will make you suffer! I will devour and burn all you care about, starting with the accursed world tree that bore you worthless scum!"*

Gwen and Virgil shared a look of concern with each other. Only the druids could defeat the general, and they were unsure of how to overcome the hulking titan of a demon.

They needed a plan.

INTERLUDE

Pierre and Marianna

"Sunbeam!" Marianna shouted the attack command to her drake. Her large, draconic spriggan made of plant material that she was riding on flapped its wings and opened its mouth wide. The drake seemed to collect energy from the sun and a large orb of white light accumulated in its maw. Utilizing this magical version of solar power, the Spriggan Drake roared and released a beam of pure magic energy at Amthoon.

Despite her and Pierre's unannounced arrival, the city somehow seemed prepared for their coming. Every single one of their citizens had taken shelter in the large city, and a large magic dome erected around the entire metropolis that emerged out of the large tower on the city's edge! She and Pierre had flown over and demanded that the city surrender Gwen and Virgil to their custody, but for whatever reason, their jarl would not comply.

Marianna scowled at the nerve of the portly half elf. The man was holding wanted fugitives, whose bounty could help Marianna gain more power. Pierre, being the ever-noble warrior, loyally stayed by Marianna's side, believing them to be on the side of truth and justice. After negotiations with the city failed that night, he and Marianna had been attacking the shield with their magic and drakes the entire next day. Despite their numerous and powerful magical attacks, the shield held. There hadn't even been a crack in the construct.

The Plant Druid was getting mad at their lack of progress until one of the Thieves' Guild spies carefully approached her with vital information about the city's defenses. He was from their branch called the Blackfoots. Apparently, the magic shield was weakest at the main bridge connecting the left and right part of the port city and the regenerative abilities of the shield were lowest there as well. As soon as the spy dispersed the information, he disappeared in a puff of smoke, likely back to his boss.

With the new information, she and Pierre had come up with a plan. Her Spriggan Drake's Sunbeam was the first part. The drake's beam fired and struck the shield in the spot she had been informed about. A large, shit-eating grin sprang up on her face as white cracks started showing as the beam kept attacking that point. After a few seconds, the sunbeam stopped and the shield was on its last leg. "Pierre, now!" she ordered.

The Moon Druid was adorned in thick metallic draconic armor. He wielded two war glaives as weapons. One white with three blades and the other red with two in honor of the two moons of the world of Imeria. Besides fighting with his weapons, he had specialized his magic into large spells that required charging time and concentration. His drake was similar in its attacks, and it had been preparing the final 'punch' to break through the shield.

"Hurricane Breath!" he commanded his Ocean Drake. The large blue dragon mount released a breath of spiraling lighting at the shield. It struck the already broken section with a loud boom. Flying sparks of electricity crackled over the entire shield covering the city. The entire shield let out one loud pulse then completely shattered, disappearing back into pure manna in milliseconds.

Marianna smiled a predatory grin. She had been informed

where the jarl's quarters were. Now with their defenses down, she and Pierre could force the jarl to hand over Virgil and Gwen.

Her and Pierre's drakes were about to descend on the city when a loud roar echoed from behind them. It sounded as if it came from miles away, but was offensive to them somehow. Their druidic senses immediately helped them realize what let out that roar: it was a demon general.

CHAPTER TWENTY-EIGHT

Concocting a Plan

The party ran along the tunnel as fast as their tired bodies could move them. There was a large section where the tunnel opened up, and the pathway turned into a bridge over a flowing river of lava. They weren't in danger of a rapid flow of lava overtaking them from behind… at least not yet. Apparently Zinthos's activity had caused the river below to bubble and churn violently. They had to move with more caution to not fall over.

Once they had made it to the other side, the ground began to quake again. A large stalactite fell from above them. They dove forward, narrowly avoiding the stone projectile. It shattered the bridge and blocked their path behind them, completely enclosing the party in another dark tunnel. It was actually a blessing in disguise, as the stone should prevent any lava flow from following them! They made it over to the door to Zemeepo and Vulpa's underground home.

Virgil began to rap on the door. Knock, knock. "Zemeepo!" Knock, knock. "Zemeepo, Vulpa, this is Virgil. Open the door, quick!" After a few tense moments, the metal safe door began to turn and creak open. Behind the door was Zemeepo, his wife behind him with a couple of glass vials with green colored liquid in each hand. She looked as if she was going to throw them at whoever was on the other side, but upon seeing the party, her hands went to her side and she placed them in some hidden pockets in her long blue dress.

"Um... Oh! Oh my goodness! Please come in, quick!" Zemeepo said as he saw that it was indeed the people he had escorted. The party entered their subterranean home, and when the small warg closed and sealed the door again, they finally felt a modicum of safety for the first time since they had encountered Zinthos. Feeling the adrenaline leave their systems, the party practically collapsed on the stone floor in front of the warg couple. Concerned, they both checked on the party.

"I take it our plan worked?" Zemeepo asked. Virgil nodded. The warg alchemist smiled, "That's... incredible! Thank you so much! We are forever grateful, druids!" Zemeepo then seemed to truly grasp the sorry and exhausted states of the party. "Wait, where is the boar? By Yggdrasil's mercy, your arm! Vulpa, go get my emergency kit of potions!" His wife took off down the tunnel. The alchemist always had a potion on hand, though, so he pulled out a glass vial with a light brown, thick material inside it. He uncorked it and began giving it to Virgil, who looked to be in the worst state of the group.

Virgil looked at the potion with a bit of trepidation. The only brown-colored alchemic creations he had ever encountered used either blood or feces in it.

Zemeepo seemed to understand the elf's hesitation because he rolled his eyes and said, "It's chocolate, okay?"

Virgil shrugged and accepted the offered potion. It was thick and delicious! It reminded him of a DQ Blizzard. He fucking loved Dairy Queen!

Immediately, his breathing eased. His body felt more energized. A notification appeared in his vision informing him that he had ingested a Chocolate Iced Brew, and it not only replenished his Stamina, it increased his Stamina regeneration rate by fifty percent for the next thirty minutes, hence the increased energy. "Thank you," Virgil said after he had finished.

"Of course," Zemeepo replied. Vulpa returned with a large canvas bag that rang with sounds of clanging glass inside it. She pulled out three more of the brews. Gwen happily took one. Virgil knew Splinter had a Trait called Survivalist that allowed her to eat anything, so he was fine with the large rodent having one. While Baphomet wasn't technically labeled as a canine, when the beastking was in its smaller form, it looked like a puppy. Granted, it looked like a purple and brown puppy with antlers, but a puppy nonetheless.

Being a vet, Virgil knew that dogs and chocolate was a no-go, and he didn't want to chance accidentally poisoning his animal companion. Instead, he had Vulpa give it a high-quality Stamina Restoration Potion. Feeling better, but still not up to the effort of going through all of what happened, Virgil had Grief recount the events.

Virgil had to do a quick introduction as the couple was notably disturbed by a talking dwarven skull, but they actually took the information in stride after a few moments. The dwarf skull definitely had a flare for the dramatic when he recounted their trek through the firebrand city, the volcano temple, and encountering the amalgam demon general.

In another life, Grief could've been a bard, because he was honestly entertaining. When Virgil thought about all the disgruntled ex-lovers the dwarf had, he realized Grief could *definitely* make a good bard!

Upon hearing about Zinthos, the wargs blanched. "Y... You mean that wasn't just the volcano?" Zemeepo asked nervously.

The druids shook their heads no.

"It was the demon, and if we don't defeat it, Yggdrasil and the entire world will fall prey to it," Gwen said grimly.

"Well, that's what you're here for, right? So, how do you plan on beating it?" Zemeepo asked.

At that, the elves' expressions turned sullen. In truth, he was so large and terrifying, they didn't know how to beat him. They had barely managed to escape from becoming his dinner, and that was from them solely focusing on retreat. Not only was Zinthos a large, fire-breathing tortoise demon, he also had some psychic powers, and if you looked him in the eye without some kind of resistance or protection like Virgil's Purifying Aura, the demon general could put you under his control!

All seemed downtrodden, except Grief. "Come on, lads, don't act like a bunch of ninnies! Sure, the bastard was big, but we dwarves know that size not be everything. I already told ye, Virgil, an amalgam's weakness be from the first thing it eats. That shaman nitwit just up and said what the amalgam ate!"

Virgil perked at that. Grief was right! They did know what Zinthos ate! Virgil distinctly remembered Ramsay saying that the general ate something called a Psy-Tortoise. Now they just needed to figure out what in the world a Psy-Tortoise was.

"Grief, you beautiful bastard, you're actually right!" Virgil exclaimed.

"Of course I be right, lad! I be Goodgrief Devilslayer! I know 'bout how to slay demons. It's in me name," the skull replied indignantly.

Virgil and Gwen chuckled, then Virgil looked at the warg couple. "Do you know what a Psy-Tortoise is? Are they dangerous? Do they have any weaknesses?"

They gave the Healer Druid a perplexed look. "Uh, yes, we know what a Psy-Tortoise is. They actually live here in the Scorched Lands. They are large creatures that make tasty stew when cooked right. Vulpa here can make a great tortoise stew. They are tough but slow. They are called Psy-Tortoises because, when threatened, they emit a mental scream that forces any predators to run away. Besides that, though, they are just like any other tortoise, docile and peaceful creatures."

"So, no obvious weaknesses then?" Gwen asked.

Zemeepo shrugged. "If you flip them on their shells, it can take them a long time to right themselves, but I doubt you'll be able to do that to the demon if it's as big as you say."

"Well, lad?"

"What?" Virgil replied.

"Ye be the beast expert, bein' a veterinarian. Go on then, tell us what be a tortoise's weakness?"

Everyone's eyes focused on Virgil. The dark elf himself gave a surprised look at the skull for the comment. He had never thought of an animal's weakness before. At least, not in the way Grief was saying. He did know what predispositions animals had to types of injury or illness, so he should be able to extrapolate. For example, English Bulldogs were prone to airway and breathing difficulties, horses literally walked on one toe per foot, which made them more likely to get serious leg and toe injuries, Maine Coon cats were prone to hypertrophic cardiomyopathy, and Labradors were prone to tearing their equivalent of an ACL.

Tortoises? Well, tortoises were herbivores, but Zinthos didn't seem to have any problem eating meat. The demon actually preferred it. They could do well without a lot of water to drink. In fact, many people confused tortoises with turtles, but one of the key differences was… "Tortoises can't swim," Virgil said, almost whispering in realization. "Tortoises can't swim!" he said, chuckling slightly in excitement.

"Um, lad, I don't want to burst yer bubble, but I think the bastard can swim. Remember he was in a pool of lava?" Grief asked.

Virgil shook his head. "First off, that was lava, not water. The demonic nature of Zinthos probably had something to do with him being able to withstand it. Secondly, the demon was massive. He was so big that he actually stood up inside the volcano, so he could actually touch the bottom of it. So he didn't need to know how to swim!"

There was a pregnant pause as everyone processed Virgil's words. Grief was the first to respond. "Ha! By me granpappy's prize-winnin' braided beard, ye be right, lad! The bastard can't swim!"

"That still leaves one problem. How are we going to get the general to a body of water deep enough to drown him?

Certainly, he's not going to just walk into a lake willingly," Gwen said.

Virgil nodded. "You're right, so we're going to have to lead him into some sort of trap. The demon uses hateflame and is clearly very willing to bring a personal end to our lives. I think we should be able to lure him. We're just going to have to be the bait."

"And this trap you speak of?" Gwen asked.

Virgil gave her a knowing smile. "Remember Glassy Cliff?"

Realization struck her face as she gave the telltale "Oh" face to Virgil. "Damn, love! You're a genius!"

"Er hem," Zemeepo cleared his throat, reminding the druids that the wargs were there too. "I know not of this Glassy Cliff of which you speak, but is there any way in which we might be able to help you?"

"If you don't mind working with a fellow alchemist, you can assuredly help. I have a plan, but it requires a certain set of potions, and for them to be administered in a particular way. Tell me, have you ever made a transdermal potion?"

CHAPTER TWENTY-NINE

Kiting the Boss

For the next hour, Virgil and Zemeepo crafted. Virgil pursed his lips in frustration at having to work with only one arm, especially since he was right-handed. It was still disturbing to him to be missing a limb. Sometimes, he even had phantom sensations that his arm was still there, but he couldn't focus on it. If they didn't stop Zinthos, he'd have more serious concerns than a missing limb. So he focused on what he could control, compartmentalizing his trauma for a later time.

During their alchemy work, Gwen and Vulpa took Baphomet to work on a special project. When the men arrived outside the wargs' abode, they saw exactly what the project was. Strapped onto the middle of the beastking's back was a saddle. It was a very rudimentary saddle, mind you, but Virgil noticed it was made of the hide of some sort of alligator. He quickly realized it was from the Sludgegator pelt he had acquired from Kygor's sewer system. Set atop the saddle was a belt made of the skin from the giant python they had killed earlier back in the jungle. On one side of it was the snake's skin, while the other side was lined with brown fur.

"I figured it would be hard to keep your balance while riding with one arm and trying to use your staff," Gwen said with a slight smile, not wanting to make Virgil feel like a burden, because he certainly wasn't.

"No, this is great! Thank you so much," he said. The ground began to rhythmically shake after his words. There was a certain cadence to them, and it was clear that they were reverberations from footsteps. Giant footsteps. The party climbed up and peeked over the sand dune that covered the wargs' home. Off in the distance was the demon general Zinthos. The amalgam was still covered in his malicious red aura. The druids visibly recoiled from the wrongness he exuded.

Zinthos was on his way in the direction out of the Scorched Lands and occasionally blasting things with a beam of destructive fire, acting like a force of nature. He was actually going in the direction that the druids entered through.

Gwen blanched as she grasped the route the demon was heading toward. "Virgil, I know we were going to wait until he made it into the jungle, but we need to get his attention now!" she said intensely.

"What's going on?" he asked.

"Judging from his trajectory, he's heading straight for Kygor, and he will go straight through Ginterbacher on his way."

Goosebumps raised on Virgil's skin. The small village would be crushed. Even with their contingent of rangers, they didn't stand a chance! They had no large stone walls or army to defend them!

"You're right. Let's go," he said, and the two elves slid down the dune back to the two wargs and beasts. It was time to enact step one. Virgil took out a jar of Enhanced Scatter Scat Paste and forced Baphomet to take a deep inhalation of it. The beast-king took a big whiff then shook its head side-to-side, trying to remove the foul odor from its nostrils. The effect had already been acquired, as Virgil noticed that Baphomet was already moving quicker with its small movements.

"Thank you so much. Your help has been instrumental to us. We have to go now. Please be safe, and may nature be ever your ally," Virgil said as he hopped onto the beastking and cinched his new belt. He had never said that phrase before, but he had heard others say it, and being a druid, it seemed an appropriate idiom for him to use.

Once Virgil was strapped in, he clicked his heels and Baphomet took off after the demon. The demon didn't notice them, as his giant singular eye was focused forward.

Time for step two. Virgil pulled out two glass vials. One was yellow and had some bubbles in it, while the other was a dark red that almost matched the aura surrounding Zinthos. Virgil uncorked the vial with the yellow liquid and downed it like a shot of tequila on Taco Tuesday. The dark elf gave a satisfied sigh, as if he had taken a gulp of soda. He gave the other vial to Gwen. There was a small metal spring partially embedded in the cork that held a small leather cord.

Gwen pulled out an arrow with the arrowhead made of shining white Mithril. She needed this shot to land, and to ensure success, she used her highest quality arrow. She wrapped the cord on the shaft of the arrow behind the arrowhead and took aim. The Hunter Druid pointed her arrow ahead of the general, accounting for the trajectory of Baphomet, the demon, and the wind resistance, all on a subconscious level. She drew in a deep breath and fired as she exhaled.

Her aim was true, and the arrow struck the demon, penetrating its blood-red aura and resisting its inflammatory effects. It hit Zinthos in his eyestalk—or was it neck?—right under the eye. It sank in about a foot deep, and the glass vial shattered as it impacted the demon's hide. The demon let out a pained roar and stopped running; he took a stabilizing step to the right to adjust to the newfound pain. A cloud went over Zinthos's singular eye then dissipated as if it had never existed.

Virgil cast Purifying Aura right before the demon general turned his gaze upon them. His pupil dilated as the party felt the invisible pressure of his psychic powers trying to cloy at and wrap their minds. They grunted, but the spell's buffer kept their minds protected. "Insects! You dare show your miserable faces again?! You dare resist my control?!"

Before the general could speak again, Virgil fired a Nature Bolt directly at his large mouth. It did barely any damage to the demon. That wasn't the goal of it. It was to piss Zinthos off. The demon snarled at the attack. It was still not enough. "Hey, great devourer, you wanna eat something? Eat this!" Virgil said as he flipped the bird at the demon. Then something unexpected happened. Baphomet groaned and whined some, then hiked its right hindleg up. The beastking proceeded to piss a large stream right in front of the demon. Zinthos just stared at the beastking in utter shock at its gall. There was a heavy silence, as if the entire world held its breath during that moment.

When it was done, Baphomet promptly put its leg back down and gave a contented moan of relief. Apparently, Baphomet *really* had to pee and couldn't hold it anymore, despite the obvious tension of the situation. Virgil capitalized on the unintended display and shouted, "Fuuuuucccck you!" He put all his will and intent in the words and action, activating Taunt.

It worked... it *really* worked. Zinthos began to visibly quake in anger.

"You insolent cur!" the demon shouted with all the hatred it possessed. A ring of fire arose around all four of its feet.

Virgil's Danger Sense kicked in, and he listened to it. He immediately squeezed Baphomet with his legs like it was a horse and shouted, "Gooo!" The obedient and much more content beast complied and took off running. Just two seconds later, a gout of lava erupted from the sand directly underneath where the party had been. Zinthos roared and began shouting obscenities in the infernal tongue at the party as he began chasing in pursuit of the despicable scum that dared to be so obscene in his presence!

Baphomet took off, as all of the party's lives literally

depended on it! The demon general started chasing them, his hateful glare focused on Baphomet and Virgil. Zinthos shot out another beam of hateflame at them. Quickly, Virgil grabbed his staff and cast Phoenix Fire just before the flames made contact. His spell converted the red demonic flames into white flames of healing Nature Magic. Virgil used his staff to redirect the spell directly into Baphomet, healing any minor injuries the beast-king may have obtained.

"Damn you!" Zinthos shouted in fury, shaking the ground around them, but the party managed to keep going.

"Blimey, Virgil! Did you tell Baphomet to do that?!" Gwen asked in partial disbelief.

"Haha! Honestly, no, but it worked out amazingly! My plan was to get the general really angry, so angry that he would focus entirely on me and forget about burning Yggdrasil," he explained. "So, I had you fire a Potion of Demonic Fury at him, and I drank an upgraded Potion of True Taunt that Zemeepo and I made to temporarily bring my Taunt skill up to seventy-five. After that, I just needed to get an effective inciting incident to piss him off and use my Taunt skill. Baphomet's natural urges seemed to do the trick! Nature seems to find a way!"

Gwen just looked at Virgil, dumbfounded. How did they not get killed then? "Well, I guess we were lucky bastards, then. If the general hadn't been so shocked, he could've burnt us all alive," she relented and shook her head, not entirely disapproving of what transpired, but not entirely thrilled by it either.

While she was not happy with how Virgil did things, Grief couldn't be happier. The dwarf skull was laughing loudly at Virgil's antics. "Hahaha! That be hilarious, lad! The big beastie actually 'pissed' off a demon! Get it? 'Pissed' off? That be brilliant! I can say that ye be the ballsiest demon hunter I've ever laid eyes on! Haha! I couldn't be prouder of ye, Virgil! If ye were a dwarf, I'd adopt ye into me clan!"

Despite the tension of the situation, Grief's rant did cause both of the druids to chuckle at the skull's bad pun. "More like the luckiest," Gwen chuckled.

Virgil turned back and gave her a wink. "Either way, as long as we make it out, I'm happy with either nickname. Besides, I think I'm still considered a Lucky Bastard for the next few hours," he said.

After another half hour of running, the party made it to the border of the Scorched Lands where they had previously crossed to enter into the warded territory. There were a few large vultures eating the burnt remains of the Amthoon guards and dead firebrands. As Baphomet neared, the beastking's Alpha Predator Trait kicked in. The scrawny carrion eaters immediately began to run then fly away in fear, not wanting to challenge the mighty Baphomet.

Virgil stored his staff inside Grief, then had Baphomet turn right to go west into the thick rainforest and toward Amthoon where they planned to trap the demon general. They had made it a quarter kilometer into the jungle when Gwen looked back. Her Enhanced Vision Trait from her high elven heritage allowed her to see that Zinthos was, in fact, following them.

After a few more seconds, the sounds of cracking and breaking trees confirmed it as Zinthos crashed into the jungle, breaking down large trees and plants in his wake. A small pulse of flame shot out from each of his massive footsteps, partially setting the forest ablaze. Hopefully, Yggdrasil's influence could help prevent a full-on forest fire, despite the increased strength of the general's flames, because the druids didn't have the time to stop it!

Now, Baphomet was plenty big. In fact, the beastking was slightly taller than a full-grown ogre when standing on its two hindlimbs. It was even able to carry the entire party on its back while on all fours. Despite that, it was but a child in comparison to the kaiju-like demon pursuing them. Virgil estimated Zinthos to be one-hundred-fifty to two-hundred feet tall, towering over almost every massive tree in the jungle. Because of the size-disparity, Baphomet had to push itself hard to gain any ground, as one footstep from Zinthos was worth many of its own.

After another twenty minutes, the party had gained a little

more distance from the demon. Virgil noticed that Baphomet had begun to breathe harder and its pace started to slow. "Time for step four," he said, as he pulled out two small clay jars. Virgil knew that despite Baphomet's impressive size and stats, the beastking couldn't outlast the demon in a long-distance sprint. Not without help, at least. Virgil also knew that they couldn't stop to feed Baphomet any potions to replenish health or stamina as they ran, as that would allow Zinthos to catch up to them and spell their certain doom. Virgil also didn't want to risk the beastking accidentally aspirating any potions if he tried to feed them to it as it ran.

To remedy this, Virgil was inspired by his veterinary work back on Earth. There were plenty of wild animals and even pets who were not very compliant in taking oral meds. Have you ever tried to pill a housecat who didn't want to take the pill? Try it, and you'll see for yourself. Thus, the clever pharmaceutical companies found alternative methods to administer medications such as injectable and transdermal medications. The latter had been a game changer for many household pets, and was the administration method he decided to copy when he was working with Zemeepo.

Virgil opened up the gray jars to reveal a green gelatinous paste that honestly looked like hair gel. Virgil scooped out the contents out of both vials and liberally applied them to Baphomet's purple skin where there was less hair to allow better absorption. Almost immediately, the beastking's breathing eased and the pace returned to a run.

Virgil gave a grin, as his plan had worked! He and Zemeepo had been able to convert both Health and Stamina potions from a form that had to be drank to be absorbed, to a trans-dermal version absorbed through the skin. The extra benefit was while it usually took more time to fully absorb through the skin, the effects would last longer. That meant that Baphomet would get a supply of extra Stamina more readily over time than just a lump sum immediately that could be wasted quickly or wasted by supplying too much extra Stamina. It would be like giving a potion that restored one-hundred Stamina to someone who could only have fifty stamina at max. Fifty points from that potion would be wasted. That wouldn't be the case with this type of alchemic creation!

INTERLUDE

Dirk

Dirk used his claw weapon to gouge out the pit fiend's throat. The large demon begged him for mercy, but the druid had none for it. The wood elf and warlock had entered the demonic stronghold. Unsurprisingly, the demons did not respond kindly to a pronounced enemy walking straight at their master's stronghold, but with Shreez's help, Dirk was able to enter unmolested. Well... mostly unmolested. A bulbous, disgusting demon covered in ruptured black wounds tried to attack him right after he entered the city, but he quickly took care of it.

Dirk's attunement allowed him to take on bestial aspects of any beast he killed, allowing him to mix and match the strongest parts of any creature he overcame. When the demon ran up to attack him with a wicked dagger, Dirk changed his feet to that of a panthera and used the legs to spring into a surprise tackle, bringing the fiend to the ground. With his hands pinning the demon's wrists and clawed feet on the fiend's large stomach, Dirk began rapidly and violently eviscerating the demon right then and there in front of a crowd of its brethren.

The other demons respected his pure savagery as he

painfully and brutally killed the fat creature, whose cries of pain were only cut short when Dirk changed his mouth into that of a Saber Bear and bit down on the demon's skull, both puncturing and caving in its festered brain. The others in the city watched the elf in both admiration and fear at his savagery. Dirk reverted back to his regular form, but was still covered in the black blood of the demon he'd killed.

He spat before speaking. "Does anyone else want some?" All of the others didn't except for a large pit fiend. That was the one who the Feral Druid was currently teaching a painful lesson. After that demon also lay still on the red ground oozing black blood, both Dirk and Shreez were allowed to pass through without incident. They eventually met a couple of winged fiends around the size of an average human, adorned in wicked black armor. Dirk could feel the power radiating from them. Shreez informed him that these were a couple of Vozremath's royal guards.

After being told that 'the master' was expecting them, they decided to follow the guards, Dirk still keeping his eyes peeled for any traps. After ascending multiple levels of the raised city, they had made it to a large and foreboding center castle. It was solid black, made of some strange metal that radiated infernal energy. Somehow Dirk could tell that it was built using a lot of pain and suffering, as the walls seemed to project that feeling to him, as if cries of the slaves who made the structure somehow gave it power too. The castle was also adorned with numerous pyres of green flame. There were more guards patrolling the walls with various hideous, bestial fiends pacing back and forth. One of them noticed Dirk and opened its mouth hungrily at the elf, revealing a long barbed forked tongue. Dirk gave it a quick scowl before continuing into the castle.

After another five minutes, the duo were led to a large set of stone doors, each possessing a hideous demonic face protruding out as the door handle. Around the carvings were various scenes of brutal and grotesque torture. One picture depicted a man's abdomen being cut open by a demon and feeding him his own intestines!

Though Dirk wouldn't say it, the pictures did make him wonder if he'd made a mistake coming here. Then he remembered that damn doc, his lies, him taking his woman, and the sheer gall of the bastard to attack him, all because he didn't want to give up his damn pet. The man could get another one, but Dirk couldn't get the loot he had rightfully deserved without killing that Baphomet. Dirk would have his vengeance. No one crossed him and got away with it.

Thoroughly reminded, Dirk grabbed one door handle. He gritted his teeth as the sharp teeth of the demon carving's mouth cut his fingers, not willing to show weakness after coming this far. Shreez, excited by the drawing of his companion's blood, placed his hand on the door and pulled as well. The door opened into a dark room. There was only a subtle green light that emanated from the hallway behind them.

"What the fuck is this?" Dirk asked, clearly pissed. Before he could turn back to the guards, the two doors shut on the duo, engulfing them in complete darkness. "Fuck!" He spat, curling his hands into fists, ready to gore anyone who came to him. "Shreez, can you see anything?" he asked.

The warlock cackled in his usual maniacal manner and then stopped abruptly.

"Shreez? Shit," Dirk said before using his Attunement to morph his eyes into that of a panthera's, giving the druid adequate Darkvision. He was just making out a form in the distance when multiple sconces suddenly lit with green infernal flame, illuminating the room they were in.

They were in a large chamber that looked like an ancient Greek temple. Two rows of large columns were present, one row on each side of Dirk. The floor was covered in blood and gore; multiple dead, mutilated bodies were chained up on each column. All the bodies were dead, and if they weren't, they wished they were.

Dirk didn't care about those miserable SOBs though. No, he

was here to get the power he wanted—the power he deserved and was promised. He was here to get the power to force others into submission. Dirk looked ahead, and somehow Shreez was about a hundred feet ahead of him. The dark elf warlock wasn't alone though, he was on both hands and feet, bowing to a large creature. When Dirk's eyes focused on the being before Shreez, his blood went cold.

Seated atop a large throne was a massive, hulking demon. His skin was a sickly shade of yellow with a number of wounds, blisters, and warts on his body. He was built like an ogre, but much more toned in musculature. The creature's face was quite unsettling. The demon had a mouth that was too big for his face that was smiling from ear to ear, revealing an uneven group of sharp teeth, a wriggling tongue that seemed to be perpetually rotting and healing before their very eyes, and a horde of maggots writhing just behind his teeth. It had no nose, just a pair of nasal septums exposed. Instead of just two, he had five eyes, two on each side with a center one larger than the others. All of the orbs were made of fire that was dark red and reptilian in appearance. The demon had two horns, each one curling over his head with sickly white hair.

Covering what parts of its infected skin weren't exposed, it wore what appeared to be the tanned skins of elves, demons, and humans roughly stitched together, their faces stuck as if they were screaming. Dirk couldn't stand to look at the garb for too long, because an indescribable sense of dread overcame his mind if he did so. The demon emanated both pure malice and power. While the presence of Yggdrasil inside him forced Dirk to be internally disgusted by the fiend's aura, Dirk wanted its power. He ignored his body's natural inclination to run or attack.

"Who have you brought before me, worm?" the demon asked Shreez. His voice, laced with pure malice, was deep, terrifying, deadly, and otherworldly.

"I bring before you, great master Vozremath, master of all

infernal magics, the great corruptor, the one and only archdemon, ruler of all fiends, and bane of Yggdrasil, a druid who—"

"Druiiiiddd?!" the archdemon interrupted the warlock, standing up from his large throne. He was clearly not happy with the answer. "You miserable, pathetic swine! How dare you bring a servant of that accursed world tree into my realm. You will pay for your insolence!" he said before grabbing Shreez up by the throat. It looked as if the demon's very touch was corrosive, as the warlock's throat and skin began to rot before their very eyes.

Dirk smiled at Vozremath. This was what he wanted! The archdemon had power, unquestionable and undeniable power. The dude ruled all of this hellish place by pure force of will! Dirk would do anything for that power. He didn't really care about Shreez. The dude always had a screw loose, but the warlock had proven helpful and was likely Dirk's best chance to accomplish his goals here. No need to get rid of a tool when it still worked well, and there still was a need.

"Hey, the great corruptor or whatever you are, I ain't no servant of that world tree bitch."

The large demon didn't let go of Shreez's throat, but seemed to lessen his grip on the dark elf slightly. "What?"

"I said, I ain't no servant of that world tree bitch. I've come to make a deal for your power," he said, giving a greedy and evil grin.

The archdemon detected the druid's familiar aura of malice that resonated deeply like his own. The ruler of the infernal realms was not an inattentive leader, nor did anything ever occur in his city without his knowledge. He had been watching the druid and warlock ever since they arrived in his realm. It was only the druid's selfishness and bloodlust that kept the demon from realizing that he actually was a druid.

If Vozremath had known, he wouldn't have let Dirk get so close, not that the small wood elf could do anything to him, however. While bloodthirsty, the elf was no match for the leader of the infernal realms!

Few had ever shown the personal qualities that the druid had, the cockiness, the strength, the malice, and the conviction to gain power no matter the cost. If Vozremath didn't know any better, he would've said that Dirk actually was a demon! Though he didn't like the elf's insolent tone, the archdemon couldn't help but smile back at the druid. "Hahahaha! I think that can be arranged, my new minion."

CHAPTER THIRTY

Druidic Reunion

For the next ninety minutes, the party continued to lead Zinthos away toward Amthoon and the Glassy Cliff, careful to avoid close contact with the demon and managing to dodge or magically intercept his fire attacks. Despite Baphomet's massive size, the party didn't attract the hostilities of any other creature inside the jungle as they ran.

Gwen managed to block an orb of lava that had shot out from one of the general's eye tentacles with her Stone Spear spell. When she saw the spear just barely block the lava orb before it was overtaken by flames and crumbled, she gasped as an important memory flashed to the forefront of her mind.

"Bollocks, Virgil, we're right and proper idiots," she said, frustration evident in her voice.

"Idiots? What do you mean?" he asked.

"We led the miffed demon away from Yggdrasil herself, but one of her roots is under the college," she explained.

Virgil gritted his teeth in frustration. Gwen was right. They were idiots. They didn't take into account that while they were leading Zinthos away from being able to kill Yggdrasil's body directly, they were still leading the demon in the direction of one of her roots. Even though her main body was safe, if one of her roots got corrupted by the demon generals, Yggdrasil and the entire world would fall prey to the demon horde.

"Crap, you're right, but we're in too deep now. This is our best chance of killing this thing before it kills Yggdrasil. We don't have a choice any longer," he said.

Gwen bunched her lips in frustration at the situation, but nodded in agreement with the Healer Druid.

Virgil turned back, and the scent of saltwater hit his nostrils. They were getting near the coastal city!

As they came near a thick cluster of trees that reminded Virgil of the huge Kapok trees in the Amazon back on Earth, Virgil's Danger Sense warned him of an imminent threat. "Turn right!" Virgil shouted the order and leaned slightly in that direction. Splinter huddled against her master to not be thrown off by the momentum as Baphomet made a ninety degree turn to the right.

Virgil saw a familiar whip shoot out from the thick canopy at Splinter and raised his shield to defend his beloved stego rat. The whip wrapped itself around both the crystalline buckler and Virgil's forearm. Thorns protruding from the whip embedded themselves into his flesh slightly. Acting on instinct, Virgil used his teeth to unlatch the buckler from his forearm. The shield detached and he managed to get his arm free from the whip. With Baphomet's speed, Virgil knew that either he would have been yanked off, or had his arm injured, or worse. He had already lost one arm. He wasn't too keen on losing another, so he sacrificed his shield instead.

Virgil wasn't injury-free, though, as the thorns did remove small chunks of flesh. He immediately cast Restore on himself, repairing the damaged flesh.

"Bollocks! Was that what I think it was?" Gwen asked.

As if in answer, a bellowing roar rang out from the dense canopy. It was quickly followed by the appearance of two drakes. The winged dragons jumped out of the canopy and descended toward the party. Zinthos had chased the party throughout the night and the morning sun was beginning to rise, providing sparse illumination to the jungle. It allowed them to see the drakes more fully.

One was blue-green with a mouth that seemed to be too wide for its face and adorned with rows of sharp teeth. It honestly reminded Virgil of some kind of Tolkien-inspired Nazgul hybrid. The other drake was made entirely out of plant material, composed of various vines, leaves and branches. Its pupilless green eyes looked like they were literally made out of emeralds, and it had a toothless mouth that was round and protruded forward like a suckerfish. Atop each drake was a single elf adorned in pristine draconic armor.

It was obvious who these were: Marianna and Pierre. Just great, they already had a literal monstrosity tailing them, and now they had to deal with Pete & Re-Pete. Each drake flew beside the running party, easily keeping speed.

"Stop this foolishness, pendejo," Marianna said. "You're seriously escorting a demon general? You know, I knew you weren't working with the demons before, I just wanted the reward. Now, though, with this damning evidence, I'm going to—"

"Bugger off, bitch!" Gwen tersely interrupted the Plant Druid. "We're not escorting the demon, we're leading him to a trap, you dimwit!"

Marianna scowled, but before she could respond, Pierre started speaking. "Marianna, are you serious? You knew that he was innocent, and yet you lied to me to attack him?" the Moon Druid asked, his face showing clear hurt at this revelation.

The dawn elf gave a flash of surprise on her expression, realizing her faux paus, but quickly recovered. "Mierda, what does it matter, anyway? It's clear they're working with the demons now!" she said and pulled back her whip to attack.

Gwen aimed an arrow at her in response. Before either could attack though, another beam of red hateflame shot out from Zinthos's lone eye at them. Virgil shouted a warning, which allowed all of them to narrowly dodge the infernal flames.

"Insects! You cannot flee forever, and when you stop, I will crush you, then make you watch as I burn everything you love!" Zinthos yelled, then gave a roar of anger, shaking the forest and the druids to their very cores.

"Does that sound like we're allies?!" Virgil said. "That fucking thing ripped off my arm!" he said exasperatedly, pointing to the lump that remained of his arm. "How dense do you have to be?" he asked Marianna, then turned to Pierre. The Frenchman was admittedly gullible, but he was a goodhearted person, and that was plain to see, though he may be a little airheaded. "Please, help us."

The Moon Druid, atop his Ocean Drake, gave Virgil a serious look as he bunched his lips before looking at Virgil's missing arm and said, "C'est naze. Je suis désolé. I will help you."

"Pierre, you can't be serious?!" Marianna said.

"Tais-toi!" he replied in French. Virgil's earring translated to a good ol' fashioned "Shut up."

"Either you help, or you leave," he said, scowling at the deceitful dawn elf.

Marianna looked back at the demon still following them. Fear pulsed through her as the gargantuan demon general plowed through large trees as if they were saplings. She looked back at the other three druids. "You are idiotas, and I'm not going to die here with you," she said, then pulled on her Spriggan Drake's reins, separating from the group and flying above the jungle's canopy.

Marianna began to fly around the demon to get behind Zinthos, giving him a wide berth. Her hopes of retreat were dashed as one of the four flame tentacles curled inward then extended out rapidly like a go-go gadget arm. In just three seconds, the tentacle wrapped itself completely around the Spriggan Drake's body, halting its flight and holding it midair.

The drake let out a pained, otherworldly howl, as if it was made from a gust of wind blowing through trees in an autumn storm.

As its body was made of plant material, the drake went up in flame. The drake's howls were now accompanied by Marianna's. Just like in Pokémon, grass was weak to fire. Excited by finally catching a druid and venting his frustrations at not catching Baphomet and Virgil yet, Zinthos actually stopped his charge to stare at the druid and drake engulfed in flames.

Pierre looked back in horror. He gave a look to the group, but Virgil raised his hand up, knowing Pierre's intent and stopping the high elf from reckless action. "It's too late for her, and she left us for dead. Don't throw away your life needlessly. Besides, with you on our side, we should be able to avenge her death," he said.

Pierre was clearly uncomfortable with that logic, but relented. Virgil had no such qualms. It was fair to say that he had grown a bitter shell around him since arriving in Imeria. Plenty had treated him cruelly based off of bigoted or selfish motivations. Marianna was one of them. It was a cold lesson, but it helped Virgil survive this far. Though he wasn't too motivated to try to save her, Vigil's analytical brain told him that there was no way they actually could now.

In a morbid way, Marianna had actually sacrificed herself for them, albeit unintentionally. Zinthos's momentum had halted, and it was allowing the party to gain some valuable distance from the demon general. The druid trio then turned their attentions forward and left the Plant Druid to her fate. Virgil began discussing with Pierre their plan and how he could help.

Zinthos began to drool lava instead of saliva, as it pulled in the burning druid and drake toward his toothy maw.

As Marianna screamed in pain from the flames around her, she freed her feet from the saddle of her doomed drake. She gritted her teeth and focused. She would not die today, not like this. It was a good thing that she was looking down at her own body, as Zinthos's stalked eye was glaring down at her and the drake. If she had met his gaze, she would've fallen prey to his psychic control. Marianna's metal draconic armor had two special enchantments aside from various stat-boosting effects. The first gave her complete control over the Spriggan Drake. The second allowed her to restore her health back to one-hundred percent once per day and remove any debuffs.

She freed herself from the drake and began to plummet down to the forest and activated that enchantment. As she fell down to the ground, she did not despair. No, that was because of the third enchantment. She activated that final enchantment, and the cape of flame-resistant pink rose petals surrounded her entire body in a protective shell. She smirked inside her barrier as she fell. Inside it, she would be safe. It would take a massive amount of damage to break through it! Unfortunately for her, Zinthos noticed the falling pink ball, and decided to bring a massive amount of damage on it!

As Zinthos shoved the burning Spriggan Drake into his mouth, he slammed his giant tortoise foot into the ground and caused a geyser of concentrated lava laced with his demonic energy to erupt violently from the ground. It shot up so quickly that the lava struck the shell just as it broke the canopy. The pink shell began to burn and erupt in flame as it was propelled up in the air like a modern rocket, flying so high that it soared miles over and behind Zinthos. The demon general was frustrated that part of his meal had flown away, but was confident that flimsy shield couldn't protect her when she descended, despite her disgusting druid powers.

That reminded him of that audacious piece of filth druid who dared urinate in his presence. Zinthos growled. He would make the dark elf burn, then he would eat him... slowly. "Druid!" he shouted and continued on his warpath toward the fleeing trio of druids and beasts, burning everything in his wake.

CHAPTER THIRTY-ONE

Unstable Ground

"Can you do that?" Virgil asked Pierre after discussing their plan.

"Oui," he said. "It is risky, but if what you say is true, it should work."

Virgil nodded and began to unlatch his belt. He felt Gwen's hand on his shoulder. He looked back to see her with serious, sad eyes. "Please... come back, okay? I... don't want to lose anyone else," she said, giving him a pleading look that made Virgil's heart ache. Here was someone who he had a deep connection with and genuinely cared for him, and he felt the same! It was a feeling that was so rare to him on Earth. He treasured it greatly.

He then glanced over to Splinter and Baphomet. Virgil not only had another person, but loyal creatures that had bonded with him. They were a part of him as much as he was a part of them now. Virgil would do his best to come back to them.

He gave Gwen a quick but passionate kiss, then scratched both Splinter and Baphomet lovingly. "Why would you think I won't come back? Don't forget, I'm one lucky bastard," he said with a wink, then reached over to Pierre's Drake. The winged dragon raised itself slightly and grabbed Virgil gently with his claws, so as not to injure the veterinarian. After a few seconds, the party finally broke the jungle's edge to the rocky cliff face by the ocean. They quickly found Glassy Cliff.

At that point, Virgil's two animal companions went left to hide in the jungle away from the path they had laid for the demon to follow. Pierre's drake flew over the fragile cliff, as it was too dangerous for Virgil to walk over, and dropped Virgil off on top of the lighthouse. "You sure about this?" Pierre asked.

"Is water wet?" Virgil asked in reply.

Pierre cocked his head slightly and gave Virgil a confused look.

"Never mind, yes. Go," Virgil said, and the drake began to soar skyward, becoming hidden in the clouds after a few seconds. It was now early morning and the sun was still rising, causing the sky to be filled with various shades of pink and orange. It was a beautiful sky that Virgil wished he could enjoy, and hoped he would see again. Finally, he turned back to face the demon that was rampaging through the rainforest behind them.

"You ready for this, Grief?" Virgil sent to his friend through their private Soulbound Communication.

"Ye bet yer ass I be ready," the skull answered excitedly. *"Let's show this walking inbred-looking abomination what the Healer Druid and his badass soulbound companion can do!"*

Virgil smiled. He couldn't have said it better himself. He gripped his staff and renewed his Purifying Aura spell to keep the demon's psychic influence at bay. He stared in the direction of the demon, hoping their plan would work and wishing he had more health, despite having the Ring of the Bound Warrior equipped. He was definitely grateful to have worn all his rings on his left hand! Virgil mentally facepalmed as he remembered that he had unused stat points from leveling. Not having much time to deliberate, he threw all four into strength, increasing his health by a total of forty points. Maybe it wouldn't matter, but every little bit counted. He had just enough time for his muscles to grow and his body to stretch to accommodate before the gargantuan fiend appeared, his single eye towering over the treetops. Upon seeing Virgil, the eye squinted, and the hulking general charged forward, bursting out from the jungle with a boom.

"Druuuiiiiddd!" the demon roared as it emerged.

"Yeah, yeah, I'm a druid, and you don't like me. Big whoop. Get a new line already," he said dismissively.

The demon let out a low growl and lifted his foot to take a step forward, then stopped. "Where are your pathetic little friends, druid?" he asked suspiciously.

"They left," Virgil answered cryptically. "I don't need them here to beat you," he said, then cast Barkskin on himself.

The demon glared at Virgil. "Lying filth, burn!" he shouted then shot out a bolt of lava out from his mouth. Reacting on instinct, Virgil cast another Phoenix Fire and transformed the lava into a bolt of healing flame. His spell didn't change the projectile's speed though, and it struck him square in the sternum. Virgil coughed as his breath was forced out of him. After a few seconds of grunting and beating his chest, he was able to breathe normally again.

Virgil began to laugh maniacally, sounding almost like a madman as he stared directly at Zinthos. "And you call my friends pathetic?! Ha! Look at you, a demon general taller than most of the jungle behind him, afraid of me? My friends are pathetic? You can't even kill a one-armed elf despite your power. Now tell me, who really sounds pathetic in this instance?" he asked, trying to incite the demon's rage.

"Afraid?! Pathetic?!" Zinthos yelled. With every word, the red aura around the demon intensified and fire started emerging from in between the rings of his massive shell. The faces stuck in horrified visages of pain also started to shoot out gouts of flame. Virgil felt the heat of the entire area go up significantly. His sensitive dark elf eyes squinted from the newfound light, and he stuck his arm out to block the light. He ground his teeth together from the sudden wave of oppressive heat. Virgil was confident that without his Purifying Aura, he would be getting burnt right now. He hoped that everyone else was farther away than he was from Zinthos.

Virgil looked at Zinthos, and noticed that the demon had not taken a step forward yet. So he taunted him further. "You heard me! Come and get some if you're not, or do I have to take another piss in front of you to show that you're my bitch?"

That was the final straw. Blinded by rage at the pure gall and insolence of the Healer Druid, the demon general began charging forward to the druid on the cliff. After Zinthos took two steps, the demon's massive weight made the ground beneath him crack. The sound of shattering earth echoed as the cliff immediately gave way to the demon general's mass.

Zinthos's eye went wide in surprise and he roared in anger as his body began to plummet. Virgil just smiled and waved bye-bye as the demon sank below his vision. Virgil was fortunately at the edge of the cliff, so it did not shatter along with the section that Zinthos stepped on, now making it an island.

Before he could hear the demon splash into the deep ocean below and celebrate, his Danger Sense alerted him that the threat was not over. From the spot where Zinthos fell, a literal tornado of flame erupted out. Virgil's heart began to beat strongly inside his chest when he saw Zinthos inside the twister, slowly emerging up out of the trap.

"Are you kidding me?" Virgil muttered as goosebumps went down his arm. Emerging from the streaks of flame on his shell were two massive bat wings made entirely of fire. He could fly! How the fuck did he get wings? He was a tortoise, not a flying koopa!

Zinthos's large mouth had an evil grin on it. "Fool! I told you I would eat you, and the great devourer will get *his fill*!" he said, punctuating his last words before diving at Virgil.

"*Now!*" he shouted through Party Chat. Immediately, a large ballista bolt shot out from way off deep in the forest, hitting the demon through the back of his massive eye and penetrating just through the front and center of the pupil. It was an impossible shot, but Gwen could now do that on command. The demon roared in pain as his trajectory was now changed from the newfound pain and blindness, and he was on a crash course with the lighthouse Virgil was on!

There was a deep howl of wind from above as the clouds gave way to something. Above the airborne demon was a massive meteor! It was Pierre's trademark spell, Meteoric Burst. Virgil was personally familiar with this spell, as it had almost killed him during their last fight with a demon general. The meteor fell onto the demon, crashing into Zinthos's back with a force of mighty Nature damage before the general could make his own crash landing.

It was as if time slowed for Virgil as he watched what happened. The large meteor's velocity and sheer mass struck Zinthos's shell, causing it to break with a loud crack that echoed for miles. Upon the shell breaking, the meteor embedded itself into the demon's back and shoved the demon straight down like an angry god smiting their enemy.

Time seemed to catch back up, and Zinthos crashed into the remaining section of the Glassy Cliff, shattering the fragile rock in a heartbeat. The amalgam was forced downward in a flash, going through the entire cliff and into the ocean below. The velocity of the meteor was slowed negligibly as it sank into the water, and it continued to force the demon downward into the ocean violently. Zinthos screamed in anger, and for the first time since arriving in this world, he also yelled in despair, as his dense and heavy tortoise body was being forced downward to his doom.

That scream was the general's first and last as he sank deeper and deeper like a sailor tied to an anchor. The demon general's lungs took in more and more saltwater, and he quickly drowned. His fire was put out.

Virgil was not able to savor that moment, though. Pierre's spell was powerful, and while Virgil was a doctor, he was a veterinarian, not a physicist. He didn't take into account the pure wave of force from the meteor impacting the cliff and ocean below.

There was a loud 'boom' that rang out as the meteor crashed through the cliff and into the ocean, and a wave of destructive force containing wind, dirt, water, and fire shot out for a mile in all directions, completely obliterating all structures in its wake. The abandoned lighthouse and the fragile rock it was on were blown away. Virgil's body was flung out with a violent force half a mile over the ocean, his body receiving a set of cuts and burns in the blink of an eye. Despite that, he was able to hold his grip on his staff with his one and only arm.

A familiar voice rang out in Virgil's mind. *"I got ye, lad!"* Before his airborne body could fall into the ocean below, a supernatural pull tugged at the dark elf's chest, and he started flying upward as if gravity worked in reverse! Virgil let out a reactive yell as he felt the sensation of someone else having control over his body.

He flew high, about a mile into the clouds before reaching his target. There, in the middle of the air, was Grief. The skull was being held by the clawed foot of Pierre's Ocean Drake, who was flapping his wings to maintain elevation. The Moon Druid sat atop the dragon, breathing heavily and clearly exhausted from his recent spellcasting.

As soon as Virgil's chest made contact with Grief, he instantly wrapped his arm and both legs around the skull, clutching the skull like a life preserver for an overboard sailor.

"Haha! Great job, lad! Good grief! I didn't expect mister dragon elf here to drop such a big load on ye! If his spell load be that big, I'd hate to see the load he'd drop on a toilet!"

Virgil was not amused. To experience no control over his body and to now be hanging a mile over the ocean with strong winds gusting brought him very little comfort.

The veterinarian hadn't told anyone, but he wasn't the biggest fan of heights. It wasn't the actual heights, mind you, it was the sensation of falling with no control. Though the direction was upward, the weightlessness he experienced being drawn to Grief was the same, and Virgil was not so pleasantly reminded that if he let go of his soulbound companion, he would plummet to his certain doom.

"Pierre, bring us down!" he shouted, squeezing his eyes completely shut.

"I take it the demon is, how you say, taken care of?" the Moon Druid asked.

"Yes," Virgil quickly answered. He then took a steadying breath, and in a forced calm asked, "Please put me down now?"

"Oh, you want down? Well then, of course I shall oblige," the Frenchman said, then his drake gently grabbed Virgil with the foot not holding onto Grief. Once Virgil had let go of the skull and was in the drake's left foot, the drake promptly dropped him.

Virgil began to shout in fear as he descended toward the water below and a grisly death. Before he made contact, though, he felt his body being caught by the drake's foot in a diving swoop.

Both Pierre and Grief were laughing loudly, the Frenchman in particular sounding nasally and pompous, like he was some rude Monty Python character, but maybe that was Virgil just being angry. "Fuck you!" he said to both of them poignantly, which only helped the two to laugh more.

"Ha! I like this lad, Virgil. He follows my ideas and has a good sense of humor!" Grief said.

"More like a sick sense of humor," Virgil muttered under his breath. Despite his two near-death experiences, Virgil felt immense relief. He was alive, and they had done it! They had killed Zinthos, the tortoise-looking bastard and the second demon general! Wait, had they? He hadn't received a notification yet! The group flew back over into the forest. There, in a small clearing, they saw Virgil's two animal companions both safe and sound. The drake landed on the ground carefully, this time setting Virgil down more gently. In a matter of seconds, Virgil was greeted by his two beasts.

Splinter ran up and hugged Virgil's leg, while Baphomet

almost tackled Virgil to the ground as it charged up and bear-hugged him. The beastking whined like a dog who had missed their master and began to lick his face with its massive tongue. Virgil grimaced, but pushed them off. "Hold up! Hold up!" he shouted. "The general is not dead yet," he said gravely.

The animal companions understood their master, as their expressions became firm and they stared past him to the water. Virgil forced himself up and turned to face the water too, running on pure adrenaline and ready to fight once more. Pierre turned to face the Ocean Drake, whom he'd named Jacque. The drake snarled, ready to resume the fight.

Gwen ran up beside Virgil with a large arrow already nocked on her bowstring. "Hurry up and die, you ugly bastard," she spat at the demon deep below in the water whom she could not see. Concern started running through the elves' minds for a couple of moments. Had Zinthos absorbed the power of a fish so he could breathe underwater? Their concerns were quickly quelled when a boom came from the underwater pit Zinthos had plunged into, causing the ground to quake slightly. A wonderful sight appeared in the druids' vision.

Congratulations, Druid Champion of Yggdrasil!
Your efforts and quick thinking have allowed you to defeat Vozremath's 2nd demon general, Zinthos the Devourer. For your service to the world tree and all of Imeria as a whole, you will be rewarded.

Rewards
+75,000 Experience
A unique treasure from Yggdrasil

Quest Update: I Need A Hero
2 out of 3 Demon Generals defeated.

Virgil also received a notification that he had reached level nineteen from his extra experience bonus! With the danger passed, Virgil collapsed onto his back in relief. Splinter and

Baphomet ran back over, concerned at first, then began showing affection for him again, seeing his smiling face. Splinter rubbed the side of her head against his while Baphomet began licking his face like an excited dog.

While he was happy to have his creatures show such affection for him, pretty soon his face was covered in drool. "Okay, okay, you two, I'm happy to see you as well. Good job to both of you. Your master is proud," he said, taking turns to scratch both of them on their heads.

As they both let go of him, he drank a Minor Stamina Potion, then stood back up to clean his saliva-covered glasses off. Once he put them back on, he was once again beset by another running hug. This one was from Gwen and despite the surprise, the embrace was definitely welcome.

"I was so worried," she said as she placed her palm on Virgil's cheek. Her eyes were watery and her cheeks were lined with tear stains.

"I told you, I'm one lucky bastard. I mean, I got you to fall for me. How much luckier could I get? Fighting a demon general? Pfft, no problem," he said jokingly.

She rolled her eyes, used her Ring of Prestidigitation to clean off all the dust and debris from his form, then gave him a tender kiss before turning to Pierre. "Thank you, Pierre, for believing us. We really never meant you harm, and we think you're actually an alright bloke. So, are we square?" she asked.

"It is I who should apologize," Pierre replied. "I was a fool, first blinded by fear then blinded by beauty. I submitted to that foul mouth asshole Dirk because of his strength, then I followed Marianna because... I wanted more than just simple camaraderie. Now I see she was just as selfish and dishonorable as the Feral Druid. If you would allow it, I wish to make it up to you lot and join your party. If that is something you cannot do, I understand."

Gwen and Virgil gave each other a look, communicating silently about Pierre, who realized they were using Party Chat. In just a few seconds, though, the pair had made their decision.

"Welcome aboard," Virgil said, and sent a request for Pierre to join. With that, the party grew by one druid more!

Name: Pierre
Level: 25 (348,522/1,276,702 experience to next level.)
Unallocated Stat Points: 0
Race: Elf **Subrace:** High Elf
Class: Druid
Specialization: Moon Druid
Attunement: True Intentions
Languages: Common, Elven
Companions: Jacque (Ocean Drake)

Pools & Resistances
Health: 400 (+100)
Manna: 400
Stamina: 450 (+100)
Armor: 150
Air Magic: 50%
Water Magic: 50%
Nature Magic: 50%

Statistics
Strength: 40 (+10)
Agility: 35
Intelligence: 40
Endurance: 45 (+10)
Charisma: 25

"You've awakened your Attunement?" Virgil asked.

Pierre gave a confident smile. "Oui, I actually awakened it after I decided to join your cause over Marianna's. It is a passive ability that increases both my physical and magical abilities if they are used for true and noble purposes. That is why my meteoric burst spell was much larger and more powerful."

Both Gwen and Virgil let out a small chuckle at that. The

description matched the honor-bound Pierre to a T. "I couldn't think of a better Attunement for you," Virgil replied.

"Let's go, boys, we should get closer to the water and check out where the demon died," Gwen said as she began to walk toward the edge of the forest. "The bastard probably left some loot and Yggdrasil promised us a unique treasure."

CHAPTER THIRTY-TWO

Heroic Rewards

The party followed Gwen to the water's edge. The cliff was gone, and a good chunk of the rocky wall that it was connected to was gone as well. The corpses of various fish were scattered across the rock wall and even in some of the trees near the party; their bodies had been sent flying from the effects of Pierre's spell. Numerous gulls and various waterfowl were starting to appear, their animal instincts drawn to the smell of an easy all-you-can-eat fish buffet.

The party looked down. The water where the cliff had been was deeper than the rest as it was much darker than the surrounding water. Virgil began to wonder if they were going to have to actually go *into* the water to get the prizes. Right after the thought crossed his mind, the water began to bubble. A geyser shot straight up, but it wasn't made of water, nor was it made of some sort of demonic fire. Instead, it was made of flowing white ethereal energy.

The elf's eyes started noticing forms inside the energy... and faces! Silhouettes of people of various races and numerous kinds of animals were seen inside the geyser of spiritual force. The spiritual conglomeration flowed upward then descended and flew right over by the party, enveloping all of them as if the spirits were a gust of wind.

All of them, elf and animal, experienced the spirits' feelings as they flew by. First was fear followed by sadness, then despair followed by rage. Finally, though, they felt peace. Instantly, the party recognized deep down that these were all the spirits of the six-hundred different creatures that Zinthos had consumed, with one notable exception: Ramsay. It appeared the demon was not freed of Zinthos's consumption even after death.

The spirits then communed with the party. It was a deeper form of communication that only those who have died or were trained in the spiritual arts could attain. From deep inside the essences of each of the people and creatures' very beings, two words were passed on. "Thank you." And with that, the spirits disappeared, finally free from the demon's grasp to go into the afterlife.

All except one.

A small, floating white orb hovered in front of Gwen. She cocked her head to the side slightly, curious as to why this particular spirit hadn't moved on. The spirit then gently booped against her forehead, and her eyes went wide in recognition. "Christopher?" she asked, her voice trembling with emotion. The orb went down to the ground and transformed into Gwen's terror boar, but now made of spiritual energy and semi-transparent. Gwen began to cry and somehow was able to hug her beloved pet who was taken from her. Christopher just grunted.

"What're you doing here, love?" The boar took a couple of steps back and wagged his curly tail expectantly at her and lifted his head a couple of times at her, like it was obvious. A notification brought an answer to Gwen's query. It was accompanied by the sound of a pig snorting.

Greetings, Druid Champion of Yggdrasil!
Your bond with your animal companion was so strong that the beast has returned from the dead to be in your service once more! The terror boar, Christopher P. Bacon has gone from

being a demon's dinner to a creature of pure spirit. Instead of leaving the mortal plane, it does not want to leave your side and desires to become your spirit animal.

Reward:
A spirit animal: Terror Boar
A new skill
A new spell
Increases to Stats
Do you accept his offer?
Yes or No

Gwen's eyes widened. She minimized the notification and looked at Christopher. "Are you sure about this, love?" The boar snorted and nodded enthusiastically. Gwen smiled, reopened the notification, and selected Yes.

Christopher turned back into a floating orb, flew up, and sank into Gwen's chest, bonding with her. Her bones grew denser and more tough. She felt her body strengthen as muscles grew and became more defined, making her both sturdier and faster. The Hunter Druid's mind also expanded, granting her two new magical abilities!

Congratulations!
You have gained a spirit animal: Terror Boar.
After bonding with a terror boar, your body has been enhanced, increasing your physical capabilities!
+10 Strength
+5 Endurance
+2 Agility

Skill Gained: Summon Spirit Animal
Summon your spirit animal to fight by your side. While not as physically strong as they were in life, the spirit can still provide valuable aid in times of need. If the spirit's health hits 0, they will return back into your body to recover. The spirit will not be able to return to the mortal plane for 24 hours.

You have learned a new Predator Magic Spell: Spiritual Fusion.
Cost: 100 MP
Cooldown: 24 hours
Range: 100 feet
Description: Your connection with your spirit animal has allowed you both to be able to use manna to create a temporary bond so strong that your forms merge as one. When in your fused form, your stats will be enhanced and you will have unique abilities that you can only use while in that form.
Effect: Fuses into a Terror Boar-High Elf hybrid, providing unique offensive benefits.

"What happened?" Virgil asked.

Gwen turned and smiled. "Guess I'm a lucky bastard too. I got my pet boar back." She went on to explain what she saw, and the other elves were definitely impressed. Both men were also happy to learn that she had recovered her beloved pet that was so tragically taken from her.

Then they all felt a familiar sensation from the ocean below, as if Yggdrasil herself was there. The world tree wasn't, but since her champions had defeated another general, her power was able to grant them some rewards.

Nature Magic pulsed from under the corpse of Zinthos and into him. The mighty demon general's body lay dead dozens of kilometers on the ocean floor. His shell was cracked from both the meteor impact and the significant water pressure on his body. The Nature Magic, whose origins came from Yggdrasil herself, was anathema to the demon servant of her enemy Vozremath, and as it traveled through the corpse, caused it to rot and decay at an accelerated rate. In just a minute, the body had dissolved into three orbs which quickly glowed white with the world tree's energy. The orbs then began to surge upward as if they were propelled by a rocket.

The three elves watched in fascination as three orbs of white Nature Magic broke the surface of the deep water and floated in front of them. Each druid had a single orb in front of them. They all knew subconsciously what to do, and all of them stuck out their hands under the orbs. They floated down and landed in their hands. After they made contact, the orbs turned to glowing white chests that opened then began to dissolve, revealing the contents inside.

Gwen received a thick black metal bracelet. Its information appeared and informed her that it was called Hunter's Recaller. It allowed her to psychically recall her fired arrows back to her, like with Virgil and Grief's Soulbound Recall, as long as the arrow was intact. It was extremely useful, allowing Gwen to now re-use previously one-time-use arrows, making her a much more deadly force.

Pierre had a thin silver circlet that seemed to slightly change to the orange color of flames before reverting back to silver. It was called Circlet of Dominant Will, and it allowed the Moon Druid to now be able to psychically communicate with his drake. Unlike Gwen and Virgil, Pierre's dominion of the Ocean Drake was through his armor enchantment, and if the drake was left alone, it was prone to hostility and hard to control unless one had the proper skills or equipment. Now with the circlet, Pierre could dismount the drake and control it with his mind, making Jacque an effective combatant and valuable teammate on his own.

Virgil's was the most interesting… in his hand was an arm. It was heavy, onyx black like his skin, and was made of what looked to be tortoise shells arranged in a plated fashion, like it was a suit of armor. Virgil Analyzed it.

You have found Right Arm of the Healer.
Item Type: Unique
Durability: 2000/2000
Item Class: Artifact
Description: A reward given to Virgil, Healer Druid and Champion of Yggdrasil by the world tree herself. His sacrifice was not unnoticed and was not in vain. Yggdrasil has used her magic to condense and transform the thick carapace of

Zinthos's tortoise shell into a new arm for her druid champion. The arm is both thicker and more durable than the arm of flesh he had before. It can also summon a shield for protection. The arm, being a magical device, cannot wear any rings, though.

Effect: +50 Armor, can partially expand forearm to form a buckler upon mental flex of will, self-regenerates.

You get to be right-handed again. Enjoy!

Virgil chuckled as the last words were spoken in his mind from Yggdrasil herself. With all the craziness that had been going on, he had honestly put his concerns to the back of his mind about being right-handed and no longer having a right hand. Virgil was even more grateful to Yggdrasil just for the sheer practicality of not having to relearn everything with a different arm. He'd tried brushing his teeth with his left arm before for a mental exercise. Even that took a lot more mental exertion and forceful effort than he could ever remember when he had used his right hand. The arm he just received would save him *a lot* of trouble!

Virgil carefully lifted the heavy item to the nub that remained of his right arm. It was ironic, but Virgil would've said that the item given to him by the world tree 'fit like a glove,' as it attached to the section of the amputated arm by the shoulder. There was an audible click as the magical arm connected to Virgil's body. The veterinarian twitched in surprise, and he realized his new arm twitched, too. He looked down at his new appendage and could feel it. He could actually feel it! He moved his fingers individually and he experienced the tactile sensation of touching his new palm made out of the thick carapace.

Virgil began to laugh in amazement, tears of joy starting to go down his face. This was awesome! With all the near-death experiences the past two days, he had compartmentalized the trauma that he had experienced in order to just survive. Now though, free from an immediate threat, the terror from losing a limb, and especially so violently, came to the forefront of his mind.

It was quickly overridden by the sheer joy at having a new and improved one, though! In the back of his mind, Virgil hoped that both people and animals back on Earth could achieve limb replacements to the same degree as this!

His musings stopped when he looked at both Pierre and Gwen, each of the high elves also wearing their new gear. Both looked at him in amazement then celebrated also. "By me non-existent beard, lad, that be some fine craftsmanship the world tree did fer ye," Grief said. "Now, let's head back to Amthoon, why don't we. I reckon we done enough to celebrate, eh?"

"I'd reckon so," Virgil replied.

"Great call, lad! We'll celebrate in the custom of me people, with a good ol' fashioned barrel of ale. I'd love to down a pint of brew with me new Space Vacuum skill!"

"Wait, I thought you couldn't actually taste or get any effects from anything you intake?" Virgil asked.

There was an awkward silence as the skull thought about the dark elf's words then somberly remembered that no buzz nor taste of alcohol would greet him tonight, unfortunately. "Good grief!"

EPILOGUE

Return

A blood-red portal tore through reality on the continent of Kygora, home of the world tree Yggdrasil. Out of the portal stepped Shreez, the dark elf warlock. The elf was now wearing a red-orange vest made from the leather of a demon's hide, along with pants made of the same material. His long white hair was now shaved into a wild mohawk. The warlock's face still possessed his signature crazed look, and he now had six deep-red vertical scars along his face as well as some down his arms and on his exposed bare feet.

While the warlock oozed malevolent power, the figure that followed absolutely radiated it. "Hehehe, this world is ripe for the conquering... general," the warlock said.

From out of the portal walked a seven-foot-tall figure. He had two large bull horns atop his head and two cloven-hooved feet below, covered with a layer of black fur. A long black tail with a wicked barb was present. The figure's upper body was heavily muscled, but despite that, his skin was yellowed, thick, and possessed a few large pustules ready to pop. While the right hand ended in a giant black crab-like claw, the other had three fingers all ending in long, sharp claws. The only clothes the general wore were two rusted iron chains around his torso, making an X.

While the figure was imposing, his face was downright terrifying. He had three solid black eyes and a snout like a vampire bat for a nose. The figure gave a smile with a mouth that was much too big for his face and stretched up and past both of his pointed ears.

Dirk, the new and final demon general, the first-ever demonic druid, and champion of Vozremath the archdemon, opened his toothy maw and revealed a large, rotting tongue that stretched down to his chest as he spoke. "Good, Shreez. Let's see how Yggdrasil does when we take the fight directly to her own doorstep."

VIRGIL'S STATS AT THE END OF BOOK TWO

Name: Virgil
Level: 19 (3,374/112,160 experience to next level)
Unallocated Stat Points: 2
Race: Elf **Subrace:** Dark Elf
Class: Druid
Specialization: Healer Druid
Attunement: A Veterinarian's Pact
Languages: Common, Elven
Companions: Grief (Soulbound), Splinter, Baphomet

Pools & Resistances
Health: 162
Manna: 430
Stamina: 290
Armor: 159
Life Magic: 50%
Earth Magic: 50%
Nature Magic: 50%
Light Magic: -50%

Statistics

Strength: 16
Agility: 56
Intelligence: 43
Endurance: 34
Charisma: 13

Traits

True Healer
Darkvision
Increased Hearing
Ally of Darkness
Beast Commander
Alchemically Inspired

Skills

Medicine Level 53
Herbology Level 55
Nature Magic (Restoration) Level 33
Spells: Restore, Leeching Vines, Yggdrashield, Nature Bolt,
Barkskin, Purifying Aura, Phoenix Fire
Stealth Level 23 – Subskill: Sneak Attack Level 3
Analyze Level 13
Danger Sense Level 19 – Subskill: Detect Hostile Intent Level 7
Skinning Level 4
Trade Level 9
Alchemy Level 41
Taunt Level 13
Soulbound Recall
Culinary Level 2
Manna Manipulation

AUTHOR'S NOTE

Thank you for reading this story! If you liked it, please take just the next sixty seconds to leave a positive review on Amazon. It really makes a huge difference! Thanks to everyone who helped make this book possible, especially the awesome people at Mountaindale Press who were willing to take a chance on me! I'm forever grateful for your help in making this author dream of mine possible.
-Maxwell

P.S. Please consult your local veterinarian if you have any health concerns for your pets. This is a work of fiction and should not be a substitute for any medical advice in regards to your animals' individual care.

ABOUT MAXWELL FARMER

Hi there, I'm Maxwell Farmer. I'm an avid nerd, gamer, and veterinarian who fell in love with LitRPG back in college. I loved it so much that I started writing my own!

I'd love to hear your thoughts on the book and would love to talk about nerd stuff in general. Keep living your best life!

I was inspired to write from the multitude of LitRPG I consumed as well as the games I've played that have made an impact on me. They opened up worlds of wonder and possibility and brought much joy to me. I hope my books will do the same for you. :)

Connect with Maxwell Farmer:
MaxwellFarmer.com
Facebook.com/AuthorMaxwellFarmer
Instagram.com/MaxwellFarmer
Patreon.com/MaxwellFarmer

ABOUT MOUNTAINDALE PRESS

Dakota and Danielle Krout, a husband and wife team, strive to create as well as publish excellent fantasy and science fiction novels. Self-publishing *The Divine Dungeon: Dungeon Born* in 2016 transformed their careers from Dakota's military and programming background and Danielle's Ph.D. in pharmacology to President and CEO, respectively, of a small press. Their goal is to share their success with other authors and provide captivating fiction to readers with the purpose of solidifying Mountaindale Press as the place 'Where Fantasy Transforms Reality.'

Connect with Mountaindale Press:
MountaindalePress.com
Facebook.com/MountaindalePress
Twitter.com/_Mountaindale
Instagram.com/MountaindalePress

MOUNTAINDALE PRESS TITLES

GameLit and LitRPG

The Completionist Chronicles,
The Divine Dungeon,
Full Murderhobo, and
Year of the Sword by Dakota Krout

Arcana Unlocked by Gregory Blackburn

A Touch of Power by Jay Boyce

Red Mage and
Farming Livia by Xander Boyce

Space Seasons by Dawn Chapman

Ether Collapse and
Ether Flows by Ryan DeBruyn

Dr. Druid by Maxwell Farmer

Bloodgames by Christian J. Gilliland

Threads of Fate by Michael Head

Lion's Lineage by Rohan Hublikar and Dakota Krout

Wolfman Warlock by James Hunter and Dakota Krout

Axe Druid,
Mephisto's Magic Online, and
High Table Hijinks by Christopher Johns

Skeleton in Space by Andries Louws

Chronicles of Ethan by John L. Monk

Pixel Dust and
Necrotic Apocalypse by David Petrie

Viceroy's Pride by Cale Plamann

Henchman by Carl Stubblefield

Artorian's Archives by Dennis Vanderkerken and Dakota Krout

Made in the USA
Middletown, DE
24 May 2022